T0594800

LITTLE
BROWN
———
LARGE
PRINT

THE NEW PEOPLE

A Novel

ANDREA UPTMOR

LITTLE
BROWN

LARGE
PRINT

New York

Little, Brown and Company
Hachette Book Group
1290 Avenue of the Americas, New York, NY 10104
littlebrown.com

First Edition: July 2026

Little, Brown and Company is a division of Hachette Book Group, Inc. The Little, Brown name and logo are trademarks of Hachette Book Group, Inc.

The publisher is not responsible for websites (or their content) that are not owned by the publisher.

The Hachette Speakers Bureau provides a wide range of authors for speaking events. To find out more, go to hachettespeakersbureau.com or email hachettespeakers@hbgusa.com.

Contact your local bookseller or special.markets@hbgusa.com regarding special discounts for bulk purchases.

Print book interior design by Taylor Navis

ISBN 9780316602211 (hardcover), 9780316607827 (large print)
LCCN 2026931150

For Liz,
of course

THE
NEW
PEOPLE

CHAPTER 1

Emma had felt the house was haunted from the moment Rachel opened the door with their new key. Maybe not literally. But the metaphorical ghosts were undeniable. For one thing, there was the smell. The pinch of new carpet and fresh paint only masked an older, more penetrative odor of mildew, which the central air-conditioning, already on, dispersed like a sour rain. In the entryway she noticed the faint outline of what must have been a child's height marks etched into the doorframe, now painted over. There was something about flipped houses that reminded Emma of a surgeon's scrubs: No matter how clean they were, you knew that at one point, someone else's life had stained them.

Rachel slipped her arm around Emma's waist as

they appraised themselves in the hallway mirror, which gleamed like a still lake. It occurred to Emma that someone—who?—must have taken time with a bottle of blue cleaner so that this, the moment she and her wife entered their new home, would remain as clear and sharp in their memories as the day they were married, just six weeks before.

Yet she saw with dismay that she looked the same as she always had, with a sharply sloping forehead and thin eyebrows that, together, gave her an expression of disapproval, even when she was trying hard to be nice. Ample hips but scant eyelashes she had to coax into existence with mascara every morning. Next to her, Rachel's body was long and simple, with hard calves from running and triceps that knotted under her slender arms. She'd been a swimmer in high school, and, despite not having been in a pool for years, she retained a swimmer's body, graceful and easy.

"I'm looking very George Eliot today," said Emma. "Don't laugh," she said, though it always pleased her when Rachel laughed. "I've got that Victorian homeliness in my DNA."

"It's not you, it's the mirror. They make everything cheap now." Rachel bent her knees and bobbed up and down. "See. It's warped."

"Yet somehow you still look perfect."

Her wife gave a coy shrug. Birdie, their Pomeranian, emerged from behind their ankles, the fur on her check still flattened from a long nap in the car. She sniffed the air and barked, skittering off down the hall to explore.

"She smells it," said Emma. "The mythical backyard. I hope it doesn't go to her head."

"Oh, it will." Rachel nodded. "No more pathetic apartment courtyard for her. She'll be drunk on power from now on."

They broke apart to explore the new world before them: A dining room where pendant lights hung over gleaming hardwood floors, a bathroom with brushed-nickel fixtures. A short hallway with a large closet joined the two bedrooms. Emma walked through rooms, touching everything. The house, a two-bedroom, fourteen-hundred-square-foot, one-story Cape Cod with a sharply pointing roof, a small finished basement, a backyard hot tub, and — the part Emma and Rachel could not get over — an attached garage, looked so different than it had when they'd first seen the place two months ago. In June the wisteria covering the side of the house had been in full bloom, its flowers hanging like pendulums and smelling sweet. That was before the renovation, when the former owners' furniture was still there, cowering along the walls like naughty children who'd been told to wait for their parents to arrive. Now the baseboards gleamed with fresh white paint and Emma could hear, faintly, the sweet slide whistle of a cardinal on a branch outside.

Emma hung her purse on a decorative wall hook by the door. The hook fell out almost immediately, leaving a hole that flatulated a cloud of plaster dust. The contents of her bag—cell phone, a tin of herbal tea bags, loose M&M's, and the rattling prescription from Dr. Casey—spewed onto the floor.

"Whoops." She pushed the hook back into its hole, but it hung loosely, incapably, like a bird's broken wing. Annoyed, she left it dangling, turned toward the garage, and opened the door.

Expecting an empty space, she nearly jumped to see that one side of the garage was crowded with furniture from the previous owners. Next to the built-in shelves on the far wall, a futon squatted beside side tables and credenzas—all the dusty pieces the real estate agent had promised would be gone after the closing. The furniture gave off the same musty smell, as if it'd been retrieved from a lake and left here to dry out. There was no room to park their car unless they got rid of all this stuff, which, Emma knew, would not happen unless she took care of it.

She stepped down into the garage and pressed the plastic button on the wall to open the overhead door. Nothing. Her eyes followed the track along the ceiling to the motorized unit. It looked ancient, with an open plastic panel and loose wires as if someone had started to fix it and then simply walked away.

"Useless," she said. "What a surprise." Still, she

stood in the doorway and savored, for the moment, another thing gone wrong. There was some satisfaction in collecting all the ways she'd been right, however small and worthless they were, like a child gathering dandelions in a basket. She hadn't wanted to move here. She'd felt heavy with bleak inevitability the first time they'd seen pictures of the house online. The real estate agent had photoshopped different furniture into the rooms to suggest their potential for livability, though the hasty crops and poor lighting conveyed more desperation than homeyness. But the price was shocking—half the cost of a two-bedroom condo on the north side of Chicago—and anyway, Emma knew as she watched Rachel click through the pictures that her wife had already made up her mind.

Emma stepped inside the garage and went to the exterior door, which had a window that looked out on the backyard. She watched Birdie sniff around the hot tub, which looked hulkish and lonely on its concrete slab. Its vinyl cover was peeling and sun-bleached, but those were things she could fix. She imagined being in the hot tub with Rachel, leaning their heads against the plastic headrests, letting their bodies float to the surface as moonlight dappled their skin.

Maybe it wasn't all going to be bad.

Stepping back in the house, Emma reached up her hand to turn out the light. A jolt of static electricity made her yank her arm back. She put her finger in her mouth, where it tingled briefly against her tongue. Wiping her finger on her jeans, she left the garage behind and closed the door.

"Rach?" she called. "Where'd you go?"

No answer. Birdie bounded into the hall, exhilarated and warmed by the sun. She touched her nose to Emma's calf and then veered into the kitchen, where Emma heard Rachel exclaim, "Ah, hier gibt mein liebehund!" Rachel was learning German, nearly fluent after only a few weeks of YouTube videos. Her cell phone chime was a mnemonic of German prepositions set to the tune of "The Blue Danube" waltz: *aus, ausser, bei, mit, nach, seit, von, zu.* It had been ringing so frequently with details of her university onboarding and well wishes from new colleagues that Emma found herself humming the tune unconsciously, grinding her teeth to its triple meter in her sleep.

Emma followed the dog to the kitchen, where Rachel was blanketing the granite counter with their overnight provisions, meant to last at least until the moving pod arrived the next day: naan, hummus, two pears, a brick of white cheddar, a bottle of wine, toothbrushes, a tangle of chargers, Birdie's food and water dishes, and two hardcovers—a novel for Emma and essays on the intersections of bodily rhetoric and feminism for Rachel. The cover of Rachel's book was a photograph of a woman's hand posing as a small body: two red-lacquered fingernails pressed on the floor like feet with the thumb like a hand on its hip. The image bothered Emma for reasons she couldn't quite place. Nor did she understand why Rachel kept dust jackets on books at all. Emma removed it as soon as she purchased a book, shedding its glossy skin off into the trash like scraping a dinner plate. Rachel went so far as to tape the jacket to the book, which ensured the entire product remained intact as the publisher intended it. Rachel was a rule follower. She was reliable like that.

Emma wrapped her arms around her wife from behind and lightly bit the place between Rachel's scapulae, firm from yoga. She felt her wife's breath deepen, and Emma slipped her hands inside the front of her shirt. She parted Rachel's curls with her nose and let her tongue graze the warm skin at the base of her wife's neck.

Rachel flattened her palms on the countertop. "Are you sure?"

Emma was.

They went to the guest bedroom, the only room with carpeting. Emma tugged Rachel's shirt up, pressed their soft bellies together. The curtainless window cast a yellow square in the middle of the floor, and they found themselves on it, drawn to its warm respite from the blasting air-conditioning. The carpet was not as soft as it looked; it left a raw patch on Emma's shoulder blades where she arched her back against it. Emma let her mind go, her body pressing on with its own agenda. She knew Rachel was looking at her—Rachel always liked to look at her—but Emma closed her eyes and let her mind run through a pastiche of fuck miscellany: skin, tongues, the involuntary flex of muscles under glistening skin.

"Oh, Emma."

Rachel unwove herself from Emma and looked down at her hand. Blood. They both stared. Rachel wiped her fingers on her T-shirt to protect the carpet.

"I'm sorry. I thought it was over," said Emma.

"Jesus, don't apologize," said Rachel. "Are you okay? Does it hurt?"

"I'm fine."

Rachel didn't move. Not until Emma said, "Please." Only when she was gone, when Emma could hear the faucet running in the hallway bathroom, did Emma hold her shirt up to her mouth and let out a sound that only Birdie, who appeared in the doorway with her ears cocked, could hear.

* * *

The moving pod did not, in fact, arrive the next day. Rachel was put on hold for forty minutes before someone told her that the pod had mistakenly been sent to the wrong state. Apparently there was also a Riverbend, Oregon.

"It happens all the time, actually," the company

representative said without a trace of apology or irony. "What do you think we have you sign a waiver for?"

When Rachel hung up, she said, "It's a real Dalloway, honey." This was a joke that had evolved over the years, ever since one of their first dates, when Emma had arrived at the bar late and breathless, unwinding the scarf around her neck as she explained that her apartment's dishwasher had spread bubbles across the floor because her roommate had used Dawn dish soap instead of dishwasher detergent. "My day has gone worse than Mrs. Dalloway's," she'd said in apology, and Rachel had burst into such genuine laughter, her teeth shining in the bar's red neon light, that the joke had stuck, the name becoming shorthand for life's inconveniences.

Without the moving pod, the house continued to feel vacant and ownerless. In addition to the backpack with their first night's provisions, Emma and Rachel had brought a couple of suitcases full of clothing and a few small boxes of meaningful items with them, enough to make do for a few days. But Emma thought longingly of all that was missing: Their couch with its back cushions flattened from years of Birdie's thick, koala-like naps. The oak bookshelves and their eclectic volumes, whose worn spines Emma would run her fingers along as she talked on the phone. The blue mason jars they drank water and iced tea and wine from. The kilim rug she had ordered from Turkey for a bewilderingly low price; when it arrived and was only two square feet, Rachel had hung it on the wall and proclaimed it art.

Back in Chicago, they'd hired two college boys in sweat-resistant tracksuits to load their moving pod, which had been delivered on a truck. The boys drank bottles of purple electrolyte juice and obeyed Emma as she pointed them around the apartment. They pushed trolley after trolley of book boxes down the elevator and across the courtyard, sweat rolling off the ends of their noses. It was hot outside, the August air wavy and thick. Each piece of her life they carried out felt like it was connected to her body, and it tugged at her stomach and heart and throat to see them swallowed into the mouth of the moving pod. When Rachel went out to pick up sandwiches for lunch, Emma finally broke down.

One of the boys had touched her shoulder and she'd jumped—she hadn't heard him come in—and when she handed him his tip, he'd said, "Indiana, right? Shit, I'd cry too."

*　　　*　　　*

On their second full day in Riverbend, Emma and Rachel went to the closest grocery store, a big-box retailer, and filled the cart with oatmeal and hot sauce and tampons and eggs and shampoo. Since their bed was on the pod, they picked out new sheets and an inflatable mattress. When Emma stooped to get it from the bottom shelf, Rachel swatted her hands.

"Go easy," Rachel said, heaving the plastic package into the cart. "Remember what Dr. Casey said. No heavy lifting."

"I feel fine. And it's not exactly heavy."

"Just for another few days, okay? Then you can go back to pretending that you enjoy strenuous physical activity."

Emma affectionately pinched her wife's arm. "Get out of here, lady. Go home and alphabetize your Woolfs and Wolfes."

Rachel groaned. "My Woolf pack! Where do you think it is now?"

"The worst fate, I'm afraid. Bouncing on a highway somewhere in Idaho."

The grocery aisles abruptly ended and dumped them into the book section before a side-cap display of new fiction. "Hey, they have the new June Gaskill," said Emma, picking up a heavy book. "I love her. The *Times* called this book 'an exercise in intellectual exhaustion.' Remember? And I was like, 'This *review* is an exercise in' —"

"You have to be kidding me."

Emma looked up to see her wife's face purpling with embarrassment. An entire pyramid display of Rachel's novel with its bright yellow cover towered above her. A hand-lettered sign, colored painstakingly with marker by an employee, read BOOK OF THE WEEK! Beside it was Rachel's author photo with her vaguely confused smile, Lake Michigan in soft focus beyond.

"Oh, wow." Emma read the card. "'*Give Me Five Moons* is a stunning debut that mixes science fiction with literary prowess. Its examination of human relationships against the backdrop of a sinister reproductive technology offers a thought-provoking exploration of both the possibilities and limitations of motherhood in an evolving world.'" She clucked her tongue. "I mean, they copied that straight from *The Guardian*, but still. Very nice for a superstore review."

"Let's go," Rachel said, putting her hand on the cart. She hardly ever mentioned the novel now that the press had died down; she worried it might sabotage the respect she'd worked so hard to earn as an academic. Rachel and Emma also both knew but never discussed how deeply the book's success had wounded Emma, the actual fiction writer, who had never been able to find an agent for her own novel. Every literary agency had sent Emma some version of the same personalized pass: *This is the hardest kind of rejection to send. . . . A book this quiet just won't sell in today's market. . . . There's not as much appreciation these days for the art of the sentence, as much as we might personally feel otherwise.* Emma's publishing career was a collection of almosts: runner-up for a number of fiction prizes, a finalist for two fellowships that each ultimately went to someone else. The worst had been two years ago when she'd secured a tentative offer from a small but respected independent publisher that folded before the deal could be finalized.

Yet it had been Emma who suggested Rachel try her hand at fiction—"Something genre, maybe," she'd said—to keep Rachel's mind busy while awaiting news of whether her dissertation would be accepted for publication. Rachel had initially considered the novel a distraction but before long had fully thrown herself into the exercise. When Emma read the first draft, she was proud, but there was something else too. A sense of yearning, perhaps, for how it might have felt to put something on the page without the weight of self-doubt slowing the process down. Rachel's novel was precise and descriptive and just the right length. It was a new idea with sharply written characters. It had all the ingredients of a great book, but there was something essential missing, something Emma couldn't put her finger on. Perhaps it was the same thing that was missing in Rachel herself: messiness.

Emma was attracted to messy books. She liked quiet, interminable scenes and sprawling descriptions of domestic realism. She liked endings that felt like the quiet sigh that escapes after a headache dissolves. Rachel's book wasn't her type, per se, but she knew it would have broad appeal. So when Rachel's dissertation was rejected by her top-choice academic publisher, Emma sent the novel to a literary agency. She'd hoped for some positive feedback to boost Rachel's confidence, but she hadn't expected the scale of the response. The agent had not just emailed back; she'd called Rachel three days after receiving the query and signed her immediately. The book quickly sold at auction for a staggering amount of money, and shortly after that, Emma filed away her own manuscript for good.

It shouldn't have been a surprise. Rachel did nearly everything better than Emma did. For Emma, writing was not so much like pecking away at something but like picking at a knot that refused to come undone. But she loved her wife, and whether Emma liked it or not, her wife was now a bestselling author.

Emma took a book and placed it along with the Gas-kill atop the precarious pile of home goods in the cart.

"What are you doing?" Rachel asked. "We have, like, twenty-five copies in the moving pod."

"But the pod isn't here. What if a neighbor pops by and I want to show you off, Professor?"

"Don't be obnoxious."

"Don't pretend it's nothing," Emma said, sliding her hands onto the cart handle and steering it toward the checkout line, "when the rest of us can see that it's something."

They decided to take the long route home to get a better feel for the city and found themselves winding through an industrial park that looked as if it had been abandoned long ago. Empty parking lots reflected the expansive, cloudless sky. FOR SALE: PRIME RETAIL SPACE blared a red sign; Emma caught the phrase *vibrant shopping corridor* and wondered if that signaled an optimism for the future or a clinging to a past that no longer existed. One apartment complex, its paint flaking, bore a patchwork of signs and legal notices. Emma could read only one, handwritten on cardboard, as they drove by: PLEASE CHECK FOR KITTENS BEFORE DEMOLITION.

"Riverbend reminds me of where I grew up," said Emma. "Except in Arcola, they wouldn't have bothered with a sign. Too much spelling."

"Right." Rachel adjusted her sun visor. "So you've said."

"Did I ever tell you I grew up half a mile from an abandoned grain elevator? I gave Kyle Richards a terrible hand job there, and a week later it collapsed."

"Thanks for that image."

"You're welcome." Emma patted Rachel's thigh. "I peaked at fifteen, didn't I? It's all been downhill since the grain elevator."

Rachel smiled. "Baby, I know your childhood was a mess of religious indoctrination and tractor races—"

"Tractor pulls."

"But Riverbend versus Arcola is not a fair comparison. Also, it's 2008. We've got a Black guy running for president. We're two ladies who are married! This is an entirely new world compared to when we were kids."

"I know." Emma looked out the window. She hadn't been to her hometown in over ten years, but its contours still shaped her thoughts. Sometimes when she closed her eyes at night she saw, without warning, a faded red-brick post office or a country road flanked by cornfields. Arcola was both a philosophical idea, something that hadn't actually happened to her, and a grim sediment that had calcified in her memory, like a tattoo she'd forgotten she had.

"I'm actually glad we're here," Rachel said. They were stopped at a red light beside a McDonald's letterboard sign that read HARD WORK, NOT HANDOUTS. $7/HOUR START.

"Because you want French fries?" Emma asked.

"I mean in Riverbend. This place needs a little queering up."

"Ah, yes. The rainbow touch."

"Funny."

"Where small town meets big gay dreams."

"Okay, never mind." The light turned green. Rachel flipped her visor back up. "I was being serious."

"Sorry," said Emma. "You know you have a heart of gold, Rachel Sullivan." Rachel didn't answer, but her shoulders drew back in the way they did when she was pleased.

As they wove through the residential streets closer to their new home, Emma craned her neck to try and get a sense of the people who lived in this part of the city. The university was north of here, where graduate students and lower-ranking faculty kept the campus bus lines full and the Starbucks open until ten o'clock at night. But the area south of campus was harder to parse, a mix of sagging porches and newly flipped homes with glossy exteriors. The houses were set back from the road, which in Chicago would have suggested Lincoln Park wealth or comfortable suburbia. But here the lawns were bald in places, the driveways cracked and buckled. The curtains were drawn over every window, and Emma imagined their interiors were all a copy of the house she'd grown up in: Green plaid cushions on a wooden couch frame coated in wax, the humming yellow refrigerator weighted with half-empty ketchup bottles, brown carpeting flattened from years of her mother's pacing. A plastic crucifix presiding over meat-loaf dinners from its spot on the kitchen wall.

On their new block alone Emma counted three McCain bumper stickers and six signs supporting the reelection of the Republican governor, a white man with a tall forehead and thin lips. He looked like he could be either of their fathers. Well, maybe not Rachel's father. Rachel's father had a low ponytail and was the chair of the philosophy department at the University of Chicago. Rachel's father said things like "Are we *not* floating in space, then?" whenever he wanted someone to reevaluate their opinions. Emma loved him; he read all of her stories, sending her handwritten notes (*I nearly had a coronary on the treadmill when I got to the scene with the doctor!*) after each publication, even the ones behind a paywall. Her own father had never read her writing. That was probably for the best.

Emma said, "We can't forget to register to vote."

"You haven't yet? I did it online last week."

Emma looked at her wife. With her hair pulled back she looked angelic, eyebrows high and innocent. "Oh, lady. Of course you did."

*   *   *

By the weekend, the pod still hadn't arrived and the moving company offered no further updates on its ETA. With nothing to unpack, Emma turned to administrative tasks. She hung a big calendar on the door of the kitchen pantry. With a marker, she neatly wrote in her and Rachel's class schedules, marking times when they'd share the car and times when one of them would need to take the bus. Emma didn't have to teach on Tuesdays and Thursdays, and she was filled with anticipation for the long hours she would spend on those days reading and cooking and easing herself gently back into writing. She hadn't had that kind of freedom in years. Rachel had dangled this promise like a carrot when coaxing Emma to Indiana.

When the calendar was done, Emma opened her laptop and reviewed her class roster. It had been nearly two years since she'd sworn she'd never adjunct again, and here she was, facing down two sections of Intro to Rhetoric, each with twenty-six nearly identical white faces.

"A Kenneth, three Brittanys, and two Michaels walk into a classroom," she called out to Rachel, who didn't answer, which was fine because Emma hadn't worked out a punch line.

As was required of all faculty, she had copied the dense brick of university policies — disability accommodations, plagiarism, attendance — and pasted it on the last two pages of her syllabus. When she'd taught in Chicago, it had been a joke among her colleagues that students never read the fine print; those pages were a waste of the precious hundred and fifty photocopies loaded onto their faculty cards each semester. One semester her friend Anna had suggested a contest to find the rare student who read the policies — "The one true undergraduate!" — and the writing instructors began dropping hidden messages into the final pages of their syllabi, things like *Email Sun Yi if you have read this and she will give you five extra-credit points* and *Announce your favorite television show exactly four minutes into class and get an automatic pass on that day's quiz.* Students rarely noticed these messages, but when they did, that teacher would be owed a beer by their colleagues at happy hour. Those friendships had buoyed Emma during the misery of adjuncting, through the low pay and crippling self-doubt she was positive her students could sense in her. It was bizarre to be stepping back into this world, and without any friends this time.

In a moment of nostalgia, Emma opened her syllabus and typed, *Congratulations on finding this hidden message! You've proven yourself to be more observant than a vice president on a quail hunt. Email Emma the name of your favorite band and receive a pass on one weekly quiz.*

When course prep was done, Emma cleaned the bathroom, scrubbing behind the toilet with enough bleach to sting her eyes. Then she paced the house, feeling each room's emptiness and vast, open space.

"You're deferring the inevitable," said Rachel when Emma wandered into the bedroom with a bottle of blue window cleaner and a roll of paper towels. Rachel, wearing Emma's Depeche Mode hoodie, was spread out on the air mattress with her own syllabus, a thick highlighter twirling through her fingers.

"How so?"

"The deal was, you were going to start writing again after we moved." Rachel looked at her over the top of her readers, which required tipping her head in a condescending way. "I wouldn't be a supportive wife if I didn't tell you to stop procrastinating."

Emma sprayed the bedroom window with cleaner and wiped, an old soreness rising. She'd become so practiced at pushing this feeling away that she only noticed its shadow, darkening like sand after the tide pulls back. She couldn't let Rachel know how deeply she mourned the loss of her vision of herself as a successful writer. Her wife would think that Emma's creative paralysis was her fault, that it was her big, successful book that had prompted Emma to abandon her own — and of course it was, but Emma didn't want to taint a new marriage with her oppressive feelings.

Instead, Emma said, "We've only been here four days. And I've been busy with class prep."

"How? You're only teaching two sections this fall."

Emma smeared the paper towel across the glass, pressing hard enough to produce a pleasing chirp beneath her hand. She'd learned long ago that the things that slipped from Rachel's mouth weren't as tinged with condescension as they seemed. Not intentionally, anyway. Rachel was a person who took things literally, and her standards were shaped by her own relentless work ethic. Still, there were times when Emma wished that her wife could just be average.

Settle for a B-plus, lady! But Rachel had never gotten a B-plus in her life.

"You know what? You've inspired me," Emma said, tossing the paper towel into the wastebasket. "I'm going to go dust off the old manuscript right now. This very second."

"All right, then. Gold star for you." Rachel looked like she was going to say something else, but instead she put the highlighter in her mouth and turned back to her syllabus.

Emma went into the kitchen and opened her laptop, settling into the ten-dollar plastic lawn chair they'd bought as makeshift seating until the pod arrived. She clicked through the folder path that led to her manuscript, feeling a wash of pity for its hopeful naming conventions — *TheCrossing_FINAL!*, *TheCrossing_Ready4Edits*, *TheCrossing_RevisedFinal*. The book had grown from a short story Emma wrote in grad school about a widowed artist into a four-hundred-page meditation on art and the limits of devotion. She'd been working on the project for years, since before she'd even known Rachel. It used to be the first thing she thought of when she woke up, the story her mind turned to instinctively on long bus rides or idle Sunday-morning walks. Now it had been nearly eighteen months since she'd opened the document.

She settled back in the chair. It was always odd to read her own work after a break from it. Sometimes she marveled at the sentences she no longer recognized; sometimes she saw immediately what had been invisible to her before and knew exactly how to fix them. Today, though. It could have been the heat or the lack of furniture or the emphasis Rachel had put on the word *only*—"You're *only* teaching two sections"—but today, Emma saw that the book she'd unreservedly devoted herself to for years was simply not good. The main character engaged in constant, obnoxious self-editorializing; the prose was thick and greedy, as if she'd written each description several ways and decided to keep them all. Even her favorite scenes seemed to float like debris in a larger ocean of overworked, murky language.

How had she ever thought this was ready to send out? What on earth had she been thinking? Emma recalled all the times Rachel read chapters and offered her careful feedback, always beginning with what she found beautiful. Rachel must have known this whole time what a mess it was, how unpublishable it had become.

Emma felt a pressure in her throat—the prelude to either a sob or vomit—and slammed the laptop shut. She needed some air. Shoving the laptop aside, she went to the front door and stepped out. As if summoned, their next-door neighbor marched over. The woman's lips were twisted in a grimace that indicated she was headed toward Emma's house for business, not social pleasure. She stopped on Emma's driveway and held out an envelope.

"I was going to put this in your mail slot," she said. "Got a letter meant for you." She was in her sixties; her hair was cut short, the color of a squirrel, and flattened against her forehead. She could have teleported directly from Emma's childhood, could've been any of the older women who piled their plates with deviled eggs at church potlucks and patrolled the children's tables to prevent dessert hoarding.

Emma saw that the woman wasn't going to step closer, so she went to the driveway and took the envelope from her. It was a letter from the university for Rachel, probably health-insurance paperwork. "Thanks. We just moved in."

"I saw. You certainly got a deal on the house." Her eyes flickered to the tattoo on Emma's inner elbow, a flock of starlings. "I'm Patty. You're Rachel, then?" She nodded at the envelope.

"I'm Emma. Rachel's my wife."

Patty raised her eyebrows. "Didn't know that was legal."

"Well, Patty, it is in California." Emma hated how defensive she sounded, but she'd grown tired of the implication that her marriage was counterfeit. "We got married there in June." Emma and Rachel had been one of a dozen same-sex couples to get married at the city hall that morning in San Francisco, on a patio lined with knobby trees whose branches had been laced with purple and silver streamers. Emma had been six weeks pregnant, dizzy with joy and the faint stirrings of first-trimester nausea. Her parents, whom she saw only every three years or so anyway, hadn't come to the ceremony—expensive flights, boarding the dog, et cetera. But Rachel's parents were there, of course. Her mother had fried their digital camera with her tears.

"You're from California?" Patty asked. The gold cross on her necklace was caught on the zipper of her hoodie, pulling the chain slightly into the soft skin of her neck like a cheese wire sinking into a fresh Brie.

"Actually, no. We're from Chicago."

"Why'd you come here, then?"

"Rachel's going to be teaching at the university. I will too, actually. As an adjunct." When Patty didn't respond, Emma felt obliged to explain. "Teaching's the inevitable end to an MFA in creative writing. That's the degree I have. You either teach or publish a book, and I haven't—"

"You're lucky to get jobs," Patty interrupted. "My son's been looking for six months and nothing. I was out there with him in Terre Haute all summer, helping him with the new baby because you would not believe the cost of diapers right now, let alone day care. I'd help him more, but our retirement account sprung a leak. This economy." She stopped there, the rest of her sentence so predictable it could remain unspoken.

Emma nodded in sympathy. Two years ago she'd turned thirty-one and decided to quit teaching once and for all. She hated the tenuous nature of adjunct life and was tired of using all her creative energy to grade undergraduate essays and stories. So she'd sent her résumé to countless office jobs and gotten not a single interview. It was only by luck that she'd landed a job as an administrative assistant in the School of Communication at Loyola—an old friend worked in development and passed her résumé along. Emma found she liked spending her days making travel arrangements for the dean and taking notes in faculty meetings. The work was boring but not exhausting; her mind was free to wander in a way it couldn't when she was in front of a classroom. She'd felt a bit ashamed by her professional inertia, especially since Rachel seemed disappointed by the lack of ambition. But it was a job, and she did have more energy to write, at least in the beginning.

Then Rachel was offered a tenure-track faculty position in Indiana, and Emma had to quit. She couldn't say no to the spousal-hiring deal. A teaching contract was a job, and in this economy, she had to take it. What's more, she was supposed to feel grateful—she was snaking her way through a recession with barely a scratch on her.

"What degree does your son have?" Emma asked. "He should look at college jobs. Higher ed is the one place that's doing well right now. Everyone's enrolling."

Patty sighed at this information as if Emma had asked her to carry something heavy. "Listen, I just came over to give you the mail. And to tell you that you need to water the spireas. They need a good soak every week or they make a big fuss and turn yellow and then the whole neighborhood looks like we're all on welfare."

Emma looked at the bushes in front of the house. Their deep red blooms were one of the only things that had appealed to her about this place. She couldn't help but identify with their resignation, the way they bowed to the grass: *I will live here quietly for three years, but a moment longer, and I swear I will uproot myself.*

"Okay," Emma said. "We can do that."

"She may have had her troubles, but Charlotte always took care of her plants," said Patty. "When she left, there were fourteen different varieties of hostas along the walk. The contractors ripped them out for these half-price spireas from Home Depot. I was gone the day they did it, otherwise I would have come over and put a stop to it."

"Who's Charlotte?"

Patty looked pained. "The person whose house you moved into. Charlotte and her husband, Dirk."

"Oh." Emma felt the air thicken with tension; the home had been foreclosed on in the summer, the couple who had lived there for decades evicted. Their real estate agent had called it the Boomer Bust-Up—retirees blindsided by the sudden dip in the economy, thinking their hardships were over after a handful of global wars and a childhood steeped in post-Depression trauma. "They're all refinancing their homes like they're still in their prime," he'd said. "It's a little sad, if you want to know my opinion." Emma hadn't liked the real estate agent, Victor Maxwell; he had a red mustache that he touched too much, and he tried to tell Rachel a dirty joke in German.

"Did they move somewhere nearby?" she asked Patty now. She felt stressed by the thought of the house's former owners driving past slowly, assessing the quality of her landscaping.

Patty sniffed. "Don't know where they are. They left while I was in Terre Haute this summer. Didn't even bother to let me know. Got back and there was a dumpster in the front yard full of their stuff. Apparently they stopped paying their mortgage and walked. Left everything behind. Then the renovation, which I very much doubt was done well, given the timeline." She tilted her head so she could look down her nose at Emma. "What's it like inside?"

Emma flushed, thinking of the hook she'd pulled from the wall. "It's nice. You know, they left some furniture here. Maybe you'd want to —"

Patty held up her hands. "Like I have the space for any more stuff in my house. If they left it, they don't need it. They probably went to live with their son, and

I can't imagine Justin having room for anything more than a mattress and a hot plate. Kid's a drug addict, hardly ever came around." She wiped her chin, where a tiny bit of saliva had landed while she was talking. "He's responsible for that horrendous Jacuzzi in the backyard. Why you didn't insist they remove that eyesore before you moved in is beyond me."

"The hot tub?" Emma said in surprise. "I think it's kind of cool."

"Honey, that thing hasn't worked in ten years. Dirk tried to fix it up, but who knows where Justin got it." She shook her head. "Lucky you don't have kids."

Emma looked toward the backyard, then at Patty again. "What makes you think we don't have kids?"

Patty stared at her for a moment, blinking several times. "Do you?"

Emma flushed. "Well, no. Not yet."

Patty lifted her hands as if to say, *See?* "You'll also have to trim the spireas," she said. "Be respectful of the place, will you?" With that, she was gone, tromping across the grass, dandelion seeds erupting in clouds at her feet.

Emma took the letter into the house. She found Rachel in the guest bedroom, which they planned to set up as an office as soon as the furniture arrived. The room seemed chaotic without the gravity of her desk. Papers and books and literary journals were strewn around like trash on a beach. Rachel was kneeling in the middle of it, holding a stapler in one hand and a mason jar of coffee in the other. Her curls were frizzy, a sign she'd been running her fingers through them.

"Hey, hey, Lady Macbeth." Emma took the coffee and the stapler and set them on the windowsill. "You need a break. Let's go for a walk."

"My syllabus is too Eurocentric," said Rachel, plunging an arm into a plastic bin full of bound course packets, one of the boxes she'd deemed too precious for the pod and shoved in the back seat of the car, where it had blocked the rearview mirror for the entire six-hour drive. "I need to find that essay on body rhetoric by the Haitian writer, the queer woman. What's her name? Do you remember? Of course you don't," she said without waiting for an answer. "I bought you the book and you never even opened it."

"I doubt anyone in a city with two Walmarts and six evangelical churches cares whether your syllabus is too Eurocentric."

"God, Emma. Listen to you! That's exactly why it's important."

Emma sighed. Ever since *Give Me Five Moons* came out, Rachel had been even more tightly coiled, feeling the pressure to prove herself as a serious intellectual and not just a science fiction writer. Emma wondered sometimes if she might have felt less resentful if Rachel had wanted the success as badly as she did or if Rachel had at least agonized over the writing process as much as Emma did her own. There was something medicinal about shared suffering. But for Rachel the novel had been at first a lark and now a nuisance because the reviews for *Give Me Five Moons* (all glowing) pushed her recently published essay on intersectionality in queer feminist rhetoric to the third page on Google. Emma didn't tell Rachel that the essay she was looking for was written by Fabiola Saint-Fleur and was probably in the material for the Caribbean diaspora course she took in the third year of her PhD.

This was how marriage worked, Emma had decided; you took your victories in private.

"You got mail," Emma said. The visit from Patty had unexpectedly cheered her up; it had been enough of a distraction that the cloud of doom surrounding her novel had passed and now had a vaguely irrelevant, long-ago feeling to it.

Rachel didn't look up from the stack of papers in her hands. "Open it."

Emma tore open the envelope. "It's an invitation for a faculty reception next month welcoming the new hires. The new full-time hires, of course. Not us plebeian adjuncts. But I guess I can be your plus-one."

Rachel dropped her papers and pressed the heels of her palms into her eyes. "I feel like I'm going to have a migraine."

Emma moved behind Rachel. She put her hands on her wife's shoulders and leaned her full weight into them. They breathed together for a minute. Then Emma straightened up and let go. She watched Rachel's shoulders rise back up and felt the vicarious pleasure of lightness.

"This will cheer you up," said Emma. "I nearly killed the neighbor by telling her that two women could be legally married. She's probably at home grousing to her husband about it over chili mac right now. And don't you think it's ironic how all the homophobic midwestern moms have the same dyke haircut?"

Rachel looked up. For a moment Emma thought she saw regret in her eyes, but Rachel's mouth straightened into a thin smile, her expression full of empathy. Her teaching face. "You know what I'm going to say."

"Oh, right."

"Sometimes you have to be——"

"Someone's first gay person. Right."

"I mean, it's true."

"I know, I know." Emma sighed. "We have to pander to the troglodytes."

"She'll get to know us, and her worldview will shift. Even if it's just a little bit. This is how change happens, Em. So be nice. It's your duty to future generations of queer kids." Rachel touched Emma's thigh. "And to our kids."

Emma dropped to her knees and leaned her head on her wife's shoulder. Rachel had been raised by intellectuals in a progressive suburb; her sexuality was just another part of her exceptionalness, like her perfect ACT score and her wild, untamable curls. Emma was dazzled by—and envious of—her wife's ability to maneuver through the world without absorbing any shame. Rachel never felt the need to justify her existence; she felt sorry for homophobes, believing they were simply misinformed, like people who believed you swallowed a certain number of spiders a year while sleeping. It drove Emma, who was raised Catholic, crazy.

Emma stroked Rachel's hair. "Speaking of kids. Maybe we could try again soon. There's an IVF clinic here. It has good reviews."

"IVF? Are we already at that point?"

"I think so. Everything I've read says that it has much better odds of success. And we only have one vial of sperm left. Don't you think we should really make it count?"

Rachel hesitated. "It's really soon, though, don't you think? You're still bleeding."

"Barely. And I feel fine."

Rachel swept her hand to indicate the mess of papers on the floor. "Can we talk about it later? Maybe when I'm not spiraling?"

"Of course." Emma stood. "I'll start dinner. Shakshuka okay?"

But Rachel was gleeful, thrusting a worn blue course packet into the air. "Fabiola Saint-Fleur! I found you!"

"As we both knew you would," Emma said, and went to their new kitchen to start dinner.

*　　　*　　　*

Boon University was more beautiful than Emma wanted to admit. Crested trees lined the sidewalks beside a duck pond edged with sandstone slabs. The campus felt busy, with flocks of students dodging bicycles on footpaths and weaving along the peony-topped medians of the pedestrian walkway, but the short buildings and wide lanes gave the whole place a pleasant sense of sprawl. As promised on the Riverbend city website, charming cafés crowded the sidewalks with their little tables, and a second-run movie theater listed its showings on an old-fashioned marquee.

The English department occupied a squat brick building on the south end of campus, ivy tangled on its sides. Emma climbed the steps and pushed through the front door. She didn't have an office, but she'd been given keys to a shared adjunct lounge in the basement. The department chair, a thick and breathless man who'd introduced himself as Paulie, had informed Emma that she was lucky to have even this accommodation.

"We believe in investing in our core faculty," he'd said when Rachel and Emma had visited campus over the summer to sign their contracts. After a brief tour of the department, they'd made a stop in the windowless lounge that had obviously been a storage room in its previous life. One of its three tables was piled with the runoff of past department events: paper plates, napkins, programs for commencements five years earlier. Underneath one table lay stacks of folded tablecloths in green and black, the school's colors. The room's most imposing fixture was the elderly copy machine, which wheezed even when off the job and doubled as a table for mismatched coffee mugs. The place smelled heavily of Band-Aids, an odor that bit the back of the tongue like an aged cheese.

"It's a fixer-upper," Paulie said, jangling his keys. "But most universities don't have the real estate for adjuncts at all." He breathed heavily, light flecks of white in the corners of his mouth. Brown hair flopped over his forehead, which Emma could tell he was proud of; he kept touching it with his thick fingers as if to ensure it was still there.

"Actually, Northwestern has adjunct offices," said Emma. "And Loyola."

"Do they, now?" Paulie nodded as if he appreciated this information. Emma could feel Rachel's chagrin, but she couldn't help finishing the thought.

"Well, we had to share, two per, but our schedules rarely crossed. It's actually not as unfeasible as most universities think. And it helps with retention." Emma thought of the semesters she and Rachel had both been graduate instructors, early in their relationship. They spent hours in those adjunct offices, grading papers in their sweatpants, sipping milky tea and sharing bags of pretzels under the light of Rachel's SAD lamp. They'd had sex in the office more than once amid the rolling highlighters and bottles of Wite-Out and stacks of course packets from semesters past. Emma had come to think of those concrete walls as the place where her life had begun; she sometimes ran her finger between the cinder blocks and felt that Rachel had carved a clean line into her life like a snowplow, filling her with orderliness and purpose.

"Well, private universities operate with private money," said Paulie. "And as far as retention goes—I mean, you're both here and not there, right?" His smile was vast; a silver tooth peeked from the corner of his chapped lips.

Rachel was given a private office in the tenure-track enclave on the second floor. Her office was the size of their bedroom at home, boasting bookshelves crowded with her predecessors' castoffs and a large window facing the river that ran past campus. There was plenty of room for both of them to work there; in fact, Emma had assumed Rachel would offer to share the space. They could grade papers in a cloud of pretzel dust just as they had in grad school. But when she mentioned it after their trip, Rachel said she didn't think it would be good optics. How would Emma make friends with other instructors if she spent all her time in her wife's office? Emma knew Rachel's logic was based on some vague sense of fairness, but she still found it hurtful and had pouted for most of the day afterward.

This morning, Emma was glad to be the only person in the adjunct room. She ran her syllabus through the copy machine, the pre-class jitters already buzzing. She thought of Rachel, still at home because her first class wasn't until tomorrow. Rachel was probably poaching an egg and boiling water for her bitter turmeric tea. Slicing a plum. She would probably eat this breakfast leisurely, in front of the window, paging through a *New Yorker* and circling her bare toes around the rung of the ten-dollar lawn chair. Rachel never had pre-class jitters. When Emma thought of her wife like this, she felt the familiar flex of lust and envy under her skin.

Emma arrived at class at the moment it was to begin. She'd learned long ago that it was never a good idea to be the first one there. You were forced to feign busyness — shuffling papers, counting syllabi over and over — while students trickled in, murmuring to one another about the concerts and cafeteria meat loaf and study-abroad trips that filled their lives. Teaching was a performance, and while Emma had never grown completely comfortable with being in front of a class, she'd learned a few tricks to fake it. As she entered now, she threw her keys casually on the table at the front of the room — establish authority early! — and looked up at the clock, which drew the students' gazes away from her and toward the time, precisely 8:30 a.m., and bought her a moment to take a deep breath.

"Morning, everyone," she said.

The students were silent, a sea of denim and ponytails and Ugg boots, backpacks pooled at their feet. This was a required course; they were mostly freshmen. Practically babies. Emma knew not to take their silence personally—for some, it was their first college course ever—but the stillness of the room felt particularly thick. She cleared her throat. "This is Intro to Rhetoric. Our goal this semester is to gain a deeper understanding of the ways that language shapes the way we think and act."

The class stared sleepily at her. Someone coughed.

"Here's how I look at it. Words are everything," Emma continued. "When you master language, you have power. You can convince anyone of anything, whether it's why they should buy a certain brand of toilet paper or who they should vote for."

A hand went up. "How many papers do we have to write?"

"Right. The most important question of all." Emma pulled the warm syllabi from her bag and handed them out. The students came to life, flipping through the pages, running their fingers down the words. She could see their minds scramble to calculate the effort that it would require of them, how to balance it against the weight of labs and lectures and presentations and athletics. And jobs — nearly 60 percent of the undergraduates were also working, many full-time, to shoulder the sharply increasing tuition. Emma had read about this in the summer issue of the student newspaper, the *Boon Beacon*. Reading the article, she had felt sorry for the college students upon whom the weight of the recession had suddenly pressed. She could relate, having barely afforded college herself. Emma had worked every on-campus job she could find, from ushering at hockey games to collecting birds that had died in window strikes for the biology department, and she still carried a persistent vestige of loan debt. Now, seeing her own students fidget in their chairs as they parsed life's impossible equations, she felt a flicker of kinship.

A boy in a tracksuit and large glasses raised his hand. "My syllabus is missing the second page."

Emma shook herself out of her thoughts and passed him a new copy. "Sorry about that. I haven't had my prescription Red Bull yet."

The class laughed, a sudden reassurance that they were on her side, which prompted her own relief: Things were going to be fine after all! They were at the beginning of a new adventure, the soft kick of a fresh semester nudging them all awake. Maybe she would even feel like writing soon. Something new.

Emma was nearly finished covering the main points in the syllabus when the door swung open and another student entered, dipping his head through the doorframe like a much taller person, though there was plenty of clearance above him.

"Sorry I'm late." He straightened his backpack over his shoulder and walked in, a slow, intentional swagger in his hips. He stopped next to Emma at the front of the room and bowed to her, his backpack sliding to the floor. "Alex Brewer, junior, begging your forgiveness, madame."

"Glad to have you, Alex," said Emma, holding out a syllabus.

"Everyone calls me Brewer." Alex's eyes dropped to Emma's tattoo. "Nice ink. I love starlings."

Emma was annoyed by the responsive lift in her chest. Alex was undeniably attractive; there wasn't a person on earth who would have disagreed. He knew it, though, and it was his currency. He had deep-set dark eyes, expressive brows. A pouty bottom lip. A white T-shirt draped over his pectorals, and beneath that were loose silk board shorts and a pair of slides that held long, hairless toes. How easily he must transition from bed, thought Emma. Ready in ten seconds without any of the agony in front of the mirror that stormed her mornings. She had a feeling about certain men that wasn't exactly attraction but admiration and envy — their simple profiles, the economy of their entire being. There weren't many layers.

Alex lightly touched a finger to the tattoo on her

inner elbow, and Emma jerked her arm back—maybe, she immediately thought, a little too forcefully. The class hummed with sudden interest.

"Hey," Alex said, looking wounded. "I'm not a predator or anything."

"No one said you were," said Emma. "Just take the syllabus so we can continue."

Alex waited a beat. His thick eyebrows rose in a way that suggested everything was funny to him. Then he pinched the paper between two fingers and slid it from her hand. Almost imperceptibly, his hand shook, the paper trembling like dry leaves in the wind. Mocking her.

"You nervous, Prof?"

Emma forced her lips into a smile. "Just bracing for the challenge of grading your papers. Since you seem to know everything already."

The class laughed, harder this time.

Alex loped through the room purposefully. He took a seat in the back and spread his legs, smiling like a hound.

Emma wanted to smooth her hair and lick her lips, but she could feel everyone's eyes on her. "Now that everyone's here, let's go around and introduce ourselves, why don't we," she said. "Have you ever played two truths and a lie?"

They went around the room. Each student had to say three things about themselves, but one had to be a lie.

The rest of the class would guess which was which. The game was always hit or miss with undergrads, but this morning they seemed to be enjoying it. One student said he was from Missouri, he'd seen Kenny Chesney in concert eleven times, and he'd never been out of the country. Another said her father was an astronaut, she wished she had curly hair, and her cat was named Jerry Orbach because he loved to watch *Law and Order.*

Alex went last. When it was his turn, he held up his index finger. "I'm Brewer. Number one, I play golf on the school team." Another finger. "Two, I believe tattoos are a sign of intelligence."

The class laughed, and Emma's face burned. She desperately wanted to touch her cheek to see if it was as hot as it felt, but half the students were still watching her.

"And three," he said. "Hmm. Let me think of a good one." He looked out the window at the bronze statue of a robed woman reaching one hand out over the courtyard. The statue was meant to represent higher education as a gift passed from one mind to the next, but student lore had it she'd fly away if a virgin walked under her arm. The myth created an impossible trap for freshman girls, who were mocked for avoiding walking beneath it and slut-shamed if they did.

Emma saw the rest of the students follow Alex's stare, and in a moment they were all looking out the window at the statue, whose bronze eyes looked tired under their gaze. Emma could see Alex was stretching the moment out, feeling its power.

"Oh, I know," he said suddenly. He flicked a third finger in the air. "My favorite book is *Give Me Five Moons*. Such a good twist at the end."

Emma kept her face even. So she had found him, the student who researched the teacher, scouring the internet for facts about her personal life, before class began. Students did this for one of two reasons: They were suck-ups who believed that aligning their interests with hers would earn them a higher grade, or they were obsessive types, eager to devour inside information to either foster a crush or harbor that knowledge for later use. Emma wondered what else Alex knew. She tried not to mentally flip through her online footprint — the story she published about her childhood dog, her membership in the Human Rights Campaign — as she looked out at the class. "Any guesses?" she asked.

The spirit of the game had withered by this point. "The book one is probably true," said a student. "The least interesting one is usually true."

"Don't *you* want to guess which one is the lie?" Alex asked, looking right at Emma.

"You don't strike me as the golfing type." She reached for the stack of essays she'd photocopied that morning. "Now, let's move on to —"

"Because of my disability?" Alex interrupted.

"I'm sorry?"

"You don't think I look like a golfer," he said. "Because of my disability."

Emma's eyes fell, involuntarily, to his legs, spread obnoxiously. She thought of his slow walk, the lopsided turn of his hip—a limp, she thought with dismay. Not a swagger. "No. I mean, I didn't know you had a disability."

The class, suddenly revived, looked at her with interest. Alex held her gaze for a moment before letting his face burst into another supernova smile. "I'm messing with you."

Flustered, Emma pulled out the essays she'd copied. "Well, I'm off to a great start, aren't I? Why don't we split into small groups for a little exercise. Read through this essay. Don't worry, it's short. Then in fifteen, we'll talk about how it uses amplification to reiterate its point."

The classroom filled with the squeak of desks being dragged into groups. Emma had each student read a paragraph aloud and then discuss the piece with their groups. It was a cop-out exercise, one she always had in her back pocket when she felt too rattled to lead a discussion properly. As the groups chatted, she walked around the room and listened to their conversations. She sensed that the confidence she'd felt at the beginning of class had been only a thread, one that had unraveled from something that would never become whole in this particular classroom again. Worse, she knew that some of the students could see this — college kids might be sleepy, but they were perceptive — and Alex, whose eyes she could feel on her as she walked around the room, was very, very pleased about it all.

*   *   *

After class was over and the students had disappeared into their lives, Emma collapsed into a chair and let her head fall back, eyes closed. She felt exhausted by the effort of teaching, of pretending to be an extrovert when she'd rather be home alone with a book and her dog. That she had to teach two of these classes, each held three times a week, for the next fifteen weeks felt impossible. The spring held only the possibility of the same, or even more, and the next fall too. She thought of Chicago and its teeming streets lined with medians bursting with marigolds and impatiens, the bus that rocked her sleepily to her apartment, the lake that impassively accepted whatever she screamed at it from its rocky coast. Homesickness rose in her like nausea, burning and urgent.

"That bad, eh?"

Emma jerked her head up and saw Paulie standing in the doorway of the classroom. His hand hovered politely near the doorframe as if he'd been prepared to knock but then saw her fragile emotional state and thought better of it. He'd grown a patchy beard since she and Rachel had signed their contracts over the summer; she almost didn't recognize him.

"Oh, hi," she said, scrambling to her feet. "Just finished my first session of Intro to Rhetoric."

"Looks like they took it out of you already," he said. "I'm on my way to get a coffee. Come with me?"

He led her to a student-run café on the second floor of the English building. The space was surrounded by yellow couches upon which young people were piled like laundry, sipping coffee and scrolling through laptops and phones. Paulie ordered two Americanos. "You're not one of those nondairy people, are you?"

"Full dairy here. Bring on the cream."

"Thank heavens." Their coffees appeared on the metal counter, and he handed one to Emma before leading her to a wide sofa with stiff cushions. "This is a brand-new lounge area funded by a generous alum. You don't get a lot of generous donations from English alumni. Not that their hearts aren't big, but as you know, the prospects for prosperity are bleak." He took a sip. "Do you know the difference between an English doctoral student and a large pizza?"

Emma shook her head.

"The pizza can feed a family of four." Paulie's mouth widened in sudden pleasure, as if he were hearing the joke for the first time. "But, really, how are you settling into Riverbend? Finding the church-potluck circuit to your liking?"

Emma smiled. "It's an adjustment. But it's nice. It's—" She tried to think of something positive to say. "The traffic has been easy."

"Oh, yes. University Avenue is no Lake Shore Drive." Paulie twisted the lid of his coffee around until the sip hole lined up with the seam of the cup. "And the house? Rachel said you bought something in the Willow Heights neighborhood. Great up-and-coming area."

"The house is fine." She shrugged. "We're learning that the flippers may have cut a few corners. The fuse blows if you plug in the kitchen kettle while the oven's on. Half the outlets work on the bottom but not the top. That sort of thing. And our moving pod still hasn't arrived." She paused, realizing how negative she sounded. "But the old owners left half their furniture in the garage, so we're using that for now. Rachel's already painted one of their cabinets yellow and put new knobs on it."

"How enterprising, not surprising." Paulie hummed a moment, and Emma felt his pleasure in the rhythm of his words. So he was a poet, or had been at one time. "Have I mentioned how excited we are about Rachel?" he asked.

Emma shifted the paper cup to her other hand. It didn't have a cardboard sleeve, and the cup's heat scorched her palm. "You've made her feel very welcome."

"She was a real find. I loved *Give Me Five Moons.*

Stayed up until two o'clock in the morning just turning pages. I haven't felt like that about reading since I was in grad school. And when I found out she was an academic!" Paulie wolf-whistled. Then he studied Emma, his expression suddenly serious. "But I know what it's like to be you."

Emma raised her eyebrows.

"Well, not in every sense, ha-ha! But Rachel's got very keen ambitions, is that right?"

"Yes."

"Even when she doesn't try, she succeeds. She's just one of those people who are wired for it. For the spouse, it can get unbelievably tiring."

Emma smiled. "It's like you wrote her biography. And mine."

Paulie nodded. "My wife is the provost here."

"I didn't know that."

"Lisa's a powerhouse. Very instrumental in getting the funding we needed for the new wing. So I know that having a partner who casts a large shadow can be depleting, creatively." He sniffed. "What I'm trying to say is, I hope you don't let it slow the momentum of your own writing. I read the story you wrote in *Granta* last year."

Emma took a sip of coffee to hide the surprise on her face. "You did?"

"Of course."

"I didn't think anyone actually read those. I've

always felt like publishing short stories in journals is like throwing them into a lake."

"Oh, it is. But there are always a few little fish who nibble at them. Anyway, it was spectacular. You have an ear for dialogue."

"Well, thank you." The lift in her chest again—but this time she allowed it. "Truthfully, I haven't been able to write much since Rachel's book came out."

"Understandable." He nodded gravely. "But you really should take advantage of the time you have right now. Rarely in life will you stumble upon such a flexible schedule."

"That's what Rachel says."

"And what about kids?"

Emma coughed as the hot drink hit the back of her throat. "I'm sorry?"

"Are you planning on having them?"

"Oh." She blushed with a sudden sense that her body was part of the conversation in a way it hadn't been before. She felt the spread of her thighs on the sofa and crossed her legs. "Yeah. Someday. I wasn't so sure at first, but it's important to Rachel, so. Do you have kids?"

Paulie shook his head. "Lisa's ambivalence always outweighed my desire. Now that ship has sailed."

Emma realized, as she looked more closely at his face, that Paulie was older than she'd originally estimated. Probably early fifties. He looked at her intensely when she was speaking, but it didn't seem to be a power move; he was simply trying to discern what she meant. Emma caught a glimpse of what he must have been like as a boy, not understanding the assignment and always trailing after his mother. She felt briefly charmed. "I'm sure parenthood isn't all it's cracked up to be."

He smiled. "Oh, life has treated us just fine. Listen, Emma, I've been talking your ear off and haven't gotten to the reason I wanted to chat."

She felt an instinctive flash of caution. "What's that?"

"We had a late surge in enrollment for Intro to Rhetoric. A serendipitous combination of recent changes in degree requirements at Boon and the Pell Grant increases. But we have twenty-three extra heads, enough to scrape together a whole extra section. Naturally I thought of you."

"To teach it?" She meant it as a clarifying question, but her voice recoiled slightly.

"What, you need to check your schedule?" Paulie cocked his head. "Most adjuncts are banging down my door for a bigger course load."

"No, I can do it." Emma willed her voice to brighten. "When is it?"

"Tuesdays and Thursdays, ten to eleven thirty. Plus office hours."

There went her empty days. She knew she was being bratty and ungrateful, but a day with even a single class in it felt ruined, a fingerprint on otherwise clear glass. Still, she smiled. "Thank you."

"Welcome. Obviously I want you to be happy here, Emma."

She nodded. "I appreciate that."

"And not just because I don't want to lose Rachel. But we do need her here. Boon got some flak last year about the lack of gender diversity among our tenured faculty. Blame my wife. She hires all the men! Anyway, Rachel being a lesbian — she's basically a double woman." Paulie petted the emergent beard on his cheeks and nodded. "Counts as two!"

Emma gave a tight smile. "Don't forget Rachel also has ten years of teaching experience and won the dean's distinguished dissertation award. On top of being a bestselling author."

Paulie was quiet for a moment, and Emma flushed, afraid she'd overstepped. But then he smiled and shook his finger. "See, that's what I love about women! You're always looking out for each other. Happy wife, happy life. Am I right?" Without waiting for an answer, he dropped his cup in the waste bin and checked his phone. "How is it ten o'clock already? I'm going to be late for a budget meeting." He gave Emma a wry smile. "The things my twenty-five-year-old self would have been horrified to hear come from my lips."

She watched him labor up the stairs to the tenured

faculty offices. Rachel would be happy to learn about this conversation. She would probably laugh about the "double woman" comment. *People are nice here,* she would say. *And I told you you're a brilliant writer—even Paulie Schinzer knows it.* But now Emma felt unsure if the comment about her writing was genuine or simply an attempt to inflate her ego in order to keep her wife happy and get her to agree to an extra course.

She checked her phone. Two hours until her next class. Not quite enough time to make a worthwhile trip home and back. So she returned to the adjunct office, which now housed a trio of faculty who were pulling the drawers of the copy machine in and out in an attempt to unclog a paper jam. Emma lifted her hand to them in greeting, and they nodded without interest. She didn't take it personally; the culture of adjuncts was naturally one of distrust. They were all figs on a tree, hoping to be plucked.

Emma sat at a desk against the wall and opened her laptop. *I will write a new book,* she told herself. *Start fresh. Just a sentence to warm up.* She drummed her fingers lightly on the keys, listening to the pleasant clacking sound they made as she tried to think of a place to start. But instead, pulled by the dopamine-rich possibilities of the internet, she opened a web browser.

She'd been to the Riverbend Family Planning Center's website so often that her browser auto-filled the address after she typed only one letter. When she'd first come across it, the name made her think it was one of those clinics where they tricked young pregnant women into giving their babies up for adoption when they came in scared and looking for help. But when she finally visited the website, the tagline surprised her: *Bringing joy to families through IVF.* The homepage featured a young white woman with blond hair holding an infant in her arms. She looked serenely upon her baby, her eyelashes full and effortless, exuding a secret wisdom available only to mothers. Emma's chest ached at the sight of the woman's self-satisfaction.

It was true that Emma hadn't wanted to have children in the first place. She thought she was too anxious for parenthood, too predestined for failure. But Rachel had talked her into it, citing stories of her own idyllic childhood filled with camping trips to Muir Woods and French lessons and two parents who packed whimsical notes in her lunch box. Lying in bed at night, tracing Rachel's collarbone with her finger, Emma had felt that Rachel was gently planting something in her mind and tending to it so that one day Emma would realize it might be possible after all. And it had worked. When Rachel's book deal landed in their lives like an impossible gift, Emma decided it was time to start trying for a baby. She reasoned that having children was a way to reestablish one's identity and sense of purpose. A chance to start over, in a way, maybe even to undo the damage your own parents had done. And Emma's parents had definitely done some damage.

Rachel had undergone a hysterectomy when she was twenty-two because of severe endometriosis, which meant Emma would be the one to get pregnant. So the process that followed—the winnowing down of sperm-donor profiles, the painful intrauterine inseminations with the pinching catheter snaking through her cervix, the monthly sense of failure when her period arrived, the hundreds of cups of red clover tea, the staggering cost—had been, for Emma, an act of love for her wife, not a child.

But the process kept failing. Every month her period came and they were crushed by disappointment. This pattern continued for a whole year, alongside the birth of Rachel's book. Through the editing process and cover design and an online prerelease campaign for which Rachel had to fly to New York to film her part in a book trailer—"You can't withhold the author's face from readers when it's this attractive," her agent had said—Emma was left to carry the guilt of the negative pregnancy tests alone. To make things worse, the rejections from literary agents continued to trickle in months after she'd shelved the manuscript. Salt in a very deep wound. Emma found herself at one of the lowest points in her life, the two failures lining up neatly as the teeth of a zipper. She couldn't publish a book, and now she couldn't make a baby. It felt

destined somehow, an implausible plotline orches-
trated by the sinister higher power that had governed
her Catholic childhood. *I didn't even want a baby!* she
wanted to scream. *I only wanted the book!*

Then one day two lines appeared on a home pregnancy test. And a strange thing happened. It was
like when she'd gotten her wisdom teeth removed in
college—not until the procedure was over did she
understand how much pain she'd been in before, how
ordinary that pain had become. Looking at the pregnancy test in her hand, Emma felt like her life had been
sheared in two, partitioning the time before this baby
and the time that began now, in which everything
she'd been holding—the internalized homophobia,
the problems with her parents, angst over her failed
publishing career, the dismay at Rachel accepting a job
in Indiana, of all places—was gone. And in its place
was the coolness of extraction, an open space that
almost immediately filled with warmth. With love. She
loved the baby—was it possible it happened so quickly
like this? She and Rachel were so dizzy with excite-
ment, they booked plane tickets to California and got
married.

The pregnancy lasted eleven weeks. And when it
ended, Emma's self-loathing quietly seeped back in,
like rain filling a footprint in the mud. The desire to
become pregnant again had grown quietly until it was
a thirst she could hardly ignore. In some ways, she

wanted it more than Rachel did. Especially now, as she tried to find herself in this strange new life that looked nothing like what she'd imagined.

Emma stared at the blond woman on the screen. Hadn't Paulie said that Rachel's happiness depended on Emma's happiness? In a way that was true. They were married. They had gone from being two planets to a universe unto themselves, orbiting together in a new shared gravity. So, when you put it that way, there wasn't any harm in Emma learning more about their options, even if Rachel said she wasn't ready yet.

REQUEST AN APPOINTMENT. The button was green and ripe as a pear. Emma clicked it.

CHAPTER 2

Charlotte knew something was wrong before she was fully awake. Her senses were sharp these days. Crackling. She could feel the weather without going outside (rain was like fingers running lightly over her scalp, humidity like being boiled from within). She knew the lamp bulb was going to burn out before it even began to flicker. And she knew now, summoning herself from a dream, that something was wrong with her husband.

Charlotte sat up too quickly and her arthritis flared in her hips, sending red coals of pain up her back. Oh, she missed her old mattress. This one was too soft and gave off plumes of an unwashed smell, sage-y and bitter.

Dirk was sitting up on the edge of the mattress. He was panting, his hands on his knees, elbows out, like he was preparing to stand but hadn't yet mustered the energy.

Please not a heart attack, Charlotte said to herself. *Please, anything but that.*

With effort, she stood, went around to his side, knelt beside him. His face was white; his cheeks were slightly sticky to the touch. His palms were trembling against his knees. She could hear his breath leaving his nostrils in short, impatient bursts.

Oh, thank heavens.

"Dirkie, you need to eat something," she said. "It's your blood sugar."

He nodded. Charlotte dug out a package of peanut butter crackers she kept in a box by the bed for this purpose. Dirk had had several of these episodes over the summer, but they'd both come to see them as an acceptable risk. The beta-blocker kept his blood pressure down, which was good for his heart, but it made him prone to sudden episodes of hypoglycemia. Even their health was a negotiation these days.

She unwrapped the crackers and started to hand him the package, then changed her mind and pulled just one cracker out. He opened his mouth obediently, and she pressed the cracker in like a coin in a vending machine. His jaws went to work on it, slow and methodical.

Charlotte was attuned to Dirk's body like it was her own. This was what marriage was: the slow pooling of another person under your skin. Charlotte had known that Dirk's father died that day in 1983 simply by the way Dirk hung up the phone, as carefully as laying a baby in its crib; she'd known he'd lost his job fifteen years later when he peeled off his watch after work and set it in the fruit bowl (only a year before retirement! They'd squeezed a full day's work out of him before letting him know his position was being handed to someone a third his age); and then there were all the colds and sinus infections and stomach bugs whose symptoms she could smell on him days before he felt sick.

Charlotte handed him another cracker. She felt her relief turn to annoyance. Her husband would have sat on the edge of the bed, two feet from the crackers, all day if she hadn't woken up to help. If Dirk looked out the window one day and saw a tornado approaching, he'd just stand there with his model car in his hand and wait to get swept away. That was the difference between him and Charlotte.

"Where's your meter?" she asked when all the crackers were gone. Dirk raised a finger toward the trunk at the foot of the bed, and Charlotte dug through the stacks of magazines and extra blankets and puzzles until she found the blood-sugar meter. She unzipped it from its canvas case and pressed the button to power it on. Nothing.

"It's out of batteries," Dirk said. "I forgot to tell you." He was looking better now, his color normal again. Cracker dust coated his dry lips.

Charlotte sighed. "I'll go downstairs and get more. I know I saw some in the kitchen drawer." She sat on the trunk and pulled on her slippers. Outside, the brakes of the garbage truck wailed and she paused to listen. When Justin was little—about four or five, maybe—he'd drop his toys at the sound of the truck to rush outside and stand on the lawn, mouth agape, as the workers loaded their trash onto the hydraulic compactor. He cried when he was too late, when by the time he got outside, the truck had already worked its way down the block and started to turn the corner. Justin's fascination with garbage trucks was fleeting, gone within a year, like most of his obsessions—but somehow, decades later, Charlotte still felt a jolt of anxiety when she heard the brakes, like she was meant to be somewhere in a hurry.

Slippers on, she stood too quickly and hit her head on the sloped ceiling, cursing under her breath. She would never get used to this place, would never stop longing for her old life. She pined for her brass headboard and solid oak nightstand adorned with a lace doily and a sprig of dried flowers in a bud vase. For her bureau with its neat vertebrae of pill bottles, her jewelry box, jars of loose change. Their new life was hollow, simplified to a mattress, a chair, some boxes, and a couple suitcases that doubled as laundry hampers. The people downstairs were always making noise. Doors slamming, music playing, the metal trash-can lid crashing like a cymbal. And that dog and its sporadic barking nearly drove her mad with impatient rage.

"I heard them leave," Dirk said as if reading her mind. "About fifteen minutes ago. Eight thirty on the dot."

Charlotte stuffed her bowl and thermos and toothbrush into a canvas bag and slung it over her shoulder. "Thank heavens," she said. "I could use some peace this morning."

*   *   *

As usual, the dog greeted her with a whine, standing on his hind legs. "Git," she said, nudging him with her foot. She walked quickly to the bathroom and peed, the relief exquisite as she watched her expression in the low mirror. She was looking every bit of her sixty-eight years today; the roots of her hair formed a seam of white above her forehead now that she wasn't coloring it anymore, and the lines around her mouth pulled down, making her look more animal than human. A mastiff ready to bite. Charlotte avoided the mirror as she washed her hands and face, brushed her teeth. She dried the sink with the towel and folded it neatly back over the rack.

Charlotte found comfort in these little motions, their familiar choreography. She had always thought of herself as the keeper of the invisible. The one who held things together. For years, Dirk and Justin—when he was home—lived in a world so responsive to their needs they were not even aware of the machinery required to make it happen. When their hunger began to thrum, roast chicken and peas or tomato soup and sandwiches would magically appear on the table. Their clothing was always clean, their dentist appointments scheduled. When they opened the refrigerator, the milk jug smiled back at them, magically refilling itself over and over.

She wondered sometimes what it would be like to be a man. To see life as an endless buffet. Charlotte only sometimes resented their haplessness, like when Justin burned a hole in her silicone spatula or Dirk wore a shirt without a middle button to work when she was sick in bed with the flu. Most of the time she found a deep satisfaction in straightening out the day, tidying its corners, so that everything was taken care of. It wasn't until she went to therapy, when Justin was in the most feral part of his teenage years, that Charlotte learned she was simply a person who wanted to control everything. This, she was told, was its own pathology. She was probably responding to her mother's messiness, a childhood of tripping over rocking-chair rails and shoving aside piles of musty lace doilies so she could do her homework. And perhaps, the therapist had suggested, blinking rapidly, it was Charlotte's need to control her environment that made Justin respond so aggressively to her presence. It was like a pendulum swinging between generations. She'd been so hurt by his assessment that she'd stopped attending her sessions. But the idea had been foisted upon her like an unwanted gift, and it worked its way into her mind so deeply that the therapist had become, alongside the ghost of her mother, a character in her head with whom she argued all the time.

Well, she wished he could see her now. She had never been less in control of her life, and she was still here, straightening towels and screwing on the toothpaste cap with steady hands.

Charlotte turned off the light in the bathroom. As she passed the guest bedroom, a movement caught her eye and nearly made her trip. But it was only a flash of colored light from an open laptop, tethered to the wall by its power cord. A hypnotic screen saver cast shifting patterns of purple and green on the wall. Charlotte glanced into the room, which was lined with stacks of books and papers—didn't these people have shelves?—and as she rounded the corner into the living room, her bare toe met the edge of a hard cabinet that hadn't been there before. A picture frame sitting on top clattered as it fell over. Charlotte sucked in air through her teeth, bent over in a silent grimace. She leaned on the cabinet while rubbing her toe against the calf of her other leg. Then she stopped, her fingers folding over the familiar edge.

It was her own credenza. The one that had belonged to her mother, with oak paneling and felt-lined drawers. Someone had painted it a garish yellow color, sloppy around the edges. On top was a pile of mail and books. Charlotte ran her hand along the edge of the cabinet. She could still feel, under the thick paint, the soft dip where her spider plant had leaked, leaving a circle of water damage.

The phrase *rock bottom* tumbled through Charlotte's mind. That was a term people used at Al-Anon meetings to describe being pushed down the porch steps by their alcoholic husband or sitting by their sister's hospital bed after she overdosed. Charlotte never liked these declarations of certainty. How did people know what shape their lives would take? That things couldn't get worse? Her own rock bottoms always seemed to have a trapdoor beneath them.

She turned the picture frame back upright. It was the two women she often saw leaving the house, either both together in the car or one in the car and the other on a bicycle. A pretty one, wiry and blond, and a brunette with bad posture. In the photo, they had their arms wrapped around each other, flushed and smug, the blurry lights behind them suggesting a party. Not sisters, she'd surmised from the way they held hands when they left the house. She could only see them if she pressed her eye against the window jamb and looked hard right. It gave her a headache, but she'd been curious about them. Even as they separated at the car — one sliding into the driver's seat and the other into the passenger's — they continued to reach across the hood, wiggling their fingers like they were casting a spell on each other. Charlotte could not imagine what Patty thought about this. Well, she could.

They'd brought next to no furniture to the house, which Charlotte and Dirk had taken to mean they were temporary. Maybe they were real estate agents staging the house for another sale. Or visiting professors, only here for the semester. There had been something childlike about the lack of chairs, the empty Chinese takeout containers rinsed and drying in the sink, the single lamp plugged in with its cord trailing across the living-room floor. The girls didn't mean any harm. They certainly couldn't have known that the house had been ripped from Charlotte and Dirk's possession. They were just doing what everyone was doing: trying to get by for a short time. Charlotte could relate to that, as she and Dirk were staying in the garage attic only temporarily too. The four of them were simply sharing a waiting room, their lives suspended until someone's name was called.

But seeing the credenza made Charlotte realize she'd been fooled. The new people were here for good. You didn't paint a piece of furniture if you simply wanted a surface to set things on, and you didn't go for such a gaudy color if you wanted to make the house palatable for a future owner. They intended to stay. To live here forever. And this, like a switch flipping, changed Charlotte's feelings about them.

She had a sudden impulse to cause harm, a twitching in her fingers as she flipped through the mail—nothing today—then picked up the picture frame again. She dragged its sharp metal edge across the top of the credenza. The feeling of the paint scratching loosened something inside of her, and she felt for a moment that all of their problems were gone. Then she set the frame back down again.

Oh, it was dangerous, tasting that kind of relief.

*　　*　　*

Charlotte found the batteries in a kitchen drawer next to packets of soy sauce and takeout napkins, a few of which she tucked into her pocket. Then she opened the refrigerator to see what promise the day held. She'd come to think of the kitchen as a game of chance, a slot machine with random payouts. Some days it was easy to take what she wanted without it being noticed. A pickle here, a quarter cup of cooked rice there. Some mornings were crackling with unexpected joys:

a family-size box of sweet cereal, a five-pound bag of tangerines.

And then there were the off-limits items. A single muffin. The last of the strawberries. When Charlotte opened the fridge last week and discovered a pizza box with only one slice remaining, its cheese congealed onto the cardboard, she felt a burst of sorrow in her chest to see yet another ordinary happiness that had drifted out of her reach.

This morning brought a rare bounty: three loaves of rye bread, a packet of Swiss cheese, grapes in a large plastic clamshell. They must have gone to Costco. Charlotte pulled out two slices of bread, paused — thinking of the yellow cabinet — then took two more. She made sandwiches at the counter, wishing she had some ham. All that bread and there was never any meat.

She liked these quiet mornings when the house was empty and hers again. For the first two weeks after the new people arrived, they hardly left the house at all. Charlotte and Dirk had to stay in the attic for days at a time, sitting at the top of the steps at night to dip their feet into the coolness of the garage like two retirees perched on the edge of a pool. But now it was easy to know when the girls would be gone, because they kept a calendar in the kitchen with all their appointments and classes and events. The print was meticulous, the handwriting of a person who was clearly trying her best.

Charlotte spread mustard on the bread with her finger. This was the same counter where she'd de-stemmed kale from the garden each summer, creasing the dark leaves until they submitted and stripped from the stem without resistance. Over in the corner, under the tacky new pendant light, was where Justin had sat with his homework every night, staring into space, tapping his pencil against the edge of his chair to the rhythm of his own private, frenzied song. To the right, the bathroom where all of them had spent one miserable Easter after contracting norovirus at the church potluck. Out the back window was that ridiculous hot tub, which still embarrassed her so much she had to look away. And as always, her eyes fell on her garden, where she'd brought to life seasons of tomatoes and zucchinis and potatoes, and where Dirk helped Justin pick lavender and tie it up in bunches for a 4-H project.

Her garden. It pained her to look at it, though it was still in decent shape. Patty had surely been watering it now that she was back from Terre Haute. Patty had always taken care of things when Charlotte and Dirk went to visit Justin in the treatment center. And now Patty was all alone, her husband, Rob, having died of a brain aneurysm two years ago. Charlotte felt a pang of guilt now as she remembered Patty showing up on their doorstep in her Garfield nightshirt, her slippers coated with snow. Her voice was calm as she explained that she'd woken up to find Rob stiff in his recliner, a small pool of vomit in his lap. Charlotte had brought Patty inside and made her coffee as Dirk called 911. Patty started trembling after a bit. She asked Dirk to go back to the house to check on Rob, to be sure, and Dirk had obeyed, blinking rapidly upon his return. "He looked very comfortable," he said. And then all three of them had cried, grasping one another's fingers over the table, until the ambulance arrived and Patty used Charlotte's phone to call her son, Benji.

Charlotte had been too ashamed to tell Patty about the foreclosure. She'd shut down, became brusque and transactional—*Here's your Tupperware; lawn-clipping pickup is tomorrow*—those final weeks before the house was taken. She wondered now if Patty was upset with her for disappearing or if she was glad to be rid of moody old Charlotte. But Patty probably wasn't thinking about her at all. Patty had three sisters, and Benji visited all the time. She was better off than any of them, Charlotte reminded herself as she filled her thermos with ice and water and wiped the crumbs from the counter.

She'd just loaded the sandwiches into her bag when she heard the front door slam.

The little dog, who had been marching in place beside her hoping for a slice of cheese, suddenly turned and skidded out of the kitchen. Charlotte's shoulders tightened in panic as she heard a woman's voice sing, "Birdie!" And then something else in another language— German, maybe—her voice deep and melodic and far too close.

Charlotte held her breath, frozen. Her senses sharpened; she could feel the change in air pressure as another person moved through the rooms. She heard keys jangle on the far side of the living room now, almost to the hallway. The keys jangled in place, as if the woman was standing still, spinning them around her finger. Then they stopped. Charlotte wondered if she was examining the scratch in the credenza, which Charlotte now regretted. *Stupid,* she heard her mother's voice say. *That was entirely stupid.*

The woman moved to the guest bedroom, the one with the laptop. She rifled through papers, murmuring something. Charlotte flattened herself against the side of the fridge and examined her options. She and Dirk had a plan for this situation that they called Hide, Run, Dementia. Should the new people appear unexpectedly while they were in the house, their first strategy would be to hide in the deep closet just off the living room or behind the laundry machines in the basement. Option two was to simply run to the nearest exit—likely the back door—and find refuge behind Dirk's old shed until it was safe to return again. But in this case, Charlotte's exits were blocked; with the girl in the guest bedroom, she had no safe passage to either the back door or the garage. And what if the girl came to get food from the kitchen? Charlotte felt her mouth go dry as she looked over and saw her blue thermos still on the counter, standing obliviously before the coffee maker like an uninvited guest.

Option three had started as a joke but held promise for the direst situations, like one of the new people opening the door on Charlotte or Dirk in the bathroom. Charlotte or Dirk would assume a drooped, medicated expression and say, "Have you seen my Betty Ann?" When the girl left the room to call 911 to report a lost person with dementia, Charlotte or Dirk would revert to option two and book it the hell out of there.

Charlotte was preparing for this scenario when she heard the front door open again. "Be the best girl today," the voice sang to the dog, and then the door closed and the house was silent. Charlotte didn't hesitate; she grabbed her bag of food and thermos and ran, the grippers on the bottom of her slippers propelling her along, until she made it out to the garage. She pulled the hidden door aside and went up the narrow steps that led her to Dirk.

He was sitting on the edge of the mattress, sleepily tucking his penis into the gallon jug he used when he was too lazy to go downstairs. His hair was matted on the side of his head; he'd fallen back asleep while she was gone. When she saw him, her body thrummed with gratitude that she was the one who had gone downstairs this morning. Dirk's heart couldn't take the drama.

"How's the world today?" he asked.

"Quiet," she said. She kissed his head and held up the sandwiches. "And full of good things."

*　　　*　　　*

The garage attic had previously been Justin's room, though prior to that it had sat unoccupied, except for squirrels, for years. In 1987, Dirk reorganized the garage and decided to use the attic as a storage space. He cleared out the squirrels with traps—Charlotte didn't want to know exactly what that entailed—and sealed the hole in the soffit where they'd been entering. Then he moved the Christmas decorations and spare lawn-mower parts upstairs to the attic to make more space for his workbench in the garage.

Not long after that, Charlotte bought a new slow cooker and decided to put the old broken one in the garage attic. Her kitchen cupboards were full and she'd felt very clever, thinking of the unused space she could fill with things that no longer worked but that she felt too guilty to throw away. (Her mother's voice rang in her ear: *Isn't it too expensive to be broken? You probably just don't know how to use it.*)

At that time, the only entrance to the attic was

through a hatch cut in the garage ceiling, a small panel that had to be lifted and set inside. Charlotte struggled to get the ladder unfolded and clicked into shape. Then she picked up the slow cooker, with its cord coiled neatly inside its bowl, and tried to take a step up the ladder. The weight and size of the pot threw her off balance and she tipped back and landed hard on her heels.

"What are you doing?" Justin stood in the doorway to the garage, licking chocolate pudding from a spoon. He was fourteen and his voice had been flat and thick lately, like he was exhausted, though he slept so deeply he was late to school every day. Each morning Charlotte had to perform acts of increasing violence to rouse him—shaking his shoulders, dripping cold water onto his forehead, turning on his stereo with its obnoxious rock music. She suspected he'd been smoking marijuana and she was certain—because she'd seen him do it—that he liked to push staples into his fingers when he was angry. In the past year he'd gotten turned around a few times walking home from school and had to call from a pay phone for a ride; when Charlotte picked him up, he would scream at her for not arriving quickly enough.

Now Justin was gripping a pudding cup in one hand, a spoon in the other, his fingers wrapped so tightly around the spoon that Charlotte could see the valley between each knuckle, the small hairs that signaled he was in a new phase of life now, slipping dangerously from childhood and into something uncharted. His hair, freshly cut, exposed the field of pimples across his forehead. She would need to remind him to wash his face, she told herself. She would practice on Dirk first, to get the request down nicely, to make sure her voice was friendly and nonjudgmental. That was what Dr. Sheffield, the psychiatrist, had said: *Be firm but kind. Draw boundaries.* Also: *Encourage him to be independent and make his own choices.*

There was so much conflicting information.

"I'm trying to put this cooker in the attic," Charlotte said. "It's broken."

"Attic?" Suddenly he was beside her, the spoon and pudding cup abandoned. He did that often, dropped his trash wherever he stood; it drove Charlotte crazy, but she'd long ago learned to be selective with her battles. He put one foot on the ladder.

"No, honey, it's not safe."

He turned to her, and for a moment his expression looked hurt, childlike. "But I want to help."

Charlotte hesitated. "It's very heavy."

Justin stepped back down, took the pot from her, and lifted it a couple of times, as if wanting to assess its weight for himself. Then he put the pot down, took off the lid, flipped it over, and set it back on so that it was inverted, a snug fit that didn't slip. Before Charlotte could protest, he hoisted the thing onto one shoulder and began climbing the ladder.

"Careful!" she called. And to her surprise, he slowed, taking deliberate steps and wrapping his fingers around each rung. When he reached the top, the upper half of his body disappeared into the hatch. She heard the pot rattle as he set it down inside.

"Why have I never been up here?" he asked. And then he was gone, his whole body swallowed by the dark hole.

"Honey, there's no floor up there," Charlotte called as she climbed up after him. "You really need to be careful."

She stuck her head through the hatch and saw mostly darkness, except for a dim rectangle of light that came from the small window on the east end. Then there was the soft sound of a lighter clicking, and a flame appeared around Justin's face. He was standing with his feet apart, each sneaker balanced on a joist. Charlotte pressed her lips together to prevent herself from asking him why he had a lighter. Instead, she smiled at him. "Kind of spooky, isn't it?"

"Yeah." Justin's eyes were scanning the place as he held his flame out. The space was sharply triangular, but fairly tall—fifteen feet long and just over eight feet high in the center, where the rafters joined along a single beam. Dirk had placed a couple of pieces of plywood across the joists closest to the hatch. They now held two squirrel traps (empty, she was relieved to see) and a few boxes of tools and model-car pieces.

Charlotte put one knee experimentally on the board closest to her. It held her weight without protest, so she hoisted the rest of herself ungracefully into the attic. She tried to figure out how to ask Justin to come down before his lighter caught something flammable and burned the house down. As she stood, she had the sensation that the whole room recoiled at her presence. Floor joists moaned, strange smells swirled in the silence. She felt, for a moment, as if there were something alive about the space, something that did not like her. *Projection* is what Dr. Sheffield would have called it.

Justin loped past her, ducking his head, his arm reaching to touch the rafters like he was a monkey swinging from tree to tree. As he passed her, the smell of his ripe body pinched through the staleness of the attic and Charlotte said, without thinking, "Oh, honey, you really need to shower."

Justin stopped and turned to face her. They were standing on opposite floor joists, sixteen inches apart. He was already taller than her, and his chin dipped down to meet her eye. She tried to smile, fortifying herself with kindness for the screaming that would certainly come next. *Hug him when he doesn't deserve it.*

But Justin smiled back. "Only if you take one with me." And he flicked his tongue out like a snake.

Charlotte stepped back and nearly stumbled off the joist, but at the last second her other foot got purchase on a plank behind her and she stood awkwardly, her legs apart.

Justin laughed. He laughed and laughed and laughed as she stepped to the hatch and lowered herself shamefully down the ladder.

That night at dinner Justin asked if he could move into the attic. He was agitated but freshly showered, smelling like the mint soap Charlotte put out for guests. He hadn't taken a bite of his stew, only pinching off pieces of the bread and rolling them like tiny cigarettes, which he flicked impatiently off his plate as he laid out his argument: It was basically part of the house, given that the garage shared a wall with his parents' bedroom. He had plans for where his bed would go. His stereo, his paperbacks and band posters of long-haired men with leather gloves, his ancient trunk he'd found at a garage sale the previous summer and that Charlotte was always digging dirty clothes from. There was room for it all, he said. So much room!

When Justin stopped suddenly to guzzle his milk, his throat bobbing up and down with new energy, Dirk picked up his spoon and said, "I don't see why not." He looked at Charlotte, anticipating her protest, and said, "We all need space from our parents." The thought flickered through her head so quickly, she didn't even register it until the guilt flooded in: *And I need space from our child.*

Getting a city permit to update the attic was an

unnecessary expense, Dirk said, when he could do the work himself. Over the next few weeks, he ran wiring up through the wall and put two junction boxes with outlets along the studs in the attic. He insulated the floor and ceiling. He built a plywood floor and painted it black, per Justin's request, and rolled a thick, sound-absorbing rug across it. He spent almost an entire paycheck on a Japanese ductless air conditioner to keep the room cool in the summer. Charlotte kept her mouth shut when she saw the price tag. Dr. Sheffield had told them that Justin needed tangible support, which Charlotte had taken to mean the prescriptions and appointments every Tuesday; Dirk interpreted the advice in a more literal way, buying Justin supplies for every fleeting hobby—a guitar, a subscription to a fishing magazine, a camera with a zoom lens. He never said no. Even years later, when Justin brought home that hot tub on the back of a friend's truck—did Dirk even ask where it came from? No, he had simply poured a concrete slab to put it on and ran wiring underground, digging up half the grass. And the thing hadn't even worked.

Men dealt with a child's illness in this way, she'd read in one of the books. They often saw it as a problem they could fix, a loose hinge that simply needed to be tightened so the door would swing properly again. Charlotte's heart filled with pity as she watched her husband work to transform the attic into a bedroom for their son. She could see most clearly in the way he snapped his measuring tape, in the little notes she found dusting the garage floor—*Sheetrock, corner*—how badly he wanted Justin to be okay and how little he understood the future that lay ahead of them.

For the first few months after Justin moved into the attic, the hatch had been the main problem. Charlotte worried every time Justin came down, imagining him sleepily catching his foot on the foldable ladder and breaking a leg on the concrete floor. Plus, they couldn't park their car in the garage anymore because it would block the entrance to his new room. Once Charlotte had forgotten and pulled the car in; Justin had dropped from the hatch and landed on the car's roof, leaving a dent the size of a watermelon.

Then one day, the water heater in the garage utility closet stopped working. It was an ancient machine that predated Charlotte and Dirk's time in the house, and like an old dog, it had outlived its projected lifespan by at least five years. They bought a new one, and in a stroke of expensive ingenuity, Dirk hired a plumber to install it in the basement, freeing up the utility closet in the garage to become the entrance to a set of steep but sturdy steps up to the attic. Dirk built a recessed door to this new alcove, lined with wooden shelves so that he still had a place to showcase his expanding collection of model cars. When the door to the closet was closed, it looked like a built-in shelf in an otherwise ordinary wall. Dirk spent the rest of the weekend covering the original ceiling hatch with drywall, standing on a ladder to smooth the mud with a taping knife until the seams were gone.

Justin had been thrilled with the result; he'd gone up and down the steps over and over, closing and reopening the door behind him as Dirk swept up the last of the sawdust.

"You'll never find me," he said, disappearing behind the shelf-door. A moment later, the door swung open and he jumped out. "But here I am!"

Charlotte started, nearly dropping the basket of clean laundry she'd been bringing up to the new room. Justin laughed at her skittishness — she did too — then he closed himself back behind the door. She waited, steeling herself for him to pop out again. This time she wouldn't jump! But he didn't come back, and after a few seconds she opened the door and left the laundry basket at the bottom of the steps.

*   *   *

Dirk watched as Charlotte put the batteries in his glucose meter. She loaded the lancet, pricked the side of his finger, and watched the bauble of blood pull itself onto the test strip like a dewdrop clinging to the edge of a leaf.

"Eighty-five," she said. His black bag full of pills

and bandages — the relief kit, they called it — sat open next to him. "You take your medicine, mister?"

"Waiting for water." He reached for the thermos, wiggling his fingers like a child. "And stop looking at me like that."

"Like what?"

"Like I'm a dog who needs to be put down."

"If I wanted to put you down, I'd have done it years ago." Charlotte spread their breakfast across the trunk. "Here we go. Your continental breakfast. On the house."

"Would you look at these spoils." Dirk plucked a slice of cheese and folded it into his mouth. "Today's already a good day."

"Food-wise, sure."

"And the mail?"

She shook her head.

Dirk examined the crust of his bread, picking off an invisible particle before taking a bite. He wasn't as clever about hiding his feelings as he believed.

"I told you," Charlotte said. "People don't send out wedding invitations until closer to the ceremony. I'd say we have a few weeks to go."

"You're checking the trash too? Maybe the new people threw it away because their name wasn't on the envelope."

"I checked the trash. And you could go down and look for yourself sometime. It doesn't always have to be me." Charlotte took a bite of her sandwich. She had come to regret telling Dirk about the little pink card that had arrived in July. It showed up during the two weeks they'd stayed in the house before the new people moved in, when it was empty and ghostlike except for their mail—overdue bills, advertisements for expensive dental procedures, grocery flyers—which kept piling up inside the mail slot by the front door. The little pink card had said, simply, *We're getting married! Justin + Amy. 12.10.08. Invitation to come.* Charlotte wished she had thought to hide it, to take the time to consider its implications on her own before involving Dirk. But the news had surprised her so much she was frozen in place, holding its cardstock edges as though it were a Polaroid blooming into life. Dirk had taken it from her hand. She'd watched as a storm of expressions crossed his face. A wedding was unfathomable for any number of reasons. That Justin would get married at all when he'd never kept a girlfriend longer than a few months. That he'd invite his parents after not speaking to them for over a year. They didn't even have his phone number. Charlotte didn't know whether the engagement was a sign that he'd matured and found stability or if it was yet another impulsive decision in a life strung together from erratic choices.

But it didn't matter, really. Because he'd invited them. Or, more likely, based on the loopy handwriting on the envelope, Amy had invited them—but he'd given her the address, hadn't he? Or had she looked them up, hoping to orchestrate some type of reconciliation on Justin's behalf? The envelope had no return address, and the wedding location said only Kansas City, Missouri.

Charlotte saw the card as a sign of two things: That Justin, or at least Amy, wanted them in his life in some way, and that she and Dirk needed to wait for the invitation that was promised before they could reconnect with their son. Kansas City had good barbecue and reasonable rents. She and Dirk could get part-time jobs and find a little apartment. Justin would live nearby with this Amy person, who would be good for him, who would fill up his pillbox and leave it on the kitchen counter so he always remembered to take his meds, and after a year they'd have a baby and go away on weekends while Charlotte babysat. The card had felt dangerous in her hands not because of how she'd found it but because it was tinged with so much hope.

"If the wedding is in December, then the invitation will probably come in October," Charlotte said now, tearing a piece of cheese. She pressed it to her tongue, feeling the sharp ache of anticipation in her jaw.

"Unless they break up."

"They won't. I can just tell Amy's a good person. He needs her."

"Lottie! You always do this."

"Do what?"

"Get carried away with a story in your head." Dirk plucked a grape. He chewed and chewed it. "You don't know this Amy any more than you know the people downstairs. Who you go on about like you're all in a book club or something."

"Oh, let's not talk about it anymore." Charlotte cast her eyes around the room, looking for a change in subject. Then she clapped her hands. "Oh! You won't believe this. The new people took my mother's credenza and painted over the finish in yellow. And put plastic knobs on it. You know that cabinet is a hundred years old? It belonged to my grandfather."

Dirk was brushing his teeth now. He held up a finger as he took a sip of water and swished it in his mouth, then swallowed, toothpaste and all. "You're not going to like this, Lottie, but you know who you sound like."

"Don't."

"Your mother."

Charlotte made a face that indicated she didn't want to continue mediating conflict between her husband and her mother, given that one of them was long dead. Dirk and her mother had always been at odds. He thought Helen was self-important; she found him unrefined. She always pointed out his oil-smeared pants or his dirty nails when they went to her house for dinner. *Imagine what his sperm must look like,* Helen would say in the early years when they were clearing the table as Dirk smoked a cigarette on the porch. *They probably already need dental work.*

"You know, some things don't need to come out of your mouth," said Charlotte. "Speaking of which, you have toothpaste on your lip."

Dirk wiped his mouth with the collar of his T-shirt. "How does it look, though? The newly yellow cabinet?"

"What do you think? It looks like a child painted it." She felt suddenly impatient, irritated by the weak breath of the attic's old mini-split. The heat was most intolerable in the hour after she returned from downstairs, the ghost of central air still on her skin. "Get up. It's time for Healthy Hour."

"Oh, not goddamned Healthy Hour."

"Yes. Get up." Charlotte stood, dipping her neck to make sure she didn't hit her head on the rafters. She led them every day in movements she recalled from old Jane Fonda tapes: tapping their toes on the mattress, balancing on one foot, twisting their hips, flapping their arms like clumsy albatrosses. It was one of the only pleasant surprises of living in the attic, Charlotte learning that all the years of squatting in the garden had left her nimbler and more flexible than one would expect at nearly seventy. All the drug commercials on television indicated that she was in a stage of life at which simply staying upright was a miracle. But Charlotte felt good when she was in motion; her arthritis quieted when her joints were active. Dirk, who'd spent his life hunched over the open hood of a car or pushing a broom down the halls of the university, struggled through Healthy Hour.

"Not now." Dirk gently lifted his model car, a 1964 Pontiac GTO, from its shoebox. "See how the glue on the chassis is dried? I want to prime it while the morning light's still good."

"Dirk Dennison."

"We can exercise later."

"We can exercise later." Charlotte tapped her chin. "Why does that sound familiar? Oh, right, that's exactly what every one of the thirty-three people who die of heart disease every minute say right before their time is up."

"Not this again." Dirk shook his head. "Not your miserable hospital-pamphlet statistics."

They wouldn't have spoken to each other this way a few months ago. But the heat—it was nearly 85 degrees in the attic—had dissolved their politeness. They were free to speak however they wished. Charlotte found this made marriage much more efficient.

"You have to stay active," she said. "That's what Dr. Sharma said after the stroke."

"It wasn't a stroke. It was stroke-like." This was technically true, at least according to the twenty-eight-year-old doctor in the emergency room when Charlotte brought Dirk there in May with one side of his face drooping like a wilted tomato leaf. A transient ischemic attack—TIA, the girl repeated, like it was a vocabulary word on a test—was essentially a preview of the stroke that was likely to come. Dirk's blood pressure was off the charts, and when they looked at his heart, they found that one of his arteries was clogged. And maybe a little bit of diabetes. The doctors placed a stent in his heart and the next day sent him home with a handful of prescriptions and a warning that things were precarious with his health unless he got his blood pressure and stress under control. The irony of the eviction notice waiting in the mailbox, small and white, like an invitation to a party, was not lost on either of them. When Charlotte opened it, the word *vacate* leaped from the page. *You must vacate the premises in twenty-one days.* Charlotte had pictured a tidal wave sweeping in, curling itself over the slate roof, ripping off shingles, pouring through the windows, and pulling Dirk and his long, hairless legs out to sea.

"Besides." Dirk picked up the can of primer. "That's not how it happens."

"Not how what happens?"

"They don't mean thirty-three people die all at once. It's more like clumps of them die, here and there, and then a period goes by where no one dies. It's an average, not a bus schedule." He set down his car. "But I suppose you're not going to stop nagging until I just give in?"

"You married me."

Dirk sighed. "Let's get it over with, then." He helped Charlotte move the trunk aside and they lay on their backs on the rug, bicycling their legs in the air. Above them the rafters joined in the center as if in prayer, with Justin's old Christmas lights still strung along the middle beam. They kept the mattress tucked behind a curtain, separated from the living area. An old striped bedsheet covered the trunk like a nice table. Charlotte had hung up another sheet to afford some privacy around the emergency commode, a plastic bucket with a fitted lid they'd taken to calling the honeypot. She'd instinctively understood, when they first came up here, that for them to survive the situation, the place would need to look good. And it did. Certainly more welcoming than it had years ago when it was Justin's room, lined with torn magazines and smelling like weed and the vinegary mix of socks and armpits.

"Do you remember," Dirk asked as he moved his legs slowly in the air, "when he brought that girl home? What was that, three, four years ago?"

"Brandy was her name." Of course Charlotte remembered. It was the only time Justin had ever brought a girlfriend around. She'd heard him laughing through the open window before he pressed the doorbell. Charlotte had thrown down the laundry she was folding, and as she ran through the house to get to the front door, she passed a mirror and saw her hair wild and uncombed, her eyes feral. A surprise visit! It had been raining, Justin soaked from it, but she'd thrown her arms around him and felt his wild, hammering heart beneath his T-shirt and smelled his sharp, scalpy smell, nicotine baked into his skin. But there was something different about his posture; it was rigid, as if he had his mind half on something else. She pulled back and saw the girl behind him. Thin as bones, stringy hair. Everything about the girl came to a point: her nose, the angle of her jaw, the sharp toe of her canvas sneakers, which were wet from the rain.

"She had to use the bathroom soon as she got here," Charlotte remembered. "Spent half an hour in there splashing around, and later I come to find one of my towels in the garbage can. I didn't even pull it out, didn't want to know. Just bagged it up and took it to the bin."

"That was a good visit, though," Dirk said. Gas erupted from his shorts now and then as he bicycled his legs; he grunted with the effort of not rolling over.

"You're right about that. Until the end." Charlotte didn't like Brandy, but she had to admit that the girl's presence did something pleasant to Justin's personality. He picked up their plates when dinner was done without even being asked, and he took the trash out, and he sat with his guitar and sang. Charlotte had even decided Brandy was quite pretty if you looked at her in a certain way.

Three days into their visit, Charlotte had woken

up with a bad feeling. She padded to the garage without bothering to put her robe on over her pajamas and opened the alcove door. Hearing nothing, she climbed up. The attic was empty, their bags gone. The bed unmade. She went to the kitchen and took down the teapot where she kept their rainy-day cash. It was empty. Six hundred dollars or so gone.

"It was a good visit until that girl stole our money," said Charlotte.

"There's only one way she'd have known it was up there."

"He probably mentioned it in passing, and she remembered."

Dirk rolled his ankle in slow circles. "Anything's possible."

Charlotte watched the skin on her thighs swing like curtains as she bicycled her legs. Why had Dirk brought that up? Now she could feel herself slipping into sadness again. The next time they'd seen Justin was months later, Christmas, and he was thin again, and depressed. Brandy was gone. He'd become upset when Charlotte asked him about the money, accusing her of never trusting him and thinking he was trash, but all the time he yelled and frothed, he never denied it.

"You know what? I think I'd like to take that credenza back. The one they painted yellow." Charlotte moved to a plank position, feeling the softness of her abdomen clench with effort. "Wouldn't that be something? They come home and all their mail's in a pile on the floor?" That was better. Her feelings about the credenza, which had at first been complicated and messy, hardened each time she thought about it. She liked the way this felt, sharp and mean in her mind.

"You were glad to be rid of it," Dirk said. "You only kept it because you knew your mother would haunt the rest of your days if you dumped it at Goodwill."

"That's irrelevant. It's still mine, is the point. Not theirs." She paused. "It wouldn't even be illegal if I took it. Not technically."

"*Legal* isn't the same as *right*." Dirk rolled onto his back and caught his breath. "As we know."

Charlotte pressed two fingers into the soft skin of his neck to check his pulse, but he swatted her away. Then he took her hand and put it on his chest, where she could feel the thrum of his heartbeat under his T-shirt. She put her head on his chest and listened.

"I understand about the furniture, Lottie, I do," he said. "But we'll get a better cabinet next time. One you pick out. It'll be a new life. Imagine it."

"I don't want a new life," she whispered. "I want the old one. Don't you?"

"Of course." He stroked her hand. "But you have to admit, the old one had its problems."

"We could have done things differently, you mean."

"Yes."

She sat up. "Like what? If you had a do-over, what would you do differently?"

"You and your hypotheticals, Lottie." Dirk let go of her hand and rubbed his calf. She thought she saw irritation in his eyes, but it was only pain. A cramp. She waited for him to tell her that he'd had enough, that Healthy Hour was over.

But he didn't. He lifted his leg and began to pump it again, slowly and deliberately.

"I wouldn't do anything differently," he said at last. "Because I have loved this life."

*　　　　*　　　　*

Charlotte and Dirk had first come back to the house in July, when it stood freshly sold but as yet unoccupied. It was late at night, and the only light on in Patty's house next door was the blue flashing of her bedroom television. They parked a block over and walked down the alley, not turning on their flashlight until they were at the garage door. Charlotte had figured that they wouldn't be able to get in. But despite the updated exterior — the vinyl house numbers replaced by bronze, the front door slapped with a coat of blue paint — no one had bothered to fix the lock on the garage's service door, which opened to the backyard and had been broken for nearly three years. Dirk had meant to fix it, but it was one of those projects that wasn't urgent enough to stay fresh in their minds; they remembered it only those rare times when one of them went out to the yard that way. When they sneaked back to the house that night, Dirk had grinned at Charlotte as the door swung open as if to say, *See? Aren't you glad we did things imperfectly?*

The intent had been only to snoop, to see what had changed. Charlotte was surprised to see the small collection of furniture in the garage, her mother's things stacked neatly along the wall as if expecting their return. But inside the house, seeing all the white paint and vinyl flooring and cheap-looking fixtures, they had been so unsettled that they'd sat for hours on the new carpeting, not speaking, the same way they had when Charlotte's doctor told them, decades earlier, that pregnancy was a dream she should stop chasing. After that appointment, Charlotte and Dirk had shared a bag of potato chips on the floor in front of their couch, tracing shapes in the carpet with their fingers. Now they sat in their gutted home and listened to the hum of the new refrigerator. Finally Charlotte had lain down to ease her aching hips, and Dirk had followed her. They'd fallen asleep on the floor like that, using their matching windbreakers as pillows, the moon glowing through the curtainless window.

The next morning, Charlotte had climbed up to Justin's old room. She needed to see the whole house, every inch of it, as if by doing so she might understand why this had happened to them. But the attic had not been touched. There was the old mattress and its tangled blankets, the stack of boxes stuffed with Christmas decorations, Justin's trunkful of comics and camera lenses and other things he'd abandoned in his haste toward adulthood. She felt so relieved to see this part of her life had been preserved that she ran her hands over all of it, touching each fold of the blanket and scraping her fingernails against the soft ridges of the aged cardboard boxes. She still existed. And—this was the part that surprised her, the depth of feeling that accompanied this thought—so did Justin. He was still here. The way he had been when they were a family.

Wasn't it odd, she thought, that the house had been so thoroughly gutted except for this one space? Everything had clearly been done in a hurry—wall paint bled onto the baseboards; the outlet in the newly finished basement was crooked—but every other inch of the house had been wiped clean. So why not here? Then her eyes fell to the opening above the alcove. She thought of the shelf-lined door at the bottom, the fact that Dirk hadn't pulled any city permits to create the room, and realized the truth was actually simple: The attic was untouched because the bastards who'd taken her house hadn't found it.

They stayed for nearly two weeks in the empty house, like hotel guests who kept extending their vacation. They ate beef jerky and granola bars and cans of pears that they bought in a late-night trip to Walmart before parking the car on a quiet side street blocks away. Charlotte cleaned every day, erasing their steps with her old vacuum, which had been left in the garage. She knew, deep down, that this couldn't last. But a small part of her felt she was performing a penance with every wipe of the counter and spray of the windows. A payment toward buying back a thing that had once been hers. As the days passed and no one came, she began to harvest a small hope that the house would be empty forever, and they could continue like this, in a new version of their old life. Moving around quietly, keeping the lights off at night. Sleeping in Justin's room as they waited for his wedding invitation to arrive.

Then one day the new people showed up, braying with pleasure at their good fortune and filling the house with their footsteps. Charlotte had been headed to the bathroom when they entered, and she managed to slip out to the garage and close herself into the alcove at the bottom of the attic stairs. She felt Dirk's hot breath as he joined her, his hands trembling at having been woken suddenly from an afternoon nap.

They heard one girl open the garage door. A moment of quiet, during which Charlotte held her breath, imagining this stranger casting her eyes over the furniture in judgment. All of her old things, which bore the scuffs and chips of the years, leaning along the concrete walls like the line outside a soup kitchen. She felt as mortified as if the girl had walked in on her naked.

"Useless," the girl had said. "What a surprise."

Charlotte nearly cried out in protest—her furniture might have been old, but it wasn't trash!—but Dirk squeezed her shoulder and she stayed quiet. They held their breath in the small space. When they heard the girl go inside the house, they climbed back up the steps to the attic. And without discussing it any further, there they stayed. Partly because there was nowhere else to go. They had food, a bed. The promise of the wedding invitation. Wasn't that more than what some people had? Didn't that make them two of the lucky ones?

*   *   *

In many ways, Charlotte and Dirk's life had been filled with good fortune. They met in a happy accident, literally, when Charlotte was nineteen and backed her mother's car into a hydrant while trying to park at the library. She'd felt her blood run cold when she got out of the car and saw the dent in the bumper. Helen was precious about her things; she spent afternoons walking through the crowded rooms of their home, touching the baskets and old books and dark, time-worn furniture, anointing them with a value beyond their actual worth.

Dirk had come out of the library in a work jumpsuit smeared with oil, a paperback crime novel in one hand and a sandwich in the other. He was on his lunch break from his job at the automotive plant, where he spent his days stamping sheet metal into chassis for Studebakers. When he passed the station wagon parked oddly on the curb, he noticed first how the paint on its roof had oxidized from red to nearly pink, how its tires looked bald and uneven along their tread. Then he saw Charlotte squatting by the back bumper, scowling, one hand wrapped around the other fist as if holding herself back from hitting something. He thought her reaction was disproportionate to the situation—the dent wasn't really that big, and the car was at least fifteen years old anyway—but he felt called to be of service and used a rubber mallet and a towel, pulled from the pockets of his work trousers, to pound the steel back into place. Then he gave her half his sandwich. White bread, butter, and jam. His thick fingers had imprinted in the soft bread; she slid her own into the mark they'd left.

Charlotte was only twenty when they married. She'd thought of Dirk as her salvation, the man who'd scooped her up from her mother's house with its old quilts and dark, thick rooms. Dirk was twenty-five and had a good job at the plant. They rented a small house with a woodstove, and Dirk walked to work every morning while Charlotte turned a few terra-cotta pots into an herb garden, which she used in tarragon chicken pies and beef stews and rosemary biscuits. She loved her new world, and her new world was Dirk. She clipped coupons and took charge of their bank statements and made jams and simmered chicken stocks and crushed dried herbs. She had no interest in going to college or working, as some of her high-school friends were, as a salesclerk at L. S. Ayres. Everything she wanted to do was in service of making a home for her and her husband and, eventually, a baby. In the evenings, Dirk would come home and rub Charlotte's freesia-scented lotion on his hands, which were dry after scrubbing off the oil and lubricants from the stamping press. Later, when he put those same hands over her body, she felt a deep and ridiculous pleasure at the idea of him changing his skin to match hers, of them becoming one body, one sweet and peppery smell.

But when the Studebaker plant shut down in 1970, Dirk, along with thousands of other workers, lost his job. Even though he eventually got hired as a facilities manager at the college, he was forced to take a pay cut for what turned out to be a glorified janitor role. They struggled to pay the rent and had to put off starting a family until they managed to climb out of the hole dug by the months of Dirk's unemployment. When they were finally back on their feet but kept failing to produce a baby, Charlotte could hardly look her mother in the eye, afraid to see the gloat that lay just under the surface. Instead she saw glimpses of Helen in her own body—in her hands as they washed out peanut butter jars or sewed the elastic waistband back onto Dirk's underwear after it had torn again, loose from age, and, worse, in her reflection in the mirror, her expression hard as stone as she rubbed Vaseline over her dry lips.

As the years went by and no baby came, Charlotte threw herself into gardening. She lined the front walk of their rented home with alyssum and snapdragons and vibrant marigolds, each a tiny sun. She stocked their pantry with home-canned jellies and tomato sauce and stewed prunes and relish. The other couples they knew were systematically maturing into families with children. Over and over she saw the process: the elation, the glow, the swelling belly, the velvet-cheeked baby wrapped in chenille and clutched by a besotted mother, the house smelling damp and milk-sour. Charlotte knitted them all blankets and hats and mittens. She visited, bringing pies and cooing over the baby, fussing over the mother and making her tea, praising everyone's resilience and beauty. And then, every time, she went home and cried.

In 1973 Charlotte and Dirk borrowed money for the first time, a private loan for the home-study and adoption fees and a mortgage for the house on Willabee Drive with its steeply sloping roof and fenced backyard. Their new house had a hallway that guided her gently to bed each night, a backyard already glutted with raspberries and tomatoes and snap peas. And then one evening, while they ate lasagna on the floor of the dining room still stacked with boxes, they got the call that their baby had arrived.

Justin was pink and pristine, with brown hair like suede and small white bumps peppering the sides of his nose. But he smelled unfamiliar; he was too light in her arms, so Charlotte had a sudden fear of dropping him, and she hurriedly handed him off to Dirk. It wasn't that she didn't like the baby. It was that she'd had an idea in her mind about motherhood that had crystallized over the years. Holding her baby for the first time was meant to be a euphoric moment of transfiguration in which she shed her old identity and became an entirely new being. But it hadn't been like that at all. She'd felt just the same as when she'd held all those other babies during her visits with friends. As if they didn't belong to each other.

It was a momentary stumble—she took Justin back from Dirk a few minutes later and found his body more familiar in her arms—but it was her initial disappointment, she came to believe, that was the cause of all his troubles later in life. As if it lay dormant in his small body for years until the day he walked past Charlotte's canned tomatoes and swept his arm out over the counter, knocking everything down into a pile of glass and red pulp. What had he been angry about? She couldn't remember. But she remembered the way he'd looked at her: as if he had seen through her act. She wasn't meant to be a mother, had no capacity to handle what was to come. He was twelve and nearly electric with a recent temper, his whole body joining him in rage, cheeks purpling and teeth bared. As she wiped the red sauce from her sweater, a tiny, insistent voice echoed inside of her:

Your fault. All of this is your fault.

*   *   *

After Healthy Hour, Dirk arranged his model car and a can of primer on the trunk. He pulled a brush from his kit and ran his thumb over the bristles. Charlotte stood before him, hands on her hips.

"Need anything from downstairs?" she asked.

Dirk looked up, surprised. "You were just down there an hour ago."

"I could get you more water."

He picked the thermos up and gave it a shake. "Still full."

"How about a snack? You liked that cheese, I could get another slice."

"It's not even ten o'clock." He opened the primer, releasing an acrid smell that Charlotte could feel on her tongue. "Why are you acting so jumpy?"

"I'm not jumpy," said Charlotte. "I have to go to the bathroom. Stomach's acting up."

"Oh." Dirk's expression softened. "Well, you better go, then. Don't waste time worrying about me."

Charlotte went down the steps. The cool air kissed her skin as she opened the door into the garage and then again as she entered the air-conditioned house. She passed the bathroom and went straight to the guest bedroom, where the laptop still sat open in the middle of the floor. Charlotte's end table, which had been placed in a corner, held three glasses of water. No coasters. Annoyed, she picked up a book from the floor and set it under the glasses. Then she knelt before the laptop and rubbed her finger over the trackpad, summoning the computer to life.

Please, she thought. *Please don't ask me for a password.*

It didn't. A photo of the dog appeared, then a scattering of file icons filled the screen. Charlotte first felt relieved, then disoriented. She had used her and Dirk's old desktop computer—where had that even ended up?—only to look up recipes and read about stroke symptoms and check her Hotmail for coupons. She clumsily navigated to an internet browser and typed *I need a lawyer to help me sue the person who stole my house* in the search bar. She paused, then added *please* and pressed send.

A list of law offices and legal aid clinics appeared. Some were free if you qualified; others were promising in terms of results but nonspecific in terms of cost. There was no time to be picky. She clicked to each website in the order it appeared, found an email address, and sent the message she'd been working through in her mind for the past half hour, ever since she got the idea. No time for pleasantries; she got right to it: *We were victims of fraud that cost us our home and we need help challenging its sale...*

As she typed, Charlotte felt as if her fingers were moving on their own, propelled by the rage that thrummed inside her. For so many years she had tried to stay calm to counteract Justin's anger—his illness, she came to understand—which was like a wild animal that wouldn't leave the house. Once, Charlotte had come home to find that Justin, then twenty, had cooked spaghetti and left its detritus everywhere. Sauce burned into the stove, noodles hanging over the edge of the pot, plates smeared with food on the counter and more in the living room, on the couch. *No,* she told herself. *I will not react to this.* But when she went down to the basement to get the laundry, he followed her and started pestering: *What's wrong? Huh? What's going on? Tell me.* When she finally said she was annoyed he'd made such a mess after she'd just cleaned, he screamed—sweet relief, as if he was waiting to blow up—that she always made a big deal out of nothing, she was a bitch and a cunt and a whore. Often when she thought of Justin, she thought of some version of this scene, the two of them facing off in the basement, laundry strung all around them, doused in the sickly sweet smell of fabric softener and wet clothes.

But Charlotte had felt closer to Justin in these past few weeks than she had during all the years they'd shared a home. And it wasn't just because she and Dirk were staying in his old room, where the tattered *Top Gun* poster still clung to the wall and, just yesterday, Charlotte had found an abandoned Jolly Rancher under the edge of the mattress. (She'd unwrapped the sticky, melted thing and put it in her mouth. Grape.) Charlotte felt closer to Justin because she finally understood what he'd meant when he said that being angry was the only thing that felt true. When Charlotte thought of the house being sold—specifically, when she thought of that horrible man Victor Maxwell and his disgusting red mustache—she felt full of ripe, hard violence. And in those moments, it was the truest thing about her.

She hit send on the final email just as she heard footsteps coming around the corner. She held her breath. Dirk appeared at the door, his nipples puckering under his sheer nightshirt. The confusion on his face and the dried paint on his fingers made him look like a boy who'd gotten lost searching for his classroom. Charlotte closed the laptop and stood.

"I was checking email. It's not a big deal," she said before he said anything. Dirk didn't think they should be touching things around the house. He wouldn't like that she'd used the computer, and she certainly wasn't going to tell him that she'd reached out to lawyers.

Charlotte had kept so many things from Dirk over the years, what was one more? She'd never told him the actual cost of Justin's first rehab or about the life insurance policy she'd taken out on their son when he was seventeen. It felt dirty and shameful each time she paid the annual premium, but she knew from the books and the Al-Anon meetings that she had a higher chance of losing her son than most parents did, and she worried that she and Dirk would inherit whatever debts he'd accumulated. Charlotte liked to think of herself as holding an umbrella above Dirk's head so that the rains of the world didn't soak his white, itchy scalp. And maybe Dirk understood this. Maybe that was why he let her run the business of their marriage: opening the envelopes, making the calls, signing the checks. Dirk wasn't a problem-solver. So there was no need for Dirk to know that Charlotte was investigating their legal options. She wouldn't involve him until she had an answer.

But he didn't scold her for using the computer. He held out his palm, upon which lay a pink tablet. "I found this in the relief kit. Something for your tummy."

Charlotte took the pill and chewed, feeling its chalky residue coat her teeth and tongue. "You could have waited until I came back. I was on my way."

"Why make you wait if I had something that could help you now?" His question was so earnest, his face so etched with love, that she slipped her hand in his and kissed his shoulder.

"Wait one second." She turned back and opened the laptop, clicked to the history folder, and cleared what she'd done. She'd learned that trick from the Riverbend library staff when she'd used the computers to pay one of Justin's medical bills. She left the laptop open this time, remembering that's how she'd found it. But before she returned to Dirk, she pulled the laptop plug from the wall so the battery would drain. A small satisfaction, but it would do. For now.

CHAPTER 3

The Riverbend Family Planning Center wasn't easy to find. Emma drove past it twice before seeing the turn. Tucked behind a strip mall and flanked by six-foot-tall green shrubbery, the building looked like it was meant to be inconspicuous. The only identifying marker was a poster in the window of a grinning white baby, resplendent in its own drool. The whole exterior gave off a grim, barren vibe — appropriate, Emma supposed, in an ironic sort of way. So inside, she was surprised to find herself in a waiting room nearly full of women flipping through brochures or digging through their purses. Most of them had men at their sides typing on their phones. The walls were lined with vinyl plants, and the air had the insistently pleasant odor of a diffuser tucked somewhere out of sight.

Emma checked in with the receptionist, then sat on an empty chair in the corner. Her seat faced two coffee tables, each holding a box of Kleenex. She examined the paintings on the walls—gently rolling abstracts that suggested either oceanic landscapes or fertile wombs. A muted television in the corner showed John McCain standing in front of a mountain in a shirt two sizes too big, the breeze flapping its pockets.

Emma had not told Rachel about the appointment. She had meant to. But Rachel was busy and distracted; she always had students emailing questions and showing up to office hours. "Lucy's applying to grad schools for rhetoric studies," Rachel said last night as they sliced peppers and tofu for dinner. "And Carmen's a senior but in the middle of changing majors to comparative literature. Which reminds me, I need to write her a letter of recommendation."

Emma had no idea how her wife was able to penetrate the innermost wishes and ambitions of her students so quickly—or even tell them all apart!—but perhaps that was why Emma was the adjunct and her wife was not. "Did I tell you the IVF clinic here isn't too far from campus?" Emma asked, pressing the tofu between two dish towels.

"Let's talk about that when the time comes," said Rachel. When Emma asked what time that would bc, Rachel slid her knife expertly through the center of a bell pepper, extracting the core without spliting it. Then she put the knife down and said, "In the spring. Okay? Can we just get through this semester?"

Emma couldn't deny the logic in this approach. Yes, they should wait to try again. Emma had finished bleeding only a few weeks ago. They hadn't even been in Riverbend for a month. Their pod still hadn't arrived! But Emma wasn't operating on logic. She pined for a baby, for the curl of newness inside her body. She wanted something to imprint itself into her blood and grow until it stretched her skin taut before emerging, fully baked, directly into her arms. It was primal, this feeling, and it tingled at her jaw like hunger.

So she decided to go to the appointment alone. It was only a consultation, after all. She was just researching their options. Seeing what was possible. So that when Rachel was ready, Emma would have their game plan lined up.

Emma watched the other women as their names were called by a nurse. They got up, tugged their purses over their shoulders, wrapped their fingers around their husbands' biceps. One by one they smiled at Emma and at all the seated women as they were escorted out of the room. Emma smiled back. It was nice to feel like she was part of a group. The waiting room at the Riverbend Family Planning Center was the antithesis of the adjunct lounge at Boon University, where the instructors barely nodded hello to one another. Just yesterday a manila folder with a note scrawled on it had been placed on the copy machine: *Paper famine in progress — remaining sheets for 3000-level courses ONLY.* Below that, someone had added a Post-it: *Classism, but make it petty.*

"Emma Sullivan?"

Emma sat up straight, jolted from her thoughts. The nurse was back and scanning the waiting room. As Emma stood, she felt the eyes of all the other women on her. *Don't worry!* she hoped her smile said. *We'll all get our turn.*

The nurse led her to a small exam room. Emma obediently held out her arm for the blood pressure cuff, stepped on a scale, and answered the checklist of questions. No, she didn't smoke. Yes, social drinking. No, she hadn't felt much despair in four of the past five days.

Satisfied, the nurse ushered Emma into a different room. This one was professorial, with a large desk and green pothos trailing over the window. A painting of sequoia trees hung on one wall next to a calendar still flipped to the previous month. Emma sat on a chair and waited. She felt slightly buoyant, like she'd passed some initial screening for motherhood with her acceptable vital signs and the low depression scores.

The doctor entered with her hand already held out. Emma shook it, wondering if she'd walked down the hallway like that. She wore her hair slicked back in a low ponytail pulled so tightly it lent her an expression of alarm—her eyes set apart, her broad mouth slightly open. A stethoscope jiggled around her neck as she pumped Emma's hand firmly up and down.

"Emma," she said. "I'm Dr. Rivera. Are we still waiting for your husband?"

"I don't have a husband."

"I see." Dr. Rivera sat behind her desk and made a note on a piece of paper. "Single motherhood. It's hard to do alone."

"I am married. I have a wife."

Dr. Rivera looked up. "Ah. Well, you're in luck, then."

"Am I?"

"If you were married legally, you'd need to have your husband here for consent. We wouldn't be able to continue." She put on a pair of purple reading glasses and examined a sheaf of papers. "But since you're not married in the eyes of the law, we can go ahead and look at your options now."

Emma tucked her hair behind her ear. The casual way her marriage was regularly delegitimized, like a knockoff purse, made her feel oafish and unpretty. "How lucky indeed," she said.

Dr. Rivera lifted her shoulder slightly and tilted her head as if to say, *Depends on how you look at it.* "What do you know about IVF?"

"Not much, really. It's my first time."

Dr. Rivera laid a sheet of blank paper in front of

her on the desk. "IVF gets a lot of flak for being both complicated and expensive. But it's only one of those things." She drew a uterus and ovaries upside down in quick, sweeping gestures. "The process is very straightforward. We'll do some bloodwork and an HSG. That's a test where we inject dye into your uterus to make sure all the parts are there and in working order. If everything looks good, we'll do a baseline ultrasound and start you on birth control for a few weeks to optimize your timing. Then comes a stimming protocol for ten days or so. You'll do daily injections at home to stimulate your ovaries to produce multiple eggs in a single cycle." She paused to stab the pen into the ovaries, creating dozens of tiny dots. "This phase can be a little uncomfortable. We'll do ultrasounds every other day or so to monitor the follicles and adjust the medicine if needed. When all the eggs are ready, you'll do a special shot to trigger ovulation. And then you'll come in for a retrieval, where we take out the eggs while you're under light anesthesia. Those eggs are introduced to sperm to create embryos."

Dr. Rivera leaned back, admiring her drawing. She drew a long arrow from the ovaries back to the uterus. "A few days later, we take the best-looking embryo and transfer it into your uterus. If all goes well, it implants successfully and results in a live birth. You do have sperm, right?"

Emma felt like her head was swimming. "Uh—yes. We have one vial left. From an anonymous donor."

"It's being held in a sperm bank, then?"

Emma nodded.

"Easy. You'll just give them our clinic information, and they'll ship it before the retrieval." Dr. Rivera picked up Emma's file. "Your intake form says you've had a spontaneous abortion within the year."

"I've never had an—"

"Miscarriage is what I mean. How was that pregnancy conceived?"

"I had an intrauterine insemination at my old clinic in Chicago." Emma flinched slightly, remembering the pinch of the catheter squeezing through her cervix. "We tried several times before it worked."

"How many times?"

"Five."

"I see." Dr. Rivera leaned back in her chair and thought. "Typically we like to see six failed attempts before moving to IVF. For a normal woman, that's six negative pregnancy tests after intercourse during ovulation. But since you're not—you know, typical, I suppose we can go ahead and run some tests to clear out any functional problems." She looked at Emma's file. "Based on the date of your last period, we can do an HSG and blood draws today."

"So soon?"

Dr. Rivera looked over her glasses. The lenses distorted the bottoms of her eyes, making her look like she was weeping. "Are you not sure about this?"

"No, I am."

"No or yes?"

"Yes." Emma bit her thumbnail. "I can do the tests today."

"Good. But first, the paperwork." Dr. Rivera pulled a folder from her desk drawer. The cover displayed the same photo of the smiling baby that hung in the front window. She flipped it open and ran a manicured finger down each margin. "Consent to treatment, privacy notice, waiver of liability, the usual. But what most women are interested in is how much this is going to cost them." She pulled a sheet from the back and laid it on top. Emma pressed her lips together when she saw the dollar amount.

"We do financing," Dr. Rivera said. "Zero interest for the first six months."

Of course Emma had already thought about this. The medications and ultrasounds would be covered by their health insurance. Rachel's agent was in talks with a production company for the movie rights to *Give Me Five Moons,* but nothing about that was guaranteed. Still, between the book money and Rachel's salary—and the fact that their monthly mortgage payment was less than half what their rent in Chicago had been—Emma's meager adjunct salary was basically buttercream frosting on their privileged situation. They'd agreed to put all of Emma's money into savings for the future. And wasn't becoming a family their future? She silently crunched the numbers. With the extra class Paulie had given her, all she needed to do was make it through three semesters. Assuming she got the same course load each time. Fifteen months of pressing through the job, and the IVF would be covered.

"I have to talk to my wife about it," Emma said. "She knows this is the next step. I've just been waiting for her to settle in at her job a bit before we deal with the logistics of this whole process."

"Of course." Dr. Rivera nodded. "Can I give you some advice?"

Emma nodded.

"The women I see in my office all face the same two barriers: money and time. Yes, assisted reproductive technology is expensive. An IVF baby can cost the same as a nice car. It's limiting for a lot of people, to be honest."

Emma thought of the Kleenex boxes in the waiting room. It dawned on her that there were several reasons to cry at this clinic.

"And then there's time. If you're a woman who wants to have a baby, the years do nothing but work against you. There's no loan option for time, no paying it back later. Money, however, is something you can work with. Not one patient has ever looked down at her baby and thought, *This wasn't worth the cost.* But a lot of them wait too long and then have to deal with that regret."

"It's not that I can't afford it. I just can't pay today," said Emma. "I'm not even ready to start."

"That's fine." Dr. Rivera clicked her pen. "This is just paperwork. It's getting the signatures out of the way so we can get you set up in the system."

Afterward, Emma was released to the phlebotomist, who drew three vials of blood. Then the nurse delivered her to another exam room, where she undressed from the waist down. Dr. Rivera came in and inserted a cold speculum—Emma longed for her gynecologist in Chicago, who always ran it under warm tap water first—and then her uterus cramped up as the doctor injected contrast through a tube threaded through her cervix. A radiology tech watched on a nearby screen. Emma gasped with the pain and clutched the sides of the table, tearing the tissue paper covering.

"It's not as bad as labor," said Dr. Rivera. "Think of this as practice."

"You get drugs with labor." Emma could feel tears pinching her eyes.

"I didn't." Dr. Rivera nodded to the tech. "All good?" The tech gave a thumbs-up. Dr. Rivera pulled out the tube and the speculum. Emma closed her legs and pulled the tissue paper over her thighs.

"We'll call you with the results of the blood draw," said Dr. Rivera, snapping her gloves into the trash. And then she was gone, whistling down the hallway "Don't Worry, Be Happy."

*   *   *

When Emma pulled into the driveway at the house, she was surprised to see Patty sitting on the front stoop, her ankles crossed. She wore a faded T-shirt that said STILL HOT...FLASHES and a vexed expression. Emma felt dread in the pit of her stomach. Yesterday, after seeing Rachel off for work with a long goodbye kiss at the car, she had turned to find Patty watching from her yard, hose in hand. As Rachel pulled out of the driveway, Patty said, "You know there are children in this neighborhood, right?" Emma had been at first embarrassed—she wasn't often publicly affectionate, but Rachel just looked so cute that morning with her top collar buttoned—and then so unmoored by the similarity between Patty's expression and Emma's own mother's, with that same twist of displeasure in her mouth, that she ran inside without thinking of a response, though one came much later, as she was washing dishes: *It's better they see our love than your hate, Patty!*

How stupid. It was better she hadn't thought of it at the time.

Emma got out of the car. "Can I help you with something?"

Patty looked up at her calmly, as if she had been waiting for this question. "You can read up on *Buddleja davidii.*"

"I'm sorry?"

Patty sighed and heaved herself to standing, her knees cracking loudly. She beckoned Emma to follow her around the house and into Emma's backyard. "Summer lilacs," she said, pointing at a drooping purple bush. "Your butterfly bush. It's dying."

Emma looked at the flowers. "I've been watering it."

"You overwatered it."

Emma shook her head. "I'm sorry, but why were you even in my backyard?"

"I come every day to check on the plants."

"I haven't ever noticed you walking around the house."

Patty pointed to the privacy fence that separated their properties. When Emma gave her a blank look, Patty walked over and pressed her pointed finger into one of the wooden slats. A hidden door creaked open.

"There's a door connecting our backyards?" said Emma.

Patty put her hands on her hips. "Charlotte's husband, Dirk, set it up so the kids could have extra space to run around. And it made it easy for us to water their garden when they were away. Just pulled our own hose through. Did you not do an inspection on the house?"

Emma was too flustered to admit that they'd done the inspection via a video call with a guy named Chip who kept hinting that if they wanted to let the house go, he'd be interested in buying it himself. He said things like "These granite countertops are nice. Most flips you're going to find laminate. Quartz at best." In the frenzy of buying a house long-distance and negotiating jobs, punctuated by a miscarriage, Rachel and Emma were relieved that this one thing had gone right: The house they'd picked was a good one. Of course, after they moved in, it was clear that Chip had overlooked a few things. The sensitive fuses, the fussy toilet whose handle needed to be jiggled aggressively after flushing. The fridge had mysteriously warmed and darkened yesterday, and Emma's gratification with this further proof that the house was conspiring against them—Rachel got annoyed when she used the word *haunted*—fizzled this morning when she had to dump their warm cream cheese and leftover tofu and homemade hollandaise sauce into the trash.

"I understand that it was normal for you to come over when Charlotte was here," said Emma. "But now we live here. You have to respect our privacy."

"Believe me, I'm not interested in your privacy." Patty shuddered, making clear what she meant. "I have to check on the garden. Charlotte probably planted this bush before you were born. Do you know how rare it is for one of these to live longer than a decade? She'd be horrified to see it going to rot."

Emma shifted her weight, a sharp twinge jabbing in her cervix from Dr. Rivera's exam. She felt it move up her body and into her throat, where it did what pain often did, which was twist itself into meanness. She walked to the shed and selected a rusty shovel that had been left there by the previous occupants. She took the shovel back to where Patty stood watching with a look of detached interest.

"Since you're so invested in the welfare of these plants, why don't you take them to your own yard?" Emma held out the shovel. "That solves both our problems."

"You can't dig up summer lilacs," Patty said. "The root system is too complicated."

Emma flushed, feeling stupid. She lowered the shovel. "Well, you can't just come over here to check on the plants."

"Why not? I'm not bothering you."

"You are, though."

"It bothers you that your neighbor wants to make sure your yard doesn't look like trash?" Patty hooted. "You really are from Chicago."

The nerve of this woman! Emma curled her fingers around the shovel's handle. "Well, at least in Chicago, people know not to go where they're not invited."

Patty pressed her lips together so hard, they turned white. Their pale pink color rushed back in as she opened her mouth. But no words came out; she simply turned and left, pushing open the fence door with her foot and disappearing behind it.

*   *   *

On Thursday the English building looked morose in the twilight. Students drained from its doors, their evening classes finished at last, sloughing bags from their shoulders and shouting about Thirsty Thursday specials. Emma and Rachel went to the second floor, where the atrium was filled with people wearing ties and plastic name tags. A sign at the door read NEW FACULTY RECEPTION. The room, with its ornate windows and gilded portraits of past university presidents, was meant for wowing donors. But the carpet was dark and there was a stale smell under the aroma of grilled salmon, which lay skewered on kebab sticks atop warming pans.

"'The Buckley Center,'" Emma read from a plate on the wall. She turned to Rachel. "What's your guess, the novelist or the ideologue? Or maybe it depends on which donor is asking."

"Please just be friendly tonight," Rachel said. She looked ravishing in a blazer they'd bought at the mall, a thin layer of green shadow at the crease of her eyelids. You'd never know she'd spent the afternoon on the couch chewing antacids. Rachel had developed GERD during her PhD, the result of too much coffee and too little sleep, and she was still haunted by episodes of heartburn when she was stressed. When Emma first met Rachel, her attraction didn't come from the fact that Rachel was pretty—which she was, inarguably; people were always commenting on how pretty Rachel was—but from her self-possession, underneath which Emma could sense something wild and loose and frightened, something Emma was drawn to taking care of. And maybe something she wanted to be? Emma often thought, as she watched her wife shrug into clothing with a toothbrush in her mouth, that she would love to have her body for a day. The things she would decorate it with, the clothing she would wear, the lovely nail polish she would glide over those clean, hard nails. Emma rarely had the opportunity to see the wounded side of Rachel, but each time her wife's vulnerability emerged, usually in the form of gastrointestinal distress, Emma felt reverent, like she was witnessing a solar eclipse.

Rachel, on the other hand, had little patience for any failing of her body. When a friend in Chicago asked how they decided on Emma as the gestational carrier for their children, Rachel said, "Oh, have I not mentioned that I'm barren?" She'd laughed, to give others permission to laugh, but when the topic shifted, Rachel's mood dimmed, her face a curtain of darkness. Even now, as Rachel straightened her shoulders and waved to a colleague, Emma could see that same shadow dulling her eyes.

It was not the right day to bring up the IVF clinic, Emma knew. And so she hadn't.

"I'll be friendly," said Emma now. "Lady, I'm always friendly."

"Well. To me you are." Rachel smiled at a trio of women who were approaching with plastic cups of wine. All had the same curly hair and big teeth and thin silver jewelry. When they descended, Rachel introduced them as the Shakespeareans. Emma shook their hands, looking to find some discernible difference among them, but they seemed to have coordinated their looks, or perhaps they had worked together so long they had simply begun the process of symbiotic integration.

"Emma," one sang, her teeth tinted with wine. "We've heard so much about you."

"Rachel told us you write short stories," said another.

"Good for you," said the third charitably.

Before Emma could speak, the tallest one wrapped her hands around Rachel's arm and said to Emma, "We actually need to snatch your other half away for a bit, if you don't mind? There are some people she has to meet."

Emma watched Rachel get whisked away to a corner of the room, where a cluster of faculty was seated at a table around a bottle of whiskey and a plate of cheese. Emma recognized a couple of them from the department's website; they were tenured, their neckties loose and wine cups generously full. Their faces lit up when Rachel approached. Everyone liked her wife. Straight women especially loved to grasp her toned arm—the way the tall Shakespearean was doing now—because Rachel wasn't the kind of lesbian who would hit on them; she was the kind who would notice when they looked nice and say something about it. Rachel was a safe person. She had been Emma's safe person for nearly seven years.

Emma joined the line at the food table and filled her plate with watermelon and grape tomatoes and feta-stuffed mushrooms. She picked up a cup of white wine and studied the projection beamed on the screen at the front of the room: *Welcome, New Faculty! "The roots of education are bitter, but the fruit is sweet."—Aristotle*

"Enjoying the evening?" Paulie appeared beside her holding a beer and a plate of miniature cheesecakes. He'd removed his jacket and there was sweat under the arms of his shirt, though he smelled like cologne. Emma imagined him disrobing from the waist up in the faculty restroom and swabbing at his hairy armpits with a paper towel dampened with gel soap.

"It's a lovely event," she said. "Well catered."

Paulie laughed. "I can't stand these things. They go on too long. Look, a faculty meeting should be like a skirt—long enough to cover everything, but short enough to keep people interested."

Emma laughed politely. "Right."

"I see your partner's been kidnapped by the Elizabethans." Paulie nodded toward the group in the corner. One of the faculty, wearing an eye patch with his name tag stuck to it, was telling a story that involved undulating his palms as if they were floating on the ocean. Rachel's head was tilted to show that she was listening carefully.

"Rachel gets along with everyone," Emma said. "She'll probably volunteer for every faculty committee there is."

"How about you?" Paulie sank his teeth into one of the cheesecakes, getting a dab of lemon curd on his mustache. "Classes still leaving you comatose afterward?"

Emma felt her cheeks redden. "You caught me at a tired moment. It's mostly fine."

"Mostly?"

"I mean, I'm glad to be here. But there are always students who press your buttons." She was thinking of Alex Brewer, who had shown up to their second class with a gallon of orange juice and drunk it steadily through the course of her lecture. She'd tried to focus on other students, but there was something about the way he swung the gallon jug up to his mouth that made her flinch, like a moth flittering unexpectedly in the corner of her vision. When she did look at him, Alex was grinning with his wet juice mouth. She'd looked him up in the student directory and learned he was the president of Boon University's Campus Conservatives Alliance. Of course, she thought. A wolf circling its prey. He'd submitted an initial draft of his position paper this week—"The Right to Life: A Personal and Philosophical Defense of Pro-Life Values." Emma had shuffled it to the bottom of her grading stack so often that now it was the only one left to mark.

"You can't take it personally," said Paulie. "Undergraduates show up to every class like it's a dental appointment."

"Oh, I know. Most of them are absolutely fine." Emma thought of Chelsea B., who bobbed her head in gentle agreement while Emma talked about using ethos and pathos in writing. And Mark F., who began all of his emails *Dear Prof!!* But the students in her morning classes struggled to stay awake, and the ones in her afternoon classes were already exhausted by the efforts of the day. She could rarely get them to talk during discussions; it was never clear whether they'd done the assigned readings. And every other morning, Alex Brewer sat smirking in the back.

"What's on your syllabus?" Paulie asked.

"For their first assignment, I had them read 'The Yellow Wallpaper' and write an essay comparing it to a recent June Gaskill story about a suburban woman trying to figure out what's causing this bad smell in her house. Have you read it?"

Paulie nodded vigorously. "She thinks her immigrant

neighbors are trying to poison her? And then it turns out—"

"It's just a dead opossum under the porch."

"Poisoned by her own weed killer." Paulie shook his head. "Great story. I hadn't associated it with Gilman, but that's a clever assignment."

Emma flushed with pleasure. "Thank you. But my classes didn't really seem to connect with it. Or maybe they didn't get it. Their comparisons were, you know, that the stories were fiction and the last name of each author began with *G*."

Paulie laughed heartily. "In as many words as possible, I assume. And in sixteen-point font."

"Exactly. And a lot of them derailed into this story about a fraternity prank that happened here."

"Ah, of course. Last year a rejected fraternity rushee put dead fish in the ventilation system of the Delta Sigma Rho house. Forced all twenty-seven frat brothers to move out during finals week while the place was deep-cleaned."

"Oh, I heard. Actually, a couple of the essays ended up comparing that incident to the Gaskill story, totally forgetting 'The Yellow Wallpaper' was even part of it." As Emma laughed with Paulie, she realized it was the first time she'd felt at ease with someone other than Rachel since they'd moved here.

"It's tradition," Paulie said. "Every year the under-grads get worse, and yet every year, the seniors somehow graduate." He shook his head. "Please tell me there were at least a few good ones in the batch."

"Of course. Several." She took another sip of wine. Alex Brewer had actually handed in the best essay, describing not just the similarities in plot mechanics but also in stylistic choices—the use of metaphor to articulate the blurring of reality, the connotative diction in word choices like *sickly*.

And then there was also this paragraph:

The theme of paranoia is highlighted in both stories. It's a common feature of female hysteria, which has historical and modern applications. Take for example a hypothetical professor who teaches a class where no one speaks up. She must wonder, is it because she has failed as an instructor and no one knows any answers, or is it because no one can respect her when she wears her self-doubt like a crown? The wondering could certainly lead to insanity, as it does in both of these illuminating fictional stories.

When Emma finished reading his essay, she'd stood up and walked a brisk lap around the perimeter of the adjunct lounge. A combination of rage and humiliation burned just below her skin. She reviewed her options: She could grade the essay fairly, in which case it was certainly an A paper, given the depth of his analysis and the fact that there was nothing in the rubric sheet that said you couldn't embed a not-so-coded insult to the professor. Or she could address the issue directly. She could email Alex and ask him to come to office hours. If he had a problem with her, they should talk about it. That's what Rachel would do. But Emma didn't think she had the grit for this conversation; she pictured herself stammering and sidestepping like a stray kitten. Pathetic. So she chose a third option. She rounded a final lap of the adjunct lounge, picked up Alex's essay from the table, and dropped it in the recycling bin. She would say he'd never handed it in and deduct five points for lateness when he resubmitted it. This was certainly the most unethical thing she could do, but it was also the most satisfying. And definitely not something she would tell Paulie. Or Rachel.

Emma finished her wine. Paulie looked at the empty plastic cup.

"I'm sure you can handle yourself," he said. "But if you have any problem students, you come to me." The small dollop of curd still nestled in his mustache. "My office door is open anytime. We want you happy, remember?"

His elbow pressed against hers momentarily as he turned to reach for another canapé. Emma took a polite step back. "I appreciate that."

"We can't have you the way I found you the other day. Beaten down." He took a bite and chewed.

"Mouth agape like one of Picasso's subjects in *Guernica*. Except," he said, licking the curd from his mustache, "fully clothed, of course."

The room suddenly felt overcrowded and loud. Emma cleared her throat and glanced back at Rachel, who was laughing as the one-eyed faculty member chopped at the air with the sides of his hands and shouted something in French. Rachel's effortless smile made Emma aware of the tightness in her own cheeks. "Thank you for the pep talk," Emma said. "I should probably mingle."

"Before you go. That's my wife, Lisa, over there." Paulie pointed to a tall woman across the room. She was talking to someone Emma suspected was a donor, an elderly man with barreling confidence and a suit two sizes too large. Lisa listened to him intently, her eyes glimmering, and when he said something amusing, she threw her head back in laughter, ironed blond hair raining down her back.

"She looks like a young Stevie Nicks," Emma said.

Paulie looked at Emma with pleasure at the corners of his eyes. "You see it. She's got a stuffy vibe, but that's just a costume for work."

"Of course."

"We've got this boat we take out on the lake sometimes. Really nice cabin cruiser with wraparound seating. An onboard electric grill where I make steaks."

"Sounds nice."

"Fridge full of chardonnay. Big, comfy bed." Paulie

lowered his voice. "Lisa can really relax when we're on the boat. Women and chardonnay! I'm sure you know what I mean."

Emma looked for Rachel again, but the group of faculty in the corner had vanished, leaving their plastic cups scattered on the table.

Paulie sucked cheesecake from his thumb. "You should come with us sometime."

"Sorry, where?"

"On our boat."

"Oh. I'm not really a water person," she said. "I get seasick."

"No one gets seasick on my boat. It's got a deep-V bottom hull. Rides like silk." He leaned in so close, Emma could smell the faint tinge of onion on his breath. "And I know Lisa would love to have your company. She's your type, isn't she? What'd you say—a young Stevie Nicks?"

Emma laughed, a short and brief bark. "Look, buddy, if your wife doesn't want to sleep with you, I can't help you there." She'd meant it as a joke to mask her own discomfort, but as soon as the words left her mouth, she knew she'd touched an open wound. Paulie's face went hard as stone. "Oh, I didn't mean—of course your wife—"

"Never mind." Paulie crumpled the paper that had held the cheesecakes and stuffed it in his pocket. "It's easy to forget your place when you're new."

Emma's cheeks blazed. The wine burned through her, warming behind her eyes.

"Well, that was a stupid joke," she said. "Very undergrad of me."

Paulie looked carefully at her. "You know, when Rachel negotiated your adjunct status as part of her contract, we initially said no. Did she tell you that?"

Emma, sensing a trap she'd already fallen into, shook her head.

"Our department has eleven loyal adjuncts, alumni who because of the economy right now are all too happy to take on a monster course load. Of all the things we need in academia, one more Intro to Rhetoric instructor is not one of them. Especially one who hasn't taught in years. But Rachel insisted. And so we conceded. I even gave you the extra section that opened up this semester. That's how badly we wanted your wife."

Emma stayed silent, pressing her fingers into the plastic wine cup.

"Just some helpful context to help you navigate moments of ingratitude." Paulie held his hands out as if he'd laid down a full house in poker. "Excuse me, I'd better get this party started."

He wound his way to the front of the room, where an oak podium bore the university's crest. He tapped the microphone and joked about the free food being the reason for the big crowd, which made everyone laugh. Emma looked around. Everything in the room seemed to be getting smaller, and she trembled as she went back to the refreshment table and filled her cup from a silver water dispenser. As Paulie introduced each new faculty member, they came up to the stage—including Rachel, with a flush in her cheeks from the whiskey. Emma drank glass after glass of cold water until her bladder was full, and then she went down the hall to the restroom. It was there, while she was sitting on the toilet, that her phone buzzed. She answered.

"Emma?" The woman's voice was friendly. "This is Julie. I'm a nurse in Dr. Rivera's office, calling with some test results."

"Oh, hi." Emma quickly stood and pulled her pants up. "It's kind of late, isn't it? For a clinic?"

"We're open until eight on Thursdays to accommodate working mothers-to-be. Did I catch you at a bad time?"

"No, not at all." Emma leaned against the bathroom stall. Across from her, the words *God loves you* were written in Sharpie. Beneath that someone else had written *Not after what you did in here.* "This is fine."

"Good. So I wanted to let you know that Dr. Rivera has looked over your bloodwork and your HSG images."

"Okay."

"Everything looks normal. She says you're a perfect candidate for IVF. In fact, her words were 'This is one fertile mama.'"

Emma's eyebrows lifted in surprise. "Oh. That's good news."

"Isn't it? Listen, we typically book months out for a fresh cycle, but just this morning I had a cancellation. Based on the dates of your cycle, this could work out well. We'd get you started on the birth control protocol next week."

"Next week? That's too soon. I haven't even talked to my wife."

There was a scuffling on the line as if Julie was moving the phone. "No problem. Then let me see next available. One sec. I'm looking at May."

The door to the bathroom opened. Heels clicked on the floor; the sink turned on.

"May?" Emma whispered. "So our options are, do it now or wait another eight months?" She pictured a montage of the seasons changing: the sky blackening early in the evening and dirty snow melting to reveal the world was still the same.

"I know it's a long wait." Julie's voice deepened with warmth. "The hardest part of the whole process is often the waiting."

The woman with the heels closed herself in the stall next to Emma. A forceful stream of urine echoed through the bathroom.

"It just feels like it's already been a long time."

"I'm sure it has. Listen, there's one option that might work for you."

"What's that?"

"You can freeze. We can get you on the books now to start the process. Bring you in for a retrieval in" — the shuffling of papers — "early November. You could see how many embryos you got. Then if you weren't ready for pregnancy, we could freeze them and transfer at a later date."

Emma thought about this. It did seem like a tidy solution. She could keep moving forward with the process without having to pull Rachel in just yet. After all, Rachel was focused on getting her footing in the department. She had a full load of classes and committee work and a university-wide lecture to give next month. It would be the right thing to do, the more she thought about it. Rachel had hand-selected their city and their house — and, apparently, Emma's job. It would be okay for Emma to decide this one thing. Wouldn't it?

The woman next to Emma flushed and clacked out of the bathroom without washing her hands.

"Do you need more time to think?" Julie asked. "Or shall I book you for a baseline ultrasound next week?"

"Next week would be perfect," Emma said without allowing herself another moment of deliberation. She opened the stall. In the bathroom mirror she looked calm, capable. A woman taking charge. "Let's do this."

*　　　*　　　*

On the drive home, Emma told Rachel what had happened with Paulie.

"The whole time that I thought we were getting friendly, I think he was hitting on me. He suggested I should sleep with his wife. Or him and his wife both? I'm not sure. But now I feel like I did something wrong." Emma stopped at a red light under the glow of a looming Walmart. She'd replayed for Rachel the entire conversation except for the part about the department not wanting to hire her. She didn't think she could endure that level of embarrassment again, not even in front of her wife, who had known about it all along.

Emma looked at Rachel. She'd tilted her seat back slightly to ease the dizziness from the whiskey. The visor threw a shadow over her eyes; the bottom of her face was cast in red from the traffic light. It was hard to read her expression. But Emma could see it in the way she opened and then closed her lips. A flicker of doubt.

"You don't believe me," Emma said.

"Of course I do." Rachel blinked. "And I also know it's been hard for you here overall."

"I'm not making it up."

"Baby, I know. And I'm sorry this weird exchange happened. But do you think there's a chance you misread the situation? Like the thing with Patty earlier. Maybe people are trying to be nice or make you laugh, and you're—"

"I'm not imagining things." Emma wished she hadn't

told Rachel about the incident with Patty. Rachel had said, "She came over to water the plants and you threatened to dig them up?" Emma hadn't liked this tidy summary, which, while technically correct, didn't feel true. But she wasn't always able to explain things the way they actually felt. People were always misunderstanding. Maybe that was the real reason her writing career hadn't worked out.

"No, of course not," said Rachel. "Not imagining. Just—*adding a layer to the narrative* is what I was going to say."

Emma felt betrayed by this diplomacy. The point of marriage, she thought, was to have an automatic ally. She didn't speak as she drove straight home, past the tiki bar they'd originally planned on stopping by after the reception. Rachel didn't seem up for any more alcohol, which was fine. Emma wasn't really in the mood for a mai tai anyway.

As they pulled into their driveway, Emma saw the sign for the governor's reelection shining in the moonlight on Patty's lawn. "You have to be kidding me." She parked the car. "Do you see that? She must have put that up today. Right after I told her to stop nosing around our yard."

Rachel squinted at the sign. "I mean, people are putting up signs everywhere now. And she's probably a Republican. It makes sense that he's her candidate."

"You don't think that sign is a direct statement to us? That guy's biggest platform is 'traditional marriage.'"

"No," said Rachel. "I don't think everything is a commentary on us." She looked tired in the moonlight, loose hair coming down from her bun and coiling like fern fronds. "Isn't that an exhausting worldview?" She took Emma's hand and brought it to her lips. Emma felt annoyed by the tingle of pleasure that crawled up her arm.

"It is exhausting," said Emma. "But sometimes it's true."

They sat in the car holding hands. The headlights were still on. Moths fluttered helplessly into them, casting confetti-like shadows against the garage door.

"Could you leave the blinds open next time you go out?" Rachel asked. "You know how Birdie likes to get on the futon and look out the window."

Emma looked at the house. "I didn't close them. Did I?"

"I'm sure you did. You were worried Patty was going to spy on us." Rachel began to laugh. "Sorry, I'm just picturing her crouching under our window with night-vision goggles. Watching to see if you water the pothos."

Annoyed, Emma turned off the engine. "I'm not crazy. I get that one shitty neighbor is just that, a shitty neighbor. But that neighbor, plus a sleazy boss, plus students who want to write essays arguing against *Roe v. Wade*—now we're talking about an environment. You know what I mean? I don't feel like we belong here."

Rachel was quiet for a moment. Then she raised Emma's hand to her mouth again and closed her eyes as she pressed her lips against Emma's knuckles. "Okay."

"Okay?"

"Just give me two years."

"For what?"

"To be here. Two years is enough time for me to get my teeth into the academic world. Get a little equity in the house."

"And then what?"

"And then we're out of here. You can make the next big decision."

"You promise," Emma said.

"Yes."

Emma brought Rachel's hand to her own mouth and bit her thumbnail, a gesture of intimacy that always, inexplicably, made Rachel laugh. She laughed now.

Birdie greeted them at the door, dancing on her hind legs with joy. Emma picked her up and kissed the top of her head, inhaling the warm, yeasty scent of her fur. As Rachel went to the bathroom, Emma tucked the dog under one arm and pawed at the stack of papers on the credenza. "Hey, Rach? Have you seen my book? The June Gaskill? It was right here on the yellow cabinet."

"No," called Rachel. "Check the bed."

Emma set Birdie down and looked in the bedroom.

Not there. She checked the kitchen, her work bag, the office. An uneasy feeling settled on her shoulders. She came back to the living room, where Rachel, already changed into a T-shirt and sweats, was now picking bits of cracker off the futon. "I can't find it."

"I'm not surprised. You're not the most organized person I've ever married." Rachel brushed the crumbs into one hand and held them up as proof. "Your book is probably underneath the pile of laundry in our room."

"Those aren't mine. I didn't even eat crackers today. Did I?"

"I definitely didn't." Rachel dropped the crumbs into a wastebasket. Then she clipped on Birdie's leash. "Let's go for a walk."

"You don't think she took my book, do you?"

"Who?"

"Patty."

Rachel looked confused. "The neighbor?"

"You didn't see her when she was yelling at me about the bushes. She's got this sense of ownership over our house. And there's that creepy connecting fence in the backyard. Did you lock the doors before we left?"

"I really don't think we need to worry about a sixty-five-year-old neighbor breaking in to steal our novels." Seeing Emma's face, Rachel added, "Of course I locked it."

"You still think I'm overreacting."

"I think you're stressed."

Emma closed her eyes. "Maybe."

"I think you're cute."

"Possibly."

Rachel pulled her close, her hot whiskey breath on Emma's ear. "Hey. Let's take Birdie for a walk around this dangerous, high-crime neighborhood. And if we make it back alive, let's go to bed."

Emma pursed her lips. She pretended to think about it. "Fine," she said at last, and let her wife lead her by the hand out the door.

CHAPTER 4

When Charlotte opened her email, the lawyer's name sat there at the top, neat and indifferent. Russell Sloane, JD, of Sloane and Cartwright LLP had written her back. His name sent a thrill through her. He was the most impressive-looking lawyer she'd found and the only one to reply. Almost every day for the past week she'd checked the computer, wasting her precious downstairs time hunting for the laptop and pecking out her email password, only to be greeted by nothing. No responses from any of the attorneys or legal aid clinics she'd written to. Until today.

She clicked on the message.

Mrs. Dennison,

Thank you for your inquiry. Given your circumstances, you may have grounds to challenge the legitimacy of the title transfer. Best option is a quiet title action disputing the ownership. Is the house vacant? If so, that's good news. New owners complicate things. I'll have my assistant set up a consult to discuss.

Russell Sloane, JD

Charlotte read the message twice. It wasn't the news she wanted to hear—the word *complicate* left a bitter taste after the initial sweetness of *good news*— and it was irritating that Russell Sloane had not taken the time to fully read her first message, which clearly stated that the new people had moved in, but there was some promise here. She sat back, feeling the grind of her spine against the wooden chair. She'd always hated these chairs; they had a carved lattice pattern on the backs that made long dinners uncomfortable. Charlotte had complained about them endlessly to Dirk, who always suggested they buy new ones, then. But she felt guilty about getting rid of the set. Her mother had been so proud of the intricate carvings and high backs with their implication of wealth, so Charlotte had simply endured the discomfort for thousands of dinners, even after her mother died.

Now, in its life under new ownership, one of the chairs had been paired with a cheap folding card table in the guest bedroom. A few stacks of papers—student assignments to be graded, from the looks of it—notebooks, and pens littered the folding table, along with two empty coffee mugs and a glass of iced tea that appeared to be a day or two old. Looking at the setup, Charlotte realized how positively idiotic it had been to keep the chairs. Had she really spent so much of her life worrying about what someone else thought (a *deceased* person, at that!) that she was willing to sacrifice her own comfort? What did this get her other than the same low-grade misery that plagued her mother?

When it came down to it, Justin was the one she should have emulated. He never bottled anything up. His emotions came flowing out of him, pure and true and alive. Charlotte felt Justin's presence all the time lately. She would be reading or knitting or scrounging in the fridge and suddenly remember the absurd wideness of his big toe or the thicket of hair that met his temple in a sharp line. She remembered the briny smell of his skin when he came in from basketball practice his freshman year in high school, the only year he played before he was kicked off the team for fighting. The way he tipped his whole body back to drink his post-practice juice before the open fridge; oh, that had always made her laugh. She wondered how Amy handled his bad times. Did she rub his back until he calmed down? Close herself in another room for safety? Maybe Amy was a loose cannon herself, and the two of them aired all their grievances at the same time, bellowing like dogs straining at their leashes before wrapping themselves in each other's forgiveness. Maybe Charlotte had been too closed off. If she'd just screamed back at him rather than trying to correct him, would he have listened? Instead of always being so righteous, she could have met him in anger, the place he always returned to. It could have been so simple.

Charlotte felt the particular ache of loneliness that always arose when she thought about Justin. She missed all of him, even — maybe especially — his complications and sharp corners. She was going to find him to make things right. And Russell Sloane was going to help.

She clicked on his message to reply, but before she had a chance, a new message appeared from his office. She opened it.

Dear Charlotte,

Thank you for your interest in Sloane and Cartwright LLP. To move forward with your inquiry, a retainer of $2,500 is required. Please call our office at your earliest convenience to set up an appointment.

Cecily Hunt, legal assistant

Of course. The cost. Charlotte said the number out loud, feeling its impossible roundness in her mouth. She reached for one of the coffee mugs and curled her fingers around the handle. The urge to throw it against the wall pulsed through her. She imagined hearing it break. Seeing it press its shape into the drywall before splitting apart and spreading its sharp bits into the carpeting, where they would lie in wait for the new people to walk through barefoot. But Charlotte couldn't leave a mark like that. Not if she wanted to stay here. And she had to stay here. Not just because they were waiting for the wedding invitation to arrive. But because—and this part she didn't like to face—there was nowhere else to go.

She typed quickly.

Mr. Sloane,

I don't know how you can sleep at night asking for thousands of dollars from a person whose house and everything in it was stolen.

I wrote to you because I thought you could
help me, but I guess the law is only helpful
for people who can afford to break it. Shame
on you.

She hit send, her fingers shaking. It was thrilling
to tell someone off like this, to sample her anger like
a sweet wine. So what if her message was ignored or
sent briskly to the trash? She didn't care what Russell
Sloane thought. She cared about no one at all except
herself and Dirk and Justin.

She tried to scoot the chair back, but it caught on
the carpet and her elbow bumped the table, which
knocked the iced tea all over the papers. For a few
seconds Charlotte watched as the brown liquid blossomed and darkened over the title "The Right to Life:
A Personal and Philosophical Defense of Pro-Life
Values." She felt a momentary flash of pleasure in seeing the damage she'd caused. She had come to hate
every object in the house that didn't belong to her.
She'd found sporadic outlets for her anger in minor
acts of destruction, like wearing her shoes downstairs
and scuffing them along the new flooring. Last week
she'd flipped the breaker to the refrigerator, imagining
the satisfying halt to the appliance's hum, the spoil-
ing of yogurts and cheese. That plan had backfired
a bit, as the new people didn't turn the fridge back on

for days, and during that time their fridge was empty and dark, which meant no fresh food for Charlotte either.

Charlotte hurried to the kitchen, walking along the far wall to avoid windows, and grabbed several paper towels from the roll. She took them back to the guest bedroom and dabbed at the iced-tea mess. The paper was soggy along the edges, the first two pages ruined for sure; she crumpled them up and shoved them in her pocket. Then she wiped up the rest of the spill and straightened the remaining papers. She ripped out a few tea-stained pages of the notebook, left it open to a blank page, and put it on top of the stack to cover the fact that some papers were missing. She set the empty glass upright and laid a pen gingerly across the notebook.

There. Looked fine.

Charlotte glanced at her watch. It was Wednesday, which meant the blond girl would be home in fifteen minutes. She was prompt and methodical, always calling for the dog in the same way, always leaving her keys hanging on the hook by the front door. She came out to the garage sometimes to talk on her phone, and once she seemed to be fiddling with the shelves on the alcove door, so close beneath them they heard her say, "No, I haven't told her yet. I just want to make sure things are—" and then her voice abruptly faded, as if she'd turned on her heel and begun pacing. Charlotte had taken Dirk's hand then, feeling his pulse before he pulled away and picked up a crossword.

Charlotte turned to the laptop to shut down her email when she saw the law office's name again, bolded at the top of the inbox. She clicked the message.

Mrs. Dennison—

A quiet title suit is complex and my retainer reflects the work involved. However, if the property is vacant, I can work on a reduced fee to cover the initial filings and title work. There is a possibility of recovering those fees if we pursue a separate fraud claim, depending on the defendant's assets. Please confirm whether the house is vacant so I can advise next steps.

She read the email again and again until some of her anger was spent with the effort of memorizing his words. After a few minutes, she felt cleansed as she highlighted the most positive aspects of the email. *Reduced fee. There is a possibility. Next steps.* She had the same thought she'd had in her old life when she opened the cabinets at dinnertime after not going to the grocery store: *I can work with this.*

Mr. Sloane,

It's not vacant at the moment, but it will be soon. I will be in touch when the current occupants are gone.

Thank you sincerely,
Charlotte Dennison

It was getting late. She logged out of her email, wiped the browser history, and closed the laptop. On her way back to the garage, she stopped by the trash can in the kitchen and shoved the tea-stained papers from her pocket beneath a Styrofoam takeout container.

*   *   *

For the first few weeks of summer, before they'd moved into the attic, Charlotte and Dirk had stayed in a budget motel off the highway called Meadow View Inn, a place that smelled of long-ago cigarettes and unwashed feet. Its nickname among guests was Mildew View, and it was the only place in the area with an available room. Charlotte had never expected that longer-stay motels would be in such demand, but she supposed it made sense in the face of so many foreclosures, with people being flung out of their homes with no place to land. Apartments were a cleaner choice, but few could scrape together the deposit required, so here they were. Recession was good for business.

On the first day as they rolled their suitcases across the cracked pavement toward their room, a boy no older than twenty with bleached yellow hair approached. He was twirling a caulking gun in one hand and cradling a cardboard box in his other arm.

"You're new," he said.

Charlotte stepped closer to Dirk, who was fishing in his pocket for the key. "Just temporary," she said. "While some things are taken care of at our house."

"Renovations, like." The boy's lips split into a wide smile, revealing a missing tooth. He jabbed his tongue reflexively into the empty place; its loss must have been recent. "Can I give you some advice? Number one, do not leave valuables in your room. I do not care if it's a cell phone or a gold chain or a firearm. Or your girl-friend's prosthetic arm. It will disappear while you are away. Ask me how I know."

"I suppose you've been the victim of theft," said Dirk. He had the key now, with its large plastic tag, but he was waiting for the boy to leave before putting it in the keyhole.

"'S'right." The boy sniffed. "Who the fuck steals a prosthetic arm? The constituency here is general lowlifes." He tapped the box under his arm with the caulking gun. "Moral of the story, put your stuff in a box and take it with you always. Also, never answer the door. That advice is my housewarming gift to you."

The boy began to walk away, but after a few steps he tipped his head back and called, "And check the mattress. Purple dots are either mold or the blood of bedbugs."

Dirk unlocked the door and as they stepped inside, they were hit with the smell. Body odor and cigarette smoke and pet hair forced its way through the weak defenses of industrial cleaner. Beads of water pressed up between the cheap planks of vinyl flooring as they rolled their suitcases in. There was a living area with a kitchenette and a separate bedroom just big enough for the queen bed. The coffee maker had a line of semipermanent crust, as if there had been a time when someone had filled it halfway and forgotten about it for a year. Everything in the room was bolted down—even the plastic tissue box—as if the motel proprietors knew the type of people who stayed here had lost everything and were looking to reclaim some furnishings for their own.

"It's only for a few weeks," Dirk said as he came up behind her. He wrapped his long arms around her waist awkwardly, like a prom date. "We'll get everything sorted and be back home before you know it."

Charlotte was stiff under his touch. "Guess we were due a vacation," she said. A stupid thing to say, really. But it was also funny, and the shudder of Dirk's body against hers as he laughed helped her forgive herself, if only for a moment.

All there was to do in the first weeks at the motel was watch television with the volume up to compete with the lashing of the rain on the window. Every news program was the same: jobs lost, savings and retirement accounts disappearing, people so desperate to keep their lives intact that they signed over their deeds to predatory buyback programs that left them homeless. The door between their room and the parking lot was thin, filling the evenings with the thunder of the vending machine and shouts from the parking lot. Sometimes Charlotte fantasized about opening her door to a group of men shoving one another over lost cigarettes and finding that one of them was Justin. She could picture him living in a motel like this with a girlfriend who looked ten years older than she actually was, both of them sleeping through the days easily on the stiff sheets, unbothered by the scritching of mice in the walls. Eating nothing but pudding and bologna and chips. She could imagine him being this close to their house but never calling, never even once considering it because of all she'd done to hurt him.

They had come to the motel on the advice of a real estate mediator named Victor Maxwell, who was negotiating new terms for their mortgage with the bank. Victor wasn't exactly a charming person—he had a habit of absently lifting the end of his tie to his red mustache and sniffing—but he was the only one who had shown up to help when the eviction started to close in on them. They'd refinanced in order to play catch-up with the long-ago debt from Justin's rehabs, and the new mortgage's interest rates sharply increased until payments were beyond their reach, especially after Dirk's 401(k) tanked. It had been a confusing time in which Charlotte and Dirk saw everything they'd thought of as stable—their house, their retirement funds—come crashing down. And being old did them no favors. When the EZ Auto Clinic posted a job, Dirk went down there in person and told the manager about his years of experience in the shop. The manager had asked, "You think you'd be able to keep up with the job?" and never called back.

Charlotte had gone through the yellow pages in the spring and called every local assistance organization she could find, from legal aid clinics to churches to housing counseling agencies. She'd sat with the phone at the kitchen table and explained their story over and over again, including the fact that the mortgage company—their own bank!—recommended she skip three payments in order to prove financial duress but then slapped them with an eviction notice when they fell that far behind. Each time she talked to someone, she was met with sympathy but little else. Aid agencies were at capacity, or they didn't have enough staff to support any additional cases, or their already limited funding had been depleted entirely by the recession. During these afternoons on the phone, Charlotte watched the tulips in the backyard twist themselves open like little lipsticks. The peonies around the Japanese maple tree unfolded, reaching greedily toward the sun. She used to love this time of year, when everything burst into existence at once. But now it seemed pathetic that these flowers and birds and insects kept regenerating when another winter was coming. What was the point? Everything would be gone soon.

Each time she hung up, Charlotte crossed another organization off her list. And then she had no more names to call. By the time the tulips had withered back into the ground, she had painted the backyard with their failures and knew she would never look upon it the same way again.

When Victor Maxwell arrived at their doorstep, a manila folder tucked under his sweaty arm, Charlotte and Dirk were three days from their eviction and had a little over eight thousand dollars to their name. He had heard about their case from a nonprofit called Silver Lining Support Services, which offered financial assistance to people over sixty-five. Charlotte had called the agency in May and left her story on a voicemail that was never returned. Victor was a mediator who didn't have the easy solution Charlotte had hoped for; his fee was five thousand dollars and he needed them to stay at a motel for a few weeks while he negotiated on their behalf with the mortgage company. Being away from the home meant they could avoid the direct summons that was required for the bank to seize the house.

"If they can't find you, they can't serve you," he'd explained, slurping the lemonade Dirk had set in front of him on the coffee table. "Our governor has a statute, bless the man, that says possession of the home cannot take place until a face-to-face summons is made with an owner if they're over the age of sixty-five."

"So we go into hiding? That's what you're saying?" Charlotte said. She was immediately suspicious of the idea, though it was hard to tell how much of her suspicion was rooted in her dislike of Victor himself, the way he spread his legs and leaned forward like he was sitting on a toilet instead of an armchair. But she could feel Dirk straighten beside her, paying attention, so she'd willed herself to listen to the man. He was the only one who'd shown up, after all. Hiding out in a motel was not a solution she'd considered, to be sure, but she did have to admit there was something unsurprising about it. After all the messages she'd left and letters she'd written that had gone unanswered, Charlotte had come to think of the law as 10 percent fairness and 90 percent evasive maneuvers.

"It's not a crime. While I take care of things with Doug Rockford at Homestead Capital, you just lie low. Doug's an old high-school friend who is up to his nostrils in foreclosures." Victor pressed his index finger under his nose, pausing a moment to sniff. "He's amenable to negotiating new terms on mortgages like yours."

"Like ours?"

"Belonging to people with a history of financial responsibility. No criminal record." Victor pointed at Charlotte, then at Dirk, his fingers shaped like a gun. "*Good* people. We can get your payments down to a reasonable amount for a couple living solely on Social Security."

"I already called the mortgage company," said Charlotte. "They said they can't help."

"I hate to say this, but it is very hard for the average person to advocate for himself—or herself—within the financial system. Hiring a mediator levels the playing field."

"Are you a lawyer?" Dirk wanted to know.

"Mr. and Mrs. Dennison, a lawyer can't help you in this particular situation."

"Why not?"

Victor looked him square in the eye. "Because, to put it bluntly"—here he shifted his gaze to Charlotte—"you're in a mess of your own making."

Charlotte blinked, her eyes burning.

"With mediation, you have a chance. We find creative solutions because we want everyone to feel like they won. In this situation, for example, you get to keep your home, and your lender, Homestead Capital, gets to minimize loss. Foreclosures are expensive for banks." Victor said this last part quietly, as if it were a secret he wasn't supposed to reveal.

They sat for a minute, Charlotte and Dirk next to each other on the couch, Victor across from them, his big, boyish hands gripping the empty lemonade glass. Behind him the wall was filled with Dirk's framed hunting knives and a glossy picture of a loon dipping over a lake. Looking at it all made Charlotte's eyes tired. She put her hand on Dirk's knee and squeezed.

"We really don't have five thousand dollars to spare," Dirk said. "But we thank you for coming."

Victor didn't seem surprised. He just swept his papers together into the folder. He stood and shook Dirk's hand. "Thanks for taking the time. And I sincerely hope you find a solution." As he walked toward the door, he nodded at a picture on the mantel. "That your son?"

The photo was from five years ago, when Justin was nearly thirty. His hair was cut just above his eyebrows, which accentuated the way they drew up when he smiled. He stood between his parents, a broad arm over each one's shoulder. They'd set up the timer for that photo. An awful fuss, pressing all those buttons, Charlotte sick with worry he might leave without her getting a photo, but then Justin had laughed and reached for the camera and said, "Let me do it, Ma."

One of the good visits. Not like last year.

"Yes," she said. "That's Justin."

"He live close by? You could stay with him instead of a motel. Save a few bucks."

Charlotte shook her head. She was surprised to hear Dirk say, "Don't know where he's living now. He's had his troubles." She was about to give him a look to hush, but then she caught the expression on Victor's face. Not pity but sorrow.

"Happened with my brother too," he said. "For him it was addiction. Just about broke my parents' hearts."

"Yes," said Dirk. "Addiction here too."

"And mental illness." Charlotte wanted to get the facts straight. The faulty wiring came first, then the problems with drugs. She wanted it to be clear it wasn't Justin's fault. That was at least one positive thing that came out of the Al-Anon meetings.

"The world will get every one of us in some way," Victor said.

At the front door he turned around. "My brother eventually did come home, you know. Got himself cleaned up, made a little apartment in my parents' basement. Got a job selling vacuum cleaners. Had a girlfriend for a while. So there was a happy ending, at least for my parents."

"They must have been proud," said Charlotte. "To see him overcome his struggles."

Victor shrugged as if this was of little connection to his story. "I do know that it was the reason they never moved. Had to stay put so when Luke decided to come home, he'd know where to find them."

Dirk reached one hand up to touch Charlotte's shoulder, the other wiping his mouth aggressively.

"They always come home," Victor said, seeing this. "There may be other pleasures of the world out there, but they are fleeting. Home is what lasts. Always in their minds as a backup." He put his hand on the doorknob. "Have you thought about what Justin will do if he comes home and some stranger answers the door? If he learns his parents foreclosed on his childhood home and moved without even telling him?"

Charlotte and Dirk didn't look at Victor. They looked only at each other. Then Dirk said, "There's a little more than five in the checking, I think. Maybe we could—"

But she was already gone, off to find the checkbook.

*   *   *

Charlotte crouched at the attic window. Through the wisteria vines she could see the clouds—cumulus, she was pretty sure—moving briskly across the sky, a sign of the weather growing cooler. The street was bathed in a golden afternoon light, illuminating the bumpers of the cars on the street, which looked small and impersonal from here. It was like looking out the wrong end of a telescope, everything distant and just out of reach.

Charlotte was feeling optimistic tonight, a rare lift in her chest as she watched the new people get in their car and back out of the driveway. A plan was forming in her mind, and she was impatient to get downstairs. The car disappeared down the block like a pesky fly buzzing off.

"Get your pants on," she said to Dirk. "We're going on a date."

Dirk looked up from his magazine. He was in his boxers, sitting on a stack of milk crates with one leg crossed over the other, his readers perched on his nose. Justin's vinyl records, which had previously filled the crates, were stacked neatly in the corner. "A date? Where?"

"Downstairs. They've gone to some big event at the university. I think we have three hours clear."

She watched as a progression of reluctance marched across her husband's face: confusion, hesitation, fear. Dirk didn't like to make the trip down the hatch. The steep stairs made his knees crack, he said, though Charlotte suspected the real reason was that it hurt him to see his house invaded and dismantled. He went downstairs every two or three days to have a bowel movement, and on those trips he was efficient, returning within four minutes. Charlotte remembered all the times during their marriage when he disappeared with a newspaper into the bathroom while she made breakfast and cut up fruit for lunches. He'd luxuriated in those trips, sometimes gone for twenty-five minutes or more, and she felt a pang of sympathy for him now that he'd not only lost his home but all the little routines he'd built inside of it.

But still. The fact that he was content to stay in the attic day in and out, disappearing into his model cars and magazines while she fetched food and emptied the honeypot and washed socks and underpants in the sink and carried around the stink and humiliation of their new reality—well, it grated on her nerves.

"Plus," she said, "you need to shower."

Dirk lifted an arm to his nose. "Do I smell?"

"Like a barn cat in August." She waited. "Well? Or do you have somewhere else to be?"

"I'm just thinking." Dirk closed his magazine. "If we're just going downstairs, why in the name of sanity do I have to put on pants?"

Charlotte went down first, stepping carefully on each stair, bracing her arms on the narrow walls beside her. She loved this part; it was like lowering herself into a swimming pool on a hot day. But it was a journey she had to approach with humility, because a fall was out of the question. Some days when she crept down for breakfast, Charlotte envisioned it in gruesome detail, the way her hip would snap on the way down, the blood that would smear the wall as her head hit the alcove door and threw it open. The new people would come across her body in the garage—no, worse, the little dog would find her first—and then their eyes would rise in horror to the open hatch above through which they'd hear the faint, amnesic sound of Dirk's snoring.

But tonight Charlotte was careful, and so was Dirk. They grunted with the effort of lowering their bodies with control, and once in the garage, they smiled at each other. It was the kind of smile they used to share when they'd left her mother's house after dinner, knowing she was watching them from the window as they carried their foil-wrapped leftovers to the car.

"Welcome home," Charlotte said as she opened the door into the house. The little dog leaped from the futon to greet them. "It's like a mini-vacation."

Dirk bent down and scratched the dog's head. "It's not the worst place we've stayed. It's no Mildew View."

"No," she agreed. "It's certainly not."

Inside, she nudged Dirk toward the bathroom, where he obediently retreated with a towel over his arm. Charlotte went to the living room, the little dog following at her heels. The room had been transformed over the past week into a vaguely incorrect approximation of her old home, missing all its essential components. Justin's futon was pressed along the wall, an ugly tartan blanket thrown over it. Their old television sat in the corner atop a small side table like an unopened gift. A leaning tower of unfamiliar shoes cluttered the entryway.

She closed the blinds in the front room. Then, as soon as she heard the shower running, Charlotte slipped quietly down the steps to the basement. All afternoon her mind had worked through Russell Sloane's promise like a dog pawing the dirt. There were countless ways to get new owners to abandon their home — a septic system failure, sudden cracks in the foundation, persistent and unfindable odors — but Charlotte cast each of these aside. She didn't want to hurt the house or inherit the expensive repairs any of these might require. No, this project needed to be entirely psychological in nature.

The solution was simple, really: wreak minor but persistent havoc. It wasn't a flooded basement that made someone want to flee but the countless cold shocks of water each morning in the shower. People were built to withstand enormous loss; they'd bury their loved ones and carry on. But make them fish hair out of a clogged drain every day and they'd come undone.

At the bottom of the steps, Charlotte stopped a moment to catch her breath at the shock — it never faded, even though she'd been down here several times now — of seeing it carpeted and drywalled with a drop ceiling like a sad little dormitory. Had she been blindfolded and dumped here, Charlotte would never have known this was the place she'd done thousands of loads of laundry, hurling heavy, wet sweaters over the clothesline that used to hang from each end.

She went to the laundry room and unscrewed the drain hose on the back of the washing machine. Not completely off, but loose enough that it would, after a few washes, begin to pool water on the floor. As she stood back up, she felt a momentary flash of pity. Not for the new people but for the floor beneath the laundry machine, which already had years of hidden water damage from the times the hose had loosened on its own and Charlotte hadn't noticed.

She knew she should stop there. But she felt so good, her anger sweet and indulgent, like running her tongue along a doughnut's glaze. She stepped out of the laundry room and stood in the middle of the basement, feeling her slippers sinking into the carpet. Her eyes fell on the crooked electrical outlet on the wall. The plastic cover stuck out, leaving a gap the width of a pencil eraser. Dirk had pointed it out when they first came back to the house, saying it was a sign the renovation had been hasty. His impulse was to fix it—she'd seen him straighten his shoulders and turn with purpose toward the stairs until it hit him, a second after it hit her, that his tools had been taken along with everything else. Charlotte's anger flared now at the memory. She wiggled her finger behind the plate and gave a tug. She was surprised when the whole plate came loose, as if it had only been tucked inside the wall rather than fastened. The lights flickered briefly and there was a momentary crackling noise, satisfying as the sound of popcorn coming to life in the microwave, as the metal electrical box lurched out of the hole in the drywall. It hung there for a moment like a dislocated body part, suspended by a sinewy cluster of green and black wires. Charlotte considered leaving it that way. Let the new people see it as a metaphor for the house itself, the way it was falling apart, its history of having things ripped from it with violence. Let them taste a moment of horror when they came down to the basement to wash their clothes. It wouldn't be a fraction of what Charlotte felt when she first saw her home hollowed and violated, her furniture shoved into the garage like debris.

Grow up, her mother's voice said. *Stop being a petulant child.*

Helen, this time, was right. The point was to be subtle, to do her work without being noticed. So Charlotte pressed the plate back into place with the sole of her slipper and went upstairs just as Dirk came out of the bathroom smelling of vanilla shower gel. A damp towel hung from his hand.

"Did you wipe out all the drips?" she asked.

Dirk saluted her with two fingers. "All evidence destroyed, Sergeant." He looked around the room. "Now, this feels odd."

"I told you. Every time I come in here, it's something new. Well, something old." She pointed at the television in the corner. "They even set up the TV you kept in the basement for baseball games."

"Can we watch it? Just sit and watch TV like a couple of normal people?"

Charlotte smiled. "Mister, that's exactly the plan."

Dirk looked at the blinds, through which the last of the golden afternoon light striped his face with worry. "What if they come back?"

"They won't." Charlotte was certain the girls wouldn't return early that night, because on the calendar one of them had written *5:00 reception, 6:00 remarks, 7:00 date night??* Those question marks reeked of desperation. They would no doubt stay out later than either of them wished, drinking flat beers at Applebee's, neither of them wanting to be the one to finally call it.

Charlotte smiled. A breakup was yet another reason to move out of a house, wasn't it? A different type of crack in the foundation.

"Sit your clean self down," Charlotte said. "I have a surprise for you." She went to the kitchen and opened a lower cabinet while Dirk hunted for the remote. She'd found the new people's bottle of rum last week when she was looking for a plastic bag and felt a burst of free-wheeling joy at the sight of its square glass shoulders and tidy label. She'd never cared much for liquor, but for years Dirk had made himself a nightcap of rum and vanilla Diet Coke every Saturday. As she poured a finger into each of two paper cups from beneath the sink—didn't these people have any real dishes?—and added an equal amount of water to the bottle, she thought of Dirk on those nights when he'd take his drink, the ice clinking in the glass, and roam the house to find her. They'd watch TV or, if it was summer, sit in the backyard so they could chat while she pulled weeds. If Justin was there, Dirk only poured Cokes. He hid the liquor bottle in Charlotte's sewing basket, and sometimes she'd come across it days later, the hardness of the glass surprising her as she reached for her pincushion.

She held the cups in her hands, a sleeve of crackers tucked under her arm, and went to the living room. Dirk sat on the futon watching television.

"Look at this, Lottie," he said. "Are you seeing this?"

Charlotte sat next to him. It was the news. Men in polo shirts were carrying cardboard boxes out of the revolving doors of a New York office building, the flash of cameras on their grim faces. Charlotte couldn't hear the report—the volume was low so Dirk could stay vigilant to sounds of a returning car. But she got the gist. One of the men carrying boxes shook his head and tucked his chin down like a boy who'd just been asked who started the food fight in the school cafeteria.

"They filed for bankruptcy," Dirk said. "Can you believe it?"

Charlotte handed him his cup. "I don't feel sorry for them in the slightest."

Dirk lifted the cup to his nose and sniffed. Then he smiled. "You know what? Me either."

They watched for a few minutes. Obama appeared in a campaign ad, gleaming with self-assurance in front of a pair of French windows. As he spoke, his head shook ever so slightly—a thing Charlotte wouldn't have noticed if the volume were higher—as if to say, *Sorry, but I'm afraid you're wrong.*

"Button your collar," Charlotte told the television. "You look like an undergraduate."

They clicked around and found a made-for-TV movie. The rum had relaxed Dirk, and he turned up the volume a few clicks. A woman detective was trying to solve the murder of her high-school classmate. She worked long days hunting for the killer; her husband griped about dinner not being ready when she came home.

"Make it yourself, bozo," Charlotte said, opening the crackers. She handed some to Dirk, who snapped them in half before putting them in his mouth. Crumbs dropped on his lap and Charlotte brushed them off. The drink numbed their lips and warmed their throats while the dog snored at their feet. It all felt deliciously ordinary.

Angry with her husband, the detective in the movie checked into a motel called Last Resort. She entered the dark room and dropped her keys on the side table. She pulled off her boots and sighed. Then she flicked the light on and a man stepped out of the bathroom, pointing a gun at her.

"Let's change it," Charlotte said, reaching for the remote.

But Dirk was already frozen, his fingers wrapped around the plastic remote. She pried it loose and he coughed suddenly, then bent over with his face in his hands.

"Are you okay?" she asked, grabbing his arm. "Dirk, do you need me to call an ambulance?"

He shook his head. Charlotte gently took his fingers from his face and saw with relief that he was only crying.

"No chest pain?"

He shook his head.

"Oh, Dirkie." She switched back to the news and muted the TV. "It was just a dumb movie." She pressed him against the futon and held his head against her neck, where she could feel the warmth of his tears pool on her collarbone. She whispered in his ear, nonsense about how things would be all right if they just stayed calm and stayed together. After a few minutes, Dirk let out a long breath and peeled himself back up. They watched the silent TV for a few more minutes. Then Charlotte, seized by compassion, reached down into his boxers and — shushing his protests — helped him feel, for just a little while, like his old self again.

*   *   *

Dirk had called living in the motel "terrible but tolerable," which became the vocabulary they used to describe just about everything there. Microwaved eggs for breakfast? Terrible. Cold cuts and canned soup for lunch? Tolerable. They took two walks during the day if it didn't rain, holding hands until the sidewalk along the highway became too cracked and narrow. Traffic buzzed by them and Charlotte thought how strange it was that the world kept on churning out its busy agenda while her own life had been diced and skewered. After their walks they returned to the motel sweaty and spent, fortified to sit for hours in front of the television.

It was during one of these evenings that someone knocked on the door. Charlotte had just finished knitting a blanket and, since she had no more yarn, was now frogging the entire thing and respooling it into a neat skein.

"Merciless," Dirk said, watching her rip the stitches. "Cold-blooded."

Charlotte was about to say that she was unraveling in more ways than one when the knock came. It was a soft tap, unsure of itself. Dirk turned down the television. It was nearly nine thirty. The parking lot outside in a rare moment of quiet.

The knock came again, louder this time.

"Don't answer," Charlotte said. "They're at the wrong room."

But a voice rang out beyond the door. A woman. "I saw your light on. Are you there?" When they didn't respond, she added in a shaking voice, "Please, I need help."

Dirk touched Charlotte's knee to indicate that she should stay on the couch. Then he rose and opened the door, leaving the chain on. Through the gap Charlotte could see a woman's pale face, her lipstick purpling her mouth like a child who'd eaten an ice pop.

"I locked myself out of the room," she said. "Can I use your phone? My kid's in my room and he's not answering the door."

"What room are you in?" Dirk asked.

"Two fourteen. I'll try calling the room, and if he doesn't answer, I need to phone the police."

"Don't you have a cell phone?" asked Charlotte. She and Dirk had no use for them — cell phones just seemed like another bill with hidden fees every month — but the girl seemed young enough to be part of the generation that always had them glowing in their faces.

"It's in the room."

"What about the front office?"

"It's never open. Please, he's only eight," the woman pleaded. "I think he's scared. He might hurt himself."

Charlotte met Dirk's eyes. There were times when they went a week without mentioning Justin. And then there were times like this, when they had an entire conversation about all the things they'd done wrong as parents and could have done differently, without saying a word. Dirk unlatched the chain, and Charlotte straightened her blouse, casting her eyes around the room to be sure it wasn't too messy. She didn't want the woman to think they were the kind of people who lived in a motel because they couldn't manage a proper home.

What happened next flashed by so quickly that it was over before Charlotte understood what had happened. There was suddenly a burst of people—three, all masked—in their room, and one of them wrapped his arm around Dirk's neck from behind and held a silver gun to the side of his head. The person was short, forcing Dirk to arch his back and bend his knees to accommodate their height. Charlotte felt the ridiculous words forming in her mouth—*He's got a bad heart, please don't stress him*—but nothing came out. She was frozen on the couch, like a chipmunk she'd once seen in her garden, who, in its panic, allowed itself to be devoured by a neighbor's cat. Charlotte watched a second person dig through her purse, which sat on the table by the coffeepot. The third person disappeared into the bedroom, and Charlotte found her voice; she yelled, "Stay out of there!" Which of course was a terrible idea, because that was what caused the second person to drop her purse and join the third in the bedroom, from which they emerged triumphantly a minute later with the envelope of cash she'd hidden under the mattress.

"Sorry," said the purple-mouthed woman, who was

still standing outside the door. "Really am sorry about this." And then they all left, the door clicked shut, and a car engine revved in the lot. Headlights filled the room briefly, illuminating Dirk's posture, which was oddly erect, his arms wrapped around himself as if he were cold. And then darkness again.

They couldn't file a police report; they understood that right away. Because if the whole reason they were staying in the motel was to avoid a direct summons, calling the police was as good as turning themselves in. When you really contemplated what was worth more, your home or an envelope with your last three thousand dollars in it, the answer was clear as a bell.

So Dirk called Victor, who didn't answer but did call back the next day. His voice was hollow and fuzzy, like he was on speakerphone, but full of sympathy. Robbed at gunpoint! Right in their own room! He promised to deliver groceries to them later.

"Tell him we'd rather go home," Dirk said loudly. Charlotte repeated this into the phone, though she was sure Victor had heard.

"We need another week," Victor said. "I'm leveraging a few things here. The bank is almost ready to sign off on a new loan that will reduce your payments by half. So there's some good news for you on a very bad day."

"And we're grateful for that, we really are—"

"I tell you what, Mrs. Dennison. Given your new

urgency, I'm going to make it six days. You know what, let's make it five. How's that? Five days. You can do that, right?"

Victor did send groceries the next day via a delivery boy, who carried four paper bags into their room and set them on the table. He waited a beat, as if expecting a tip, but Charlotte crossed her arms and met his eye until he left. The bags were surprisingly generous but full of things they couldn't cook without a kitchen—a rib eye steak, chicken breasts, frozen pizza, dried pasta—so Charlotte picked out the things they could microwave and took the meat to the front office to see if they had a freezer she could store it in until they went home.

There was no bell on the office door, and inside the only sound was the whirring breath of an oscillating fan. Charlotte didn't like coming to the front desk because it smelled like uncooked sausage and there was often someone dozing on the yellow vinyl sofa by the mailboxes. But today the place was empty. No one behind the desk either. Charlotte rang the bell and waited. There was a handwritten note, adhered to the counter with a generous amount of packing tape, that said:

> *Effective immediately the "weekly rate" will increase from $300 to $340. "Thank you" for your understanding. —Management*

"A robbery," said a voice behind her, and Charlotte jumped. It was the boy with yellow hair, now armed with a can of roach spray and a Sprite. He pointed to the sign. "Highway robbery."

"Oh. Yes."

He leaned over the counter and yelled, "Mike! Got no hot water again!" When no one answered, he sighed and set his roach spray on the counter. "How's the renovation going?"

"Pardon?"

"Renos on your house."

It took Charlotte a moment to remember. "Oh. Almost done. We have just a few days left here."

"You're not the only ones. I heard Mildew View's on its last legs." He nodded at the sign. "They think having us pay more is going to dig them out of the hole. But they'll probably close down anyway in a month or two. Good riddance."

"We were robbed last night," Charlotte said. "They put a gun to my husband's head."

The boy sucked air through his teeth. "Did they get a lot?"

"Everything," Charlotte said.

"My sympathies." He seemed to mean it. "The world is full of predators." He opened his Sprite and drank it all in three long swallows, then set the can down and burped. "I don't think Mike's here today. Or maybe"—here he raised his voice and projected it toward the office in the back—"he's ignoring me because this is the third time this week my hot water went out!"

Silence. The boy sighed, picked up his roach spray, turned to go.

"Wait," Charlotte said. "Do you have a stove in your room?"

He turned back and considered. "I got a hot plate. Ten dollars at Walmart and does everything a stove does. Grilled cheese, hot dogs, pancakes—"

"Then take this." She held out the bag of groceries. "We don't need these. I mean, we can't cook them."

He took the bag and looked inside. "Damn. You're sure?"

"Yes."

"Thank you, ma'am. And here I thought this was going to be a bad day." He whistled as he bumped open the door with his hip and turned the corner to his room, his sandals flapping cheerfully.

Charlotte went back to the room and said, "Dirk, I am done. I can't stand this place for one more second."

"Me either," Dirk said. He'd jumped when she first came in, a momentary flash of animal fright at the sound of the door opening. He'd spent the morning on the floor, fixated on repairing the broken sink drain, cursing under his breath each time he pulled himself up to turn the water supply off. Trying to keep his mind busy, and it wasn't working.

"It's not good for your heart here," she said.

Dirk wiped his hands on his jeans and stood, shakily. "Or yours."

"I would think that if the bank is this close to a new mortgage, they're not looking to evict us anymore."

"I was thinking the same myself."

Charlotte wrapped her arms around Dirk and said, "Let's just go home, then." The words were easy and delicious in her mouth.

Victor did not answer his phone or return their call. But they packed up their things anyway. They stripped the bed and swept the floor of their loose hairs and coffee grounds and dust from their shoes, which they never took off inside except to sleep. They locked the door and left the key at the front desk. Charlotte felt like a weight had been lifted as they put their suitcases in the trunk. She was buzzing with new energy, thinking of her shower and her garden and the way the windows welcomed the light after she cleaned them. She could feel the spaciousness of her house and its rooms; when she got home, she wanted nothing more than to walk through them again.

Charlotte's happiness clung to her like a tattered cloth as she and Dirk pulled out of the parking lot of Mildew View. The rain was gone, and as the afternoon sun glared through the windshield, for a fleeting moment, she let herself imagine that they were crossing some great divide between the past and future. The story of what had happened to them in the motel was only that, a story they would tell someday. They might even laugh at it! She reached over and squeezed Dirk's hand. But the spell broke the moment they turned onto their street.

At first, it didn't register. Just another patch of white against the green of their lawn. But as the car crept closer, her chest tightened. The word screamed at her from the yard.

SOLD.

For a moment Charlotte was confused about time, as she sometimes was when she woke in the night and saw the red lines of the motel's digital clock form its meaningless numbers. How long had they been gone? Had it only been three weeks, or had time outside the motel moved differently? How on earth could twenty days be long enough to uproot and dismantle an entire life?

Dirk stopped the car in the middle of the street. The windows of the house had been stripped bare of their curtains, exposing the dark, empty rooms. The yard had been mowed in crooked diagonals, leaving furry tufts along the edges of the sidewalk. Charlotte's potted geraniums were still there, but the welcome mat was gone. Half her hostas ripped out and replaced with cheap spireas. Victor Maxwell, they would learn, had disappeared forever into voicemail, his phone number soon disconnected entirely.

They sat there for a long time, until a truck needed to pass and Dirk had to move the car. But he didn't pull over; he just started driving again, and they left the house behind them without saying a word. Back toward the motel.

Charlotte watched the morning's brief rain evaporate from the road as they tried to piece together what had happened. Victor had not had a friend at the bank at all; he had let the clock run out on their eviction, then probably bought the house himself, did a slapdash job at updating it, and left with a pocketful of money. She had a long list of philosophical questions about this: How could something so undeniably hers be taken? Was fairness only an illusion? But they were quickly replaced by a more practical question: Was this even legal? And then the terrible realization that, yes, it must have been; they'd signed everything Victor put in front of them, so desperate were they to find a solution to their problems.

Your fault. All of this is your fault.

The world outside the car looked like it was cooking itself. Steam rose from the pavement of the big, shimmering parking lots and the long lines of cars wrapped around fast-food restaurants. Every few moments the light would catch a wet surface and send a piercing glare into Charlotte's eyes, but she didn't blink. She just watched the road pull them back to Mildew View.

Made sense, she thought. Motels were a place where lives ended.

But when Dirk parked by the office door, a strange thing happened: Charlotte's heart suddenly lifted. Because there was Justin. Squatting on the sidewalk, petting a gray tabby. Justin's shoulder blades pressed through the thin T-shirt he wore, and he had a cap pulled down over his eyes, and for a moment every system in Charlotte's body was activated. She flung open the door to the car before the engine was cut. He looked up.

Not Justin. The boy with the yellow hair.

Charlotte dropped to her knees next to him. She'd thought the pain of seeing her house gone couldn't be surpassed. Only a half hour or so old, it had already solidified inside her like candle wax, coating her insides. But the disappointment of seeing not-Justin was worse. It stabbed at her viciously. She wondered at this, how much a heart could take and still continue beating. But here she was, feeling the hardness of the concrete on her knees and the merciless sun on her back, the smell of oranges and cigarettes coming off the boy. Dirk pushed through the office door to see if they could get their terrible but tolerable room back.

"How old are you?" Charlotte asked.

"Twenty," the boy said.

"Do you have parents?"

He thought about this and then nodded.

"Will you go and stay with them?" Charlotte asked. "When the motel closes?" She felt she simply must have an answer. Everything had taken on new urgency in this new world she was living in; nothing would ever be light or inconsequential again. "Don't you think they would want to help you?"

"No. They just go on accusing me of every little problem in their lives. They even called the police and said I stole their laptops and power tools. I had to spend the night in jail before they let me go because there wasn't any proof."

"That's awful that they would make that up about you."

"I didn't say they did." He sniffed. "But I needed the money."

Charlotte briefly closed her eyes. "Last year I called the police on my son. I don't know if he'll ever forgive me for it."

"What'd he do?"

"He locked himself in the bathroom. Wouldn't answer when I knocked. I got frantic. He was so depressed." Even now, Charlotte's anxiety rose as she thought of how she'd gone outside without her coat and pressed her face against the bathroom window, fogged from the inside. The cold had cut through her shirt like a knife. Dirk had been at the store buying ice cream for the Christmas pie, and she'd felt helpless without his calm body beside her.

"You thought he was slicing up his wrists." The boy nodded. "Was he?"

Charlotte shook her head. "When the police got there, he just opened the door and walked out. Wrapped in a towel. Said he was in the bath and just needed a break from me." Justin's words had actually been *Here's an idea—why don't you kill yourself, Ma?*, but she didn't need to tell the boy everything. "One thing led to another, he got angry like he does, and the police—oh, they overreacted. Before I knew it they had him on the ground. His towel was off and he was naked, and they handcuffed him like that even though I begged them not to."

"Pigs," the boy offered.

"They took him to a hospital and put him under an involuntary hold for three days. Wouldn't let us visit or anything. This was Christmas! And when we went to pick him up, he'd already left. I haven't heard from him since."

"Oh, I bet he was pissed at you. But you were just trying to protect him."

"Yes." Charlotte nodded. "Of course I was."

Dirk returned from the front office with the plastic key in his hand. As he dragged the suitcases back down the sidewalk to the room, the boy leaned over suddenly. He was hugging her. Charlotte's body stiffened against his frame, which felt bigger than it looked. But he seemed like a nice boy; she tried to relax and patted his back. As she pulled away, she felt a tug on her jacket and realized his hand was in her pocket. Trying to find her wallet.

"Well, now!" she said, pushing him away. "I'll save you the trouble. There's nothing left to take."

The boy pulled back and shoved his hands in his pockets. "Sorry for everything," he mumbled before standing and running to his own room.

Much later that night, when Charlotte was looking for her glasses so she could knit, she found the jacket slung across a chair and put her hand inside the pocket. Her fingers closed around some folded paper. She pulled it out. A ten and two ones.

Twelve dollars, the boy had given her. And she didn't deserve any of it.

*   *   *

It was only a quarter after seven when they saw the flash of headlights through the front blinds. Charlotte was tucked under Dirk's arm, cradled in the hard fold of his shoulder. Not asleep but drifting in and out of detached thoughts, watching the sun's final flicker warm the curtains like cherry syrup. They were home, surrounded by their things. And then the headlights. The new people were back early.

They heard the car doors close in the driveway, the sound of two women talking in displeased tones. The dog shook itself off and trotted toward the door.

Dirk turned off the television. He crushed the empty Dixie cups in his hand. "Time to go."

"No." The word escaped her mouth on its own. "I don't want to go back up there."

"Don't be ridiculous. We need to hurry." Dirk snapped his fingers at her like she was a dog.

"Let's talk to them. Tell them that it's our house."

"That's not a good idea." He was trying to brush cracker crumbs off the futon, but it was futile; they'd been ground into the microfiber.

"But *we* live here, Dirk!"

"No." Dirk took her arm. "We don't, Lottie." He pulled her up gruffly. She resisted at first, thrashing her arms and planting her feet on the floor. Her hands clawed at the air as if she could sweep the entirety of the home into her arms and take it with her. Her eyes landed on the book atop the yellow credenza. In one motion she scooped it up and pressed it against her chest like a baby. To her surprise, Dirk didn't tell her to put it back. He just pushed her through the room, down the hall, and into the garage. Up the hatch and into the thick heat. Dirk kept shoving her along until she was on the mattress. Only after he took off her socks and folded them gently so she could wear them again tomorrow did she press her face into the pillow, the book's sharp corners digging into her breasts, and howl in silence at the unfairness of all of it, of life itself.

CHAPTER 5

In October, student conference week arrived as both a relief, because Emma didn't have to teach, and a trial of endurance, because instead she had to meet personally with each student to discuss their position papers. She held the conferences in the adjunct lounge, at a table in the back corner where she'd placed a bowl of chocolates wrapped in gold foil. Other faculty scheduled their conferences at the local coffee shop, but Emma didn't like the campus café, which was crowded and sticky and served day-old muffins for four dollars apiece. But after a few hours of meeting students in the adjunct lounge, she'd come to regret her choice, seeing the expressions of pity cross her students' faces, one by one, as they entered the cluttered room. Or maybe she was just sensitive because of the birth control pills that Dr. Rivera had prescribed to help time her IVF cycle. Emma had been unprepared for the side effects of the pill, the worst of which was a low-grade irritability that rumbled in the background like an oncoming storm. It was just hormones, she assured herself, or a natural reaction to having tender breasts and a constant headache. But sometimes her mood snagged on something, like when Rachel turned the bowls around in the dishwasher right after Emma loaded them, and she had to go take a shower just so she could cry.

Most of the student paper topics were surprisingly benign: the impact of social media on mental health, the benefit of shortening the forty-hour workweek. Four students wrote about the recession, three of them sharing the opinion that Americans were experiencing the consequences of their own greed. Charlie, a freshman on a baseball scholarship who drummed his fingers on his thighs as if he were transcribing their conversation, blamed the banks.

"My parents defaulted on their mortgage," he told Emma near the end of his conference while dipping into the bowl of chocolate. "Not because they're irresponsible. Their interest went up and the value of their house went down. My baseball scholarship is the only reason I'm here."

"Your parents talk to you about money?" Emma was amazed. Her own parents had never shared much of themselves with her. Once, as a child, she'd had to accompany her mother into the voting booth, where her mother had covered up her ballot with one hand. "None of your business," she'd hissed when Emma tried to peek.

"Sure," Charlie said. "My dad is, like, my best friend."

"That's sweet."

Charlie unwrapped another chocolate and scraped his teeth across the side experimentally, testing for filling. After confirming there was none, he popped the rest in his mouth. "Can I ask you a question? You're from Chicago, right? Have you ever been mugged?"

Emma tried to hide her smile. She felt touched that he cared enough to linger after his conference to ask her earnest questions and listen intently to her answers. This must be what every student meeting was like for Rachel. "I have never been mugged, Charlie. Never murdered either."

"But don't you feel better here in Riverbend? Like, you're safer?"

She thought about this. "I suppose safety means different things to different people."

"But Chicago?" Charlie shook his head. "I can't imagine feeling safe living in a city with another murder every week."

"Well, things are rarely as bad as the news wants you to believe. Just a few years ago we were all told that there were weapons of mass destruction in Iraq. Now we all know that was a lie to justify a pointless war."

A shadow crossed Charlie's face. "My brother's in Balad right now. I don't think he would consider it pointless."

Emma put her hand to her forehead. "Shit. I'm sorry. I didn't mean—"

"It's okay."

"It's not, though." She could feel Charlie's allegiance to her slipping, his eyes drifting to the clock behind her head as he put a hand on his backpack. "My point was that the news misrepresents threats sometimes. Not that I don't support our troops." The words sounded ridiculous coming from her mouth, but she was in free fall now. "It's awful they were sent over there under false pretenses, is all I meant."

Charlie stood. "I know. It's really no big deal. But I think the next person is waiting at the door."

Emma held out the bowl of chocolates, but he shook his head. "I've already had too many." He smiled, but it was hard not to read a tightness in his cheeks, a slight pucker of disappointment in his lower lip. Then he was gone.

Emma was still replaying the conversation and berating herself when Alex Brewer walked in, wearing a silky designer T-shirt and a silver crucifix on a chain around his neck. "Hey, Prof. You're wearing your favorite cardigan."

Of course Alex of all people would notice. Emma put her hands on the table and willed herself not to adjust the collar of her sweater, which she'd forgotten she'd worn earlier this week. She was operating on a limited wardrobe, as the moving pod still hadn't arrived. Last week the customer-service representative told Emma that it had been mistakenly marked as empty and sent to a storage facility in northern Oregon. "It's been over two months!" Emma had complained. The woman sighed as if this was a subject she had anticipated but dreaded. "You can't really put a timeline on solving these things," she said. Between the lost pod and all the things going wrong with the house—just when they'd figured out the fridge issue, the washing machine started leaking—Emma was feeling like she couldn't catch a break. Even the hot tub wouldn't turn on after Emma had spent an entire weekend scouring the inside with white vinegar and filling it with the hose. "Told you," she'd heard Patty holler from the other side of the fence. And now she'd just offended Charlie, the one student who'd seemed to like her.

Alex sat down across from her and pulled a Tupperware from his bag. When he peeled the lid off, the briny smell of fish erupted into the air. "My mother's cod," he said, lifting the dish in offering. "She puts crackers on it and drowns it in butter. Want some?"

Emma turned her head to shuffle through her folder of student papers. "I'm a vegetarian."

"Of course." He pinched off a portion of the fish and

ate it with his fingers. "Well, I hope the smell doesn't bother you."

"Well, maybe you could eat before our appointment next time." She clicked her pen and pushed his essay to the center of the table. "Let's talk about your position paper."

"What's this?" he asked, fingering the brown edges of the paper.

"Coffee, I think. Sorry, my travel mug must've loosened in my bag. And—"

"It's missing the first page too."

Emma grimaced. "Yes, I know. I apologize about that as well. It must have torn off at some point when I was pulling it from the bigger stack. But I'm sure I graded it and logged all my comments on the rubric sheet while it was still in one piece."

"Maybe I should start printing you backup copies. Seeing as this is the second time I've had issues handing something in."

Emma flushed. She regretted throwing out his "Yellow Wallpaper" essay and making him resubmit it at the start of the semester. It had been a petty and cowardly response to him mocking her in his analysis; Alex was barely more than a teenager, and she was a professional educator. Why was her first instinct retribution instead of guidance? It was karmically inevitable that she would accidentally spill coffee on his position paper after this and be forced to apologize. "Anyway,

I want to commend you on your paper, Alex. Overall, you have a solid structure. A good grasp of compelling language. And—"

"You can stop." A white flake of fish fell from Alex's fingers. Emma winced, imagining it burrowing into the carpet, where it would become part of the ancestral aroma of the adjunct lounge.

"I'm sorry?" she said. "Stop what?"

"The compliment sandwich." The fish left his lips glistening with oil. "Laying it on thick so your criticism will be more palatable. I already saw in the online portal that you gave me a B-plus."

"A B-plus is not a bad grade."

"It is, though, when it's clearly an A paper."

Emma looked down at the stained essay to find relief from Alex's gaze. "It sounds like you want to focus on the places I've docked you. Yes?"

"Please."

"Okay. There's a lack of nuance in your argument. Abortion is a complex topic, and when you're presenting a position like this, you should address the gray areas. It demonstrates intellectual honesty and builds credibility."

Alex opened his mouth and flicked out his tongue to lick the butter from his fingers. "What else?"

"I made notes on your bibliography. You need to have three credible sources."

"I do."

"The pamphlet by the Family Research Council doesn't count."

"Why not?" he asked.

"Nothing in it is based on evidence. They're not even researchers, they're a hate group." She regretted the last sentence as soon as it crossed her lips.

Alex's eyebrows lifted in interest. "A hate group? That sounds very nuanced."

"What I mean is," she said, hastening to clarify, "they're neither credible nor objective. In order to support your position, you need to provide evidence like research articles. Facts and data are your friends here. Not ideological extremism."

"I don't see anything extreme about saying that taking a human life is wrong."

"That's another flaw in your argument. For a college-level paper, you need to engage with scientific reasoning as well. What's the definition of human life? That's the kind of evidence your paper is missing."

Alex closed his Tupperware and wiped his fingers on his jeans. "See, I disagree. The core issue is pretty straightforward for most people. Taking life is immoral. Didn't you just do a lecture on how overexplaining simple concepts is insulting to the reader?"

"Providing a clear foundation for your argument isn't overexplain—"

"Let's pretend you're right." Alex leaned back in his chair. "If an abortion isn't the ending of a life, then women would feel nothing when they had a miscarriage. It's just a clump of cells that didn't come together, right? But my aunt had a miscarriage last year and she didn't leave her bed for a week. Because she lost a baby. A *person*."

Emma felt something sulfurous under her skin, and she touched her cheek. How did he know? Then she realized that he didn't; he couldn't. He was just saying whatever came to mind without considering how his words might land.

She cleared her throat. "That's another example of a nuanced human experience you're trying to distill into a logic problem."

"Emma, I hope your own ideologies aren't getting in the way of you grading my paper fairly."

"I didn't give my personal opinion," she countered, fighting to keep her voice even. "I'm just critiquing the way you've presented the issue in your essay. That's my job."

"Right." Alex smirked. "But I can see the 'Yes, We Can' pin on your bag. You're not hiding where you fall on the political spectrum. Although Obama agrees with me on this. He said that abortion is a moral issue that goes beyond women's freedom of choice. I suppose if I quoted a Barack Obama speech, that would qualify as an objective source?"

Emma felt a wave of nausea rise, the smell of fish souring the back of her throat. She swallowed. "You can subscribe to any political ideology you want. But when you're writing a college paper, you have to follow the rubric."

Alex looked at the clock. "Looks like our time is up."

"Right. I assume you'll have this sorted out before you present your paper to the class next week?"

"Sure. Have a great weekend, Emma." He saluted her before throwing his bag over his shoulder and leaving. The lounge door groaned shut behind him.

An adjunct who was marking papers over a can of soup sent Emma a solemn look from the next table. Emma held up her water bottle as if in a toast to solidarity. "Long day," she said, taking a drink. It tasted metallic, warmed from the afternoon.

"Maybe next time you should hold your conferences at the coffee shop." The instructor gestured at the papers he was marking. "I'm trying to get through these."

"Oh. Sorry." Flustered, Emma scraped her papers into her folder. The instructor watched her empty the uneaten chocolates into her bag and push the chairs back into place. She felt his disdain trailing after her as she left the lounge and headed toward Rachel's office.

"What's wrong?" Rachel asked from behind her oak desk when Emma knocked on the doorframe.

"Student conferences. A real Dalloway." Emma threw her bag down and collapsed into one of the chairs facing the desk. Over Rachel's shoulder, she could see the rowing team slicing across the water, their oars dipping into the river like paintbrushes. It struck her as funny that their coordinated movements would dissolve the moment they got off the boat and turned back to their phones. "Can we go for pizza tonight?"

"Of course. Pizza sounds truly healing. Just let me finish this one thing, and we can go." Rachel turned back to her laptop, her head dipped in concentration.

Emma pulled the Gaskill book from her bag. It was the one she'd lost, or thought she'd lost, and then this morning it was back on the yellow cabinet, under a stray *New Yorker,* as if it had always been there. Rachel swore she hadn't touched it. Emma didn't think it was likely that Patty had broken in a second time to return the book—that would mean she'd taken it simply to read it, and why not just ask to borrow it or go to a public library?—plus the doors had been locked all night. It made her feel a little crazy. Seeing the book on the yellow cabinet this morning made her wonder if the birth control was starting to cloud her judgment. Maybe she did spend too much time ruminating over Paulie's comments about the boat and Patty's hostility about the plants. Were people as unwelcoming as she suspected, or was she just paranoid? But then she thought about Alex licking his fishy fingers and staring at her with contempt. No, she decided. She was not paranoid.

Emma opened the book but didn't feel like reading. She felt like staring at her wife, whose expressions flickered lightly across her eyebrows as she worked at her computer. Emma imagined Rachel was emailing a student to justify a grade or offer additional thoughts on a reading. She was always lending them books and giving them extensions on assignments when their love lives crashed and burned. Once, in Chicago, Rachel had paid for a student to stay in a hotel for a weekend after she was kicked out of her parents' house. Rachel couldn't help it; she loved helping abandoned baby birds. Like Emma.

"You'll be such a good mom, Rach," Emma said now. She bit her lip; she hadn't meant to bring up family planning again, even tangentially, until next week, after Rachel's departmental lecture. Rachel had been chewing antacids every night as she prepared. Emma planned to take her to dinner after the lecture to announce that she'd soft-launched the IVF process. It was the perfect time: The mood would be celebratory, Rachel full of relief and self-satisfaction.

Rachel looked up. An expression of surprise made her face look briefly unattractive, childish, as if her prettiness were held together only by her constant awareness of the world. "What made you say that?"

"I was just thinking about how good you are to your students."

"It doesn't always feel that way." Rachel sighed. "I

got a complaint earlier that reading Judith Butler is like trying to run through wet cement."

"Clever. And true."

"Yeah," Rachel said absently, raking her fingers through her hair.

Emma stood up. She felt a sudden need to get close, to press her face to her wife's neck and touch the line of her collarbone. But as she came around the desk, Rachel jerked her fingers from the keys and shut the laptop suddenly. She looked up at Emma, her lips in a tight smile.

"Is everything okay?" Emma asked.

"Of course."

"You just shut your laptop, like, really fast."

"Just done with work. And glad to be done." Rachel slid the laptop into her bag. "Ready to go? Pizza, right?"

"Sure." Emma started to say something more about the laptop, but Rachel surprised her by lacing their fingers together, and they walked out into the hallway like that, holding hands.

*   *   *

On Monday Emma's students were scheduled to give individual presentations on their paper topics. Emma loved this part of the semester, when she could turn off her performative self and sit among her students, a tall chai from the campus café perched on the narrow desk arm. All three Brittanys separately presented papers that addressed social media use; Emma suspected they'd worked together but found the accusation too tiring to follow through on. Charlie used his hands expressively as he explained why bailing out banks only encouraged more reckless behavior on the part of financial institutions, and after he was done Emma clapped loudly. From her seat Emma felt like she had a private view of each student's inner self as they stood before the class, and she wondered if she, too, was so deeply exposed while she was teaching.

"All right, who's next?" she asked when Charlie sat down.

Alex Brewer's hand went up in the air. She nodded at him, and he walked to the front of the room in that slow way of his, his foot dragging slightly.

"I faced a lot of criticism for my first paper topic," he told the class once he'd taken his place. He looked at Emma. "Some of it was fair. So I scrapped it. Today I'm going to present a totally new topic."

"Alex." Emma shook her head. "We didn't discuss this."

His eyes grew wide. "What? I mean, you strongly suggested that I should start over."

"I suggested that you gather more credible sources, not change your topic. In any case, it's too late in the semester to pivot."

"I think this could be an exception. I've already done a lot of work on it."

Emma tried to keep the annoyance from her voice. "There are no exceptions. Read the syllabus. It's not fair to other students who have worked hard on their papers if you're able to switch at the last minute."

"I don't mind," said Anita, who was usually silent behind her wall of beverages — coffee, a water tumbler, a green smoothie from the campus café. "I think he should be allowed to change if he does the work."

"Thank you, Anita," said Alex. "I appreciate your input."

"Same," said Brittany J. "It doesn't bother me."

The class murmured a general agreement that no one cared about the policies in the syllabus.

"My new topic is Proposition 8," Alex said. "Is everyone familiar?"

Emma's heart quickened. She took a sip of her chai to steady herself as Alex explained to the class that Proposition 8 was a current ballot measure in California that aimed to preserve societal norms around marriage, defining it as possible only between a man and a woman.

"Since we can use anthropological data as a source, I'd like to take a quick poll here today. I want to know where everyone here stands on it." Alex flipped open his notebook and clicked his pen. "Who supports Proposition 8?"

Before Emma could say that no one should feel obligated to participate, that this wasn't part of the class, she saw the hands go up. It was as if oxygen had been leached from the room. She fought the urge to glance around the class to identify the dissenters. Instead she focused on Alex, who was making a show of counting the hands with one finger, his mouth silently moving.

"Alex, it's too late to change your paper topic." She hated how her voice shook when she faced confrontation, even when she was right. "There's not enough time to do the outline and the thesis proposal and get a revised draft in by next week."

Alex held up a sheaf of papers. "I have a draft right here. Just need to add today's anthropological research. Besides, it's related to my original idea. It's both an argument protecting the Constitution's integrity and a moral imperative."

Emma feigned coolness, crossing her arms, though her face was hot under the students' gaze. "Just talk to me after class, Alex, and stop wasting everyone's time."

"Brewer." He narrowed his eyes. "How many times do I have to ask you to call me that? I need to do one more survey."

"No." She could feel that she'd lost the classroom. The students were ping-ponging between them, but most were watching him, their mouths half open in interest, looking much more engaged than they ever did when she was lecturing.

"It'll take twenty seconds, then I'm done. I just need to know the fundamental basis of the class's perspective. For context. How many of you oppose same-sex marriage because it disrupts the natural reproductive order? Two men can't have a baby. Two women can't have a baby."

The hands hesitantly rose around her, less sure this time. In spite of herself, Emma said, "Of course they can."

She regretted it immediately. Alex's eyes lit up. "Not from a biological perspective. Not according to the natural order of things. That's not my idea, of course. That's Thomas Aquinas."

Emma felt the prickle of rage on her neck. She tried to pick up a paper for the next lesson, but her fingers crumpled it instinctively, her hand shaking. "You need to sit down. I've been very clear that it's too late to switch topics, Alex."

"Would you say that you are forbidding me to write this paper?"

"Yes."

"What would happen if I did it anyway?"

"I'd fail you. Your grade point average would nose-dive, and you'd lose your place on the golf team. Maybe then they'd start winning."

The class laughed. Emma felt the victory momentarily until Alex joined them, his mouth open like a pelican searching for fish. Then he clicked his pen again. "Thanks for clearing that up, Prof," he said as he scraped the pen over the paper.

*　　　　*　　　　*

After class, Emma ducked into the auditorium at the end of the hall, where Rachel was halfway through her departmental lecture. She slipped into a seat in the back. The audience wasn't quite full, but close, with rows of students and faculty lined up like a field of wheat. Now and then a few would cross their ankles or adjust their posture, giving the impression of a gentle breeze moving through the room. Onstage Rachel looked dazzling in an emerald sweater, her hair twisted atop her head.

"Intertextuality can be thought of as a conversation between forms of content," she was saying. "Anyone who's watched *The Simpsons* has ingested—knowingly or not—references to Shakespeare and Steinbeck and Dumas. European and American literature have played an important role in the building of humor on the show, and the recognition of these references by the viewer builds on a shared cultural knowledge, which in turn deepens the viewer's devotion."

She leaned on the podium and propped her chin on her hand, a gesture that she knew made each person in the audience feel they'd entered a private conversation, as if Rachel were a friend sitting across from them at a bar. "But it's a mistake to think of the interplay between these two forms as a dialogue. Because in this case, only one conversant is in a temporary position of power. That's the risk you take every time you write or paint or make a mixtape for your beloved. It may become an inside joke or a private door through which another idea is suddenly understood. Just last week I saw a *New Yorker* cartoon depicting the Lehman bankruptcy. Men in suits are pouring out of a building, holding boxes, and one guy turns to another and says, 'But I like big banks. They're so intimate. At small banks there isn't any privacy.'"

She looked out over the quiet audience expectantly.

"Please tell me you know what this quote is referencing."

"*Gatsby*!" someone yelled from the back, and Rachel wiped her brow in mock relief. Everyone laughed, even Emma, who'd read the same issue and hadn't noticed the cartoon. This was quintessential Rachel; she was like an oyster who pearlized the grains of sand she took in. She often prowled the house with an earbud in one ear, the long cord vining from beneath her curls as she listened to audiobooks on indigenous histories and essays about poetry and memoirs of long-forgotten women. She folded laundry and brewed tea while performing her own private photosynthesis, absorbing information and converting it into fresh ideas on restorative justice or identity politics, which she chatted about breezily over dinner, explaining things in a way Emma could understand without context.

Emma suspected the ease with which Rachel

processed the knowledge of the world was a gift from her parents, California transplants who'd come to Illinois for university jobs and stayed until they got tenure. Her mother was a scholar who'd won a prize for a feminist retranslation in German of Pali Canon Buddhist texts. Fiona wore one-piece linen jumpsuits and encouraged her daughter to ask questions not to sharpen her understanding of others' ideas but to create her own. Their home was a rushing river of books and theories and unconditional love. It was one of the reasons Rachel wanted to have children; she thought of childhood as a chrysalis that protected a new person from harm while filling them with confidence about the possibilities that lay beyond. It was one of the only naive things about her, Emma thought.

"That's about it, folks," Rachel said. "We have time for a question or two. Anyone have any burning inquiries?"

A student near the front raised a hand. "I don't have a question. I just wanted to say I loved *Give Me Five Moons*."

Rachel smiled. "Thank you."

"And I wanted to say congratulations on the Luminary book award."

"It's just a nomination," said Rachel. "But I appreciate that."

Emma was confused. Rachel hadn't been nominated for a Luminary. Had she? She pulled her laptop from her bag and did a quick search. There it was: Rachel's name and book appeared in a long list with nine others. The title was highlighted as the only debut novel, described as "a masterful fusion of literary depth and commercial appeal, which intricately explores the complexities of female empowerment while delivering a thrilling narrative that resonates long after the final page." Emma's confusion sat inside her like a knot waiting to be unraveled. The Luminary was one of the most prestigious book awards in the country. Every year she and Rachel read the list together. Why hadn't Rachel told her? It had been officially announced only this morning, but certainly Rachel's agent would have given her a heads-up that it was coming.

Then, as another audience member called out a question about metafiction, Emma remembered Rachel slamming the laptop shut in her office. She thought of the furious emailing Rachel did in the evenings lately, the way she always seemed to be finishing a task when Emma walked in the room. There was only one, humiliating, answer: Rachel had known about the nomination. But she'd wanted Emma to find out on her own so that she didn't have to be the one to deliver the news. This truth, reeking of pity, sank in Emma's stomach like a stone.

Worse, now they'd have to talk about the nomination tonight at dinner, which would hijack Emma's plans to discuss their IVF road map. Maybe she should just pretend she'd gotten held up by a student and hadn't come to the lecture at all; they could go on side-stepping reality politely in order to protect each other's feelings.

Just then Rachel looked up from the podium and searched the crowd. Her eyes met Emma's, and Rachel smiled, her relief unmistakable. She was glad the lecture had gone well and glad Emma had heard the news without having to share it herself. Two birds, one stone! Things were so easy for Rachel. The world always cleaved itself so she could pass through.

Emma smiled back and wiggled her fingers in a wave. As Rachel waved back and turned to take a final question, Emma knew that she wouldn't bring up the IVF just yet. Not tonight, anyway. She would keep it to herself just a little longer.

CHAPTER 6

Charlotte couldn't wait to show Dirk what she'd found in the recycling bin that morning. Finally, they would have something new to talk about! The quiet was starting to get to her. Lately conversations between herself and Dirk had become more like the dialogue of two monkeys in a cage: hand gestures, wide facial expressions. She often wondered what it would have been like to be in this situation with her son instead of her husband. She certainly would have told Justin about the emails to the lawyers and her plan to drive the girls out of the house. Justin would have appreciated her slow campaign of sabotage. He would have even encouraged her to take it further. Loosen the window latches even more. Unplug just one more clock. Take a hammer to the windows. Together she and Justin would have made more noise, shouting their grievances into the empty house instead of sitting upstairs like a couple of tired orangutans.

But today's trip downstairs had been full of interesting things. She was so giddy after noticing the open tabs on the laptop, she'd even brewed two cups of coffee. One was a real estate website with a map full of little red dots on the left side and pictures of apartments on the right. Condos in Chicago, each with a price tag that made her blink the moisture in her eyes away to be sure she was seeing it right. And another tab, open to a page of search results for *Home sale calculator*.

It was happening. Someone in this house was searching for a new place to live. Charlotte had nearly shouted with joy. After weeks of flushing coffee grounds down the toilet and unplugging appliances and sprinkling sugar along the baseboards to attract ants, she was finally seeing the fruits of her labor. Soon she'd be able to email Russell Sloane and tell him that the house was vacant, just as she'd promised it would be. She'd been so happy, she even stopped to scratch the little dog's belly.

Charlotte balanced the warm paper cups against her chest as she opened the door to the garage with her hip. The window blazed with red; it was the sugar maple in the backyard licking the window like flames. Hard to believe that they'd been up here long enough for a season to turn. The downstairs was now warmer than the attic, as if the house had been flipped upside down.

She took the steps two at a time despite the tremendous effort in her thighs and set the coffee on the floor just inside the hatch. Dirk was sitting on a milk crate with his 1959 Chrysler Imperial and a paintbrush in his hands, but he had the stupefied look of someone who was urging himself awake. Last week Charlotte commented on how much Dirk was sleeping these days, and now he had begun to hide it like a child sneaking candy.

"Guess what I found in the recycling bin," she said.

"It came," he said, suddenly alert. His eyes were huge behind his readers. "Oh, Lottie, let me see it."

Charlotte saw right away her mistake. "Oh, no. Not that." She pulled a newspaper from the waistband of her pants. "Just this."

Dirk looked at the paper for a long moment. He blinked several times. "Ah. He won, did he." Then he turned back to his car without looking at Charlotte.

She sat on the mattress. "Well, yes. By a mile. But he took Indiana too. The paper said it's the first time since 1964 a Democrat won here. Isn't that interesting?"

Dirk didn't respond as he held up the Chrysler to the light. Charlotte hoped he couldn't see the misalignment of the chrome trim around the window or the drips of paint around the fenders. Yesterday he'd spilled the red paint on the floor and hastily mopped it up with a T-shirt, which, when he wore it later, made Charlotte gasp with the sudden bizarre thought that his heart had exploded and was bleeding through his chest.

"Obama is a very pleasant speaker," said Charlotte. "Don't you think?"

No answer.

"Still, you don't suppose our not voting had anything to do with him winning in Indiana, do you? Not our votes on their own, of course. But all together, people like us not voting?"

Dirk finally looked at her. "People living in other people's attics, you mean?"

"Oh, you," she scoffed, pleased to have his attention. "You can stop grousing now."

He put down his paintbrush. "Where is the invitation, Lottie? You said it would be end of October at the latest."

"It's only the first week of November. And don't you remember how Justin always did his homework the morning it was due? You can bet Amy's like that too. A little scatterbrained. I'm not surprised it's late." Charlotte turned the page of the newspaper. She could feel Dirk's eyes on her, the thin heat of his anger.

"You probably missed it," he said. "I don't even know what you're doing down there half the time. You need to stop messing around." He set his car down and rubbed his temples as if to indicate the headache she'd given him.

Charlotte pressed her lips together and looked back at the paper. It was true the wedding invitation had not been her priority lately. Getting the new people out was what was important. Because once Charlotte and Dirk got the house back, they could drive themselves to Kansas City and knock on doors and put up signs. They could dedicate themselves to finding their son and bringing him home. They'd have all the time in the world, and wasn't that better than the pressure of an uncertain but looming deadline? Yet she couldn't tell Dirk any of this. His heart wasn't up for the risks that came with this kind of hope.

"I'm sorry," she said. "But it's all going to turn out fine. You don't need to worry."

The plastic car clattered to the floor, and Charlotte looked up. Dirk was bent forward, his hands pressed to his forehead. His mouth was an O of despair, a thread of saliva reaching down to the drawstring of his pants.

"Dirk?" Charlotte dropped the paper and rushed to his side. She took his thin shoulders in her hands. Slowly, Dirk lowered his hands. His eyes were dry.

"Just a headache," he said gruffly. "Comes in waves."

"When's the last time you ate?" She looked at his face closely. The whites of his eyes looked yellow, blotched with broken blood vessels. Charlotte's heart quickened. This was not a blood-sugar issue. It was something deeper, more invasive.

"Do you think you could be having a stroke? Do

you have any numbness? Tingling?" She thought of the signs the doctors had told her to look out for. "Raise your arms and say something," she demanded. "I have to check your speech and motor control."

He lifted his arms in the air and looked right at her. "Sometimes I get so tired of you, Charlotte," he said with perfect clarity. "How's that?"

Charlotte felt her eyes well with tears and quickly looked away. The coffee cups still sat by the hatch. She fetched them and placed one in front of Dirk.

"We're almost there," she said. "I promise this will be over soon."

But he picked his car up and didn't touch the coffee. As the day went on, it grew cold.

*　　　*　　　*

That evening, Charlotte stretched her legs out on the rug and tried to read. Dirk slept with a word-search book across his chest, his readers dangling off one ear. He twitched and mumbled in his sleep, an unhappy sound that filled Charlotte with guilt. She needed to accelerate things, that was for sure. Maybe not a hammer to the windows, but the Justin in her mind was right. They'd been here too long. The new people might be thinking of moving, but nothing was certain yet. They needed another nudge. Something decisive to make up their minds.

She sighed and looked back at her book, one she'd swiped from downstairs a couple of days ago when she returned the first one, which had been far too boring. This one was called *Give Me Five Moons*. It was a strange sort of story—an obstetrician named Daisy learns that all the wombs removed during hysterectomies at her hospital are being harvested by an evil corporation to grow motherless children to work in their factories. Not a book Charlotte would ever have picked up on purpose, but she found comfort in its predictability, the way it swiftly escorted her through each scene toward what she was sure would be a happy ending. Books like this always made sure things worked out, and when you were reading them, you felt temporarily certain that the whole world operated that way too. Charlotte was nearly three-quarters of the way done with the book, at the part where Daisy finds all the children imprisoned in an old warehouse. Because Daisy herself had a hysterectomy when she was younger, she wonders if some of them were grown from her own womb. When they ask how soon she can break them free, she says, "Give me five moons." Because all they have to keep track of time is a single window where they see the moon rise every night.

The whole book was surprisingly clever, and Charlotte wished Dirk weren't angry with her so she could wake him up and tell him about it. She wanted to explain the story aloud to someone and describe all the things it made her feel. Daisy is a misfit among her friends, whose lives closed her out when they started getting pregnant. She feels sad each time she delivers another woman's baby. The scene where she meets a gap-toothed teenage boy whom she's certain came from her womb—*She felt his presence like an old wound*—filled Charlotte with sadness, thinking of Justin and all the ways she'd failed him. She read that part over and over. Who knew a novel could capture the problem at the root of motherhood better than any psychology book?

The story was easy enough to follow that Charlotte had plenty of room in her mind to think her own thoughts while she read. And she thought a lot about Justin. Sometimes memories of him popped up, fully dressed: Justin standing in the backyard after school, backpack still on, plucking cherry tomatoes one by one and eating them. Justin holding her hand as they crossed the street, his snow boots tromping in the slush. Bending over a puzzle at the library, his fingers moving like little bird wings. His square white teeth; the chewed rim of his favorite juice cup.

When Justin was a toddler, Charlotte had been surprised by how quickly she'd forgotten what he'd been like as a baby; as a middle-schooler he hardly resembled the precocious preschooler who'd made up songs for his bath toys. Each stage of his life seemed to erase the memory of the previous one, and every time Justin came home as an adult, transformed again—tattoos here or there, a piercing, his skin ballooning and then deflating, draping over his bones—Charlotte felt as if he'd broken her heart for taking away her sweet baby. As if the two people weren't one and the same.

The book was at an exciting part. Daisy hears an alarm go off (a shifty security guard alerted the president of the evil company to Daisy's mission), and she runs to hide in a closet. As her eyes adjust to the dark, she finds herself face-to-face with the gap-toothed boy. He puts his finger to his lips in warning. "You brought this on yourself," he whispers.

Charlotte let the book drop to her lap, suddenly remembering. Fifteen years ago. Charlotte had found a note stuck in their mail slot. No envelope or anything, just a folded piece of paper. On the outside had been a crude drawing of an hourglass. When she opened it up, it said *Not much sand left.* And at the bottom of the page: *You brung this on yourself.* Charlotte had been terrified. Everyone in town was talking about the recent stranglings in central Indiana; the police were still looking for a suspect. All the victims had been men from the Indianapolis gay bars, but what if the killer had branched out to women? Families? She'd stood there feeling the dirtiness of the paper in her hand, certain that someone was out there watching. She closed all the blinds and locked the door. Two decades of living in their home, and it had taken only seconds to decide to abandon it. She wasted no time packing, and by the time Dirk got home from work she'd lined the living room with boxes. She explained to him they had to leave or they would be murdered. Her instincts were tingling; she felt that Dirk was an idiot for laughing at her. Men! They were supposed to be the protectors of the home, but when it came down to it, who developed relationships with the neighbors and ensured the lights were on a timer during vacations and kept a heavy flashlight by the door in case they needed to grab something to stop an intruder? Women, that's who.

Still, Dirk had been right. The truth behind the note was what she should have suspected from the moment she opened it: Justin owed money to someone, and that someone was angry. Charlotte and Dirk had to withdraw over eleven hundred dollars at the bank to pay it off, and then they'd sent him back to the treatment facility for another expensive and ultimately unsuccessful round. When he returned, he felt guilty about the trouble he'd caused and dragged home that awful hot tub as an apology. But even after everything was settled, Charlotte couldn't shake the memory of unfolding that note. She remembered how quickly her fear had dissolved all her sentimentality about the house. How easily she would have left everything behind to protect her family.

Charlotte closed the book. That was it. That was the feeling she wanted to conjure in the girls downstairs now.

She would leave a note. Something terrifying. The new people would read it and understand it was the last straw. First the house was a problem, and now the whole neighborhood would feel unsafe. They were two women, after all. There was no man around to tell them they were overreacting. No one to stop them from listening to that voice, deep inside, that said something was wrong.

Besides, the thought of frightening the girls made her happy. She felt Justin's smile. *Give them a taste,* she imagined him saying.

Charlotte put her bookmark in and quietly opened the trunk. She pulled a notebook from the bottom and ripped a piece of paper out slowly, one perforated circle at a time. Dirk didn't stir. She laid the paper flat on the trunk and clicked a pen.

CHAPTER 7

Yes. It was beautiful, seeing him on her laptop screen. Live from Chicago with his blinding smile, the thin sheen of sweat glowing as if he were lit from within. And Michelle, goddess of radiance! Shepherding their two daughters, cloaked in tufted dresses and leaning against their parents as they waved to the howling crowd. Obama made things clear: He was a family man. A man of hope and promise. Emma couldn't help, as she listened to him talk about rising and falling together as one nation, feeling charmed.

Of course, there were a few things to overlook. Like his opposition to gay marriage. And the fact that he was responsible, in a big way, for all the Black and

Hispanic voters surging to the polls in California and voting for Proposition 8.

It was a bittersweet day.

"It's weird not to be married anymore," Emma said. She was cradled in the dip of the sagging air mattress, her laptop on her legs, as Rachel folded laundry. The moving pod had miraculously been rerouted and would arrive within ten business days, their bill wiped clean after Emma posted a complaint on the Better Business Bureau's website. At least that was one problem neatly solved. But now Emma couldn't imagine the things from her old life joining her here. She felt embarrassed by her inability to write and her struggle to get control of her classroom. And her home—just yesterday she'd walked into the backyard and found Patty on her knees patting a layer of mulch onto the dirt around the butterfly bush. "Your friend said I could," she'd said when Emma started in surprise, and it took Emma a moment to realize she meant Rachel. "In fact," Patty had said, drawing back on her haunches, her denim knees muddied, "she even said thank you."

Yes, Emma's response in the moment had been childish, but she'd been caught off guard by her wife's secret diplomacy. She'd said, "Sometimes people are polite, Patty, because it's easier than telling you to get lost." Patty had huffed something about the rudeness of Emma's generation and flounced home, leaving behind a trail of wood chips.

And the house—ugh, she didn't even want to think about the house and its endless roster of problems. They'd had to pay a plumber two hundred and fifty dollars when the toilet inexplicably backed up, and he'd found, of all things, a clog of coffee grounds. When Emma said she didn't know how they got there, he'd laughed and said, "Is that right? Well, maybe that busted hot tub in the backyard started a café."

No. She couldn't bear the thought of her old, beloved furniture arriving to witness these humiliations.

"It'll be challenged in the courts," said Rachel, pulling her suitcase from the closet. "The people who fight for marriage equality aren't exactly the type to call it a day and go home." She put a bottle of extra-strength antacids in the suitcase. The Luminary book award winner would be announced in a ceremony next week, and Rachel's publicist had lined up a last-minute series of readings and dinners, plus a conference panel, leading up to the big event. She was heading to Denver in the morning, then Iowa City, then Seattle, and finally New York for the ceremony. It was a lot of flying, which always darkened her mood and made her stomach hurt. Rachel, who typically navigated the world with ease, was unnerved by the concept of aviation. Emma had learned this the first time they took a trip together when, during a bout of turbulence, Rachel had grabbed her arm in fear. Emma had distracted her by reading long passages of Elizabeth Barrett Browning's *Aurora*

Leigh in a thick Southern accent—"An' Ah who've written much in prose an' verse / For othuhs' uses, will write now fer mine"—until the plane leveled out and Rachel's face emerged from Emma's shoulder, flushed with embarrassment and gratitude. For the rest of the flight they held hands, and when they landed they had both known that they wanted to spend their lives like this, implicated in each other's happiness.

They'd never been apart for a week before. But when Rachel told her about the book trip, Emma's mind quickly lined up excuses for why she couldn't join her. What would they do with Birdie? They couldn't leave her at the Bark and Stay boarding service near campus, where Emma had once seen a staff member break up a dogfight in the outdoor play area by throwing her cell phone at the dogs. Plus Emma hadn't ingratiated herself enough with the other adjuncts to find a sub for her classes.

The real reason Emma couldn't go on the trip was that she'd miss the appointment for her egg retrieval, which was scheduled for tomorrow. Several times over the past two weeks Emma had wanted to tell Rachel about the IVF, but it hadn't happened. The whole purpose of going through the process in secret was to spare Rachel the stress. And Rachel was often lost in the glow of her laptop, grading papers or answering emails or cowriting an academic paper with colleagues. Now the book award had pulled her even farther out to sea, leaving Emma on a distant shore, her ovaries plumped to the size of golf balls. The stimming drugs had made her weepy and hormonal, and she was no longer sure whether it made sense to tell Rachel at all until after the retrieval, when their embryos were safely frozen at the clinic and she could take her wife's hand and say, *I did it. The hard part is over.* At any rate, she was certain she wouldn't be able to bring up the subject without crying.

But it hadn't mattered what excuse Emma came up with for missing the trip, because Rachel hadn't invited her. She'd just reminded Emma to roll out the trash bins on trash day.

"Eighteen thousand marriages were annulled," Emma said now. "Including this one."

"It'll get overturned. Just watch."

"You don't seem very upset."

Rachel paused, a pair of rolled-up socks in her hand. "I'm taking a broader perspective. Prop 8 isn't going to kill us. It's not like when Reagan refused to give money to fight AIDS. *That* killed gay people."

"Do you even want to be married?" Emma meant the words as a joke, planning on following them up with *Or are you just here for the cooking?*, but she heard the tears in her voice before she felt them in her eyes.

Rachel looked wounded. "How can you even ask me that?"

Emma lifted her shoulders. She regretted saying it,

but she also felt the heat of anger rising. "You're just not very present lately."

This was true. Rachel stayed late in the office. She went out for drinks at Applebee's with the medievalists. She hadn't noticed the soft yellow bruises on Emma's belly from the IVF shots or the way Emma kicked the blanket off at night because of the hot flashes from the medicine. Yet Rachel invited her entire graduate seminar over for dinner one night without asking and as they all ate paella picnic-style on quilts on the floor, Emma listened to Rachel tell the story of the missing moving pod as if it were the plot of a hilarious movie. The students in turn fawned: *Give Me Five Moons* gave voice to their generation's growing wariness of technology, their woes about lost identities in the digital age. Rachel had protested, trying to shift the topic, but Emma knew that she was warming to the idea that writing fiction wasn't as frivolous as she'd thought. She'd even, to her agent's delight, begun outlining a second book.

Now Rachel sat on the mattress next to Emma. "Just because I'm busy doesn't mean I'm not committed to doing life with you, Emma."

"You stay on campus all day, even when you don't have an afternoon class."

"I have meetings. I have grading and advising for a hundred and thirteen students. This is a full-time job. It's not—" Rachel stopped. She twisted her mouth.

Emma raised her eyebrows. "Not a three-course pity contract?"

"That's not what I was going to say."

"It sort of sounded like that's where you were headed."

"Jesus, Emma. What is up with you this week?" Rachel disappeared into the bathroom. Emma heard the rattle of hair-product bottles being swept into a bag. When Rachel returned, she said, "I feel like we're having a disconnect. What am I missing?"

Emma began to shrug, but then it dawned on her: This was it. This was the moment to tell Rachel about Dr. Rivera and the clinic and the shots. She could stand up and go to the closet where she'd hidden the medicines and syringes behind the giant pack of toilet paper they'd bought at Costco and lay it all out before her wife like an offering. Rachel would wrap her arms around Emma and press her lips to her ear and say, *You did this for me?* Emma opened her mouth.

But Rachel kept talking. "Actually, I don't even have to ask. I know why you're upset. It's your writing. Or your lack thereof."

Emma felt her face grow hot. She had pretended not to notice when, a few weeks earlier, Rachel had rearranged Emma's desk space—her messy and slightly stained school papers tucked neatly under her notebook, open to a blank page, the pen arranged just so, as if to say, *This is how easy it can be if you just try.* Emma was hurt, but at least Rachel had saved her the humiliation of a direct confrontation. Now it was out in the open, Rachel was actually saying it, and Emma realized how angry she was about being treated like a child who needed to finish her homework. She suddenly had no desire to tell Rachel any good news right now.

"Sorry you're married to a failure. Or *were* married, rather."

"Oh, please." Rachel tucked her most sensible bra, the one with wide straps, into her suitcase. "We both know you're brilliant. The opposite of a failure! But you have to move the needle. Think of how many creatives would love to have as much time on their hands as you do."

"How did this conversation turn from me saying that you're never home to me not using my time well?"

Rachel zipped her suitcase. "Maybe the thesis is that someone has to keep us afloat while you're sorting out your creative block."

Emma thought she might cry. But just then a notification appeared on the laptop screen, covering Obama's face with a red empty-battery icon. "Ugh," Emma said, though she was grateful for a distraction from the subject at hand. "I need to plug in." She dug her power cord from the pile of laundry by her side of the bed and pressed the plug into the wall outlet. Nothing.

"Only the bottom plug works on that outlet," Rachel reminded her.

Emma wanted to scream. This goddamned house! She yanked the cord out and plugged it into the bottom socket. The computer screen lit up, but Obama's face was now obscured by an email notification.

"Paulie just sent me a meeting invite," Emma said, sitting back on the bed.

"At midnight?"

"He wants me to come to his office tomorrow before class." Seeing Paulie's name was a jolt; he'd been avoiding Emma since their disastrous encounter at the faculty reception. When she saw him in the hallway or at the campus café, he never broke from conversations with other faculty or from pecking at his phone to say hello. At least, she thought he was purposely ignoring her. Maybe he felt he'd put in his requisite friendliness at the beginning of the semester to ensure that she wasn't going to convince Rachel to leave, and now Emma was invisible to him, nothing more than a pesky administrative duty swept away.

"He probably wants to talk about your course load for the spring," Rachel said. "You're going to get more than three."

"I know," Emma said glumly. She'd heard about these meetings from the other adjuncts, who spoke with both glee and trepidation of the end-of-semester check-ins when Paulie officially handed them their spring course assignments. Word in the lounge was that enrollment had gone up so much that adjunct loads were expected to increase, which pleased every-one except Emma.

"I'm sorry I snapped." Rachel sat on the edge of the air mattress, which sent Emma's body up in a moment of buoyancy, knocking the laptop off her legs.

"You're just nervous about your trip."

"I am." Rachel closed the laptop and pushed it off the bed. She ran her hand under Emma's shirt. "That's enough news for one night, don't you think?" And Emma closed her eyes and said that yes, it was.

*　　*　　*

Paulie sat princelike among his collections, his thick fingers folded on his desk. Before him a row of bobble-head figures served as the infantry for his other trea-sures: a pair of stress balls with the Boon University logo nearly worn away, a trophy engraved with MASTER OF OVERSTATEMENT. Beside them was a framed picture turned toward him so Emma couldn't see it, but she imagined it was him and Lisa on their boat, the sky a blank piece of steel behind them, a sun hat pulled firmly over his head.

"There's nothing to be stressed about," he was say-ing. "Just a casual conversation."

"Of course," Emma said, touching her hair. Did she look stressed? She'd dropped Rachel off at the airport early, and while heading to campus, she'd made the decision to come in friendly and eager, the picture of a model instructor who wanted extra classes next semester. As much as she hated teaching, she needed the full load to pay off the IVF.

A light rap at the door. Emma turned to see Lisa enter the office, her hair blown out and expensive-looking, a prix fixe smile on her face.

"Your wife is here," Emma said stupidly.

Paulie stood. "Well, Lisa is the provost."

Lisa wiggled her fingers at Paulie and perched one thigh on the front of his desk. Her thumbs began to punch aggressively at her BlackBerry. "Just one sec. I need to finish this email."

"You could have finished the email in the hallway," said Paulie under his breath. Emma could see that he was hesitant to sit again; the position would put him both lower than and behind Lisa, who sighed as she set the phone down on the desk.

"I didn't want to be late." Lisa pushed aside the row of bobbleheads and hoisted herself onto the desk. The hem of her pants rose as she crossed her ankles, revealing a patchwork of Band-Aids under her high heels. "Hello, Emma!"

"Hi," Emma said.

"I'll get to the point. We've received a complaint about you."

It took Emma a moment to register what Lisa had said. "Wait, what? What about?"

Lisa leaned forward. "Did you tell a student that they were not allowed to write an academic paper on a certain political topic?"

Emma felt the room close in. Of course she should have seen this coming. "That's not quite accurate," she said. "Alex tried to change his topic after the date set in the syllabus."

"Alex says you indicated that you wouldn't grade his first idea fairly."

"What? No."

"No?"

"I mean, he's right that I don't agree with his point of view, but my comments were completely objective. Alex wasn't using proper sources. His argument was weak. That sort of thing. It's all in the rubric."

Lisa held a hand up. "No need for all that. I'm completely on your side, Emma."

Surprise ballooned in Emma's chest. "Oh. Thank you."

"But we have to follow due process for matters like these. You understand. We're at an interesting moment in history. Campus climate is changing."

"Sure," Emma said, though she wasn't.

"Last year there was a story in the *Beacon* about how conservative students were feeling marginalized in academia, certain faculty publicly praising Obama, et cetera. Somehow the article made its way through the cyberspace cosmos and landed in a state senator's inbox."

"The guy calls me," Paulie said. "Me, of all people!

Got my number from the department website. He says he's got concerns about freedom of speech on campus. 'I'm accountable to taxpayers, Paul,' he keeps saying. 'Taxpayers expect their money to support education for everyone, not just the cultural Marxists.' He really said that."

"Student concerns like these can have an impact on resource allocation for public universities," Lisa said. "Alex Brewer is very active in the Campus Conservatives Alliance. He'll make a big stink out of this, get it in the *Beacon*. And I'm sure you don't know this, but his father is the state policy advocate for the Family Research Council. Randy Brewer has several senators' phone numbers on speed dial."

Emma closed her eyes. "I might have told Alex the FRC was a hate group."

Lisa clucked her tongue. "I see. Well, that probably put a target on your back. And ours. Because if Alex chooses to air his grievances in public—"

"The state legislature could cut Boon's funding," Emma said.

"I mean, it's often just male bluster." Lisa smoothed her hair with one hand. "But we have to play to it sometimes. You understand."

Paulie grunted.

"We just want to solve this problem today," Lisa went on. "It could get messy if we don't. Obviously no one wants that."

"So what do I do?" asked Emma. "It doesn't seem fair to let one student change his paper topic just because he's a political liability."

"Sometimes you just have to—" Lisa began, but she stopped at the knocking at the door. "Come in."

The surface temperature of Emma's skin shifted—first icy, then hot with rage—as Alex Brewer walked in, his backpack over one shoulder. Out of the corner of her eye, Emma saw Paulie straighten, a brief pinking of satisfaction on his face.

"Brewer," said Lisa. "Thanks for meeting today."

Alex slung his bag on the floor and sat in the chair next to Emma. A halo of citrus wafted from his shampooed hair.

"Emma," Paulie said. "Alex has brought to our attention some concerns about the atmosphere in your classroom. And I have to say, I'm not comfortable with what I've been hearing."

"I'm sorry?" She raised her eyebrows.

"Alex tells us that he presented you with two research-paper topics, but you rejected them both on the grounds of political disagreement."

"Are you kidding? I thought you just said—" Emma looked at Lisa, whose eyes had drifted back to her phone. "That is a gross misrepresentation of what actually happened."

"I know these issues are sensitive to you personally,"

Paulie went on. "But you can't let that cloud your pedagogical objectivity."

"It's not about you being a lesbian," said Lisa, looking up from her phone. "We'd be having this same conversation if you were straight."

Emma sat back, betrayed. She hadn't been outed in a long time and never in front of a student. But it always felt the same—like a curtain she'd been holding up in front of her had dropped. The first time was after a summer arts camp in high school; her bunkmate had sent a postcard that fall saying, *Jessica told me you kissed her after the exhibition, how did I not know this?* Emma had walked down the stairs to see her mother holding the mail, a stricken look on her face.

"Let me first say," Emma said, struggling to find solid ground, "that the piece of legislation that Alex wants to write about—the kind of legislation that tries to sanction marginalization—is objectively harmful. There are studies on this. One came out this year specifically about Proposition 8. I mean, you wouldn't allow a student to write a paper denying the Holocaust, would you?"

Paulie and Lisa exchanged an inaccessible look. "That's a bit of a stretch," said Lisa. "As a pre-law major, Brewer wanted to base his paper topic on a current piece of legislation. While you might not agree with the new law, and of course we can understand why, the fact is that this is a public university. Freedom of speech is one of our core priorities. You can't create political boundaries in the classroom."

"I haven't."

"There was a joke in your syllabus," Paulie said. "About Dick Cheney? Brewer and a few other students found it inappropriate."

Right. *You've proven yourself to be more observant than a vice president on a quail hunt.* Emma squirmed in her seat. It seemed like ages ago that she'd written that. What had she been thinking, injecting a joke about politics *and* gun violence into her syllabus? Paulie was right; it had been completely unprofessional, a sign that she'd been out of the rhythm of leading a classroom for a while. But hindsight didn't do her any favors now. Equally embarrassing in the moment, somehow, was that multiple students had found her syllabus surprise and hadn't tried to use it for extra points.

"It's just that jokes like these can be alienating for students, can make them feel like they don't have a voice." Lisa recrossed her ankles and glanced at the clock. It occurred to Emma that this meeting, which was so steeped in humiliation and sting for Emma, was simply a rectangle on Lisa's calendar.

Emma tried switching tactics. "I'll remove the joke from the syllabus, okay? But the real point is, Alex was free to choose whatever topic he wanted for his paper. But by pivoting to a new paper, he's avoiding revisions on his first, which is one of the main learning objectives of the class. Besides, it's too late in the semester to adequately make up—"

"Actually, I have the work done," said Alex. He pulled a folder from his bag. "It's right here if you want to see it, Paulie. And it actually cites the observational study that Emma referred to earlier. Which has clear problems with methodology." He turned to Emma. "Since you lose track of things sometimes, I brought another copy."

Paulie generously held up his palm. "You don't need to show me the paper." He turned to Emma. "Will you accept his work? You can grade it on your course rubric, of course. Whether things are spelled correctly, et cetera."

"No." Emma crossed her arms. "I've been very clear about this. And to be honest, I don't think it's possible to separate education from the political context in which it exists. What about modern European history? Is there any way to present the atrocities of that period without a moral perspective?" She was relieved, after the stumble over the syllabus joke, to hear the confidence in her voice. Rachel would be proud.

Paulie didn't blink. "Emma, this isn't the first complaint we've gotten about you."

She sat back. "Okay?" Her voice was small again, uncertain.

"Brewer came to us earlier in the semester to let us

know you mocked his limp," Lisa said. "From a knee injury that cost him his place on the basketball team."

"What? I didn't—"

"You said he didn't look like a golfer? The team would win if he weren't on it? In front of the whole class." Paulie looked at Alex. "You're still in rehab to sort out that leg, right?"

"Yup," said Alex, his voice hollow.

"That was a misunderstanding," Emma said. "And not political."

"What about making students listen to your views on the Iraq war?" Alex asked. "You basically told Charlie his brother's service is a waste of time."

"That is—I mean, you're missing the context of that conversation, which was—" She could hear herself stumbling. "You weren't even a part of that conversation!"

"Emma, it's not atypical for a new adjunct to make a misstep," said Lisa. "But we're seeing a pattern of behavior here that's getting a little too close to discrimination."

Emma closed her eyes. She saw, briefly, the negative afterimage of the room, with the windows blackened and Paulie's round shape a flare of light in the center.

"But Brewer has agreed to withdraw his complaints on two conditions," Lisa continued. "An apology and acceptance of his final position paper on the topic of his choosing."

Emma opened her eyes. "And if I don't agree to either?"

Lisa looked surprised. "Then your behavior falls into what the faculty handbook defines as 'egregious censorship of a student.' Which can be grounds for ending your contract."

Out of the corner of her eye—she refused to look at Alex directly—Emma could see the paper on Alex's lap. "Defending Traditional Marriage: The Case for Proposition 8." She thought about her options. She supposed she could apologize for the golfing comments; she hadn't known about his knee injury. But if she refused to accept the paper, what would happen? Would she really be fired? It was a risk. She wouldn't be able to find other work in Riverbend, not during a recession, leaving her unable to pay for the IVF, which she'd already financed like a car.

Or she could take the paper, which would mean reading it and marking it up—it would, of course, be obnoxiously well written—and, worst of all, conceding. Not just to Alex and Paulie and Lisa but to the invisible machinery that governed their lives and their opinions about one another. In that moment, she felt as if accepting the paper was the same as surrendering to Prop 8 and all its supporters, the angry people she'd seen on the news last week waving yellow hand-lettered signs on the steps of the same city hall where she and Rachel had been married. One shot showed a young girl holding a sign, her arms stretched wide to reach its edges: I NEED A MOM AND A DAD. The braids in her hair were impeccable, laced with ribbon; her mother was no doubt nearby, either holding her own sign or looking on proudly at what their family had done. It made Emma feel as if her own mother were hidden around the corner as well, distaste tightening her lips the way it did whenever she looked at her daughter.

While Emma was thinking about all this in Paulie's office, the worst thing happened. She began to cry. She felt its warning signs—a salty taste in her mouth, a tightening across the front of her neck—but she was helpless to stop the wave because these tears weren't just about Alex and this moment. Everything was surfacing at once—the sorrow that had followed her since the miscarriage, the weight of keeping the IVF a secret from Rachel, her ache to be back in Chicago. She turned her head so Alex couldn't see her face, though it meant that Paulie had a better view. He cleared his throat and looked at Lisa, who plucked a tissue from a box on his desk.

"Do you want to take some time to think this over?" she asked, holding out the tissue.

But Emma batted it away. "No," she said. "My answer is no. No to the apology and no to the paper." She wiped her eyes with the backs of her hands, knowing but not caring that her mascara had smeared and that she had just crossed a line she would not be able to walk back. "So am I fired?"

Paulie blinked in surprise. He looked at Lisa, who was studying Emma with her lips pursed in pity.

"I'm going to recommend we table this for the moment, given how emotionally charged the discussion has become," Lisa said. "You two can go."

As Paulie held the door open for them to leave, Emma realized that she and Alex now had to walk to class together. She had to teach with red, swollen eyes and the salt of injustice under her tongue. As they walked through the hall in silence, Alex a few feet ahead of her, Emma's tears turned into a smoldering rage.

At the door of the classroom, Alex turned to her. "Hey, I didn't know they were going to be such bureaucrats about the whole thing. I'm just concerned about my grade point average. I have to keep it up to stay on the golf team, you know."

She stared at him in disbelief. His expression was open and innocent. He regretted making her cry, she supposed.

"Maybe we could get a coffee after the semester is over," he said. "Talk about books. I read a lot of fiction. You could give me some recommendations." Alex wanted her to take his guilt from him; he was like a boy who'd gotten a puppy and realized its needs outweighed his expectations. He wanted a grown-up to lift the squirming thing from his arms so he could go out and play.

Emma took a deep breath. "Let me make this clear, Alex. I don't care who your father is or whether he has any influence over the university's funding. You do understand that, right? That none of this was about you?"

She paused, seeing the flinch on his face. "The most useful thing you can do is stop coming to class. In fact, I will give you an A if I never see you again. You don't contribute anything productive to discussions. You hide behind some freshman-grade humor to mask an overall lack of intellectual talent." She could see that she'd hit a bruise as his face darkened. But saying these words felt too delicious and she couldn't stop herself, even if she knew that at some point she'd pay for them. "Please go away. I don't ever want to see you again."

The playfulness on his face vanished. She saw his jaw clenching and unclenching as he thought of a response. Then he turned and walked away.

*　　*　　*

The Riverbend Family Planning Center was undergoing a renovation. A sign in the lobby said OUR LITTLE CLINIC IS GROWING! PLEASE PARDON OUR DUST AS WE BLOSSOM AND BLOOM! The receptionist waved at Emma as she came in, and Emma smiled back. It was a relief, after the terrible morning she'd had, to be in a place where she felt like she belonged. She was a regular at the clinic now. She no longer had to watch the street signs on the bus ride there; she could feel the rhythm of the three stops after crossing the bridge, pulling the cord without looking up from her book. She knew all the nurses by name; the phlebotomist always asked to see pictures of Birdie when she drew Emma's blood. It was here that she felt whole, even during the appointments where a nurse pushed an ultrasound wand into Emma's vagina and cranked it around like a joystick until follicles began to emerge on the screen. It felt, in these moments, as if something that was meant to be hers was finally within her grasp. Even Dr. Rivera's gruffness had become charming; she always greeted Emma with a salute and said, "Ladies and gents, she's back for more!" At the clinic Emma felt aware of the magnitude of all that the world could hold, from the invisible eggs in her body to the Boon campus teeming with strangers to all of Riverbend and, beyond that, to the great soup of other lives unknown to her.

Today the waiting room was halved neatly, chairs pushed together on one side while the other lay draped in plastic. Makeshift scaffolding stood in the corner like a giant spider. Behind the thick plastic sheeting Emma could make out the shadows of people working. Now and then the shriek of a drill rang out, the coarse laughter of men.

"It's the big day!" said the receptionist. Her voice was muffled behind a dust mask. "Do you have a ride home after the procedure?"

"I made a reservation with Med Transport," Emma said. She had initially been embarrassed she had no one to call for a ride after the retrieval, which would be done under anesthesia and leave her groggy. But today she was relieved to have paid an anonymous stranger fifty dollars to drive her home. There would be comfortable silence, and Emma wouldn't need to be effusive with gratitude. She could just sit back and relax.

"Then you're all set, Emma." The receptionist's eyes crinkled with kindness above her mask.

Emma sat in the only empty chair, near the windows overlooking the shrubbery by the parking lot. Next to her sat a sniffling woman who clutched her husband's hand with such force that he kept clearing his throat and tapping her knuckles to loosen up. After a moment he whispered loudly, "Crying's not going to change the situation."

Emma opened a magazine, feeling judgmental about the scene playing out next to her. The overburdened and sensitive wife beside her dim-witted husband, each oblivious to the other's needs. She'd seen this exact scenario so often in sitcoms that there were times, like now, that Emma felt she could hear a laugh track. Of course, she thought with some vexation, her own wife was thirty thousand feet up in the sky right now, flipping through an *Atlantic* and sipping ginger ale on her way to a book signing in Denver, completely unaware that Emma was sitting in a half-demolished fertility clinic about to have dozens of eggs scraped from her tender, ballooned ovaries. And Emma had had to hire a stranger from a medical-transport service to give her a ride home, whereas the two people beside her, despite their disequilibrium, would get in their car together after their appointment and collapse into a conversation about dinner. Pasta or dumplings. Something easy to bring them back together again.

The crying woman let go of her husband's hand. She leaned away from him as if repulsed, and Emma felt the woman's soft shoulder press into her own. She closed her eyes at the moment of warmth, but the woman abruptly scooted away.

"Sorry," she said.

Dr. Rivera's nurse appeared in the doorway, looking as if she were under construction herself, with loose strands falling from her ponytail and two necklaces tangled around her neck. She called Emma's name. When Emma stood and pulled her bag over her shoulder, the woman next to her looked up. Her eyeliner was smudged around the edges, but Emma could see that it had once been carefully applied in a neat line, perhaps that morning when the woman's day was still full of promise.

"Good luck," the woman said. "I sure hope it works out for you."

*   *   *

After the Med Transport driver dropped her off at home, Emma tucked herself into sweatpants and burrowed on the futon with Birdie curled next to her. She'd been cleaned out, her stuffed ovaries deflated and their contents — twelve eggs, a tidy dozen — dispatched to their mysterious duty in a petri dish. The nurse had given Emma a paper bag of progesterone suppositories, which Emma had groggily accepted even though she'd been disappointed; she'd hoped the retrieval was the end of the medicines. The bag, full of its individual cardboard containers, was big and clunky, and Emma felt, as she was wheeled out to the Med Transport van, like an old lady who'd been politely rolled through a grocery store before being returned to her group home.

The nurse would call tomorrow to let her know how many of the eggs had been fertilized. Until then, Emma felt entitled to an irrefutable sense of calm. She sank into a deep sleep.

When she woke up, the sky was darkening. She rose shakily and took Birdie for a walk around the neighborhood. The air was chilly, but one street over, a couple of kids wore T-shirts as they carried a watering can from the spigot to a plastic wading pool on the front lawn. They looked around seven or so; their faces were grubby and flushed in a way that suggested not just an afternoon of play but an entire season of evenings spent outside the house.

"Going for a swim?" Emma called to them.

The children looked at each other as if deciding something. "No," one said. "We're making soup."

"How delicious. What are you putting in it?"

The other child, bolder now, held up a bulging plastic sack. "Mud and stones."

"And a squirrel from the road," said the first child.

"Squirrel soup?" Emma rubbed her belly. "Sounds rich in protein. That must be why you're so tall."

"We're making a salad from leaves and sticks," one cried excitedly.

"Well, duh. Vegetables make you grow tall and wise."

The sound of the children giggling made Emma's heart lighten for the first time in days. "I suppose you grow all your leaves and sticks in your own garden," she said.

"They grow on the tree," the first child said with a touch of impatience. They turned back to their watering can. Emma could sense she'd lost them, but she didn't take it personally. It was hard being a child, with adults always pressing their fingers into the permeable membrane between reality and make-believe. Life was hard from the beginning, wasn't it. She waved to them before turning back to her own street.

*   *   *

She and Birdie took the long way home, circuiting the quiet streets. By the time they got back, the sky was dark and so was the house. Emma fumbled for a lamp and clicked it on while Birdie ran to her water bowl. As the living room materialized in the light, Emma felt a shiver run up her spine. Something was off, though she couldn't name what. Had she tossed the blanket over the arm of the futon like that, so that its fringes caught on the coffee table? Did she really leave her soup bowl on the floor? The paper bag of medicines dropped in the middle of the rug? She looked around the room slowly. Rachel was right, she *was* messy. She would need to set aside some time to clean before Rachel got back on Tuesday. But for the next few days, she promised herself as she picked up the mail and rifled through it, she would be messy. Fully, authentically herself. She would leave things where they fell, she would use four towels per shower, she would—

A note fell from the stack of envelopes in her hand. Emma picked it up and held it between her finger and thumb. In crude letters, it said *GET OUT.* Below that: *THIS IS A WARING. YOU DO NOT BELONG HERE.*

Emma stared at the words for a moment. There was a sort of poetry in the missing *n*—*waring* conjuring both its homophonic cousin *wearing* as well as *warring,* its *Verwechslungspartner,* as Rachel would call it. The sentence *I am weary from this warring* arose in her mind. She could see the note had meant to frighten her, but the missing letter gave it an air of absentmindedness that felt more pathetic than threatening.

Emma crumpled the note in her fist and shoved it in her pocket. It was obvious that Patty had written it. She hadn't liked the fact that a lesbian couple had moved into her neighborhood, and she'd disguised her bigotry behind an endless wall of criticism about their landscaping. For someone who clearly found their presence offensive, Patty certainly spent a lot of time watching them and clomping across the grass on their side of the property. Emma imagined her peering from behind her curtains, swigging wine coolers and stewing in fury that the world was changing. Two women could simply sign a paper and — poof — they could get married and have children, one after another, right in full view of her vegetable garden.

Emma couldn't decide what angered her more, the blatant homophobia or the fact that Patty was wrong about how easy any of it was. She wondered if Patty's position would change if she knew more about Emma, like how she'd been fired from a summer job as a tutor because some kid's parent saw a rainbow pin on her bag. And how she was banned from prom for having a girlfriend. And how, after being outed to her parents at sixteen, Emma had to move in with a friend's family, who fed her and gave her gas money but also removed all the razors and painkillers from the house so her last two years of high school were a blur of leg hair and headaches.

Patty might soften if she heard these things. Rachel certainly believed that. But Emma didn't care if Patty softened. Emma was in the mood for sharpness; she wanted to hurt Patty's feelings.

Emma didn't bother putting her jacket back on before she went outside. The neighborhood was still. The streetlight cast an orange glow over the last few hardy moths, frantically circling in the chilly air. She turned on her phone's flashlight and found the shovel in the backyard, dragged it through the dried grass to the butterfly bush. Emma propped up the flashlight against the side of the house so she could more precisely aim the shovel, which pressed easily through the layer of mulch that Patty had left and then struck the hard dirt. She leaned onto the handle until she felt the pleasant snap of roots. The cold air stung her skin, but she ignored it and kept stabbing at the exposed dirt, channeling all her anger into her arms, which felt strong and capable. When she hit resistance, she stood on the shovel's metal lip, pressing her whole body against the thick obstinance beneath the ground. Then she stepped off and tried to lift the shovel, but it wouldn't budge. Furious, she slammed all her weight into the shovel, feeling a shock of protest from her tender ovaries. The shovel suddenly moved, and she pulled up the plant and its undergrowth.

The bush was no longer in the ground but impossibly heavy on the base of her shovel, its roots dangling like nerves. A sulfuric smell, organic and fetid, rose from the hole it left.

Panting, Emma hoisted the plant up on the shovel like she was pulling a pizza peel from the oven. She was careful not to let it fall as she carried it across the yard and dumped it on Patty's front step. And then she went home and locked the door.

CHAPTER 8

Charlotte awoke in the night mid-dream, as if a hand had reached down and pulled her from somewhere deep in her subconscious. She blinked. The attic was dark and still, the smell of the new people's garlicky cooking still filling the air.

It took her a moment to realize that Dirk was not beside her. His presence had become such an integrated part of her own self, his smells mixing with hers and his skin nearly always within reach, that his absence was like a rush of cold air. There was literal cold air too, because Charlotte had cracked the window after Dirk complained of feeling too warm at dinner. She'd had to wrap a blanket around her shoulders as they ate peanut butter crackers and drank water. The lack of fresh food had made them irritable. The car had stayed stubbornly in the driveway all weekend, a layer of fallen leaves blanketing the windshield. Once, thinking the girls were out, Charlotte had gone downstairs, realizing only after pouring orange juice into her thermos that the brunette girl was there, just feet away, asleep on the futon. She had a pillowcase over her face that rose and fell softly with her snores. The little dog, curled up on her chest, had lifted its head at the creak of the floor; seeing Charlotte, it dropped its chin back on its paws. Heart slamming in her chest, Charlotte had left a puddle of juice on the floor in her haste to return to the garage, where the concrete pressed cold and hard through her slippers. During the last weeks of summer there had been so many times she'd longed for the weather to cool so that the attic didn't feel so sticky, but now that the temperature had dropped, she wished she could go back to the heat, which had at least reminded her of days in the garden. Coldness had no soul; it felt like it existed only to remind you that something was missing.

She sat up. "Dirk," she whispered into the dark. In the gap between the wall and the edge of the curtain, a strip of moonlight pierced the room, landing on his model car and jars of paint. Charlotte had a sudden, violent thought: What if Dirk had taken the pills from the relief kit? Just a few at first, to knock out the headache, but feeling no better, what if he took more? Just kept swallowing them with his cup of warm water? She felt panic rise in her throat as she scrambled off the mattress. She stood too suddenly, knocking her head against the wooden rafter. The impact made her vision go white for a moment and she instinctively crouched back to the floor, holding her head in her hands. She swallowed the wail in her throat.

After rubbing her head, she stood more carefully and stepped out from behind the curtain so she could see the whole room. She turned on the lamp and braced herself for what she might find, picturing Dirk's body splayed on the floor. But then she saw him standing in the corner, facing the wall. His shoulders stooped.

"Dirk," she whispered. When he didn't respond, she said, "What are you doing? You need something?"

He didn't answer. Then Charlotte heard a splattering that took her a moment to recognize as the sound of urine splashing down the side of the wall. "What on earth!" She hadn't seen her husband sleepwalk before, but Justin used to do it from time to time, stomping messily through their room with his eyes nearly closed, searching for the bathroom. He always just needed to pee, and afterward, he would rub his hands together over the dry sink, pantomiming washing them. Charlotte, who never saw Justin wash his hands when he was awake, found it funny every time.

She touched Dirk's shoulder and he turned to her, his eyes milky and concerned. His height, which she'd always found comforting and protective, now felt frightening. She realized how small she was next to him, how incapable she'd be of supporting his body should he need help getting down the stairs or off the floor.

"Honey, let's get you to bed." She reached for his hand to guide him to the mattress, but he pulled back forcefully. The jerk of his arm was so unexpected, Charlotte nearly fell forward.

"Where'd you put my glasses?" His voice was hoarse but loud. "I can't see a damn thing."

"Keep your voice down." Charlotte reached for him again, gently this time, but he swatted her away. "You don't need your glasses to sleep. Come back to bed."

"If I had my glasses, I could find them."

"Find what?"

"My tools." He cast his gaze wildly about the room, and as his head moved so did his body, tipping dangerously to each side. "Where'd you put them?"

"What tools? You don't need—"

Dirk brushed past her and headed toward the hatch. Charlotte's breath caught at the sound of his dull, uncareful footsteps.

"Where are you going?"

"Downstairs," he said, irritated. "For my ratchet set."

Charlotte grabbed his hand. "Dirk, you're just having a dream."

"No, I'm not. I'm awake." He looked down at

Charlotte with such intensity that she knew this was true. When Justin sleepwalked, his eyes were unfocused and glazed, the way they sometimes got when he drifted off in front of the television. But Dirk was looking right into her eyes in a way that scared her.

"All right, you're not dreaming, then." She stepped back. "But what on earth are you talking about? What do you need tools for?"

"I told him I'd fix it."

"Told who—"

"Who turned off the overhead lights? Why is it so dark everywhere?" Dirk lurched toward the wall, his hands out as if searching for a light switch. She grabbed his arm again, harder this time. Her fingers sank disturbingly deep into his skin, as if the muscle had softened and spread.

"For heaven's sake, Dirk, keep it down," she whispered. "What are you doing?"

"You took my tool bag and put it somewhere. You're hiding it."

"Now, why on earth would I do that?"

"How would I know? Maybe you want everything broken." He looked down at her again, and this time she saw a bubble of blood forming at his nostril. It began its slow trickle through his mustache. "You never let me fix anything."

"Oh, Dirkie." She let go of his arm, suddenly understanding. Not long after his stent was placed last March,

Dirk had had an episode of confusion in the garage. Charlotte had found him standing in front of the open hood of their car, pawing at tubes and plugs, his face flushed and angry. When his nose started to bleed, she drove him straight to the emergency room, where they clocked his blood pressure at 210/140. The nurse who administered an IV of medicine that cleared the red from his face explained that an episode of abnormally high blood pressure reduced blood flow to the brain. Not only could it cause severe confusion, as Dirk had experienced in the garage, but it significantly increased his chances of a stroke as well as a heart attack and kidney damage and other things Charlotte stopped hearing because these hypotheticals were too much to bear. She'd once driven past the cemetery and seen a woman her age sitting on a grave like it was a park bench, her lunch spread across her lap as she chatted away to the headstone. At the time, Charlotte hadn't felt sympathy for the woman, only disgust at the way she'd made her grief into such a performance. But sitting in the hospital and squeezing Dirk's warm hand, she realized it hadn't been a performance at all.

Now Charlotte rushed for the relief kit. She pulled out the blister pack of tablets the doctor had given her that day in the emergency room. Nitroglycerin. All Dirk had to do was let one melt under his tongue, and his blood pressure would go down. She stood with the pack in hand and paused. Dirk was lumbering around, rubbing his hands on the walls as if looking for a door. Would the tablet be enough? Was this a true emergency? Should she—she could hardly believe she was thinking it—go downstairs? Wake the new people and ask them to call 911? They'd certainly call, but perhaps not just to help Dirk. The police might arrive too; they'd arrest Charlotte, separate her from Dirk, and haul her to jail while he rode off to the hospital in an ambulance. And if that happened, when would they see each other again? And who would care for Dirk in his hospital bed? Who would fill his pink plastic cup with juice from the vending machine because he thought the hospital water tasted like pennies? Who would untuck the bottom of his sheets so his big feet didn't feel trapped?

Charlotte shook the idea out of her head. Instead she popped a tablet from its pack and brought it to Dirk's lips.

"It's just medicine," she said. "Put this under your tongue."

Dirk balked at the touch of her fingers, trying to move away. Charlotte pressed the tablet through his lips and into the warm, soft inside of his mouth. Then she felt a sharp bolt of pain and instinctively pulled her hand out of his mouth and slapped his cheek, hard.

They both looked at each other, stunned. The lamplight illuminated the contours of Dirk's face, making his skull more visible. Charlotte brought her finger to her mouth and felt with her tongue the indent of his teeth, the taste of blood. If she'd been handed a snapshot of this moment when she was twenty years old and newly married, she would never have believed it was them.

"You bit me." She wiped her finger on her sweatshirt. "I'm sorry. But you bit me."

A moment passed and sorrow crossed Dirk's face. "Lottie, I don't know what's happening."

"It's all right." She put her hand on his back and guided him toward the mattress. "Let's just go back to bed."

* * *

Somehow Dirk fell into a deep sleep that lasted until late in the morning. Charlotte had trouble turning her mind off and lay awake for an hour, feeling the pulse of fear and guilt work itself out of her body. In the morning she woke early and pulled out the blanket she'd knit and reknit so many times over the past few months that the yarn had grown thin and fuzzy. The pattern required concentration to alternate stitches, and she found her mind grateful for the task, focused on only her fingers and counting and the slip of the yarn.

When Dirk woke up, he reached for his pee jug. His hand trembled slightly.

"There's not much for breakfast," Charlotte said. "I

had to hurry because their schedule's been off and I wasn't sure if someone would come home." She nodded at the trunk, where she'd unwrapped a soft granola bar and placed it on a tissue next to a few dried apricots. "I'll try again later."

Dirk put away his jug and stretched his arms. "Okey-dokey." He reached for an apricot.

Charlotte put down her yarn. " 'Okey-dokey'? That's all you have to say?"

He blinked. "What am I supposed to say?"

"You don't remember last night?"

His face remained blank.

"You were going on about needing tools to fix something. Wandering around making all the noise in the world. You peed on the wall, Dirk." She pointed to the dark spot on the wood.

Dirk's eyes followed her finger. "I don't remember. Was I sleepwalking?"

"I thought that at first. But then your nose started bleeding. You remember when that happened last time? Scared the life out of me." She picked up her knitting again.

Dirk rubbed his forehead, as if willing the memory back. His wrinkled skin moved up and down. "God, Lottie. I'm sorry."

"Then I gave you a nitro tablet and you bit me." She held up her finger, wrapped in a Band-Aid. "Broke the skin like a damn dog."

"I don't know what to say. I have no memory of it."

"It's okay." She paused. "I slapped the daylights out of you."

"Oh." Dirk's fingers drifted to his cheek.

"I'm sorry about that."

"Sounds like I deserved it."

"Are you not taking your medicine?"

He pulled at his beard.

"Dirk?"

"I'm taking it."

"But?"

"But I'm running out."

Charlotte shook her head. "That can't be right. We filled your prescription the day before we came here. You got a six-month supply." She watched his face. "Right? You had to wait in line for so long behind that woman with pink eye that I worried you'd get it yourself."

"They only had enough in stock for two months. Told me to come back in a week for the rest."

"Two months!" Again she set her knitting down. "That was—how long, that was the end of July—"

"Little over three months ago."

"You've been out that long? No, that's not possible. I saw you take your medicine yesterday."

"I've been rationing." He picked up a granola bar and broke off a corner, placed it on his tongue. "Every other day, every three days. Half a pill here and there."

"Why didn't you tell me when we were at the pharmacy?"

He spread his hands out as if he couldn't believe the question. "How was I supposed to know we were going to hole ourselves up here like mice for the rest of our lives?"

"It's not the rest of our lives. It's only until—"

"Right, the wedding invitation." Dirk pulled at his beard again, this time hard enough to flash the pink interior of his lower eyelid. "It's not coming. You have to know that by now. It's time to face reality. You've been so busy playing house and having your adventures downstairs that you haven't taken a minute to acknowledge how awful this is. I hate it, I am miserable every minute. How can you not see that?"

Charlotte looked down at her blanket. She knew that she should feel sorry for her husband. And maybe a few months ago she would have. But the attic had changed her. Her emotions had been rearranged like a puzzle and now, more often, anger slid into place before sympathy. She thought of Dirk on the nights in their old life when he wore a headlamp to work on his car, circles of grass illuminated before him when he walked back to the house. That was Dirk, she thought. Moving through life looking just at the little spot ahead of him. Not thinking about all the big black dark that he'd inevitably have to pass through. There were some ways that her mother had been right about Dirk; he was often like another child.

"It's not forever," she said. "It's a few months, nothing in the grand scheme. We're so close—"

"But at our age, Lottie"—his voice broke—"a few months cost a lot." He was trembling with anger now; he wouldn't look at her.

"How many pills do you have left?" she asked. When he reached for his pill bottle, she leaned over and snatched it from his hand. She rattled it. A single pill clattered against the plastic. "One! This is all there is?"

He took the bottle back. "Yes. This one is the last." He opened the bottle and dropped the blue pill on his palm. It was the shape of a bowl; he'd already snapped it in half. Dirk swallowed it without water.

"I really can't believe it," she said. "I work so hard to keep you well. And you sit here and lie to me about your medicine."

"It's stressful, Lottie!" Dirk barked. "You think this is good for me? For either of us? You go on and on worrying about my blood pressure, but this right here—sitting up here day in and day out—is the most stressful goddamned thing I've ever gone through in my life!"

Charlotte blinked. She felt a response swell up in her, rise in her throat all on its own—*You think it's stressful for you? Try being the one who's always getting the food and taking care of everything*—but the words died quietly before she opened her mouth. Because what he said was true. It was maddening that they were up here. What a stupid idea it had been! But they were here, and they couldn't leave now. Not when the people downstairs were researching condos and were so close to leaving. They were going to get their home back at last. Charlotte could feel it—something in the house had changed, there had been a subtle shift in its energy, like when the air grew heavy before a storm. Her note was doing its work. Something was going to happen. She didn't need evidence of this any more than she needed proof that Amy was good for Justin. Some things a woman just knows.

Charlotte took the pill bottle from his hand. "Then I'll go to the pharmacy tomorrow and get this refilled."

"Don't be ridiculous."

"Walgreens opens at seven. I'll leave here early, before anyone is up." The plan unfolded in her mind as she spoke. "I'll drive the car." She felt a shiver of delight at the thought of her hands on the steering wheel, the world bright and wide through the windshield. Air on her face.

"It might not start. It's been months."

"Then I'll walk. It's only three miles."

"What if someone sees you and says, 'Lottie, where have you been?'"

"Who cares if they do? I'll just tell them the truth. That we've been away for a bit." She could feel the idea solidify in her mind; what had not seemed possible just five minutes ago was now weighted with inevitability. Her skin tingled with the thrill of it. She was going to leave the house.

CHAPTER 9

One embryo. Of the twelve eggs scraped from Emma's ovaries—eggs that had been summoned from twenty-nine self-injections, weeks of transvaginal ultrasounds, and handfuls of pills—only four of them had been mature, and only two of those had been fertilized. By day four, there was only one left. The news was a surprise to Emma; she'd expected to have several viable embryos, not only as a safeguard in case their first transfer didn't work but also for the future. What if they wanted to have a second child down the road? It occurred to Emma that while there was only one possible successful outcome of IVF, there were infinite possibilities for failure along the way. You could undergo the painful hysterosalpingography only to learn that your fallopian tubes were blocked and no sperm had ever stood a chance. You could look at the price sheet and realize you couldn't afford the medications and the ultrasounds. Your body might not respond to the drugs and fail to produce more than one egg. Emma had made it so far in the process, her hopes growing a little more at each appointment. And of all the disappointing outcomes she'd prepared herself for—a negative pregnancy test, another miscarriage—somehow the possibility that she would have only one embryo hadn't crossed her mind.

"One is all it takes," Julie the nurse told her when she called on Sunday. "And it looks like a grade B. Very nice."

Emma began to pace across the bedroom. Birdie watched from her perch on the air mattress, where the two of them had spent much of the past few days. It had been four days since the meeting with Paulie and Lisa and no word on the status of her contract, so Emma had taught her Thursday and Friday classes, in which she turned on *Twelve Angry Men* and told the class to write down examples of pathos and ethos, then took a seat in the back of the dark classroom with her laptop and watched as, one by one, the students put their heads on their desks and slept. Alex had not shown up to class at all, much to her relief. Aside from those brief trips to campus and her walks with Birdie—she avoided passing Patty's house, which had been eerily quiet, the butterfly bush gone from the front porch—Emma stayed home. She took long, late-morning naps on the futon with a pillowcase over her face to block out the sun and Birdie curled on her chest. She inserted the progesterone suppositories responsibly into her vagina after brushing her teeth. She ate cans of soup from the cabinets and stacks of cinnamon toast, leaving the kitchen messy. An increasingly stale smell was coming from either the garbage, which she hadn't taken out, or the laundry pile, which she kept toeing back into the closet. Once she went to the kitchen to make a sandwich and found that she'd left a pool of orange juice on the floor in front of the refrigerator. She'd felt shocked back into her own body as her bare foot pressed into its cold wetness, as if she'd been inhabiting some other space, not in this house at all.

"A grade B?" Emma asked. "Is that a good thing?"

"The lab grades all the embryos on their size and fragmentation. A B is what it sounds like. When you were in school, wouldn't you have been happy with a B?"

"I would have wondered why I didn't get an A."

"As are rarer, of course. An A implies a perfect cell shape and little to no fragmentation."

"Don't you ever grade on a curve?" Emma wasn't sure why she was trying to make a joke when she was fighting back tears.

Julie's voice was warm. "Look, all I can tell you is

that there are plenty of wonderful people in the world today who came from fuzzy little B embryos. Have you been taking the progesterone?"

"Yes."

"Good. That will make your uterine lining nice and thick for a transfer tomorrow. We have you down for ten o'clock."

"I'm not doing a transfer now. We're freezing, remember?" Emma stopped pacing. "Wait, was that what the progesterone was for?"

"Oh. Yes. It prepares your uterus for implantation." Emma could hear the furious clicking of keys on the other end of the phone, the gale of Julie's breath against the receiver. "I'm so sorry about the mix-up," she said. "I see now your file was marked wrong. One of the construction workers sawed through an internet cable in the wall, and we've had to do our appointment tracking with pen and paper. It's been a mess."

Of course. Emma closed her eyes. Not a single thing was going right this week.

"Okay, I fixed it," Julie said. "Emma, I do apologize. But you shouldn't worry about the progesterone. It won't hurt anything if you already took it. Well, as you've noticed, it might affect your mood, maybe make you a little — hello? What's that sound?"

Emma winced. A piercing sound filled the room. It warbled, like when the batteries die on a toy. Birdie's ears pricked up.

"Doorbell," she said. It was the first time she'd heard it since moving in. "I'd better go. You'll freeze the embryo today, right?"

"Tomorrow. Day five is when the blastocyst is—"

"Okay, thanks, Julie." Emma hung up and tossed the phone on the bed. She went to the living room and opened the door.

Two policemen stood on the front step. One was bald with a square goatee; the other's eyes were framed with pale skin, below which began a sunburn that was starting to peel. He had the relaxed posture of someone recently back from vacation. The last notes of the doorbell faded, off-key.

"Afternoon, ma'am," said the sunburned officer, tipping his hat.

"Is there a problem?" Emma tightened her grip on the door. She instantly pictured Patty, one fleshy arm cradling the uprooted butterfly bush, the other pressing a receiver to her ear. Was it a crime to dig up a bush that someone else had planted? Or maybe it was the discarding of the thing on Patty's porch that had gotten her in trouble. What would she be charged with? Illegal dumping? Harassment?

"Can we come in?" His face was solemn.

Her heart was in her ears. "Do you need to?"

The officers both looked briefly at the ground, then back up. "If you don't mind, ma'am, we'd like to come in and sit down," said the bald one.

Emma's hands shook as she opened the door wider and gestured the officers inside. The policemen wiped their feet aggressively on the doormat before stepping into the room. They took in the place with a glance that indicated they had not expected so little furniture. Emma felt embarrassed by the half-eaten bagel resting on the frame of the futon and the bra that hung over the side of the yellow cabinet. The smell of the house seemed fishy and neglected, worse now that strangers were standing in her living room.

"Sorry, I don't know what that smell is," she said. "The house is clean."

"Can we sit?" asked the bald officer.

Emma gestured at the futon. They sank into it, hats on their knees. There were no other seats, so Emma knelt on the floor.

"So," the bald officer began.

"I just want to say that Patty comes into my backyard all the time," said Emma in a rush. "My wife and I have asked her multiple times to stop. That's trespassing, isn't it? Isn't that a crime?"

The officers looked at each other.

"Wife?" the sunburned one asked.

The bald one held up a hand. "Ma'am, if you have an issue with a trespasser, you can call the precinct. We're looking for Charlotte and Dirk Dennison. Are they your parents?"

Emma's relief blossomed into confusion. "Who?"

"Charlotte and Dirk Dennison," the sunburned one said. When Emma stared at him, he added, "They live here?"

It took a moment for Emma to understand. "Oh, right. No, they don't live here anymore. They moved out a few months ago, I guess."

"You guess?"

"I mean, we moved in a few months ago, so..."

The bald officer cocked his head as if deciding whether to believe her. "Are you family?"

"Of theirs? No."

"Did they leave a forwarding address? Something that can help us track them down?"

Emma shook her head. "They were friendly with the neighbor I was just telling you about. Patty. But I don't think she knows where they are."

"That's too bad," said the sunburned cop.

Something about the disappointment on his face made Emma want to help. She thought and snapped her fingers. "Oh—maybe they're with their son?"

The men exchanged glances. "They're not with their son," the bald one said. "That we know."

"We're here to deliver bad news," said the sunburned one, slapping his cap against his palm. "Regarding the son."

Emma could see that the bald cop was displeased

that his partner had made this announcement; she guessed, not being family, she shouldn't be hearing about the reason behind their visit.

"Well," said Emma, standing. "I'm sorry I can't help you."

"He is deceased," the sunburned officer announced. He'd obviously rehearsed the words ahead of time, their delivery clear but his voice soft with compassion, his cap pressed to his chest. He'd rung the doorbell intending to impart the news and now was unable to stop its momentum. "It's our job to notify the parents in person."

Emma sucked in a breath of air. She thought of her one embryo. There was no end to the ways that things could go wrong. "That's awful. I wish I could help."

"We're sorry to bother you, ma'am," the bald one said. "On the off chance you do find out where they might be, you call us at the Fifth Precinct." He handed her a card.

They put their hats back on and started to leave. Just as Emma was about to close the door behind them, the sunburned cop said, "Hey." He pointed to the window where she'd hung a small rainbow flag, six inches wide. "I like your flag."

"Oh," she said in surprise. "Thanks."

"I just went to my nephew's gay wedding in Newport Beach a couple weeks ago. Gay people know how to party. Am I right? They served tiny little beef

Wellingtons, each with a gold leaf on top you could eat. And don't even get me started on the music." He began bobbing his knees, making a percussive noise with his tongue and teeth.

Emma felt politeness tug at her face. If Rachel were here she'd have laughed to make him feel comfortable, to show him that his allyship was appreciated in whatever form he was capable of producing it. But Emma didn't understand why there was any need to make straight people feel comfortable. Most seemed perfectly comfortable on their own.

He stopped bouncing and put on his sunglasses. "Shame about the Proposition 8, isn't it? My wife and I were just discussing this today. My view is, the world needs more tolerance, not more hate. Don't you think?"

"Actually," Emma said, "I can't stand that word."

"What, *hate*?"

"Tolerance."

His eyebrows peeked above his sunglasses. "Why's that?"

"Well, *tolerance* implies that there's something unpleasant to be endured," said Emma. She spoke slowly, patiently, like she might to a student who was doomed to fail the class. "Right? You tolerate slow traffic or bad weather. Why is it that when anyone talks about the way that straight people should feel about the queer community, they think tolerance is the ideal? Why not respect? Admiration? Love?"

The police officer looked at his partner. His brow wrinkled and he shifted his weight onto his heels, like a little boy who'd been chastised.

"There's no need to get political, ma'am," he said. "We get enough of that on the news."

Birdie began barking behind her. "Well, I have your card," Emma said. "In case anything comes up."

"Ma'am," said the sunburned officer, tipping his hat in goodbye. As he turned away and she closed the door, she heard him murmur—she did, didn't she?— "Fuckin' lesbians."

✳   ✳   ✳

After the squad car disappeared down the block, Emma went to the backyard and used the shovel to scrape dirt and mulch into the hole where the butterfly bush had been. It seemed suddenly important to cover the evidence of what she'd done. In the daylight she saw more clearly the plant's complicated root system and the thick woody center she'd snapped in half. She felt terrible about how quickly she'd been able to uproot something that had spent so many years anchoring itself in the earth. The whole thing must have been only a seed at one point. Its roots, now severed, had wrapped themselves around tiny relics from another time: a corroded screw, an aluminum Pepsi bottle cap, a toy car. She picked up the car and ran a thumb over its wheel, which turned with some effort. She wondered if it had belonged to the son who died. If he had buried it here on purpose years ago or if it had simply been left out in the rain long enough that the earth swallowed it up. She put the car back in the hole and noticed a flattened gray cable that was so coated in dirt, it looked like another root. Emma squatted to look closer. She could see where her shovel had nicked the cable, revealing a braided cluster of wires that caught the light of the sun. The bush had been like an octopus, she thought, hoarding its shiny treasures. She couldn't help but feel, as she finished filling the hole and brushed her hands off, like someone who had just taken a life.

Inside she called Rachel to tell her what had just happened with the police. It was a relief, in some ways, to have something she could tell Rachel. They'd talked on the phone every day since Rachel left, but Emma had yet to mention the meeting with Paulie and Lisa and Alex or the note that Patty had left or the fact that Emma had dug up the butterfly bush and dropped it on Patty's front step. Emma wanted to maintain the illusion of normalcy while Rachel was gone. She didn't want to admit that things unraveled the moment Rachel stepped away, even if that seemed to be true. So mostly she talked about Birdie and asked lots of questions about what Rachel was eating and if the hotel had a pool and if she was selling a lot of books at the readings. It seemed to Emma that the list of things she wasn't telling her wife was getting longer.

When Rachel answered, there was noise in the background, a cacophony of voices and music.

"Is it a bad time?" Emma asked.

"No," Rachel said. "But give me a second. I'm just—" There was a scuffle, and then the background noise abruptly disappeared. "I'll step outside for a second."

"Where are you?"

"Lunch with Tristan and Sylvie. I told you, remember?"

"Right, right." Emma did not remember. "I'll call you later."

"No, don't go yet. I could honestly use a breather. Tristan keeps asking if I'm going to expand my social media presence and Sylvie just borrowed my last brain cell telling me her ayahuasca story again. Anyway, how's home? How's Birdie?"

Emma felt an ache in her chest; she wished her wife were here now so she could lay her head on Rachel's lap and feel the thrum of her energy. Smell the bergamot lotion on her skin. She no longer felt like telling her about the visit from the police. It suddenly felt like a waste of precious time to spend these minutes talking about anyone but themselves.

"I miss you," she said, her voice breaking.

"What's wrong?"

"Isn't that enough?" Emma wiped her nose on the back of her hand. "I just miss you."

"I miss you too, baby." Rachel sighed. "Just two more days."

"Want to run through your acceptance speech for tomorrow? Since you're obviously going to win? I was thinking you should say something about how you couldn't have written such an amazing book without being grounded by an extremely average wife."

Rachel laughed. "Shut up."

"You're writing it down, aren't you?"

"No! And I'm laughing because you're funny, not because you're average. You're—" Rachel paused. "Emma, you're absolutely the most exceptional person on this planet."

This cheered Emma up. She lay back on the air mattress and stretched, feeling the tension in her muscles pull and release. It was nice to have all of Rachel's attention again. It made Emma feel like being confessional. "Since you're going to find out soon anyway, I might as well tell you now. I got in some trouble at work."

"What happened?"

"Remember how I told Alex his abortion paper needed revisions? His *B-plus* abortion paper, just to remind you how generous I am. How equitable, et cetera."

"I remember."

"Okay. And then he did the whole Proposition 8

song and dance in front of the class. And I told him he couldn't submit that topic."

"Right."

"Well, he spun it into a formal grievance against me. Paulie and Lisa told me I had to apologize and accept an anti-gay paper or they'd fire me."

"*Fire* you?"

"Well, yeah, that was the implication."

"Well. At least it's an easy choice. I mean, they didn't say you had to give it an A, did they? So dock a few points for not following the syllabus and move on."

Emma tugged at the drawstring on her hoodie. She had anticipated this response. Anytime she faced a challenge that felt insurmountable, Rachel could collapse it into a nonissue with a single stroke of logic. But while Emma had had a few moments of near regret the past few days over refusing the paper, she had replayed the meeting in her head over and over and each time stood by her decision. And the longer she went without hearing from Paulie and Lisa, the more confident she felt. She might not even lose her job. The optics of firing a gay faculty member for refusing an anti-gay paper were not great for Boon.

"You accepted the paper, right?" Rachel said. She sounded so confident that Emma had chosen the high road. Emma felt a flash of pity for her wife, who rarely was this oblivious. She couldn't bring herself to tell the truth.

"What, do you think I want to lose my job?"

"Oh, honey." Rachel's voice came through with a sudden fullness. Emma imagined her in the foyer of a restaurant, a finger in her ear, the cold outside air making her shiver each time someone opened the door. "I'm sorry you're dealing with all this drama and I'm not there. Do you want me to come home?"

Emma felt a stir of hope. "Would you?"

The briefest moment of silence. It could have been Rachel stepping aside to let a couple in, or simply a delay in the phone connection. But under the weight of the question, Emma felt as if Rachel waited a beat too long.

"Sure," Rachel said. "I can ask about changing my flight."

"Lady, I was just joking. You can't miss accepting the Luminary, which you are most definitely going to win."

"Yeah, maybe."

"One hundred percent."

"I am looking forward to coming home, though."

"Me too."

A pause. "Maybe we can open a bottle of wine when I'm back and have a proper conversation about what's next for us."

"What do you mean?" Emma asked.

"Hey, I have to go. Sylvie's waving at me from the table—our food's here—but I just want to say, I feel like it's time for our next big adventure. Don't you?"

"I do," Emma whispered.

"I thought so. I love you. I'll see you soon, okay? Good things are coming our way, baby."

Emma listened until after the phone was silent, after Rachel had disappeared back into a world lined with hotel pools and fifteen-dollar appetizers. She didn't even mind that the conversation had been cut short because she could still hear Rachel's last words echoing.

Good things are coming our way. A baby.

Emma didn't set the phone down after she hung up. She went right to her contacts and scrolled to Dr. Rivera's office. When Julie answered, Emma said, "I changed my mind. I want to do the transfer tomorrow."

"Oh," said Julie, surprised. "Are you sure?"

"It's not too late, is it?"

"Let me check. Can you hold for a minute?"

"Yes." Emma closed her eyes and lay back on the air mattress. In the darkness behind her eyelids she saw the roots of the butterfly bush again, tangled and labyrinthine. A transfer tomorrow would mean, if all went well, an August baby. Maternity leave would free her from the shackles of another fall semester. That is, if she still had a job. And if she didn't have a job? A baby would be a sort of redemption, a symbol of starting over. She could apply for an office gig, lose herself in the comforting mediocrity of file folders and breakroom birthday cakes. And she could write. She would.

She would spend the whole pregnancy writing, and when the baby came, her new project would be born alongside. It wasn't the craziest thing. Was it? She had already taken the medicine; she couldn't help but see it as a sign.

"Emma?"

"Yes?" Emma snapped her eyes open and sat up.

"You'll need to be here by ten tomorrow morning."

A feeling, cool and expansive, filled Emma's chest. "Thank you," she said.

"Oh, and Emma? Drink three to four glasses of water, starting at nine. You'll want your bladder full to push your uterus down and make the transfer go more smoothly."

"I will do exactly that," Emma said, and hung up.

CHAPTER 10

Charlotte woke up before the sun and got dressed. Clean underwear and socks. Jeans and a sweatshirt with the university's emblem on it, which Dirk had received as his ten-year employment award. When Charlotte pulled it on, she felt as if she were arming herself with the softest parts of Dirk, his optimism and patience. Things she'd need today.

Charlotte ran her fingers through her hair. While she brushed her teeth, she did ten squats and ten leg lifts, each time placing her foot down gently. She'd learned to be so silent, even her toothbrush made no noise with her lips wrapped around it. She swallowed her toothpaste. Slid the last of her cash—a crisp fifty-dollar bill—into her pocket.

She was tired after a night spent worrying that Dirk would wake up again. She'd placed a tablet of nitroglycerin in a sandwich bag under her pillow, just in case. Every time he shifted in his sleep Charlotte jerked awake, ready to grab him. But she hadn't needed the pill; Dirk had slept through the night starfished on the mattress, his mouth open like a baby bird's waiting to be fed.

Dirk had told her to wake him up when she left for the pharmacy, but they both knew she wouldn't. Their argument yesterday still hung in the air, making it hard to know what to say. And she wouldn't be able to handle the worry in Dirk's eyebrows; she might change her mind if she felt his fingers touch her cheek in goodbye. So she patted his sleeping face, his beard stiff and warm, and laid out a granola bar and some raisins.

"I'll be back before you're even up," she whispered.

She swung her purse over her shoulder and picked up her shoes. She listened for a full minute before beginning her descent in her thick wool socks. The service door with its faulty lock loomed before her. She put her hand on the knob and paused. The garage smelled odd, of bad cooking, perhaps, something fishy and pungent. The odor was sharp and alive, blanketing the air around her. Charlotte held her breath as she opened the door with a gentle pull.

And then she was outside.

The morning cold was a shock to her system,

especially without her shoes on. Charlotte speed-walked around the house and across the lawn, which shone in the moonlight still; she hardly stopped for the jolt of grief at the sight of the spireas, which had not been pruned and had begun to sulk under the weight of an early frost. Her joints cried out in surprise from her quick movements, but Charlotte did not stop, so alarmed was she by the immensity of the outdoors under a big sky, so empty and alive. She felt the chill of the grass dampen her socks and then the gravel on the road press sharply against her bunions, but she did not stop until she reached the end of the block, where there was no streetlight and she could pull her shoes on. She realized how comfortable she'd become being hidden, that the thought of moving into the street where she'd be exposed by the lights made her anxious.

Their car was still parked on Tulane Avenue, a dead-end street three blocks down, in front of an apartment complex with high turnover. It was covered with bird droppings but otherwise intact. She'd known the car would be safe there for as long as they needed to leave it, because the cops in the neighborhood didn't care about abandoned vehicles; they didn't even bother to boot them. Charlotte knew because she'd called to complain about a few herself over the years — vagrants, car camping for the spring — and nothing ever came of it.

She climbed into the car and saw that everything

was as they had left it. A handful of change in the cup holder, brown paper bags full of impractical shoes and silverware and other useless pieces of their lives tucked along the floor. It was a jolt to see the crumpled hamburger wrapper on the passenger seat, evidence of the last thing Dirk ate before they went to the attic. She remembered he was angry they'd left the pickles on, and he'd stuffed them in the wrapper, where they were still emitting a sour, vinegary smell.

The engine gave a brief complaint as Charlotte turned her key, clearing its throat before roaring to life. She was lucky, she realized now, that the car started at all after sitting unused for so many weeks. It felt like a good sign, and she allowed a small tremble of hope to pool in her chest as she eased the car out into the morning. What freedom, her hands on the wheel, the road unspooling in front of her.

*　　　　　*　　　　　*

The pharmacy opened at seven o'clock. As soon as Charlotte saw the clerk unlock the door, she got out of the car and marched in, the automatic doors shrugging open and pulling her into the bright fluorescent lights. The clerk gave her a disinterested smile as she pecked at the register. The boy who ran the photo department pushed a broom across the floor with one hand and held a Starbucks cup with the other. Charlotte never realized how much she had taken for granted the presence of other people before. So many times in her life she'd moved around in a sea of them, buying things, pumping gas, thumbing through books in the library, never once considering that she was any different than they were; other people, it seemed, were just an extension of herself, a part of her environment that wasn't very interesting. But now, as she picked up a shopping basket and wrapped her fingers around its chipped plastic handle, she felt separate from all of them, as if she had been dropped in from another world. She took Dirk's pill bottle to the back, where a pharmacist who looked younger than seemed possible told her it would be at least fifteen minutes.

Steering herself through the aisles, Charlotte felt overly aware of her rumpled shirt and the white stripe of hair at her roots, which beamed in the reflective security mirrors on the ceiling. The smell of the attic, musty and woodsy, clung to her. She heard the beep of the little gun the clerk was using to check prices. The chime of the door announcing another customer. A murmur of pre-coffee voices from the pharmacy window, the clatter of pills in a bottle.

Then she turned a corner and found herself in the aisle of children's things. Nerf guns and off-brand clay and card games and painting books where the colors appeared after you smeared a brush with just water on them. It was the brightest aisle, and the widest, as if the store knew that this was where people would gather, where the towering racks of stuffed animals and half-price plastic cars offered themselves like the arms of a mother. Charlotte had always tried to steer Justin away from these aisles. Otherwise he would swat pinwheels off the shelves and peel stickers from their sheets while Charlotte, never strong enough, would pull at his arm and apologize to other parents, who glowered at her as if she were the one causing the destruction. Standing there now in the sea of neon colors and bleating toys, Charlotte had a sudden understanding that Justin hadn't been behaving badly for the sake of naughtiness, as she'd assumed. He'd been overstimulated by the too-muchness of all of it. She felt the same way right now, an urge to knock down a display of plastic rattlesnakes tingling her fingertips.

"Charlotte?" A voice came from behind her, snapping Charlotte out of her reverie.

It was Debra Brewer, looking very urbane in a gray blazer and wispy white hair, long for a woman their age. "I thought that was you," Debra said. She was holding her own pharmacy bag, folded crisply at the top, and a packaged mascara. "It's funny, too, because I was just thinking about you this morning. I mean, you crossed my mind. Isn't that funny?"

The shock of seeing Debra settled like a cold wave under Charlotte's skin. It was surreal to see someone she knew, though Debra had just been a minor character in Charlotte and Dirk's life, the chatty parent of another kid in Justin's class, a girl named Kelsey who half-heartedly invited him to a handful of birthday parties. Even more shocking was the world Debra seemed to have stepped out of, a world that appeared to be teeming with hot showers, full breakfasts, lipstick.

"Oh." Charlotte patted her hair, which she felt had half escaped from its clip. "That is funny."

"It's like we're psychically connected, you think?"

"Well. That makes it sound like I'd thought of you too, though."

Debra laughed at this and pointed behind her to a sullen boy of about nineteen or twenty wearing a collared golf shirt, his neck dipped to read a text on his phone. "You remember my younger son, Alex." When he didn't look up, she snapped her fingers close to his face. "Don't be rude, Alex."

The boy looked up from his phone and nodded at Charlotte. "Hey." His hair was parted on the side, with a gentle wave where he'd combed in some type of mousse or gel. Clean face, freshly shaved. Charlotte's throat pinched; at that age, Justin would never have emerged in public looking so put together this early in the morning.

Debra sighed. "I'm certainly glad we bought you that phone so you could ignore all of us."

The boy dipped his head back down again and Charlotte had a flashing memory: Debra getting pregnant in her forties, when Kelsey was already in high school with Justin. It had been something of a scandal among the other mothers, who felt that the window for such endeavors had long closed. And who would help her with a baby? Debra's husband, Randy, traveled most of the year for some political job and never came to school events or dropped the kids off at birthday parties. Debra herself had been chastened by the pregnancy, flushed with resentment as she waddled the length of the gym to find a seat at basketball games. "If it weren't for Randy," Charlotte overheard her say once, "I wouldn't be going through with it at all. But when you marry a man of principles, you rise to meet him."

Oh, yes, Charlotte thought now. *That's why I don't like you.*

"We're running some early errands before Alex's golf match, trying to keep the house quiet," Debra said. "Randy's resting from his hip replacement, and Kelsey and her husband, Tanner, are visiting to help keep an eye on him. Did you know she's pregnant again? She's got that second-trimester exhaustion, and I just said, 'I remember those days! You stay here and sleep, dear.'"

"Congratulations," said Charlotte.

"Her husband's a real estate investor. Things are going well for them. And actually"—Debra dropped her voice and moved a bit closer; Charlotte couldn't decide whether to step away from the onslaught of rose perfume or lean in so she could hear—"actually, they just bought us a house. Can you believe it? We're moving out to Middletown this fall once Randy's hip is better. It's a new construction."

"His hip is?"

Debra threw her head back and laughed with a force that made Charlotte wonder who it was for. "No, but I love that. The house is a new construction. There's a whole development going up over there. We'll be on about three acres."

"That's a big piece of land." Charlotte stole a glance at the pharmacy. She could see the back of the pharmacist's white coat as she bent over a counter. Hopefully filling Dirk's prescription, counting the pills to make sure they were all there.

"Kelsey insisted. She sat us down and said, 'Mom, Dad, you helped me through law school, and now it's time for me to pay you back.' She knew we'd talked about wanting a country house years ago, something with a wraparound porch. I can't believe she remembered that." Breathless, Debra looked at Alex. "It's a good thing we've got Kelsey and Tanner to help, because you wouldn't believe the cost of tuition these days when you don't get a scholarship."

Alex didn't look up from his phone, but a little shadow appeared at his jaw, as if he were biting down on something hard.

"Well," said Charlotte. "Lots of fresh air out there in Middletown."

"But how are you, Charlotte?" Debra lowered her voice again. "Have you heard from Justin lately?"

"Of course." Charlotte was annoyed by the implication that she and her son were estranged, however true it was. "He's getting married, you know. Amy—his fiancée—is a nurse. And an excellent cook. You'd die if you tried her apple crisp."

Debra clasped her hands together near her heart, an inflated gesture of gratitude on Charlotte's behalf. "I'm *so* glad to hear that. He's getting better, then?"

Charlotte looked at Debra's lower lip and thought of the slugs that left trails of slime on the sidewalks after rain. "Well, Debra, in my view, there was never anything wrong with him."

"Of course. You're his mother, after all." Debra ran a finger under her bangs, pressing them back into shape. "Well. We think of you all the time, Randy and I."

"What a kindness," Charlotte said. "Thank you *so* much for that."

*　*　*

Picking up the prescription was simple; the pharmacist handed her the paper bag without making eye contact. Charlotte had harbored a private fear that something about her situation would be exposed in this transaction—would they ask her to verify her address again? Ask for a utility bill to prove where she lived?—but she was invisible to the pharmacist and the rest of the staff, who either didn't care who was accepting the medicine they'd packaged or simply wanted Charlotte and her dusty sweatshirt to leave.

The parking lot was where Charlotte's luck ran out. The car wouldn't start. The engine gave no indication that it had another trip left in it; when she turned the key, it moaned at first, then simply clicked. She tried not to curse often — she could never shake its rudeness, even in private — but Charlotte tightened her stranglehold on the steering wheel and howled a great, monstrous *"Shit."*

A tap at her window. Debra, her head cocked in concern. "Car trouble?" she asked as Charlotte opened the door. "Can I help?"

"I don't suppose you have jumper cables?"

Debra looked at her Lincoln where it idled. "Do you know how to use them? I doubt my son could figure it out."

Charlotte let out a long, stale breath. "No. Dirk always takes care of those things."

"You'd better call him, then. Want to use my phone?"

"No. I mean — " Charlotte hesitated. "It's just, he's sick in bed today."

"Well, why don't I give you a ride home? Then you and Dirk can come back later when he's feeling better and he can get you fixed up."

"That's really not necessary."

"Or I could call Tanner and have him come do the jumper cables." Debra squinted. "But it is awfully early."

"No, no." Charlotte looked at the dashboard of the old car, which only an hour earlier had greeted her like an old friend; now its dials and knobs glowed with betrayal. "I suppose the best thing would be for you to give me a ride. If you don't mind."

In the car, Debra shooed Alex to the back seat and turned the heat up high. She was teeming with self-congratulatory energy, doing her charity work for the day. Charlotte clutched the paper prescription bag. She wondered if her personal body odors were as obvious to Debra and Alex as they were to her. The syrupy morning sun drove straight into her eyes, and when she flipped the visor down to block it, she saw her reflection in the mirror. No wonder Debra had such pity in her voice.

"You know what I was thinking about recently," said Debra. She was wearing wide sunglasses, the kind that bent around her temples to prevent wrinkles. "Remember how you had the knitting club at the school for a while?"

Charlotte looked out the window at Riverbend rolling past like a film: the enormous concrete Meijer where she never shopped; the Toyota dealership with its rows of shining cars waiting like puppies in a pet-store window; steak houses and gas stations and American flags and a sky that held it all to its massive bosom. Charlotte wished Debra wouldn't talk. She didn't want to think about the knitting club. She wanted to lean her head on the window to watch the city, but she refrained, knowing her head would leave a grease spot on the glass.

"Do you remember that?" Debra asked again. "The knitting club?"

"Of course I remember." The knitting club had started when Charlotte volunteered for a classroom demonstration during Craft Week when Justin was in the sixth grade. She had wanted to see Justin in a different element; she knew very little about what happened during the hours he was at school. Each morning he left with his backpack tight against his shoulder blades, his hands working methodically to rotate a piece of toast around so that he could eat the crust first. In the afternoons Justin would return dragging the backpack on the grass, looking as if someone had plunged the life force from his body. This was at the beginning of his change, when he'd gone dark like someone had pulled a light chain inside of him.

And so when there was a call for volunteers to demonstrate a skill during Craft Week, it seemed like an opportunity to dip into his world like a paintbrush. She'd hauled a garbage bag of yarn scraps to the school and shown them how to do the garter stitch on the overhead projector, her hands enlarged monsters, every hangnail magnified on the screen at the front of the classroom. The students, each supplied with a plastic set of knitting needles donated by a local sewing-supplies store, sat obediently clicking away at their desks.

She'd regretted the whole thing almost instantly. It was painful to see Justin in the context of twenty-two other children. She hadn't realized how much other kids' eyes lit up when they spoke, how they would fling their hands in the air when they had something to share, which was often, reaching their arms so high, they would lift the sides of their bottoms off the chairs. How they wanted so badly to laugh that they were primed for it, for any moment that could be slightly funny, so they could throw their heads back and howl. They were like a garden of sunflowers craning their necks toward light.

Justin did not raise his hand. Nor did he knit. He only leaned against his elbows on his desk as if he hadn't slept. Worse, he was invisible to the other children, who didn't look at him as they giggled conspiratorially at the teacher's soft snoring in the corner. When the class passed around the basket of skeins and needles, the girl next to Justin slid it on his desk without looking at him, as if she were simply dropping a letter in a mailbox.

It physically hurt, somewhere deep in Charlotte's body, to see her son in this world. It would have been easier to see that he was prone to despondency and anger only at home, that he saved his best self for school. But watching him in the classroom, she felt embarrassed on his behalf. And as she walked around checking on the students' work, she knew his small eyes were looking right under her skin and seeing her shame.

She'd expected the knitting demonstration to go no further than that afternoon in the classroom. But a few days later, Justin's teacher called and said that the other kids had been asking when she'd come back. So every Friday afternoon after the kids had recess, Charlotte would drive to the school and pull the skeins out of the classroom closet where she kept them. She even began to enjoy it. She would walk around the classroom with her hands behind her back, pretending to inhabit an alternate life, one in which she'd become a teacher.

When summer came, knitting club continued at Charlotte's house. On Saturday mornings, ten or so kids would arrive, with their own skeins and bags this time, and spread their work on the dining table. She demonstrated knitting in the round and the rib stitch with its satisfyingly stretchy columns. They moved on from pot holders and scarves to hats and socks. And while their needles clacked, they talked—the kids did, that is—about television shows and magic tricks and basketball scores and whether certain kids in their class had held hands or kissed yet (at this, they lifted their eyes to Charlotte, where she sat working on sweaters for Justin and Dirk and pretended not to hear). Sometimes they asked Charlotte for help counting stitches or unraveling a mistake, and when she patted their backs in encouragement and they smiled at her, she felt sick with longing for something she couldn't name. Even Debra's daughter, Kelsey, came a few times, her hair in a tight ponytail with ribbons, her politeness strained through a sieve.

Justin never appeared for these meetings; he was always still sleeping in his room. Yet years later, when he was in his late twenties, he blamed the knitting club for all his problems. He said it embarrassed him to have those kids over to his house. He said it was clear that Charlotte had been ashamed of him, and he'd sat in the classroom—and, later, his own room—listening to her instructions for knitting and growing sick with fury at the sound of her voice, the way she was performing a kind of sentimental motherhood for all these other children when she'd never had any patience for him his whole life, not once.

Charlotte told him he was looking for any excuse to blame others for the ways he'd suffered in life. She said he was always playing the victim, that he should take a look around the world at people who'd had truly difficult childhoods and come out of them without drug addiction and spite. Like who, Justin had asked. And she'd said righteously, "Oprah Winfrey!" Her voice was so loud that Dirk came in and put his hand on her shoulder, walked her out of the kitchen and into their bedroom. As soon as he'd deposited her on the edge of the bed, she looked up at him and whispered, "Oh, Dirkie, it's true what he said." And Dirk said that was nonsense, she shouldn't let him get into her head. But that was Dirk for you, a hopeless diplomat.

"I still have the pot holders Kelsey made," said Debra. "I even use them sometimes." She glanced at Charlotte, hunting for gratitude. Charlotte caught the look out of the corner of her eye but kept staring out the window, watching the businesses clear and the curbs flatten as they made their way toward her subdivision.

"Actually, *I* made those pot holders," Alex said from the back seat.

"What? You did not." Debra squinted in the rear-view mirror. "You weren't even born when knitting club was around."

"Kelsey's fell apart. Remember?" Alex leaned forward, his head between the women. Charlotte could smell his shampoo. "Then she was home on break from college and we were all snowed in and she showed me how to knit. It's not hard. So I made new ones for you for Christmas." He sat back in his seat. "Black and brown, to match the cat."

Debra was quiet for a moment. Then she burst into laughter. "So at six you had the coordination to make pot holders? When at twenty you can't even keep your swing out of the sand trap?"

"I guess I peaked at six, then," Alex said. Then he muttered something under his breath that Charlotte didn't quite hear. Debra didn't ask him to repeat it.

"You can just drop me here," Charlotte said.

"Don't be silly, we're so close. You still live in the same place, right? I remember because after I dropped Kelsey off, a few of us would take our magazines to Willow Park for an hour. None of the moms could get over the fact that you offered what was basically free babysitting on a Saturday."

Charlotte looked at the clock. It was already eight. The new people might be up by now, brewing their coffee. She might be able to slip in the garage from the back, through the service door with its broken lock. But it would probably be safer to hide nearby, perhaps behind the church down the road, until she saw their car leave for work. "I really don't mind. If you drop me here, I can walk. It's good for my heart."

Debra laughed as if this were a terrific joke. "I'm not going to drop you off like some vagrant, Charlotte. We're almost there anyway." Debra turned down Willabee Drive. Charlotte's heart was slamming in her chest. She twisted the paper prescription bag so hard, it tore under the sweat of her hands. But when Debra pulled up in front of the house, she let out a breath of relief: The car was not in the driveway. The new people were gone already. Next door, Patty's shades were drawn, the windows dark. Ever since Rob died she liked to sleep late, and when she woke up she often stayed in bed playing a game on her phone until she got hungry.

Debra shifted the car into park. "Alex, make yourself useful and walk Charlotte to her door."

Charlotte shook her head. "Oh, that's not necessary at all. I can—" But Alex was already out, eager for an excuse to escape. Charlotte opened her door, and he swiveled his hips neatly to avoid being hit.

"Wait, Charlotte." Debra touched Charlotte's hand, her fingers cold despite the heat blasting in the car. "I just want to say that I'm really glad things worked out for you. Some of us were worried about you over the years. I know things were hard with Justin, and with only one income, I'm sure money was a struggle. But you've always managed to persevere. It's inspiring, really."

"All right," said Charlotte, putting one foot out the door.

"But I have to ask you, Charlotte—" Debra tightened her grip on Charlotte's hand. "Are things okay at home? You're looking a little—how do I put this? I mean this kindly, but—" She scrunched her face in preemptive apology. "You look like you could use a spa day. Joanne at Salon Delphinium works miracles with color touch-ups. She's always booked out, but I'm sure if I called and said it was an emergency, she'd move things around."

If Alex hadn't been listening next to her, Charlotte would have given a short laugh and said no, she was fine, and gotten out of the car just to be done with the conversation. But she thought, with sudden conviction, that it was important for the boy to hear an outside perspective on his mother. Charlotte herself certainly would have appreciated a grown-up offering a different view of her mother when she was young, someone who said, *Wow, you're right, kiddo, this is crazy.*

"Is your life so totally empty, Debra, that the only pleasure you get is from humiliating other people?" Charlotte asked.

Debra's chin pulled back in surprise. The lines on her neck suddenly appeared like rings on an old tree. "Excuse me?"

"I'm the one who should be inspired, really," Charlotte went on, feeling the thrill of her words. The anger that had built up over the past few weeks found its way to her tongue and her teeth, which tingled with energy as she spat the words out. "The way you've always managed to convince other people of your superiority. It's impressive. A party trick, almost. But I have bad news." Here Charlotte pulled her face in exaggerated pity. "The trick has stopped working. You're just an invisible old woman like the rest of us. And I might not look in the mirror as often as you do, but at least when I do, I can live with what I see."

An unattractive noise escaped Debra's lips. She

leaned over Charlotte and snapped her fingers at her son. "Alex, get back in the car."

Alex opened the back door. As Charlotte peeled herself ungracefully from the leather seat and hoisted herself out, her face met Alex's for a moment by the roof of the car. He was tall enough to blot the sun, and for a moment he was only a shadow with an arc of smooth hair. But Charlotte thought she could see the shape of a smile. She squinted against the light and smiled back.

"Don't listen to my mother," Alex said. Then he leaned down—was he going to hug her? No. He stopped just inches from her face. Charlotte blinked and saw that she'd been wrong—it wasn't a smile but a smirk. "I think we both know you're more of a Great Clips girl," he whispered. Then he straightened and shut the back door. "I'll get up front, actually, if you'll excuse me."

Charlotte was struck with regret for ever comparing Alex to Justin. Her son might not have ever woken up and put on a clean shirt to run errands with his mother, but she would take a thousand of Justin's fits of anger over one more second of this kid's arrogance.

"You're excused," she told him, and shut her door just as he reached for it.

Charlotte felt electric with satisfaction as she walked toward the house, pretending to dig through her pocket for a key. At the porch, she turned. The car still idled at the curb. Debra was on her cell phone, no doubt informing Randy about the drama that had just unfolded. Alex was fiddling with the radio buttons. As Debra spoke, her eyes lifted to Charlotte. Charlotte stared back, her hand on the doorknob. She kept staring until Debra finally eased her car silently down the street and back to her own house.

Charlotte let out a breath and stepped off the porch.

"Can I help you?"

The door had opened. One of the girls was standing there, the door held back with her hip, phone in her hand. She was the frumpy one from the photograph, and though she looked nicer in person, with clear skin and a well-fitting sweater, she seemed flustered, her eyes distracted. The misery was abundant on her face. Charlotte could have been looking at a picture of herself from years ago, really. The feeling of recognition and pity was so strong that Charlotte briefly forgot that this was a dangerous moment, one that could spell a lot of trouble for her.

"Can I help you?" the girl repeated. Then, inexplicably, her voice softened and she said, "Sorry."

Confused, Charlotte touched her own cheek, felt the dryness of her skin. What was she apologizing for? The girl was looking at her as if Charlotte were a lost soul. A helpless, abandoned old lady.

A lady with dementia.

"Oh, dear. I thought this was my house," Charlotte said feebly. "I get confused sometimes."

The girl frowned. "I saw someone drop you off."

"Oh. Yes. I think I gave her the wrong address. It was a mistake."

"Why didn't she know where you lived?" The girl wasn't looking at Charlotte but behind her, where Debra's Lincoln had idled just a minute before. "She just drove off and left you?"

"I'll be going. My house is just a couple blocks away."

"I'll go with you. Just let me get my coat."

"No, no. I'll be fine."

"To be honest, I could use—" A beeping noise interrupted the girl, and she glanced over her shoulder. "That's the kettle. I was just making tea. Come in for a second, will you? I'm Emma." She put a hand on Charlotte's arm, and Charlotte had no choice but to let herself be guided through the door like a blind person. She'd felt from the moment she'd allowed herself into Debra's car that she'd lost control over the day. She was simply being swept along like a leaf caught in the wind. But Emma's hand on her arm was like an anchor, and without realizing it, Charlotte put her own hand on top.

Inside, the house was warm and expectant. The fishy smell was stronger here than it had been in the garage, competing with the aroma of baked goods. Charlotte's stomach growled; she'd eaten only a handful of nuts early that morning.

"I'm sorry about the smell," Emma said. "I've been thinking there might be a dead animal in the wall or something."

"It's not so bad." Charlotte kept her gaze low, sure that her eyes would betray her connection to the house if she looked around.

Emma seemed pained. "So you can smell it too?"

Charlotte struggled to find the right answer to this question. Emma saw the look of confusion on her face and held up her hand. "Don't worry about it. Cup of tea before I walk you home?"

Charlotte hesitated. How long had it been since she'd had a mug of hot tea? She used to brew chamomile in her mother's old kettle on cold afternoons when the snow outside filled the house with light. How pleasurable it had been to wrap her hands around a hot mug and sit in the living room—this room!—and listen to the quietness of the house nestled in the otherworldliness of winter. The thought was too enticing to resist. She'd have one cup and assure Emma she was back in her right mind. Ten minutes, max. Then she'd say a polite goodbye and walk down to the church parking lot on Greenleaf, sit on the steps for a half hour or so, and return discreetly through the backyard. She'd get through the service door and up to the attic before Dirk even finished his breakfast.

"Tea would be nice," Charlotte said. She sat on the futon, the little dog scuttling over to sniff her ankles. She bent over to scratch its head.

Emma disappeared into the kitchen and came back a few moments later with a tray holding two mugs of tea and a plate of chocolate chip cookies. "Aw," she said, setting the tray down on the coffee table. "Birdie likes you."

Charlotte picked up a cookie. It warmed her fingers; she imagined chocolate melting onto her skin, leaving sweet traces that she would rediscover later when she licked her finger to turn the page of her book. She broke the cookie in half, and when the girl bent over to scoop the little dog onto her lap, Charlotte pressed the other half in her pocket to take to Dirk. She picked up the hot mug and took a sip. Mint. She closed her eyes so the tears wouldn't show.

"You're lucky I was here," Emma said. "I'm normally not home now. I was leaving to go teach, but—" She looked at the phone, where it rested next to the plate of cookies. "The department head called to say they don't need me today."

"That's nice."

"Not exactly. You've caught me on a bit of a stressful day." Emma twisted her wedding ring around her finger. It caught the light and sparkled, making Charlotte think about her own diamond, tucked in a wooden jewelry box upstairs. The gold band was worn thin on the underside, its diamond sunk low in its prongs. Dirk had been so proud of the ring and the fact that he'd selected it on his own. It had never crossed his mind that the setting, with its high prongs, was completely impractical. It had snagged on Charlotte's clothing every day for the past forty-eight years and she'd never said a word. Her eyes felt warm now as she thought of this, of how much she loved her husband. She needed to go to him, now.

Charlotte set her mug down and stood. She picked up her pharmacy bag. "You've been very kind. But I'm feeling better now. I should get home to my husband."

"Wait. I said I'd walk you."

"That's not necessary."

"Don't be silly. It's the least I can do. Just hold on— I'm going to use the bathroom quick, and then we'll go." Emma disappeared around the hall corner. The bathroom door clicked shut.

Charlotte took three large steps and opened the front door. She stepped outside and then hesitated. It was getting colder, and she was only wearing Dirk's sweatshirt. Her plan to wait on the church steps until it felt safe to come back suddenly seemed foolish without a coat. Charlotte thought of Dirk above the garage, peeling the wrapper off his granola bar and looking at his watch. He'd be wondering where she was. He probably pictured her framed in a restaurant window, eating a hot breakfast and turning the pages of a newspaper like someone from a movie. Contemplating never returning to him, not after that argument they'd had.

Charlotte stepped back inside. She heard the toilet

flush. Without pausing to weigh the pros and cons, she crossed the room, opened the coat closet door, and closed herself inside. The smell of fish and cookies was replaced by the thick musty odor of an old house. She slipped behind the few hanging coats and boxes into the deep pocket of unused space that ran over the stairs leading to the basement. The odd, narrow depth of this closet was one of the quirks she loved about the house. It was where they kept the two plastic shopping bags full of wool caps and mittens and scarves to be dragged out when winter came, where she hid Dirk's birthday presents and the plastic Christmas tree in its soft cardboard sarcophagus. Justin had called it a spy tunnel and spent hours in its darkness with a flashlight and his comic books.

The closet now was dark and empty save for a few coats and boxes, which Charlotte sank behind. She pulled her knees to her chest and held her breath. She could hear the sink running, then footsteps. A moment of silence. Suddenly, the closet door opened.

Charlotte froze. She involuntarily held her breath, though she was at the end of an exhale, and as carbon dioxide built up in her blood, the panic swelled. Still, she didn't move as Emma reached her hand in and pulled out a jacket, leaving its hanger swinging wildly. After she shut the door and Charlotte was alone in the dark again, the metal hanger continued its dance, seemingly as rattled as Charlotte. She drew in a shaky breath, her heart pounding so hard she worried it was audible.

She leaned forward to listen, but there was only silence. She imagined the girl stepping outside, looking down the street. Confusion warping her face unattractively. Maybe she'd even gone down the street to look, assuming an old lady couldn't get very far in just a couple of minutes. Charlotte swallowed, thinking of the sip of warm water she'd had that morning up in the attic. A lifetime ago. She felt for the sack with Dirk's medicine and gave it a pat.

Hold on, Dirk, she thought. *Don't worry. I'm coming.*

A moment to escape had to present itself at some point. Maybe Emma would take the dog for a walk or fall asleep. And then Charlotte would open the closet and tiptoe out until she was finally — how funny, she'd almost called it home.

CHAPTER 11

It was the strangest thing. The old woman had just disappeared. Emma came out of the bathroom, and the front door was standing ajar, like the world had opened its mouth and swallowed her. Emma had grabbed her coat from the closet and walked to the edge of the front yard. She looked down the street. The morning air was sharp against her cheeks, the sky sullen and white. A teenager wearing no coat bounded down his front steps, backpack slapping, and leaped into a car that waited for him. The car jerked a U-turn and headed toward the high school, trailing exhaust and rap music. But no old lady.

She hadn't really been that old, when Emma thought about it, maybe sixty-five? She was probably still managing early symptoms of dementia, sporadic periods of confusion. Maybe she was trying to hide it from others, like an alcoholic storing bottles in a sock drawer. But there were signs that her family would surely pick up on soon, like the vaguely musty smell about her, as if she had been hasty about showering. Her skin was pale and free of makeup, giving her a ghostly effect, and her hair was loose and indignant, as if it had been pinned a certain way its whole life and was trying to decide where to fall now that no one was brushing it. Emma could feel that she was right about these things; her instincts felt as refined and clear as polished gems. The embryo nestled deep inside her had brought with it a sense of buoyant confidence that was unfamiliar yet trustworthy. And she decided, in this state of clarity, that the woman must have found her way home. Everything would be fine.

Yet as she stood on the grass, still tipped with morning frost, Emma felt a brief longing for the woman to come back. She needed to know that she was right; the world felt too undetermined, with too many possibilities. The woman had made it home and had not made it home. Emma was married and not married. Emma wasn't pregnant, but she was also not *not* pregnant. Everything was in a dusky in-between state, where it felt like something momentous was about to unfold.

At least, she thought ruefully, she had an answer about her job now.

She closed her eyes and tried to summon a good memory. The embryo transfer yesterday—which she'd had to squeeze in between classes—had been both less climactic and more meaningful than she'd expected. Dr. Rivera had turned the lights down low and played soft Debussy as she inserted the speculum—warm this time!—and eased the familiar catheter through Emma's cervix. Then a partition in the wall slid open and a hand reached through, holding a small vial. "The embryonic lab," Dr. Rivera explained when Emma crowed with surprise. "The little one stays in her incubator until we're ready. Minimizes any environmental stressors." She disappeared between Emma's legs. The nurse indicated that Emma should watch on the ultrasound screen as a small white line wove its way into her uterus. Then Dr. Rivera pressed the plunger, and a tiny, glowing bauble shot forward and came to rest.

"That's it," Dr. Rivera said, removing her tools from Emma's body. "The little one is home." She patted Emma's shoulder on the way out, her hand so warm and strong that for a moment Emma had wanted to grab and kiss it. The nurses wheeled the ultrasound screen from the room and left Emma to rest for ten minutes in the dim lights, "Clair de Lune" tinkling in the background. A part of her wished that Rachel was there to touch her forehead and fuss over the hospital gown, which had tangled while Emma's feet were in the stirrups. But mostly Emma was glad to be alone because she didn't want to speak. Rachel always wanted to talk things through; she would have wanted to know what Emma's cervix felt like, if the transfer had hurt or whether she felt like her bladder was going to burst. Instead Emma could place her attention completely on the warmth of possibility blooming inside her. Her embryo. Her one and only. She was almost sorry when the nurse appeared to tell her it was time to leave.

The whole lovely experience had left Emma in a state of dreamlike hope that had lasted all the way until this morning. She'd been pulling the sheet of cookies from the oven, one eye on the clock so she'd get to class on time, when her cell phone rang.

Lisa's voice was wet with pity as she said, "Emma. I'm glad to catch you. Look, I know this isn't the news you were hoping for, but——" and then Emma held the phone away from her ear so that Lisa's voice thinned and she caught only the heavy, inescapable words: *regret, effective immediately, unpaid.* Emma's eyes wandered over the kitchen counter, which she'd cleaned carefully in preparation for Rachel's return today. The toaster crumbs had been swept away, the dish towel folded over the faucet of the empty sparkling sink. She heard Lisa say, "We wanted to make sure we had someone to take over your classes for the remainder of the semester," just as Emma noticed a smudge on the window——and, beyond that, a car out front. An old woman got out as a younger person dipped in, taking her place. The woman strode purposefully toward Emma's front door, satisfaction curling her lips.

"Do you have any questions for me, Emma?" Lisa was asking.

No, Emma had no questions. She simply pressed the button to end the call. Then she'd gone to the front door.

Now Emma shivered as she stood outside looking for the woman. She needed to pick up Rachel from the airport in a few hours, and the unpleasant truth was that her good news was going to be spoiled by bad news. Maybe she should tell Rachel she'd been fired first, then soften the blow with the announcement that she was maybe, possibly, pregnant. Or would good news temper the bad? She could tell Rachel about the IVF first, then drop the bombshell about her job, letting it simply flash and disappear like a shadow at sunrise.

But there was no time to think about this because there was still the smell to deal with. Emma turned back and crossed the yard to her house. She'd spent last night cleaning out sink drains, blasting the bottom of trash cans with bleach spray, throwing even slightly suspicious food away. She'd walked through the house, her nose lifted like a dog's, sniffing the air to track down the odor's source. It was slightly stronger in the basement, potentially near the washer and dryer, but she still couldn't figure out where it was coming from. She'd had a fleeting hope that it was her imagination, an early sign of pregnancy hormones, but then the old woman had wrinkled her nose the moment she walked into the house, and Emma realized the simplest answer was true: Her house stank. Of course it did. There was always something wrong with this goddamned house.

Inside, Emma took off her coat. She hung it in the closet, buttoning the top button so it wouldn't slip off the hanger. Yesterday she had worked to curate a seamless and comfortable arrival for her wife. This morning she'd even moved aside the last of the furniture in the garage and fit their car in, a project they'd talked about but never gotten around to. It had been a challenge without a garage-door opener, but Emma had persevered, nearly throwing her shoulder out pulling the door along its squeaky track until it finally slammed shut with a louder-than-expected bang. Today it was especially important for things to be perfect because Rachel had lost the Luminary award. The author who'd won had fictionalized her own childhood in a Burmese refugee camp where she'd been disfigured by a drunken guard's knife. The audience gave her a standing ovation. As Emma watched the ceremony live-stream on her laptop, she caught a brief glimpse of Rachel sitting at a table in the ballroom, her blazer on her chair and her bare shoulders catching the red light of the chandeliers as she clapped. Rachel had said the award wasn't important, and Emma believed her, but she knew that Rachel was still embarrassed in the moment. Not for losing, but for being there at all.

Emma also knew that when she picked Rachel up, her wife's body would be soft with the relief of a safe landing, her bones loose and primed for good news. She would be weak with gratitude, full of desire for Emma and their solid, square house. It was the perfect time, really, to tell her that she might be pregnant. But if Emma's getting fired didn't spoil the mood, the smell would. It was too strong a metaphor for Emma's own incapabilities, a sign that she couldn't keep things running smoothly without Rachel. So she needed to hustle.

Emma found the box fan that sat dusty in the corner of the garage, holding it above her head and squeezing sideways around the car, which now took up the whole space. She brought the fan to the basement, where the smell was strongest, and looked around for somewhere to plug it in. There was only the crooked outlet, which she'd tried to use once to charge her phone, only to find that it didn't work. Or was that just the top socket? She nudged the plastic faceplate with her finger until it straightened, then plugged the fan into the bottom. To her surprise, the fan whirred to life, sending the pages of a stray *New Yorker* flapping like an agitated pigeon. She turned the fan's knob from LO to HI and pointed it toward the laundry room, hoping the circulation would push the smell out the dryer vent.

Then she took her laptop upstairs to the bedroom and searched *Why does my house stink.* The browser window populated with ads for home deodorizers, essential oil diffusers, candles, and deep cleaners. Beneath that was a tidy gallery of articles with a shared theme: "Seven Ways to Get the Old-House Smell Out"; "Moved Into an Older Home? Here's Why It Stinks"; "Smelly House? Mold Is the Likely Culprit." Emma was about to click on a recipe for homemade potpourri when she saw a forum thread near the bottom of the window. The title was "Evicted? Put Dead Fish in Vents as a Final FU!"

Emma clicked on the post and scanned. It was a funny story, actually: After being given two weeks to move out so the landlord could sell, ProfessorPizzaRolls43 left a parting gift of frozen pollack, seventy-five cents per fillet when purchased in a bag at Kroger, in each of the house's vents. The comments on the post vibrated with approval. Someone asked how to do it to a house they couldn't get inside of—their neighbors had a SOCIALISTS NOT WELCOME HERE sign in their yard—and the suggestions were as follows: *Dryer vent, my dude* (146 upvotes); *Would it work to pour fish juice along the windowsills?* (85 upvotes); and *Crawl space, you can shove literally anything in if you go at night* (14 upvotes).

Emma shuddered, remembering the story about the scorned Boon fraternity rushee who had done the same to a Greek house on campus. They'd had to evacuate the entire building, the smell was so bad. Then she stopped scrolling.

Was it possible? Could it be—

"Alex motherfucking Brewer," she said aloud.

She felt it all clicking into place. Emma had perhaps even given him the idea by assigning the story about the racist woman searching for the smell in her home. She thought of the oily fish he had eaten during their conference. The curl of hatred on his lip when she told him off after the meeting with Paulie and Lisa. Then, with great clarity—her ability to project was sharp today—she saw him walking in a black hoodie along the edge of her fence, cloaked in the darkness of the evening. A cooler in his gloved hand. Squatting along the back of the house, feeling for the dryer vent. Pulling frozen fish from the cooler and shoving them inside. It would take a day for the fish to thaw, another few hours for the smell to start seeping into the house. Working backward, she realized he could have done it right after she told him never to return to class again. Maybe he'd done it during last Friday's session, when she was pressing play on the movie. She saw the whole scenario so clearly in her mind that it hardened into a thing she was remembering rather than a thing she was imagining.

Emma closed the laptop, relieved to be certain about something. After nearly a semester of second-guessing everything she did, of being incapable of discerning when she was right and when she had simply gone too far to turn back, she finally had clarity about this one thing. Alex *was* messing with her. She found a pair of rubber cleaning gloves under the kitchen sink and snapped them on. She pulled a plastic shopping bag from the bundle of baggies they kept for Birdie's walks and grabbed a small flashlight from a drawer. Then she went out the back door.

The November air felt personal, almost vindictive, as it sliced through her thin shirt. Emma shivered and crouched down by the dryer vent. The ground seeped cold through the knees of her jeans. She opened the metal flap and felt a flash of disgust thinking of Alex being here, so close to her bedroom window, one hand on the brick as he probed the vent with the other. She hesitated, then reached inside with her gloved hand.

Nothing.

She turned on the flashlight, got flat on the ground, and shone it inside the small metal corridor. There was nothing there except a fluff of dryer lint, smelling of clean laundry.

Emma lay on the ground for a moment to examine her feelings about this. The lack of evidence did nothing to sway her conviction that Alex was somehow responsible; in fact, it made her angrier, as if this too—her looking in the wrong place, lying on the cold ground—had been part of his plan. It was cruel. Very Old Testament.

A flutter at the periphery of her vision made her glance up. A stray leaf, pushed along by the breeze, tumbled against the house's foundation until it landed at the hole where the butterfly bush had been. And then, as quietly as it had come, Emma's grasp of the world was gone. She didn't know why her house smelled bad any more than she knew why, of all the difficult people she'd met in her life, Alex Brewer was the one who'd ultimately gotten under her skin. Or why she'd pressed on with the IVF without talking to Rachel. Why was it so hard to do the right thing? Maybe it wasn't a child she wanted so much as a different version of herself.

She lay on the ground until the cold became unbearable. Shivering, she climbed to her feet and went back into the house. She pulled off the gloves and rounded the corner, where a figure stood by the front door.

Emma screamed.

"Jesus," said Rachel, pulling off her coat. "I didn't mean to scare you." Birdie bounded from Emma's side and danced around Rachel's ankles.

Emma put her hand to her chest. "What are you doing here? I was supposed to pick you up this afternoon."

"There was an opening on an earlier flight." Rachel knelt and rubbed Birdie's belly. "I wanted to surprise you."

"Well, obviously you did." Emma tried to laugh, putting her hand over her pounding heart. Rachel gave her an odd smile as she opened the closet door, and Emma felt a rush of panic. Did she look different? Could her wife already tell that something had changed? She moved her hand down to her belly.

But Rachel just asked, "What's that smell?" as she tugged off her coat.

"It's a long story." Emma expected Rachel to probe further, but she didn't seem to be listening. Her gaze was vague and unfocused as she pulled off her boots, like she was doing some calculation in her head. She put the coat and boots in the closet and turned back to Emma.

"It's been a long week, actually," Emma said.

"Yes, it has." Rachel finally opened her arms and Emma fell into them. She wrapped her arms around Rachel's waist and pressed her face into the side of her wife's neck, feeling the pulse of artery against eyelash.

"I'm sorry about the Luminary," said Emma. "Maybe they should call them the Gloominaries."

Rachel kissed Emma. "Myat deserved it. I'm just glad it's over." She pulled back and studied Emma's face. "Hey, what's wrong?"

"Nothing." Emma felt the largeness of her unspoken news crowding the room. Whereas before the tiny embryo had felt like a pocket of warmth tucked inside her body, now that Rachel was home, it had unleashed its presence in the house, pressing up against the windows and thickening the air. Her hands trembled. "Do you want tea?"

Rachel shook her head. "I had too much coffee on the plane." She picked up a stack of mail and went through it, slowly thumbing the envelopes. "What's this?" she asked, holding up the policeman's card.

"Oh. I forgot about that." Emma sat on the futon, suddenly tired. "Two cops showed up the other day asking if I knew where the old owners of this house were. Their son died."

Rachel sucked air between her teeth in sympathy. "How sad."

"I felt bad I couldn't help. Patty next door mentioned he was a drug addict. Hadn't been around much the past few years."

"Was it an overdose?"

"Probably." Emma shrugged. "I suggested they talk to Patty, but I don't think they'll get very far with her either."

Rachel dropped the mail back on the cabinet and joined Emma on the futon. They curled toward each other with their knees touching. Birdie sank happily into their shared lap. Emma decided: Start with the good news first. "It's been a long week without you," she said. "But I have something really incredible to tell you. Something you'll be excited about."

Her heart was racing. As they faced each other, Emma thought of their wedding day. How strange it had been to say such normal things with a feeling of anxiety underpinning everything. They said "I love you" every day, yet now there were people watching them do it, Rachel's mother snapping pictures and sobbing, as if these words suddenly meant something to other people too. Emma had felt, in that moment, that marriage was completely preposterous, a performance that soured what had come before.

"Actually, can you hold on a second?" Rachel took Emma's hands in hers. "I also have something good to tell you. And I'm sure mine is bigger, so I should go first before I explode."

Emma felt her wife's hands pressing into her knuckles with a desperation unlike Rachel. "I mean, I doubt that, but sure. Go ahead."

Rachel took a deep breath. "Let me start by saying that you were right."

"About what?"

"I mean, everything. But Riverbend specifically. It's not a good fit for us. I thought we could make it work, that it would just be a few years. But I see now that this move wasn't the right one."

This was a surprise. "Okay," Emma said.

"I know you've been unhappy," Rachel went on. "And I haven't helped. You were right when you said I've been distant lately. Busy all the time. I've been distracted by something."

"It's okay. The book award—"

"It's not that. Fuck the Luminary. I've been talking to the University of Chicago about a job."

Emma tilted her head as if she hadn't heard correctly. "I'm sorry, what?"

"One of their assistant professors in linguistics decided to leave suddenly. I think her husband wanted to be closer to his family in Singapore or something. Anyway, Mimi Wellwood, who chairs the program—you remember her, right? She was on that panel with me at MLA last year? Anyway, she called about a month ago and told me to send my CV."

"Why didn't you—"

"I didn't tell you because I didn't want to get your hopes up. But they called, and we did a phone interview Friday while I was in Seattle. I had to pay a grad student twenty bucks to borrow their library carrel for the call." Rachel smiled. "But it went well. This morning they called and offered me the job."

Emma's mouth dropped open. "You mean—"

"Yes. We're done here. We can go back to Chicago for the spring semester. I'm going to tell Paulie tomorrow."

Emma felt her wife's fingers tighten around her own. Rachel could be cute when she was nervous, and her anxiety usually had the opposite effect on Emma, who found that her own worries dissolved when tasked with comforting someone she loved. Yet now Emma felt caught off guard by the presence of good news. It seemed almost menacing, as if it were meant to trick her or take the place of her own. As if it weren't possible for two good things to happen at once.

"Wait, I forgot the best part," said Rachel. "There's an administrative opening in the Diversity and Equity office that Mimi says you should apply for. It's not a dream gig, but it's not teaching either. What do you think?"

Emma leaned back and let out a breath. How many times had she imagined a moment like this, in which Rachel gave in? She'd fantasized about the possibility of leaving Riverbend so much, it still hung in the realm of the imaginary, the absolutely impossible, and it felt disorienting now to touch the reality of the moment with Rachel so close to her she could smell her lavender hotel shampoo. Back to Chicago. That was what she wanted, wasn't it? The thing she'd longed for since the moment they'd walked into this house? So why didn't she feel happy?

"How long have you known about this?" she wanted to know.

Rachel blinked. "I mean, like I said, it was about a month ago that they asked for my—"

"You should have told me then."

"You would have gotten worked up and obsessive about it."

"That's not true."

"It is," Rachel insisted. "You're not good with waiting for answers. Like every month when we were trying to get pregnant. You peed on so many sticks and thought every little twinge was a sign."

But I'm not doing that now, Emma thought. What Rachel was saying had been true for a long time, but somehow in the space of a few days it had all changed. She hadn't been tempted to take a pregnancy test—it was still too early—and she had gotten good sleep, uninterrupted by worry. She'd even tapped out a few hundred words of a new story last night before bed.

"Why is it that you're always the one who makes the decisions?" Emma asked.

Rachel scoffed. "I'm not."

"I mean, you moved us to Riverbend. You decided I should go back to teaching. You were the one who decided we should have a baby in the first place. And now you're telling me we're moving back to Chicago."

"I didn't force you to do any of those things, Emma. They were choices we made together. And you've been saying you miss Chicago every day."

"Yes, but I want to choose something for myself." Emma bit her lip. It was the truest thing she'd said all day.

"I hear you. I know." Rachel took out her hair band and shook her curls loose. "I know I am probably the most paternalistic feminist on the planet. It's my core conflict. And you're right, I should have listened when you said you didn't want to have a baby."

"Well, that." Emma waved this off, wishing she hadn't added it to her list of grievances. "I mean, it just had never crossed my mind before you. Before us."

"No, I mean it. You had so much anxiety about the idea of becoming a mother, and I pushed it anyway. All because I was trying to fulfill some bougie fantasy of private education and catered birthday parties." She shook her head as if trying to dislodge an image that had nested there. "Maybe you were right all along."

"About what?"

"I mean, maybe your reluctance was more of an instinct."

"How so?"

Rachel cast her eyes around the room as if she were looking for the answer to Emma's question. "Like." She paused. "Not everyone's meant to be a mother. And that's not a bad thing."

Emma heard these words, but it didn't seem as though they entered through her ears. It was more like she had been dusted with them all over her body, and after a moment they settled under her skin, gritty and silt-like.

"Obviously I don't mean that in a critical way," Rachel said. "I just mean that you know yourself. And your first instinct was that it wasn't right. I didn't listen to that."

"That's true. You didn't." Emma was angry, though she found her head bobbing in agreement, remembering the way that Rachel had dismissed her fears. She thought back to one of their early conversations about parenthood. They'd been naked in bed in the quiet fog of post-lovemaking. Emma had laid her head on

Rachel's chest, listening to the slowing thunder of her heartbeat. It was an odd time to bring up children, but Rachel often got excited about the future after sex, as if orgasming expanded her notion of what was possible in life. She'd mentioned it a few times before, and Emma brushed it off, saying that she wasn't sure, they felt too young. But this time, as Rachel talked about family vacations and starting new traditions and evolving their vision of themselves to something bigger—a family, not just a couple—Emma felt open to being honest. She told Rachel the truth: That she wasn't sure she was capable of offering the nurturing and support a child deserved. That she worried about unintentionally re-creating the conditional love she'd experienced from her own parents. Rachel had listened, running her fingers lightly up and down Emma's back. Then Rachel told her that it would be all right. Her fears were normal, lots of people had those worries. But they would do it together, figure things out as they went. They had plenty of resources, including her own parents.

Odd that not once in her catalog of rebuttals did Rachel say, *Of course you'll be a wonderful mother.*

Now, as Emma faced her wife on the futon, she allowed herself to feel something that had perhaps been festering under the surface for a while: Rachel didn't believe in her. She loved her, of course, but did she really believe Emma was capable of motherhood? Of writing a book? Of cobbling together a rewarding and academically challenging career? And how much of Emma's self-doubt had been fed by Rachel's view of her? How different would things have been if she'd married someone else? The thought washed over her like a cold shock of water.

Emma looked at Rachel's face. She took it in—the earnest expression, the almost imperceptible tightness across her cheeks, dry skin from hours on the airplane. The terra-cotta mole next to her nose that Emma had found impossibly cute when they'd first met. Emma hadn't noticed the mole in months, maybe years now. It felt strange to know someone so intimately that they became invisible over time. The air grew thick around Emma's face. The smell in the house grew stronger, pressing itself into her eyes, nose.

Birdie leaped off the futon, her ears cocked. She barked.

"What is that smell?" Rachel looked up.

"I told you—"

"Not that." Emma saw her wife's face take on the light from the window; the sky, in her presence, was no longer blank but bright. Suddenly, Rachel's expression changed. Without warning, she was pulling Emma up from the couch, her grip urgent and strong, then yanking her toward the door. The kitchen, she noticed in a daze, was gray, as if a giant watercolor brush had dabbed it out, the colors blurred and muted.

Smoke.

CHAPTER 12

Charlotte's legs were asleep. She felt nothing below the knees; it was as if someone had come in and erased that part of her body. Her feet were gone, cast off into the depths of the floor that ran beneath like a dark ocean. Perhaps the rest of her would disappear too. The thighs that had always disappointed her, the soft middle that folded over the waistband of her pants. Bit by bit her parts would be wiped away until she was gone.

The girls had left the closet door open, so their voices easily found her where she sat behind jackets and cardboard boxes. Their words had gathered like a stench in the air and forced themselves inside her; there was no stopping them.

Justin was gone. Justin had died.

She had imagined this moment so many times over the years. Not on purpose; she would be doing something ordinary, like having her hair cut or checking the expiration on a carton of milk at the store, when the inevitability of her son's death would seize her in its cold, unforgiving hands. In her mind it was a phone call. From a hospital, perhaps. They would tell her that a friend dropped him off unconscious in front of the ER, then sped away. They would tell her that he'd never woken up, that it was the drugs, that he'd simply nodded off and never come back. She worried sometimes that her imagining his death was somehow contributing to its inevitability, that their lives were bound by invisible threads that still pulled at one another even when they were apart. So when the thought of his death came to her, she forced herself to imagine it away. He was alive; he was safe.

And never in their months in his room in the attic had the thought of Justin's death visited her. Instead she'd become certain he was coming to the door one day, and that was the image she held in her mind: His sneakers scuffing up the front step, his bag slung low on his shoulder as it had been when he was in grade school, a sliver of his pale wrist flashing from the cuff of his jacket as he raised his hand to the doorbell. Amy's hand rubbing his back to keep him calm.

The new people had continued to talk about him

for a minute, like his life was nothing more than a plot point in a book they'd read. Then they forgot about Justin entirely, turning the conversation to their own ridiculous problems, picking at their life's imperfect edges, their voices full of impatience for the future.

Charlotte felt a flare of anger under her skin as they spoke, but only briefly, an ignition unable to click to life. She could have burst out of the closet then. Let them see her. She could have pretended to wake from a long nap, a demented Goldilocks who thought she'd crawled into her own bed. Or she could have told them the truth—it wasn't any less bizarre, really—and then gone up and told Dirk to gather their things. The two of them could put their water bottles and their underpants and magazines and beef jerky into the bags they'd brought with them and march down the steps and out of the house, past the women who would probably only stare because when it came down to it, they were both too stupid and cowardly to do anything. And what did it matter anyway? There was no reason to stay in this house any longer. Their candle of hope had been snuffed out.

But Charlotte didn't move. She sat. She let their words continue to pelt her as the circulation in her legs gave out; the prickly feeling climbed into her thighs, the eraser moving higher and higher.

From within the hollowness inside her rose a memory: Justin, age fifteen. They were going through a car wash together, just the two of them, on their way home from a trip to Sears, where they had put a gas grill on layaway for Dirk's birthday. The salesman had been an old high-school classmate of Charlotte's, a boy named Kevin who was now a slick-haired store manager with a gold watch that revealed a slight green rectangle of skin when it slid up and down his wrist. Choosing a grill had been difficult in Kevin's presence. He had circled them like a wolf and wrapped his bony fingers around the handle of the Kenmore Elite, a stainless-steel monstrosity with wheels and four burners, lined with hooks for hanging unimaginable cooking apparatuses. The grill cost two hundred dollars more than the Kenmore Classic, which Kevin had tried to block with his massive body as he described the rotisserie capabilities of the Elite. The Classic was painted steel, he told her in a hushed tone, which was really only acceptable for filing cabinets that no one touched.

Charlotte had nearly given in to the pressure, but Justin—who had until that moment been silently brooding nearby on a display porch glider—came up to Kevin and said, "Are you deaf or do you just not listen to women? We want to buy the cheaper one." Charlotte braced for the mortification to flood her face, but it didn't. She wasn't embarrassed at all. In fact, she was proud in that moment that her son moved through the world without the veil of politeness that had always slowed her down. And when she signed the layaway slip and made the first payment at the desk, she caught a glimpse of Kevin straightening the grills on display, his shirt coming untucked with the effort, and she realized she should have seen his powerlessness from the beginning.

Afterward, they'd gone to the car wash because Dirk had mentioned the Chevrolet was dusty and they were in the mood to do nice things for Dirk. Charlotte had never driven through a car wash before and was confused when the man told her to put the car in neutral. He'd grown frustrated that she didn't understand, reaching his sweaty body into her window and pulling down the gear shifter himself. Charlotte had leaned away, pressing her shoulder into Justin's, which was shaking with silent laughter. She looked up at him and saw that he wasn't laughing at her in mockery but at the absurdity of the situation. He was happy.

When the man retreated, her car was grabbed by a conveyor belt, and it began to drive along without needing her. The feeling was so strange and exhilarating that she forgot to roll her window up, and when the pre-rinse came blasting down, it spurted directly into the car, pelting her pants and shoulder with warm water. Charlotte had shrieked, stamping her foot on the accelerator, which revved the engine. Justin had undone his seat belt and leaned over her, rolled up the window himself. Charlotte felt helpless, the wetness of her clothes making her angry, but when she turned to look at Justin, she saw only delight in his eyes. Despite her embarrassment, it really was a funny situation, wasn't it? They both howled with laughter, loosening up Charlotte's chest and throat in a way she hadn't felt in years. They were free and wild, two baby elephants trumpeting just to hear the delicious sound of it.

In the darkness of the car Charlotte had felt as though she'd been transported to another life, one in which her son was happy, and in those few minutes she saw that he did love her, that it was an inescapable fact of his life. She was his mother. The feeling made her indescribably happy. Then the car wash was over, their gleaming car pulled back into the sunlight, and the laughter died. Charlotte looked over and saw that Justin had closed up and something in him had darkened again. She had known it would happen. But she also knew that those moments in the car wash had been real. His joy with her hadn't been a symptom. It had simply been the raw aliveness of her son.

Charlotte could have sat like this forever, letting the closet erase her. She felt herself absorbing its darkness, felt it entering her skin and taking root. Her spine pressed against the wall, each vertebra grinding into the wood like a marble. She could stay. Push herself deeper into the wood until she became a part of it. Let the house swallow her, wrap her in its creaks and corners and impossible angles. Its terrible smells of old moisture and years of tired bodies and ghosts of cooked food, of something rotting away like fish, of smoke —

Charlotte opened her eyes, suddenly back in her body, which had registered a change in her environment like a deer sensing a predator. She shifted slightly, her legs howling in protest. The voices had stopped. The front door slammed. It was quiet, yet she could feel the presence of something moving in the house. It made her skin tingle with alertness, something primal.

Fire.

Her house was on fire.

CHAPTER 13

"We don't even have our coats," said Emma as Rachel pulled her outside. Birdie followed at their heels, pressing her nose against their ankles as if herding them. Then she tried to turn around and go back inside, scratching her nails on the door. Emma picked Birdie up and carried her to the edge of the lawn, shivering, while the dog barked into the afternoon chill, her attention fixed on the house.

"She's cold too," Emma said. "We should have at least grabbed a sweater."

She was still confused. Something was happening, and her mind would catch up to it any moment, but right now she was caught in yet another in-between state where she was reading the world like it was fiction.

The wind had calmed; tree branches sliced the sky like jagged blades. The mouths of driveways were lined with blue trash bins, emptied this morning. She felt a pang of guilt, realizing that she'd forgotten to wheel theirs out. Now they would have to wait another week, and each time Rachel put another bag in, she would be reminded that Emma had forgotten to do this one simple task.

Rachel was pacing the edge of the road, calling 911 and reporting a fire. Emma looked. There was no fire. There was only a house. White siding and peeling gray roof and sagging bushes. Seen from the curb, its crookedness was obvious. Emma often forgot, amid the new vinyl flooring and shiny fixtures and granite countertops, that this house was old. But out here, the house looked back at her honestly, tiredly. She saw how small the place was. How impossible it would ever be to fit their entire lives into a square.

Sirens began to wail in the distance. Curious neighbors, most of whom had only held up a palm in greeting when they saw Emma and Rachel—whether it meant *Hello* or *Don't come closer,* she was never sure—began to trickle from their homes and gather in the road. The older man from across the street, who wore shorts no matter how cold it was and spent hours hacking away at the bushes in front of his house, let out a low whistle. "Hope you got good insurance."

"We do," said Rachel.

Emma still didn't understand what they were looking at until she saw within the house a spark. A light. Flames.

"The house is on fire," she said out loud.

"No kidding," said the old man's wife. "How'd it happen?"

"I don't know," said Rachel. "We were just sitting there." She turned to Emma. "Did you leave something on the stove?"

Emma shook her head, her mouth open and silent.

A few other neighbors joined them; one handed Emma and Rachel fleece jackets, which they obediently put on. The crowd stared at the house like it was a television. Then, as the sirens grew louder, an impossible thing happened.

The front door opened.

Everyone watched as a woman—the old woman, Emma realized, the one who had been delivered to the wrong address—came bounding out. Smoke followed her, released like a hostage into the cold white sky. She ran like something was wrong with her legs, as if she were being pulled into motion without complying, running and tripping and stumbling straight to Emma—of all people—and she shouted, her eyes wet and feral, "Your car is blocking the door! I can't get to him!"

Emma stepped back. The woman had somehow found her way back to Emma's house? How had she gotten in? Birdie squirmed in Emma's arms, craned her neck to lick the woman's hands.

"Who are you? What were you doing in our house?" Rachel asked, her voice shrill with shock.

"She has memory issues," Emma said. "She was here earlier today." She turned to the woman. "Ma'am, this isn't your house. Remember? You don't need to worry about the car."

"This is my house," the woman said, now clutching Emma's arm, her hands hot. "We've been staying in the garage attic. But now you parked your car where I can't get to my husband."

Emma looked at Rachel, their faces mirrors of confusion.

"We don't have an attic, do we?" said Emma.

"Please." The woman pulled on Emma's arm. "I'm Charlotte Dennison. It was my son who died. I can't lose them both."

A sudden clarity came over Emma, and without thinking, she shoved Birdie into Rachel's arms and ran with Charlotte to the garage door. She heard, faintly, Rachel shouting her name in a bewildered voice as she tugged on the garage door. It wouldn't budge. As Charlotte wrung her hands beside her, Emma thought of the loud bang when the door had shut earlier.

"I think it's broken," she said.

Their eyes fell on the front door of the house, still open. Emma ran inside. The living room was filled with a cloud, wisps of white and gray rising from the floor. The futon where she and Rachel had sat just minutes before was slowly sinking into it.

"Over here." The woman pulled Emma through the haze and into the garage. There was less smoke here, the temperature lower, and Emma had the absurd thought that time was moving backward and the fire was receding into itself, sinking into the house like a frightened animal. Maybe this entire day could be reversed. Maybe everyone would have a do-over.

"The door is over here." Charlotte pointed to a shelf on the wall. "You need to move the car so we can open it."

Emma patted her pockets, bewildered. "I don't have the keys."

"Where are they?"

"I don't know! Somewhere in the house."

Charlotte turned and charged back into the house. Emma followed her into the smoke. She coughed, her lungs seized with a burning sensation. She covered her mouth with her arm and felt panic rising in her chest, realizing she couldn't get a normal breath. She thought of the path the smoke would take once it entered her nose: down her throat, into her lungs, and diffused into millions of cells, each of which would deliver its heat to different parts of her body. Her arms. Her stomach. Her uterus.

A hand on her arm. Then someone tugging her

back. Emma stumbled, trying to keep up. As she was dragged toward the front door, she caught one last glimpse of the horrid yellow cabinet and felt pity in her heart. If she anthropomorphized—and she did, even in crisis—the cabinet looked like a face, with knobs for eyes and the long bottom drawer a mouth pulled in resignation to its fate.

Outside the sky was sharp and clear, sheared by the tidy rooftops across the road. A fire truck and an ambulance were parked in the street, their lights flashing. Emma rubbed her eyes. The firefighter who'd pulled her out still had one hand on Emma's arm. The other one held firmly to the older woman, who was trying to squirm free. "Can you breathe?" the firefighter asked Emma.

Emma realized she had been holding her breath. She let it out and nodded. Beside her, Charlotte was yelling, "He's in there! I'll get him myself if you won't!" She wasn't strong enough to pull away from the firefighter, but she slapped at her hand anyway.

The firefighter held on firmly. "Not your job, ma'am." There was kindness in her voice. "Let the big boys get him."

Emma and Charlotte were taken to the ambulance. They sat on its bumper as a paramedic slipped oxygen masks over their faces and wrapped a silver blanket around their shoulders. Rachel was there, Birdie in her arms, tears streaking down her cheeks. Emma felt as if something between them had been severed; her mind prodded for the source of this feeling. Was it because she'd forgotten the trash bins? Then their conversation came back to her like a hot wind, the things Rachel had said and the things Emma had not, and she had to look away.

From next door Patty came bounding over, her heavy breasts swinging under a T-shirt, her feet encased in pink fur slippers. It struck Emma that Patty was much older than she'd originally thought, probably in her seventies. She saw it in the effort of her stride, the ways that life had pressed down upon her. Emma braced herself for a confrontation.

But when Patty arrived at the ambulance, breathless, the earthy smell of her own home clinging to her, she didn't even look at Emma. Instead she threw her arms around the older woman.

"Charlotte," Patty cried. "In all my born days!"

"Patty." Charlotte's voice cracked. "I'm sorry—" She started to pull off her oxygen mask, but Patty took her wrist firmly.

"Leave that on, dummy." She pressed the mask back on. "What the hell is going on?"

"Dirk is still in there," Charlotte cried. "They won't let me go in."

Patty clutched Charlotte to her chest like a child. "Of course not. Let the people in the protective suits go in."

Rachel and Emma looked at each other, the answers to their questions passing silently between them. Charlotte. The woman who had lost her house and then her son. And now maybe her husband. Rachel reached for Emma, but Emma pulled the silver blanket around her shoulders and stepped closer to the house, the plastic tube connecting her mask to the oxygen tank uncoiling at her feet.

She watched as two firefighters blasted water into the front windows. Two more hoisted a ladder and propped it against the wisteria climbing up the side of the garage. She watched as one of them took out a cordless saw and began to cut the vines, the high pitch of the tool slicing through the chatter of the growing crowd of neighbors. The firefighters tore through the vines, throwing them down to the lawn, where they gathered like snakes in the grass.

The first firefighter yanked a stubborn vine so hard that when it released, he nearly toppled off the ladder. And suddenly there was a window, and they were opening it, and—Emma felt like she was dreaming—they were pulling out an old man dressed in boxers and an undershirt. He wasn't moving; one firefighter cradled him like a baby, the old man's body pressed up against the ladder, and together they slid him down and placed him on a stretcher that waited beneath. Then medical personnel descended on him like flies, covering him with blankets as they wheeled the stretcher to the ambulance. Emma stepped aside to make room as one paramedic pressed a plastic mask over the man's face. Another squeezed a bag connected to it. They worked rhythmically as a third paramedic started an IV in the man's arm. Emma caught bits of their conversation: "Airway clear. Check for the seal." She heard one murmur, "Any improvement?" and saw the slight shake of another's head.

"What the fuck," Rachel whispered.

Charlotte pulled off her mask and strained to touch her husband, but Patty blocked her with a firm hug. "No," Patty said, putting the mask back over her friend's face. "It's better you don't see. Trust me."

"Move aside," called the paramedics as they collapsed the stretcher's metal legs and slid it inside the ambulance. Emma saw a flash of the man's shoulder, white as bone, slip from under the blanket.

"Is he alive?" Charlotte asked. Her face had sharpened with anguish; she seemed so fully aware of everything that was happening that Emma could hardly believe she'd thought the woman had dementia. "Oh, please tell me, is he alive?"

"He's alive," one said. "Give us room." He turned to the driver. "We're going to need to move fast on this one."

"Oh, Dirk!" cried Charlotte. "This is all my fault!"

"She's his wife," Patty told a paramedic. "Can she come with him?"

"Not on this vehicle. You can follow us to Midwest Regional. Emergency department." And with that, the paramedics slammed the door and the ambulance took off down the street, its sirens filling the neighborhood. Bystanders parted to let it through. Birdie threw her head back and howled.

"Pull yourself together," Patty said, holding Charlotte firmly. "I'll drive you."

"I can't lose them both," cried Charlotte, her face streaked with dirty tears. "Not both."

"Are you the homeowner?" A firefighter, a different one than the one who'd pulled Charlotte and Emma out of the house, stood before Charlotte, his yellow helmet clutched to his chest.

"Yes—I mean, no." Charlotte shook her head.

"We are, actually," said Emma, gesturing at Rachel.

"I'm going to be up-front with you," he said. "You're facing significant damage to the structure of your home, and some areas may be worse than others. We've got it under control now, though. We have a team in there checking to make sure there's no risk of flare-ups."

"How did this happen?" asked Rachel.

He nodded at the house. "We'll do an assessment, but I've been on this job for twenty-two years. This was an electrical fire. No doubt about it. Signs are all there: The burn pattern around electrical outlets in the front room. Melted fuse box. You got a Jacuzzi back there?"

"The hot tub?" Emma asked. "We never used it."

"Don't matter. I'd bet money the wiring coming from that thing's been trying to burn the place down for years."

Emma closed her eyes. She saw the gray cable beneath the butterfly bush, its frayed innards shining in the light.

"But it's more the smell," the fireman went on. "An electrical malfunction has that distinctive odor." He wrinkled his nose. "The chemicals in circuit breakers and wiring insulation overheat and it smells sort of like ammonia? Or dead fish?"

"I can't believe this is happening," Emma said. She pulled off the oxygen mask and felt the sting of the chilly air touch her lips.

"There's no easy way to say this," said the firefighter. "But you're facing a significant loss. Most of your furniture and belongings have been destroyed."

Emma almost laughed. The pod! The pod full of her things, which was due to arrive any day now, had circumnavigated this entire disaster.

"Can we go in?" asked Rachel.

"I'm afraid no one can enter this home until we do a complete safety check. We'll recommend a restoration company to help clear smoke and debris."

"How long will that take?"

"Weeks, maybe." He pulled his mouth together in sympathy. "Do you have somewhere to go?"

Emma could see that Rachel was flipping through a

mental list of reluctant possibilities—probably Natasha in modern lit, who lived with her husband and two young boys in a three-bedroom house; Rick the semiotics scholar, whose home Emma had never seen but that she assumed was sterile and unwelcoming; the Elizabethans, who perhaps lived together somewhere on a commune with chickens and solar panels. Was it normal to live somewhere for three months and have no real friends? No one who came to mind when they were in need? If they had their car, they could drive back to Chicago right now. But their car was gone too.

Then Patty stepped in. "Oh, for Pete's sake. They're coming to my house. The whole lot of 'em."

CHAPTER 14

The strangest thing about Patty's house was not that it was scrupulously neat, or that she had a taxidermied fish mounted on a board in the living room, or that it was chilly but filled with lamps, every single one on—although all these things were true—but that, propped up on her couch, legs crossed, was a body. At least, that was the word that came to Emma's mind. It was actually a set of men's clothing—jeans, a red flannel shirt, work boots—stuffed with newspaper. His head was one of those Styrofoam wig holders topped with a Hoosiers cap. On his face someone had taped a set of glasses and drawn crude lips, a nose, and eyes that were half closed, as if he were either falling asleep watching TV or slowly waking up to an unfamiliar world. Birdie approached the dummy hesitantly, taking a step forward and then back, stretching out her nose to sniff at his boots.

"That's Rob," Patty had said, and offered no further explanation. She'd herded Emma and Rachel and Charlotte into her house, then disappeared into a back room to find her purse so she could take Charlotte to the hospital. The fire trucks' lights still flashed outside, but the flames were gone; the first responders were wrapping yellow caution tape around the blackened home. Much of the siding was scorched, and a small section of the roof had collapsed, exposing tufts of pink insulation. Earlier, as Patty had led them all across the yard to her house, it had begun to snow, and the tiny white flakes fell on the destroyed home like salt on a wound.

The three women stood in the living room being silently appraised by Rob. Charlotte stood by a plant in an oversize pot wrapped in burlap near the front door, her small hands folded in front of her. She wore a sweatshirt three sizes too big, the neck so wide Emma could see the collars of two more shirts, each tinged with gray where they touched her neck. She had been living in their attic this whole time. An attic they hadn't even been aware of. This revelation was so preposterous Emma couldn't wrap her mind around it, and yet in the context of the entire day, it wasn't so strange at all. Her whole life had been rattled by a seismic shift, and a stranger in their attic felt like an inevitable aftershock.

Rachel snapped her fingers at Birdie, who was licking Rob's boots. Birdie stopped. But instead of coming to Rachel, she walked to Charlotte, who looked down. Then slowly, as if it hurt her body to move, Charlotte bent over and scratched the dog's ears.

Emma hoped Rachel would say something to break this awful silence, but Rachel seemed to be doing some mental calculus, trying to piece together what had just happened, and she stood chewing on her thumbnail while staring at Rob. Then Patty emerged, a purse slung over her shoulder and a baseball cap on her head. She carried two coats and pressed one into Charlotte's arms.

"There's pop in the fridge," she told Emma and Rachel as she put her arm around Charlotte and guided her toward the door. "I don't know when I'll be back." Then she left, her arm draped over Charlotte's small shoulders. It wasn't until the door closed behind them that Emma recognized the plant by the door. The butterfly bush, repotted and trimmed down to less than a foot. The flowers were gone, and at first Emma thought it must be dead, but when she looked closer she saw a sliver of green under the scraped bark.

Through the window Emma watched Patty reach over Charlotte to buckle the woman's seat belt like she was a child. Emma understood now that there was no way Patty had written the note she'd found in their mail. She wasn't cruel; she was just an old woman who had been taught to see things a certain way and was frightened by the idea of that changing, of not recognizing the world she lived in anymore. Who wouldn't be? The fire had loosened the judgment from Emma's heart, prying it out like old paint with a knife. More likely the note had been left by Alex. Or maybe it had been left at the wrong address. Or it was a dumb prank. Emma was surprised to realize that she no longer cared. It didn't matter! Things that had seemed so important and so certain just this morning were now as distant and insignificant as dust.

Rachel went to the kitchen to call her parents while Emma sat on the couch with Rob. Emma wondered where her own phone was. She might have left it on the air mattress. She wondered what it looked like now, if its plastic parts had melted like chocolate on the bed. What happened to an air mattress in a fire? She imagined it exploding, splattering melted plastic across the carpeting.

Rachel cleared her throat and said, "Hi, Dad. We're okay. But something terrible has happened." Emma listened to her explain their situation in a neat narrative: There had been a fire in the house; they'd escaped with Birdie; they were at the neighbor's house; their car was inaccessible and possibly gone. She did not mention that an elderly couple had been living in the attic.

Instead she asked for his opinion on when to call the insurance company and how to file a claim. "Mmm-hmm. Okay, yes," she said, a pen scratching on paper. After a moment, she laughed and said, "Oh, that's okay. Myat deserved to win." When she hung up, she brought the phone to Emma. "My parents will be here tomorrow. Do you want to call yours?"

Emma shook her head.

Rachel stretched her arms over her head. "I need a shower."

"Take one."

"Should I? Is that weird?"

"I think you taking a shower at Patty's house will not be the weirdest thing to happen today."

They went to the bathroom together and shut the door behind them. The toilet and bathtub were both green and looked as if they'd been purchased as a matching set during the Nixon administration. There was a dull yellow circle at the upper end of the tub, the place where the oils of human hair had touched the surface over and over, eroding the porcelain. Emma felt that she understood a lot about Patty just then, that her life had been filled with decades of nights where she sank in the tub and pressed the back of her head against the green surface and closed her eyes to the world.

Rachel turned on the shower. Emma sat on the closed toilet lid with Birdie on her lap and watched Rachel take off her clothes. She looked like a Polaroid picture of herself, her skin washed out in the bathroom light, the bright Os of her eyes widening when she stepped in the shower, which had not yet warmed up. Emma listened as Rachel talked over the noisy water stream about how tomorrow they'd need to take photos of the damage to their house for the insurance claim and how lucky she was that her wallet had been in her pants pocket so that she still had her ID and credit cards. Emma waited for an opening to say something of her own, but Rachel was deep into her monologue about how the timing of this worked out fine, actually, because they were moving anyway, and the pod not coming was a blessing in disguise. Her voice lurched from uncertain to confident, as if she could talk the universe into righting itself.

Emma had been imagining the moment she'd finally tell Rachel about the IVF for so long that she'd forgotten she actually had little control over the context in which it would happen. She'd been so excited to see Rachel's astonishment at the idea of Emma having done such a big thing on her own; she had an impression of Dr. Rivera that she knew would make Rachel laugh. But in the dim light of Patty's bathroom, Emma began to feel in the pit of her stomach that the whole thing had been a bad idea to begin with. She felt like she'd been under a spell for the past few months and only now was she coming back to reality and all its sad, inevitable shapes.

Rachel turned off the shower and stepped onto the green bathmat, wrapping herself in one of Patty's thin towels. She bent over the tub and scrunched her hair in her fists over and over again, each time squeezing another forceful jet of water into the tub. When she stood up she looked momentarily dizzy, the wet curls falling over her shoulders as she steadied herself against the wall.

"I got fired," Emma said.

Rachel blinked. "Just now?"

"This morning."

"How—"

"I didn't accept his paper. Or apologize. Also—" Emma let out a breath. "I told him I'd give him an A if he never came back to my class."

Emma expected Rachel to launch into a lecture about the importance of modeling professionalism in order to set expectations in the classroom or about separating the student from the behavior. Or maybe she'd pick up her phone and search for instructions on filing an appeal. But Rachel just let out a breath and sat down on the edge of the tub. "Why didn't you tell me?"

"I don't know. Why didn't you tell me about the job in Chicago?"

"I did tell you."

"Today, you did."

"Yes." Rachel's eyes were ringed with red. "Today. A real Dalloway, wouldn't you say?"

Emma laughed because the air in the bathroom had

suddenly become thick with steam and all that was unspoken, and she needed to make some sort of animal noise. Rachel laughed too and reached across the narrow bathroom to take Emma's hand.

"You hated that job," Rachel said.

"I did."

"And now it's gone. And we're moving anyway."

Emma lifted Rachel's hand to her lips. "When you put it that way."

"I won't keep anything from you again," Rachel said. "That was stupid. I should have told you."

Emma pressed her lips against Rachel's fingers. She breathed in deeply.

Through the door they heard the front door open and close. Keys jingling. A pause.

"You here?" Patty called.

"In the bathroom," Emma called back. "Be right out."

She heard Patty shuffle over. "It's time to make supper." Her voice was close, right on the other side of the door.

"Okay," Rachel said. "Give us five minutes."

A pause. Then, incredulously: "You're *both* in there?"

*　　　　*　　　　*

Patty dumped a bag of frozen chicken breasts on the counter, where they clattered like rocks. She wanted to make something hearty, she told the girls, to wrap up and take to Charlotte, who had stayed behind at the hospital. Dirk was unconscious, on a ventilator—plugged in like a jukebox, in Patty's words—but Charlotte refused to leave his side to eat. As she slathered each chicken breast with a pastry brush loaded with barbecue sauce, Patty pointed with her chin to various tasks for Emma and Rachel to do: melt butter, heat up canned green beans, mix together a bag of cheddar cheese with frozen hash browns. Emma was glad to have someone tell her what to do. She didn't have to think; her mind was free as a child's to wander. She and Rachel chopped onions side by side, their elbows touching. At one point, when Patty handed Emma a can opener, Emma said hesitantly, "Patty, about the butterfly bush—" but Patty waved her pastry brush in the air, spattering little dots of barbecue sauce on the backsplash.

"That plant would be crispy as bacon by now if it hadn't been dug up. Get the plates from the top cabinet, will you?" Emma handed her the plates, and Patty licked sauce from her fingers and said, "There was root rot, anyway. It needed to be trimmed. All in all, you probably saved it in more ways than one."

Emma didn't realize how much she needed to hear that until she felt her throat tighten with tears. But she held them back as she spun the opener around a can of green beans. That was the nicest thing Patty had ever said to her, maybe to anyone.

When dinner was ready, Patty filled a paper plate

for Charlotte and covered it with foil. Then, to Emma's surprise, she filled three plates with food and put them on the table. She sat down and pointed at the other chairs. "Why are you standing around? Sit and eat."

Rachel and Emma sat.

"We should have made our own plates," said Rachel. "We don't eat meat."

Patty ignored this. "You need to know that Charlotte and Dirk are good people," she said, using the side of her fork to saw through the chicken breast. "I can vouch for that. They're good people who were dealt a hell of a hand in life."

Rachel and Emma glanced at each other. "How long had they been in our attic?" Rachel asked.

"Few months. They were there when you moved in. But you have to understand, they didn't have anywhere else to go."

"Did you know?" Emma asked.

Patty shook her head. "I did not. Like I told you, I thought they'd gone to live with Justin." Her voice trembled, and she quieted it by shoving a forkful of chicken in her mouth.

Emma took a bite of hash-brown casserole. It was warm and comforting and excessively salted, like the homemade noodles her grandmother had always served on Thanksgiving. Suddenly she realized how hungry she was—had she eaten anything today?—and began to wolf it down, swallowing bite after bite without chewing.

"They were victims of a fraud," said Patty. "Charlotte told me the whole story. Some con artist pretended to be a fancy lawyer or something, and he got them to stay in a motel while he ran out the clock on their foreclosure. The whole time they were thinking he was settling something with the bank and they'd get to go home. I wish she'd have come to me so I could have warned her off. I saw this exact story on the news a few months ago. Con man gets them to sign away the deed, saying it's a contract for a new mortgage, then flips the house and sells it again."

"That's awful," Emma said. "And totally illegal, right? Won't he be arrested?"

Patty scoffed. "None of the bad guys are people. They're all companies. LLCs with no way to trace 'em."

"Why didn't they call the police?" Rachel asked.

"I take it you *haven't* seen things like this on the news, then." Patty tapped her fork on the table to emphasize each word. "Police. Do. Not. Care. About. Poor. People."

"So they were in foreclosure," Rachel said. "When the lawyer came along."

Patty looked irritated at this line of questioning. "Yes," she said. "But like I said, he was not a lawyer."

"I don't think we need to understand how they got there," Emma said, touching Rachel's hand. "It happened and it's over and no one got hurt."

Rachel raised her eyebrows. "No one got hurt?"

"You two look fine to me," Patty said.

"Our entire house is gone!"

"Insurance." Patty shrugged. "You'll probably get more than it's worth."

"The fire wasn't the first strange thing to happen in our house," Rachel said. "Our washer started leaking because a hose had somehow become disconnected. The toilet backed up with coffee grounds, which we definitely didn't put there. The fridge stopped working completely overnight, and we had to throw out all our food and call an appliance repair company. Turns out someone had just flipped the breaker."

Patty stopped chewing. "You didn't check the fuse box?"

Rachel ignored this. "My point is, that's strange, right? That these things kept happening, and now we learn that people were in our house this whole time."

"Rach," Emma said.

"Our house basically burned down, Emma. What if that had happened while we were sleeping? Or when we weren't home to get the dog out?" Rachel's fork clattered against her plate, and beneath the table Emma felt Birdie jump with surprise. "The firefighters are telling us it was an electrical issue. I don't want to jump to accusations. But do you see the connection here?"

"The connection is, you bought a house that got flipped in less than three weeks," said Patty. "You think just because something's cheap and shiny, there won't be problems? Let me tell you, there will be problems specifically *because* it's cheap and shiny."

"Maybe. Or maybe those people were causing problems to get us out, and this went a step too far. Maybe they put us in danger."

Patty lifted her fork in the air. Emma thought for a brief second that she was going to throw it at Rachel, and she flinched reflexively. But Patty only pointed the fork, still clinging to a bite of chicken, at Rachel like a fencer poised for a duel. "When you're under my roof, you do not accuse those people — my friends — of anything. You have no idea what they've been through the past few months. Right now Charlotte is sitting by Dirk's bedside, half praying he wakes up and half hoping he doesn't, because if he opens his eyes, she's going to have to tell him that their only child is dead." Spit had gathered in the corner of her mouth, and she wiped it away angrily. "You young people have no idea about the real price of anything."

Rachel listened, tilting her head not in condescension but in genuine interest, as if Patty were a student describing a paper topic. Emma knew that Rachel's parents had never spoken to her like this, never chastised or shamed or belittled her, and she was processing this new experience in an adult way, with a slightly detached academic interest.

But Emma thought she'd die of shame. Emma thought she might melt through the wooden chair she was sitting on and disappear into the earth below, where she'd rot with the roots and worms, so ashamed was she of her wife, who sat with her arms crossed and no intention of touching the chicken on her plate. Emma wished someone had scolded Rachel like this when she was young, when her brain was still world-building, because now it was too late for her to be changed by it. It struck her that Rachel would always be like this—a person who had escaped the necessary suffering of childhood that produced a self-loathing adult.

"We're sorry," said Emma. "We're just shaken up right now. But we're not accusing anyone of anything." As if to prove her loyalty, she cut off a piece of chicken and ate it. Her first taste of meat in twelve years. It felt insignificant in her mouth, a meaningless salty chew. It tasted like all the chickens her mother had laid before her throughout childhood, roasted and fried and broiled and baked, all of which, at their center, were just flesh and sinew. Her body had no allegiances in the world; it would turn this chicken into energy just as it would any other food. She took another bite.

Rachel picked up her fork. "Obviously we're not going to press charges against a couple of homeless people. That's unconscionable. But I don't know what the insurance company is going to say."

Patty got up to get more bread, a sign that the conversation was over. Emma felt a shift in the room, as if she and Patty were on one side of the table and Rachel on the other. She did, in some ways, have more in common with Patty. The plates were the same ones from Emma's childhood. Her mother also had the same wall plaque in her kitchen, a fisherman praying over the words *Give Us This Day Our Daily Bread*. And Patty, she could see from her chewed cuticles and the lifeless man in the living room, roiled in the same world of self-doubt and fear that Emma found so familiar.

Patty returned and they ate in silence for a few minutes, the only sound besides chewing and the scrape of utensils on plates being the slow tick of the bird clock above the table. Emma looked out the window. The streetlight briefly illuminated a couple walking, holding hands, their necks swiveling to stare at the black carcass of house next door. Her appetite had disappeared. She stared at the wooden bowl in the center of the table, which Patty had filled with store-bought rolls. The side of the bowl had a decorative pattern burned into it, a meticulous design of vines that in some places transformed into bird wings.

Patty touched the bowl and said, "My husband made that." Seeing Emma's confused expression, she added, "He passed almost two years ago now."

"I'm sorry," Rachel said quietly, and Patty nodded and said thank you, as if she accepted this as a blanket apology not just for her loss but also for the conversation that had come before.

"It's a beautiful bowl," said Emma.

"It's not finished." Patty dumped the rolls onto the table, one of them rolling off the edge, and held the bowl up to the brass dome light above the table. "See this line? Just sort of ends abruptly? And all of this would have had shading. His other bowls were much more detailed." She ran her fingers over the lines burned into the bowl. "But I like this one. Feels like he just stepped away for a minute and he'll be right back." Patty set the bowl down and crumpled her napkin onto her empty plate. "I'm going to take this food to Charlotte before it gets too cold."

"We don't know how to thank you, Patty," Emma said.

"You can clean up." Patty pushed her chair back. "Dishwasher's been broken for a year."

*   *   *

That night, Emma and Rachel lay on the foldout couch in Patty's living room. They wore billowing T-shirts Patty had fished from her closet before heading back to the hospital. On Emma's was a picture of Garfield wearing a Christmas hat, and Rachel's said AGE IS JUST A NUMBER (MINE IS UNLISTED). The light from the streetlamp pierced the thin curtains and cast Rob, who had been relocated to a chair in the corner, in a silvery glow. Birdie lay between them, curled into a cinnamon roll. Emma felt, for the first time since moving to Riverbend, the heavy weight of relaxation in her bones. Now that the confetti of emotions had settled, she realized she was excited about moving back to Chicago. She thought about the slow rocking of the train and the sharp wind that came off the lake in the winter. They would get a new apartment, a bigger one this time—living in a house had spoiled them—and Emma could walk Birdie to the shore, where she loved to throw her head back and smell the briny air that came over from Michigan.

"You said you had good news," said Rachel. Her voice was already sleepy, faraway-sounding.

"I did?"

"Today. When I got home from the airport."

"Oh." Emma felt her heart quicken. "Yeah. Do you want to hear it now?"

"Yeah. I could use some good news."

"I might be pregnant."

Rachel's head swiveled on her pillow to face Emma; she was suddenly awake. "What?"

Emma put her hand on Rachel's cheek. "Obviously this was not the way I planned on telling you. I thought we'd go out to dinner to celebrate—"

"How are you pregnant?"

"I mean, I can't take a test until next week. But I went to the IVF clinic. I did the whole thing—the medicines, the ultrasounds, I gave myself shots—and it sucked. But now the hard part is over. I mean, I hope."

Rachel was blinking hard and fast. Seeing this, Emma prepared herself for what her wife might say next: *You shouldn't have done that. You should have let me be a part of it. We're married. I should get to be with you for the hard parts too.*

Instead, Rachel said, "Emma, I don't want to have a baby."

Emma stared at her. "Yes, you do. It's all you've talked about for years."

"No. We took the whole conversation off the table this semester."

"And during that time—"

"I changed my mind. That's what I'm telling you."

Emma sat up, sending Birdie toppling over. "How?"

Rachel stayed lying down, her hands covering her face. "I've spent my whole adult life picturing what it would be like to have a kid, Emma. And I just can't see it anymore. Everything would change on such a fundamental level. Life is already so stressful as it is, you know? With all the issues with the house and trying to figure out our careers. I don't know how my parents did it."

"I mean, yes." Emma's mind was spinning; she tried to pull the conversation back to the positive. "That's the point. Everything will change. Life will be more interesting, more complicated. We'll have more skin in the game. That's the whole idea of parenthood, right? That's what you always said."

Rachel shrugged underneath the sheet. She uncovered her eyes. "You don't think we have enough skin in the game now? Just you and me?"

"But those were *your* words. All those times when—" Emma rubbed her face in frustration. "I mean, this was your idea to begin with, Rachel. You pushed the idea of parenthood onto me, and now what? You're backing out just because you can?"

Rachel sat up, the couch bed creaking with her movement. "Oh, no. Do not try to frame this as something I forced you to do. You were the one who found Dr. Casey in Chicago. You were the one who ordered the sperm."

"Because you wanted to—"

"At the time I wanted to have kids, yes. But you threw yourself into the whole thing because you couldn't deal with the fact that I sold a book and you didn't."

Emma turned away. She felt the shift of the thin mattress as Rachel lay back down. The thing that had hung between them unspoken for two years had finally been said, and it felt like neither a relief nor a blow but something quieter, like the gentle closing of a door. She looked out the front window of Patty's house, at the silhouettes of tree branches stabbing at the sky. "I mean, I did it, though. The IVF. It's done."

"So you tell me." Rachel let out a long breath. "Emma, this was an insane thing to do. You understand that, right?"

"Insane or not, what are we supposed to do now?"

Rachel thought. "I mean, you don't know you're pregnant yet. And even if you are—I mean, nothing's for sure, right? Let's just see what happens."

It took a moment for Emma to understand what Rachel was saying. "You're hoping I'll have another miscarriage."

"Emma! That's not what I'm saying. You're just—"

"I get it. You're saying you hope it doesn't work out."

"I'm saying that I'm being given very little space to process this huge thing. And I'm reacting in real time."

"Do you have any idea how hard losing that pregnancy was for me? It felt like I'd lost the first really special part of myself." Emma heard her voice tremble, and she realized they'd never talked about this either, about how much the miscarriage had jolted Emma into a state of perpetual grief, how badly she'd hurt, how it had coated every day since with a feeling of loss. They'd spent all these months talking about books they liked and whether Emma was writing and politics in states they'd never lived in, but Emma had never come out and said she'd been fundamentally changed as a person on a cellular level, that grief coursed through her veins every day, and Rachel had never asked.

Rachel pulled Emma down to her. Emma sank into her arms. She felt like she wanted to cry, but the tears wouldn't come; she was too exhausted.

"It's almost midnight," Rachel whispered. "And this

has been the most upside-down day of our lives. Let's just get some sleep and talk tomorrow."

Emma wiped her face on Rachel's T-shirt. They nestled their bodies together the way they used to sleep when they were first dating: Rachel's head on Emma's chest, Emma's legs wrapped around Rachel's waist. The perfect cuddle, they'd called it. Rachel would say, "Locked in?" and Emma would say, "It's a go for sleep." And they'd drift off like that, sometimes not waking until late morning, delirious, arms and legs numb.

Emma waited until she felt Rachel's breathing deepen. Then she gently untangled herself and rolled over. She was exhausted but couldn't sleep. She looked at Rob and imagined Patty crumpling newspaper and shoving her arms into those pants. Sitting on the edge of the couch and holding the shirt collar by her teeth so she could button it properly. Buying markers at the craft store so Rob would have eyes to see beyond his glasses. Patty was someone who really cared, Emma thought. She was not off the hook when it came to her homophobia, casual or not, but people were complicated. And Emma would probably never see Patty again after tomorrow. But even after their short history together, Emma was glad to be in her house, under her blankets, with Rob watching over her like a lighthouse scanning the sea.

It was nearly two in the morning when Emma heard the door open. Moonlight fell across the room in a neat rectangle as Patty came in and, behind her, Charlotte. Patty murmured something about having a bed made up for her in the spare room, and Charlotte nodded. The door closed. Emma lay there as the two women shuffled through the room, trying to be quiet. As Charlotte walked past the couch, she crossed the yellow square of light on the wall and was illuminated like a painting. She looked down at Emma and held a tentative hand up. She wiggled her fingers. Emma waved back. Then Charlotte let herself be led back to a room where she could finally get some rest.

CHAPTER 15

EIGHT MONTHS LATER
JULY 2009

The kitchen was covered in chopped tomatoes, their goopy innards spreading over the edges of her cutting board and spilling onto the laminate counter. Charlotte used a spatula to plow the mess into a pot held firmly between the cabinet and her thighs. She felt a small stir of pleasure, nearly imperceptible: The gratification of not spilling any on the floor, the sight of her biceps flexing under the thin skin of her arm. The cool prickle of air-conditioning on her face, the bright yellow walls and leaf of cilantro in her mouth releasing its soapy flavors.

Rebecca, her grief counselor, had taught her to look out for these moments of happiness because they appear only if you notice them. She said it was like seeing constellations for the first time. Or learning the word *serendipity*. Once you learned what it meant, you saw it everywhere, crawling through magazine articles and flying out of people's mouths at the grocery store. But that word had always been there. You just hadn't been paying attention. It was important to count the small things, Rebecca said, because most people's happinesses were made up entirely of small things. Charlotte liked having Rebecca's voice in her head; it was wispy and light, full of promise. There were times when her mother's voice would barge in, but Rebecca would step in and say, *Come on, Helen, let me take you for a walk so Charlotte can get some rest.*

Charlotte picked up an onion and inspected it for discoloration. They hadn't grown as big as she'd have liked this summer, but they were firm and heavy in her hands, with dry papery skin that sloughed off with a swipe of her thumb. Maybe next summer she'd plant them on the south side of the garden, where the zucchinis wouldn't cast them in afternoon shadow. The new backyard was small, boxed in by a red cedar fence and plagued by poor drainage. In March, when they'd moved in, the ground had been overrun with hostas, a desperate and sloppy planting by the landlord, whose arthritis made it too difficult to mow the lawn any longer. Charlotte had seen, beneath the crust of late-melting snow, the scalloped leaves of ground ivy forming a thick mat at the edges of the walk, the broken bricks of the footpath. She'd felt a strange stirring of pity for the place. The inside of the house had needed work too; the carpet was matted down in places, tape from posters had peeled some of the paint off the walls, a kitchen cabinet hung loose from a lone hinge. The landlord was Charlotte's age, a retired professor named Nia who sat down a lot during the walk-through. The students who'd rented it last had broken the lease mid-spring, citing incompatible living habits, and dispersed to their hometowns. It was hard to find spring tenants in a college town, even if the rent was cheap. Nia was tired of tying the lease to the academic year and dousing the showers with bleach every summer when people moved out.

"You wouldn't believe the mildew students leave behind," she'd said. "I'm too old for this shit."

Nia had wanted to sell the place altogether, but people were still spooked by the past year or so and hesitant to take on a mortgage. And even if there was interest, she couldn't compete with the short sales that still popped up throughout the city.

But the black spots in the shower didn't bother Charlotte. She was much more forgiving of the world these days. It was an odd side effect of having been through what she had; there was a kind of freedom in knowing that you'd already sampled the worst life had to offer. Rebecca called it post-traumatic growth, though Charlotte thought that was unnecessarily clinical. It just boiled down to, there were worse things in life than a backyard that needed extra care. Plus—she couldn't explain why—she loved the little house. She'd felt an indescribable sense of belonging in the place when she first saw it, as if it had been waiting for her to come home. There was a bright alcove off the living room that cast rays of sun over the scuffed wooden flooring, and a brick fireplace—decorative only, Nia had warned—whose pinkish bricks stretched up to the ceiling. The place was yearning for love. Her love. And she suddenly, without understanding why, had so much to give.

So she spent the early spring on her hands and knees, digging trenches around the hostas and prying them up. Patty had helped, meaning she'd shown up with a bag of beignets and talked Charlotte's ear off about Obama's plans to take away her health insurance. While Charlotte put down compost and sprinkled grass seed, Patty frothed about government overreach and not being able to choose her own doctor anymore. When Patty needed a refocus, Charlotte had her wrap the plants in wet newspaper and load them into a box to take to the farmers' market.

All it took to quiet a furious mind was the touch of something green. To smell the loam of long-ago decayed plants whispering through the earth. Charlotte watched as Patty laid each wrapped plant in the box gently, one hand on its roots and another under its leaves, like she was putting her own child down for a nap. Charlotte continued to be surprised by Patty's gentleness. She'd brought homemade dinner to the hospital and sat in the waiting room for nearly six hours after the fire while Charlotte stayed at Dirk's bedside, rubbing his fingers and arm and listening to the rhythmic breath of the ventilator. When Charlotte grew exhausted and the nurses shooed her away, Patty was waiting, with an arm outstretched and her keys jingling, to take her home. And when they'd arrived—stepping around the young girls on the foldout bed, their dog curled between them—Patty had tiptoed to the closet in the guest room and pulled out a box. Charlotte had let out a cry when she saw what was inside.

"Your dumb books," Patty whispered. "Even I felt bad seeing them in the dumpster like that."

With Nia's permission, Charlotte sold the hostas at the spring farmers' market, along with seed packets and fresh herbs grown in her kitchen. With the money she made, she bought mulch and a wrought-iron arbor she found in a secondhand shop for the wisteria to climb. Next year she'd add jams to the farmers' market haul, once the raspberries were coaxed into life. Every time she called Nia to ask for permission to add something—pavers for a walking path, a compost bin in the south corner—Nia laughed and said, "You can put whatever you want back there, but don't be disappointed when nothing but ancient beer caps come pushing up through the dirt."

*　　　*　　　*

The sun cast the kitchen in a honey glaze as Charlotte pressed her knife into the first onion and waited for its compounds to release. She'd read that onions turn your own tears into sulfuric acid, which was what caused the burning sensation. Incredible to think that something as slight and sincere as an onion could change the molecules in your own body without even touching you. These days she marveled at things like that.

A hand on her back. The warmth of it went right through her T-shirt.

She smiled. "No free samples, mister."

Dirk reached for a sliced tomato anyway and scooped it into his mouth. He was wearing a new shirt, crisp at the collar. His arms were still thin, but when he put his hands on her shoulders, she could feel the strength of his grip. He took his medicines without complaint and ate the vegetables Charlotte put on his plate, but he often had to stop during their nightly walk and catch his breath. The attic still lingered in both of them, in their joints when they rose from the table after dinner and in the red rash that sometimes spread down the thin skin of their arms, which they smeared with tubes of antifungal cream. Dirk's mouth drooped at the corners, but his eyes were more focused now, brighter. He said he was just like Obama, who after just a few months in office had developed lines under his eyes and a dusting of gray around his temples.

Dirk kissed Charlotte's cheek, then licked her tears from his lips. "Did you know you're crying like a big whiny baby?"

She held up the knife. "I'm making salsa. Lots of onions."

"And jalapeños, I see. Don't make it too spicy."

"Wimp." She touched her shoulder to his briefly, like horses touching noses. "I'll put poblanos in yours instead."

Dirk surveyed the vegetables blanketing the countertop. "I see a lot of tacos in our future. You're going to have twenty jars at least by the end of the day."

"Don't panic. I'll take a few to Emma when we go see the baby." Charlotte held the cilantro stems and slid her fingers down, her palm filling with the detached leaves. "And pickles too. Maybe some bread. I don't get the feeling that girl cooks often."

"How's she doing?"

"Due any day now." Charlotte swept the cilantro leaves into a pile on her chopping board and picked up the knife. "Terrified as ever. But she'll be all right."

Oh, Emma. That girl had moved back to Chicago after the fire and got an administrative job at some college, where she managed calendars and organized trainings called sensitivity classes. She said it had to do with reducing discrimination and fostering understanding between different types of people on campus, but Charlotte couldn't help picturing students sitting around in circles, plucking Kleenex and complaining about the ways their parents had done them wrong. Why couldn't people just be decent without making it into a curriculum? But Emma seemed happy in her small apartment with a little balcony that overlooked a courtyard of white alyssum and yellow marigolds. She'd described it over the phone as her sunny-side-up view, and when Charlotte visited in May, she'd looked down and laughed at the eggy way the white blossoms surrounded clumps of yellow flowers. Of course, she also could see the irregular growth among the blossoms, a sign of poor watering, and the thick knit of chickweed pressing through and strangling the ground cover. The landlord could do a better job with upkeep. But she'd kept that to herself. If she squinted, she could see what Emma meant: circles of white, circles of yellow. And sometimes that's all a person wanted — for others to share their delight, to see the things that made them happy.

It had been a lovely moment on the balcony, with the sun dropping behind the brick building and two men flipping burgers on a grill across the courtyard. But then Emma had started crying. She'd turned to Charlotte and, without warning, pulled her into a hug. Charlotte had felt the girl's shaking breath against her ear and the unexpectedly firm press of her belly into Charlotte's soft middle.

"What if I'm a bad mom?" she'd whispered.

Charlotte had shushed her like a baby, and the two of them stood on the balcony, their bodies rocking, while Charlotte combed through possible responses. She could have said that the world would come in with its many hands and shape Emma's child in its own private ways; a mother has less power than she imagines. She could have said there was no such thing as a bad mother, or that everyone was a bad mother sometimes.

Instead she said, "If you followed an old lady you didn't know into a fire, imagine what you'll do for this baby." And it was true. Emma was good. She'd asked Rachel not to tell the insurance company that Charlotte and Dirk had been living in the house, successfully convincing her wife to lie on the official report so that there was no chance of trouble down the road for Charlotte.

Emma hadn't even told Charlotte about this kindness; Patty had.

Charlotte felt Emma relax in her arms. Charlotte probably could have said anything, really; all that child needed in the moment was touch.

Rachel had been convinced by the Boon administration to delay her new job and stay behind to finish the year in Riverbend, in faculty housing. She and Emma saw each other every other Sunday, when they met at a diner in Logansport, a small city halfway between Riverbend and Chicago. They ate lunch and exchanged the dog, splitting custody of the yappy little thing. Their plan had been for Rachel to come to Chicago over the summer and for the two of them to begin to work things out.

But Emma spent the spring growing into another person, alongside the new person growing inside her, and by the time the days grew to their longest and the humidity thickened, she'd stopped mentioning Rachel much. Instead she talked about her Palestinian neighbors who'd taught her how to hollow out a zucchini and stuff it with rice and pine nuts, and how it felt to have the baby's elbow sliding across her abdomen—like being unzipped from the inside—and her job, where a coworker led lunchtime yoga sessions by the copy machine. Emma was writing stories about it all, which she promised to send to Charlotte but so far never had.

Charlotte supposed Rachel would come up in conversation again at some point, and so she remained neutral when Emma did mention her. It wouldn't do if the two of them got back together, only for Emma to be weighed down by Charlotte's opinion that they were a bad match to begin with, each holding the other back from relaxing into life. Who wanted a marriage like that? Anyway, she suspected Emma was approaching that realization on her own. It was like watching your child learn to walk; you couldn't rush over at every stumble.

Dirk plucked another tomato slice from the counter. "Have you checked the mail yet?"

Charlotte lit the burner, watching the blue flame lick the bottom edges of the pot. "Haven't you already asked me that today?"

"Have I?"

"I would have told you if something came."

"I know."

"We'll hear one way or another one of these days." Charlotte turned from the pot and put her palms against his cheeks. She could feel the work of his jaw as he chewed. "Now stop eating my tomatoes."

*   *   *

That evening Charlotte turned on the sprinkler and stood barefoot on the pavers as fat droplets of water made their way over the garden. The zucchini leaves fluttered with the rhythms of the water; the marigolds dipped their golden heads. Through the fence came the sound of a neighbor plucking his guitar. If she listened carefully, she could hear the hum of traffic along the interstate. The sounds of people rushing home from their jobs, hoping to scrape together an hour to themselves before the day was over and they had to begin again.

She sat on the lawn chair and drank a glass of iced tea as the rest of the day drained quietly away. Always as the sun began to fall, Charlotte felt like it was pulling some part of her down with it. Grief, Rebecca told her, had a way of sliding in when you were relaxed. That was because grief was actually the tender and painful side of love. Charlotte was supposed to write down how she was feeling in these moments, to try and put into words the heavy molten movement happening inside her chest. But she rarely did. Instead she just let it burn through her. Sometimes she cried. Sometimes, like now, she fetched her new cell phone and texted Emma. It was a good distraction because her brain had to work to figure out how to write a message using only numbers. You had to press each button a certain number of times to create a single letter. *Hello* was 4 twice, 3 twice, 5 three times, 5 three times again, and 6 once. At first Charlotte hated communicating in this way, but she grew to like how its inefficiency made her strip out unnecessary chatter and get right to what was important. No point wasting minutes of your life with filler words.

Watering the zucchinis feeling sad. Baby here yet? she wrote.

Emma responded quickly. *I wish. Tired of lightning crotch. Why r the zucchinis sad?*

Charlotte hooted. *They're feeling grated.*

LOL. I'm just making a(nother) snack. Want 2 call?

No. Just going 2 bed myself.

Nite-nite. Bed bugs, etc.

Night, Emma.

Charlotte turned off her phone. She already felt better. Emma had been the first to help Charlotte work through her guilt over the fire. "I caused it," she'd confessed to Emma a few months afterward. She told Emma about how she'd pulled the loose outlet from the wall in the basement, heard a snapping sound, and seen the lights flicker. And then when she heard the fire was caused by an electrical issue! The guilt was almost too much to bear.

But Emma had read to her, over the phone, the report the fire marshal sent to the insurance company. The fire had been caused by a problem with the electrical system, yes, but it was more complicated. The renovation had been done badly; Victor's guys had rerouted the wiring Dirk had laid for the hot tub so many years ago and used it for the basement outlets. Charlotte pulling it from the wall had caused some arcing, yes, but it was also Emma's fault for hacking through the conduit with her shovel when she dug up the butterfly bush.

"Or," Emma had said thoughtfully, "it was Dirk's fault for laying that wiring to begin with."

"Or Justin's," said Charlotte. "For bringing home that monstrosity in the first place."

"How many homeowners does it take to burn down a house? It was really an impressive collaboration. Truly all our faults."

"All our faults," Charlotte had repeated, and—yes, of course, she had cried.

Charlotte smiled now. She turned off the sprinkler and went inside, where she knew she would find Dirk dozing in his rocking chair, a magazine in his lap, and she would gently pull him to bed.

*   *   *

Justin's life was good when it ended. That had been the first surprise. He'd had a job as a peer support specialist at Blue Prairie Community Clinic in Kansas City, where he was known as Coach Justin or, among a few of the regulars, the Hope Dealer. When Charlotte called there, his supervisor, Andy, said that he'd hired Justin because of the way he'd turned his life around in the previous year.

"He'd been a frequent flier for a few years, you know," Andy said. "Starting therapy, quitting therapy. Getting his meds straight, going clean, then disappearing for six months and coming back raving about his neighbors trying to get him evicted. But Amy was good for him."

"Yes," Charlotte said. "I knew she was." She felt a wave of sadness, thinking of the Amy she would never meet. Amy had been in the passenger seat when they'd hit a loose guardrail on I-70. It was foggy that night, Charlotte had been told, and just a mile past where Justin and Amy had spun off the interstate was a twelve-car pileup. In the chaos, no one noticed Justin's car until the next morning, when the fog cleared. But it was instantaneous, the coroner said. Charlotte tasted this word for days after she heard it. One second Justin was driving, his hand on Amy's leg, the car warm from their breath. The next second everything gone. She couldn't wrap her head around what this transition was like; she cried every night for weeks that Justin knew and could not describe it for her.

"You see it sometimes in this line of work," said Andy. "Not nearly as often as you'd hoped when you were starting out. But he changed." He told her Justin was taking his medicine, going to therapy at the center, and attending a local recovery group with Amy. For his job, he mentored a group of regulars at Blue Prairie, many unhoused and struggling with addiction. He'd talked a local music store into lending the center a few guitars and was teaching them how to play. He made a pot of coffee each morning and kept the dayroom tidy, the fridge stocked with cream and fruit, a mindless action movie always playing on the corner television.

"Oh, yeah, and the pot holders." Andy laughed. "Can't forget that."

"Pot holders?"

"Justin taught our Wednesday recovery circle to knit. Said it was important to keep your hands busy. Now we've got so many pot holders here, we started using them as cleaning rags."

Justin had lived in a small yellow house sandwiched between an appliance repair shop and a tattoo parlor. He had two or three roommates—the arrangement was vague, not necessarily in accordance with the lease, from what Charlotte could gather—who verified that Justin paid his rent on time and had twice helped shovel snow off the walk. His music was loud at times, and he rarely scraped his dishes before dropping them in the dishwasher, but he was generally well liked because he kept to himself and brought home leftover doughnuts and sandwiches that had been donated to the clinic. Charlotte was amazed by this information, the way she could piece together a picture of her son's life in its final months. It was more than she'd ever known. But one of the roommates—Bill, with a nasty, phlegmy cough—said that Justin had had good times like this before and it wouldn't have lasted. Bill said that good spells happen to everyone at some point or another but they never stick around.

"People don't actually change," he'd told her. "Like rivers. Rivers can change their shape, but in the end they're still water."

Charlotte asked if any of Justin's things were left in the apartment, if there was anything they could send her, but that's when the roommates stopped responding and she understood that what was left of his life had already been absorbed into their own. His guitar was probably in Bill's room right now, if he hadn't pawned it yet. Justin's green Honda was certainly gone. She'd seen it in photos, crumpled like a soda can after the accident. She wasn't looking for the photos; the insurance company had made it part of their official documentation during the claims process, and she'd come across them while paging through the packet sent last winter.

Because that was the second surprise: Justin had his own life insurance. Andy believed in providing his employees with a fair compensation package, dental and all. Justin had listed Amy as his primary beneficiary and Charlotte as his second. Charlotte had lain awake nearly every night since finding out, her heart working through all the implications. After his fiancée, the person Justin considered most important was her. His mother. After all their difficulties, he had still loved her. And he had contemplated — just as she had — the awful possibility that she would outlive him.

Since the policy was new — Justin had been at the job only eight months when the accident happened — and because the payout amount was triple in the case of accidental death, the insurance company, Everguard Life, had stalemated the claims process, alleging that Justin was under the influence when he drove that night. The first toxicology screening had turned up positive for several substances. Some were his medicines, but others weren't immediately recognizable, so they'd started the monthslong process of retesting the results.

"No word from Neverguard Life," Dirk would say after he checked the mail. He tried to hide his anger, but Charlotte could see it in the way he set his glass down and how he scraped his fingernails over the arm of the sofa while they watched TV. Justin's death had shocked him, not just the circumstances surrounding it but the fact that it had been a possibility at all. He hadn't been imagining it all these years, steeling himself the way Charlotte had. She saw now how strongly he'd believed in the simple inevitability of children outliving their parents and how much this new world confused him. But his love shone fiercely in his grief; the two were sides of a coin.

It seemed to Charlotte that the insurance people were simply betting that her life would end before the situation was resolved. Everguard was simply running out her clock. But she had more fuel left in her than they understood, and more time. She would fight for her son's vindication. She didn't care about the money, but it was important to her that there be official documentation that he hadn't been at fault for the accident. That his life had been good. That he had been good. She felt sure in her heart that his life hadn't ended in relapse. He'd had a job with benefits. A fiancée. No debt. In fact, a year ago Justin was in better shape financially than she and Dirk had been. Wasn't that something.

*   *   *

Nia came over for coffee once a week. She liked to run her fingers over the dusted shelves and watch Dirk patching the holes in the wall, put there by the fist of some crazed sophomore years ago and since covered up with a poster. She would sit in the backyard on a lawn chair with her bare feet stretched out in front of her and gaze upon the garden with its rows of frilly carrot tops and the dense jungle of zucchinis.

"Charlotte and Dirk," she'd say, sipping her coffee. "Y'all are dream-come-true tenants."

Nia didn't mind, unlike other landlords, that they'd had a recent foreclosure, especially since they'd paid the first six months up front. Nia had taken over the management of this house when her husband died, a responsibility she'd never wanted but had appreciated, for a while, for the distraction it brought during her grief. There were always students locking themselves out in the freezing cold or clogging a toilet with tampons or blowing a fuse after plugging in too many speakers for a party. Taking care of the property kept Nia busy those first years of her widowhood, a time when she might have otherwise, in her words, "locked the doors and taken a bath in vinegar and bleach."

On Saturday Nia brought half a coffee cake wrapped in foil, and she and Charlotte sat in the garden while they ate the crumbly mess over paper towels. Charlotte had set aside three jars of salsa for Nia; they were waiting in a box by the door.

"How's Dirk?" Nia asked.

"Taking his medicine. Eating his greens, as much as he complains about it." Charlotte wiped crumbs from her mouth with the back of her hand. "Last week his doctor said his cholesterol was down for the first time. So we're doing something right."

"That's good. I'm sure it takes time to get back to a baseline after the year you've had."

Charlotte nodded. Nia didn't know about the attic—no one did except for Emma and Rachel and Patty—and she and Dirk had agreed that it wasn't a story they'd ever tell. It was too outlandish, too primeval. People would have questions, and their perception of Charlotte and Dirk would change once they heard the answers. As much as Charlotte had come to like Nia and appreciate her friendship, she was sure that Nia would never be able to relax during these visits if she knew that just months ago, Charlotte was sprinkling coffee grounds over their bathroom bucket to mitigate the smell. So they'd given her an accurate if incomplete overview: The bank had foreclosed on their house, they'd moved into a motel, and their son had died, which left them with a small amount of money from the policy Charlotte had taken out on him years ago. It was enough to fix their car and pay for half a year of rent, which to Charlotte and Dirk was all they needed for now.

"Do you like it here?" Nia asked. "You like it here."

"Is that a question?"

"It's more like a vision. I'm right, though, aren't I?"

Charlotte looked at the little square of yard that had in just months bloomed in response to her touch. The place was small, and it needed care, but she'd come to appreciate the simplicity of things. Running water, a bathroom of one's own, ceilings tall enough for you to walk upright. The squashed tomato on the bricks near her feet, abandoned there by a squirrel after an early-morning feast. "You know, it's crazy. But I love it here."

Nia smiled. "Then I have a proposition for you."

"What's that?"

"I'm getting old. And I'm tired of this place." Nia shook her head. "Not just this house or the one I live in, but Riverbend in general. People have gotten too opinionated. You have to be loud to be heard. Plus I'd like to go somewhere with more sky. Colorado, maybe. Or outside of Vegas. High desert."

A circling gnat landed in Charlotte's coffee. She fished it out and gently wiped it on the bench next to her to dry. "I'm listening."

"What if we came to an agreement? Reduced rent in exchange for you and Dirk looking after the place while I'm gone. And I'd rent out my house during the academic year, come back in the summer. We could do everything through the computer."

"You've thought this through."

"I mean, if I thought you'd buy the place, I'd sell it to you in a heartbeat. But I'd settle for this arrangement."

Charlotte touched her friend's arm. "I'll have to talk to Dirk about it."

As if summoned, Dirk appeared, the screen door slamming behind him. He held an envelope in his hand. "Mail," he said. He laid the envelope on Charlotte's lap. Everguard's logo, a circle joining two clasped hands, looked up at her like an unblinking eye.

"That from your son's insurance company?" Nia, who knew about the saga with the unsettled policy, leaned over to look. Then she stood to leave. "Keep the cake. I have the other half at home." When Charlotte moved to stand, Nia held up her hand. "I know my way out. Open the letter and be together."

She left, closing the screen door quietly behind her. Dirk sat beside his wife.

Charlotte felt a pressure building inside her chest as she picked up the envelope. The sensation was unpleasant; her instinct was to shove the envelope at Dirk and let him do it. But Rebecca said these were the moments Charlotte should be more open to.

Let it unfold, Rebecca would say. *It might not be fear that's pressing up inside of you. It could be love.*

"I just need a minute," said Charlotte. She leaned against Dirk, feeling her breath moving in and out. "Aren't you anxious?"

Dirk put a hand, heavy and warm, on her arm. "I don't think the answer is going to change anything."

"I disagree. What's in here could change everything." She looked at the envelope. If the toxicology results showed that Justin had been using drugs when he died, it would mean that everything good that had been happening in his life wasn't real. It would mean that Charlotte would have to rethink the conversations she'd had with the people near him and wonder, forever, which one of them knew. It would mean that nothing on earth that was good could last. Really, inside this envelope was the answer to how she would conduct the rest of her life.

"Then let's get on with it." Dirk squeezed her arm.

She opened the envelope and pulled out the letter. A piece of paper fluttered out and fell to the ground. They both looked at where it lay, face down, atop the squirrel's abandoned tomato. A pink bead of juice darkened the paper's corner. A check. She knew by the endorsement box staring up at her.

"You want me to read it aloud?" she asked.

Dirk shook his head. "I can read it by looking at your face."

Charlotte looked back down at the paper in her hands.

After careful review and thorough investigation, we write to inform you that the life insurance claim associated with the policy held by Justin Derrick Dennison has been finalized.

The toxicology analysis conducted on the deceased in accordance with our policy terms and conditions has confirmed the absence of any illicit substances in his system. Please contact us if you would like to request a copy of the complete toxicology report.

The approved life insurance payout in the amount of $270,000 has been issued and is enclosed with this letter. Please deposit it at your earliest convenience.

Charlotte felt unsteady, a violent swell of emotion propelling her to her feet. It was strange — she'd talked about this with Rebecca just last week — how big feelings all felt the same. They all pressed themselves up within you like a balloon. Whether you were filled with rage or brimming with ecstatic hope, it was just movement working itself out. This was how Justin had felt, she thought. All this time and she never really understood until now.

Dirk ushered her inside to the kitchen table. As he helped her into a chair, she felt his shaky weakness and tried to compensate by lowering herself down with her arm on the table. By the time her bottom hit the chair, they had their arms wrapped around each other, holding on, both crying into the other's shoulder.

Oh, they were getting old, old. And this life was long. They sat there holding each other like they had all the time in the world. They only let go when their backs began to ache.

"What happens next?" Dirk asked.

Charlotte looked out the front window at the white oak's canopy, which reached over the street and left its shadow like fingerprints on the pavement.

"Well, the mailbox needs to be painted," she said. "We can't have the neighbors thinking us shabby."

Charlotte smiled at her husband, whose face was crinkled in confusion. He looked like Justin, actually. Wasn't that funny. There were things that tied people together that were bigger than genes.

"I'm not in the mood for jokes," he said.

"I'm not playing."

"What do you mean?"

"Dirk," she said. "Don't have a stroke on me. We can own this house now. It's ours if we want it. And we want it, don't we?" Her voice quavered. The question was simple, and they both knew the answer. Still, it felt like a miracle, the small impossible math of it: *I want this. I can have it.*

"There's just one problem," Dirk said.

"What?"

He looked through the screen door at the check, which still lay on the bricks, pinking with tomato juice. "Can we even cash that?"

Charlotte felt her own laughter ring out of her like a bell. She felt her cheeks pull up to her eyes, which released tears that didn't sting anymore. She felt her pelvic floor loosen. The leak of urine didn't bother her. Her joints didn't hurt. They would again in a minute, but for right now she was in the middle of something pain-free, a burst of lightness that lifted her out of her own body and brought her to another realm, nestled right in this moment.

She was home. And she would tell every person she ran into how she'd come to live here. She would work it into every conversation, no matter how short. She would tell everyone, "My son, Justin, bought me this house."

She knew he would have, if he could have.

ACKNOWLEDGMENTS

Just a couple of hours before this book deal materialized, my beloved fifteen-year-old dog, Shirley, died. What a weird day, full of equal parts grief and elation. Because of this odd synchronicity, I have held a private belief that there was something magical about the way this book came about. It's a nice thought, isn't it? A final gift from Shirley?

Of course, the forces behind a novel are less mystical than that; they're the culmination of a lot of hard work and trust from so many people.

I am so grateful to my brilliant agent, Natalie Edwards, who saw potential in this story before the ending was even right, who is deeply attuned to both the language and the spirit of literature, and whose wisdom I trust completely.

ACKNOWLEDGMENTS

This book is stronger thanks to my editor, Gabriella Mongelli, who moves with ease from thematic insights to discerning line edits, and whose enthusiasm helped me overcome (some of) my imposter syndrome.

So many people at Little, Brown and Trellis Literary Management put their time and talent into this book, including Sally Kim, Peyton Young, Michael Barrs, Elizabeth Garriga, Monica Stanton, Karen Landry, Kayleigh George, Sabrina Callahan, Nicole Cunningham, and Tracy Roe. I'm grateful for the support of Kit Nevile at Hodder. Thank you to Kirin Diemont for the gorgeous cover design and to Tara Conklin for your mentorship during my debut year.

Thanks to my friends, whose support and creative energy sustain me even when distance separates us: Adrienne Gunn, Anne Nepokroeff, Laura Mosquera, Louise Delagran, Douglas Heintz, Chris Keimig, David Malley, Angharad Davies, Lauren O'Connell, Chris Lawson. Deep thanks to Charles Baxter and Julie Schumacher, who made the MFA experience the most fun and enriching three years of my life. To my parents, Pam and Gene Uptmor, thank you for letting me follow my own path.

But the best of all is Liz, my wife, my first reader and moral support, without whom I would never have found the four other loves of my life. You're my favorites.

ABOUT THE AUTHOR

Andrea Uptmor received her MFA in fiction at the University of Minnesota, and her short fiction has appeared in *McSweeney's*, *PANK*, and the *Masters Review*, among other publications. She lives in the Chicago area with her family.

RAISING READERS
Books Build Bright Futures

Thank you for reading this book and for being a reader of books in general. We are so grateful to share being part of a community of readers with you, and we hope you will join us in passing our love of books on to the next generation of readers.

Did you know that reading for enjoyment is the single biggest predictor of a child's future happiness and success?

More than family circumstances, parents' educational background, or income, reading impacts a child's future academic performance, emotional well-being, communication skills, economic security, ambition, and happiness.

Studies show that kids reading for enjoyment in the US is in rapid decline:

- In 2012, 53% of 9-year-olds read almost every day. Just 10 years later, in 2022, the number had fallen to 39%.
- In 2012, 27% of 13-year-olds read for fun daily. By 2023, that number was just 14%.

Together, we can commit to **Raising Readers** and change this trend. How?

- Read to children in your life daily.
- Model reading as a fun activity.
- Reduce screen time.
- Start a family, school, or community book club.
- Visit bookstores and libraries regularly.
- Listen to audiobooks.
- Read the book before you see the movie.
- Encourage your child to read aloud to a pet or stuffed animal.
- Give books as gifts.
- Donate books to families and communities in need.

BOB1217

Books build bright futures, and **Raising Readers** is our shared responsibility.

For more information, visit **JoinRaisingReaders.com**

Sources: National Endowment for the Arts, National Assessment of Educational Progress, WorldBookDay.com, Nielsen BookData's 2023 "Understanding the Children's Book Consumer"

LB
LITTLE
BROWN
LARGE
PRINT

THE NEW PEOPLE

A Novel

ANDREA UPTMOR

LITTLE BROWN
LARGE PRINT